HALFIE

Stephen Palmer

ISBN-13: 979-8378441211

Author's Note

This novel is set in and around my home town of Ludlow. The town and its buildings, the River Teme, and the A49 are all real. The characters and their homes however are entirely imaginary, and any similarity between them and anyone, or any place, living and real is coincidental.

I would like to thank my editor Keith Brooke and Stanton Stephens of the Castle Bookshop.

CHAPTER 1

Halfie knew there must be an important reason for the outdoor lunch because her dad had made proper hummus sandwiches. Where had he got hummus from? The nearest shop was in Ludlow, a mile away, and it was not his style to prepare in advance.

All three of them sat in glorious May sunshine: Mum, Dad, herself. Halfie glanced at them both. Her mum – in a flowing multicoloured dress as usual – looked distracted. Her dad, in shorts and a sweat-stained shirt, appeared embarrassed more than anything else. She knew there would be an announcement soon.

"Couldn't you find any cheese then, Dad?" she asked.

He looked at her. For once, he seemed to wrestle with his usual understated irritation at her jibes before replying. "I thought it would be good to have something different on the first day of the Whit holiday," he said. "Don't you?"

Halfie turned her attention to her mum. "I expect it was your idea," she said in a softer voice.

Halfie

For a few moments her mum drifted in a reverie, perhaps listening to elf music inaudible to Halfie. "I can't remember," she replied.

The awkward atmosphere continued. Halfie glanced down at the spring bubbling beside their three chairs, sending a brook into the fields of Stone Farm next door.

At length she said, "Mum, was there any reason for us all coming here to have lunch?"

"Yes, there was."

She had not expected so definite an answer. "Oh. What?"

"The time has come for you to choose."

Halfie could not imagine what this statement referred to. "Choose what?" she asked.

Her mum smiled. "I am an elf, but your father is human. You are a half-elf, Alfreda. So to you comes a difficult decision. Will you side with the folk of Faerie or will you go to the mundane world? I am sorry this has to be done, but such is the way of it. At least the choice is yours, and not a thing to be forced upon you."

Halfie felt shocked. She understood her own nature as the child of a mother and a father from two different worlds, but there had never been any suggestion that she would have to choose one side over the other. "When do I have to decide by?" she asked. "Not today?"

"Yes," her mum replied, "today."

"But I can change my mind?"

"Your decision will be irrevocable."

"But…"

"If you choose me and the world of Faerie," her mum continued, "you will retain a little of your freedom in the mundane world. But if you choose to side with your father, you'll lose touch with the elves forever."

"And… with you too?"

"Eventually, Alfreda. But at least you have the rest of the day to think about it. Dusk is your deadline."

"Which comes quite late at this time of year," her dad added.

Halfie said, "But that's nowhere near enough time!"

"It is how the Elf King wishes it," her mum replied. "We submit to his law."

"But… how can that be fair? It's one o'clock already."

"Well," her dad said, "that gives you about seven hours to think about it."

Halfie glared at him. "That's not *enough*. Why didn't you tell me about this before? What about school? You're not allowed to miss school, unless you're ill."

Her dad shrugged. "Your mother didn't know until this morning, when the Elf King told her."

Her mum nodded, a sad smile on her face. She glanced over her shoulder at the nearby trees then said, "I was at the shee in Snittonwood when he told me. I'm sorry, Alfreda, but a king is a king for a reason. All the elves of Snittonwood Shee, me included, submit to his laws. And…"

Her dad cleared his throat, leaned forward, then said in a low voice, "And his laws are precise. They can't be deflected or sidetracked."

Halfie sat back in her chair, staring into the wood. Convinced this must be one of her dad's terrible jokes, she tried to think of a way around the dilemma. But shock bemused her; and there was the melancholy expression on her mum's face to consider, an expression which spoke of deep sorrow. Yet she had encountered no elf other than her mother – nobody else to ask for advice. She felt trapped now.

"Mum," she whispered, "is this really true? That I have to decide by dusk?"

Her mum nodded. "Before the sun's limb leaves this world and night arrives."

"But... it's not fair."

"It is the law. Nobody is above the law except the king himself, because he makes the laws."

"Then you could petition him for more time," said Halfie. "I didn't know anything about this–"

"No," her dad said in a loud voice. "Not this time. You do as the king wishes."

"But he isn't *my* king, is he? I'm only a half-elf."

"He is the ruler of Snittonwood Shee," her mum replied, "and of Snittonwood. We live here because of his magnanimity. You come under his protection because you are my daughter."

"But, you don't mean I'd have to move out, do you?"

"Out?" her mum said.

"Of home. Wouldn't an elf have to live in the shee?"

Her mum shook her head. "I don't. No... you would have to follow the king's laws, pay your respects to him, and spurn the human world, living naturally, and only here, where it is green and so peaceful. It is why I go out so rarely, Alfreda."

Halfie glanced across the field to the hedge marking the border between their smallholding and Stone Farm. In the adjacent field she saw old William Ordish driving a tractor, his son Billy standing on the trailer hitch. She glanced at her dad. The field they sat in was disputed territory: William and her dad were at daggers drawn.

"Drink from the Faerie spring," her mum said, indicating the water at their feet. "It will guide you. It brings inspiration."

4

Halfie

Her dad nodded. "Do as your mother says, Alfreda."

Again she glared at him. "What if you're wrong, and this really is Ordish land? They'd have control of the spring."

He grimaced. "You've got a decision to make, haven't you?"

Halfie jumped out of her camping chair. "I'm not siding with *you*," she said, before turning around and walking away. "Not *likely*." Then she ran to the bridleway at the eastern edge of the field, and followed it down to the western track. A few minutes later she stood in the smallholding yard.

To her left stood their huge barn, behind and opposite it sheds and livestock buildings. Tractor parts littered the yard. Goats bleated, chickens clucked and pigs grunted. Ahead stood the farmhouse: enormous, dilapidated, lichen-covered. Upon the chimney a yin-yang weathervane squeaked, while from her parents' bedroom window a line of Tibetan prayer flags fluttered in the breeze.

Now she felt horrified. She loved her home, yet she did not want to live *only* here, missing school. Besides, choosing between her parents felt wrong. She sensed tears coming, but forced them back. She had to think, and quickly.

She ran upstairs to her bedroom, a large, long chamber at the end of the farmhouse, full of clothes – mostly on the floor – and dusty old furniture with peeling paint and moth-eaten cloth covers. A few framed pictures hung askew on the wall. Her school desk was almost invisible beneath stacks of paper and exercise books.

She glanced at the corner by the window, where lay a tiny dais fashioned from corrugated iron. There Badb stood, her tame crow, named after one of the Gaelic war goddesses, the Morrigna.

She approached. "You'll help me, won't you?" she asked Badb.

Badb cawed, then fluttered up to the window sill.

"No, I'm not letting you out yet," she said. "You've got to *talk* to me, tell me what to do. Mum says I've got to decide by dusk, and it's almost half past one. What shall I do? They never told me this was coming, not a word. They sprung it on me. Well… the Elf King sprung it on me. It's his idea, his fault."

Badb cawed again.

"But I can't go against his laws, can I? They'll curse me. Oh, Badb… what will I *do?* I want to choose Mum, but I can't just let go of this world, can I? I mean, there's school, my friends…"

Badb stared at her, now silent.

"Well, not many friends, I suppose," she murmured.

She glanced out of the window to see a distant tractor in the lane, crossing the brook bridge, heading towards Stone Wood.

"Probably just Billy," she continued, "though I bet he hates me because of the dispute."

Badb fluttered up, flying against the window pane. Halfie let her out, watching her flap away. A tear trickled down one cheek. Her room felt chill, the sun not yet westward enough to brighten it. And she felt miserable.

Then she saw her mum and dad walking down the track, he carrying the camping chairs, she carrying the picnic hamper. Seeing her mum's colourful clothes flapping in the breeze made her cry.

She could not forsake her mum and the elf world.

She knew what her decision must be.

Evening lay deep and shadowed over Snittonwood.

Ten minutes earlier Halfie had watched the sun dip below hills on the horizon, her mum standing to her right, her dad to her left. A few squirrels ran up and down nearby tree trunks, while in the sky a flight of geese passed by.

Now the wood was dense with silence, full of mystery. "Is it nearly time?" she asked.

Her dad put a forefinger to his lips. "Shhh."

Halfie turned to watch her mum. She felt that this was a turning point in her life, the end of her childhood perhaps, the beginning of being a young woman. Yet that felt wrong to her. Though she knew her decision was the correct one, she felt a strong sense of injustice. Fifteen was surely too young to make such a life-changing decision.

And she had never seen or heard an elf, except her mum, though that apparently was the norm for a half-elf. Tonight, everything would change.

Her mum turned to glance at her while her dad raised the lantern he carried to light the wick inside. Rich orange light illuminated the glade they stood in.

Rustles in the undergrowth… a distant bark from a farm dog. Then Halfie heard twigs cracking behind a stand of trees.

She leaned towards her mum. "Is that them?" she whispered.

Her mum seemed in a reverie again, gaze defocused.

Halfie glanced at the bamboo flute that her mum held. "Can you hear elf music?" she whispered.

"Yes, Alfreda."

Without delay her mum began to play the flute, rocking from side to side with her eyes closed, and as ever the music was passionate, almost wild. Halfie could see that

7

she was channeling musical forces from another world, the Faerie world, whose sounds and substance were beyond human. Then her mother fell to her knees, as if spent, taking deep breaths which were almost sobs.

Halfie began to fret. She felt uncomfortable now. There was too much waiting and not enough certainty. But she knew her mum might be preparing to communicate with the elves via music, as often happened in the wood, so she decided the best thing to do was stand close and wait. Surely that flute playing would draw them out of their shee.

After a few silent moments, her mum began brushing dead leaves and undergrowth aside. Halfie crouched down as her dad leaned over to provide lantern light. Then her mum pressed fingers into soil and pulled out a handful of earth.

"The king has assented," she said.

Tapping away loose earth, she revealed a shoot growing from an acorn. It was black, so Halfie knew it had been in the earth for a while. "What is it?" she asked. This felt like a let-down now.

Her mum handed over the sprouting acorn. "This is the future tree that he has given you," she said, her voice quavering with emotion. "Oh, Alfreda, he accepted you! How wonderful."

Halfie nodded, unsure what to say. A nagging doubt entered her mind. Why was her mum always so intense about things like this? Could it all be real?

"Is it just this acorn?" she asked.

Her mum continued, "Each of the elves of Snittonwood Shee has a special tree in the wood, to which their spirit is tied. Such trees can never be cut down – the king forbids it. Thus the permanence and sanctity of the shee are guaranteed." She wiped tears from her cheeks. Halfie stared; her mum almost never showed any feelings. "Inside that future oak," her mum continued, "your spirit has a home, a home for centuries. Though in body you will always be half me and half your father, your spirit has been accepted into the elf host. This wood, which you always loved when you were little... it will be your true home, as it is for me. Bricks and mortar will crumble. Humans of the mundane world live and die. But our spirits will live on." She smiled, her eyes bright with tears. "Isn't it marvellous?"

Halfie felt neither joy nor wonder. She felt sick from anxiety. "Yes," she said. "I... I knew... I knew it must be the right decision."

"Now what you have to do is replant the acorn in a location of your choice. The elf herald will announce the news once we leave the wood."

"Won't I see any elves tonight, then?"

"Not yet. They don't feel your spirit at first. It takes time."

Her dad said, "Take the acorn to a place you like, then plant it."

"Just plant it?"

"Not with nonchalance," her mum said, "with intent, with joy! You have to plant it just right. Elves follow *laws,* remember? The king's laws, and to the letter. This is not an acorn, it is the symbol of your future here, telling the whole world that you are an elf. That acorn is your life, Alfreda."

Halfie glanced down. Again the twinge of doubt returned. "This?"

"Don't be so flippant," her dad said. "Didn't you hear? King's laws."

Halfie nodded, looking around but feeling uncertain. Seeing a patch of dandelions she moved towards it, but as she did her dad turned, then tripped over a root. The lantern fell to the ground. Startled, Halfie spun around, but then felt something brush her cheek – a tree branch. In her fright she jumped backwards, dropping the acorn.

Her mum gave a little scream. Halfie turned to see her frozen, her hands at her mouth, staring.

The lantern went out and darkness fell. In so little light and with lantern after-images blinding her, Halfie could not find the acorn, so she scrabbled around at random. Yet although her fright passed she felt increasingly alarmed, and she could sense presences now, watching her, judging her, even mocking her. Breathing quick and shallow she patted the ground, aware that her mum was beginning to moan in some unearthly language. Darkness cloaked her – she felt its weight. And darkness confused her.

But then she felt something small and hard.

"It's okay," she said, picking the object up. "I found it."

Yet her mum continued to stare. "An inauspicious omen," she murmured as the lantern beam shone out again.

"No," said Halfie, "I only dropped it." Trembling, she checked to see what she had picked up. It looked like it might be her mum's acorn, but she was not certain. "Look, it's not damaged," she said, trying to sound pleased. "It'll grow really well by those dandelions."

Her mum shook her head, eyes wide. Muttering to himself, her dad raised the lantern. "Can't you do anything right?" he grunted.

"It wasn't my fault! You made me jump. *You* fell over, *you* dropped the lantern."

"Blame me for everything," came his reply. "Just plant the seedling, then we can go."

Halfie did as she was told, recalling what had been said: her future, her life. Yet the wood did not seem so pleasant

10

now, so familiar, and she wondered if she had stirred Faerie enmity. Suddenly this was all real, even perilous.

"I finished," she said, standing up.

In a more amiable voice, her dad said, "Good. That's done, then. Now you've got your tree ready, all it has to do is grow." He paused for thought. "It'll grow like you, depending on how you turn out." He glanced at her. "If you grow up twisted, it will be twisted, but if you grow up true it will grow true, all the way up to the canopy." He nodded. "It's a lesson to you, you see? Be good. Do as you're told. Follow the law. We all have to do that, you know, Alfreda."

Halfie nodded, cowed by his firm tone of voice.

Again he grunted, as if only half pleased with the evening's events. "Better get back indoors," he said. "Still a bit of chicken hotpot on the Aga."

"Yes," Halfie replied, feeling an urge to please them both. "I'll dish it up. And there's that loaf of bread you got yesterday from the Ludlow market bakers to finish."

He nodded. "No preservatives. It goes off quickly. Yes, we'd better eat it up."

Halfie glanced at her mum. Eating natural food with no artificial preservatives and colours was an article of faith in their household. "Are you all right, Mum? Are you hungry too?"

But her mum looked away, walking slowly, her body limp, as if she was fatigued. Halfie, familiar with such taciturn responses, said nothing more. A bit of supper would help, at the end of a strange and stressful day.

They ate in the kitchen, sitting around the great pine table. Two dogs scratched themselves beneath it, gnawing bones, while one of the ginger toms sat purring on a nearby window sill. The kitchen was too warm, though, from the Aga and the day's heat.

"Shall we turn the Aga off soon?" she asked.

Neither of them replied. Her mum dipped a spoon into her dish of hotpot, gazing into thin air. Her dad seemed once again to be repressing irritability. Feeling exhausted, Halfie excused herself when she finished her meal and went upstairs.

Darkness covered the smallholding. Badb had returned, so she closed the window and drew the curtains. She switched off the main light and lit a candle, and soon the odour of Nag Champa filled the room. Badb croaked, shook her feathers, then settled down on her perch.

Halfie looked at the bird. "I did the right thing, didn't I?" she said. "I'm an elf now. I wonder if they'll like me? Do you know, Badb? You're always flying over Snittonwood. You have magical insights into the world, I know it."

Badb gave a quiet caw.

"And Stonewood next door too," she continued. "Is there a shee there? I bet there is. There's got to be. Probably it'll have a ditch filled in a bit, like our one."

She let her mind's eye conjure images of the wood that she loved: tall trees, deep earth, winter snow, green spring shoots, summer flowers, and fireweed in autumn sending fluffy seeds to the air. All hers, now. Safe, secure, beautiful. *Her* place.

"I'll be seeing the elves soon. I'll meet the king. I'd better decide soon what to wear. You have to be careful not to insult him, Mum said. Elves are strange folk... their whims turn on a moment, and you must never cross them. But Mum'll help me."

She smiled, then undressed and got into bed. As she leaned over to blow the candle out she heard steps on the wooden floorboards in the corridor outside her bedroom. There came a rat-tat-tat upon the door.

"Is that you, Mum?"

The door opened and they both walked in. Dad looked serious: Mum distracted.

Sensing that something was wrong, she said, "What's the matter?"

Her dad sat on a stool beside her bed. "Um... it seems there's been an error."

Halfie glanced at her mum, now standing beside the curtains, pulling one back to peer out; and as her mum looked she raised a single pink rose to her nose.

"Yes," her dad continued, "an error in elf procedure." He attempted a laugh, but it sounded more like he was clearing his throat: utterly false. "It's like law in the mundane world, and you know what they say about lawyers getting rich off the backs of ordinary people's problems."

Baffled, Halfie shook her head. "No," she replied.

"Well, anyway, your mother has just heard the elf herald's proclamation, and it's not good news I'm afraid."

"Why not?"

"Because you dropped the acorn before it was planted," her dad replied. "That's a bad omen, you see..." He glanced towards the window.

"Inauspicious, Duncan, inauspicious. Use the correct wording."

"Yes, Jane."

Halfie looked from one to the other. They rarely spoke like this. "So... it's bad news?" she asked. "Won't I be an elf?"

Her dad sighed. "Your mother's not sure yet, it's far too early to say."

"But it wasn't my fault," Halfie said. "You scared me, in the dark."

"You dropped the acorn–"

"You *frightened* me," Halfie interrupted, sitting up and pulling the sheets around her shoulders. "You're to blame, not me."

"It doesn't *work* like that!" he said in a loud voice. "For goodness' sake, haven't you learned anything off us? Faerie law is all about the wording. You have to follow the letter of the law, and they never let you off if you don't. It's their way – the king's way. You have to follow what he states."

Halfie stared at him, shaking her head. "But that's... stup–"

"Halfie!" her dad shouted, leaning in. "*No.* Don't say it. This is absolutely not the time for insults. You've got to be grown-up, take this seriously. But you haven't let me finish yet. It's not the end of the world, your mother says. You may be able to claw back your elf status."

"Claw back? What do you mean, they've rejected me?"

"Cursed you more like," he replied.

Halfie shrank back. "Cursed me?" she whispered. "Like... a proper, real curse?"

He nodded, lips compressed. "We're both sorry."

For once, his expression told her that he meant what he said. Halfie looked at her mum, silent and withdrawn. "Will you help me?" she asked.

She shrugged. "I don't know if I can."

"But you can speak for me, can't you? The king knows I'm your daughter."

"Yes, but kings are notoriously fickle. I will find out for you tomorrow what the situation is, then tell you straight away."

"Yes," her dad agreed, "we'll both do what we can, though tomorrow I've got to go into Ludlow to do my missionary work. Sunday, you see. Got to speak against the vicar at St Laurence's."

Halfie nodded, feeling relieved. "Yes, Mum will tell me the situation... won't you?"

Her mum stared out of the window and made no reply.

"Listening to the elf music," her dad whispered. "The proclamation is being repeated over and over. Terribly inauspicious."

Halfie nodded. Her heart beat fast, her breathing shallow and quick. "Will they do anything horrible to me?"

He shrugged. "Elves are sticklers for accuracy. It's all about the words, as I told you. Perhaps we can sweep it under the carpet, I don't know."

"You mean, the error?"

"*Your* error, yes. Elves aren't perfect, they make mistakes too, and then they have to take the consequences."

Now Halfie felt a twinge of guilt. Her initial reaction had been all about denying her own part in the spoiled rite, yet, truth be told, she was the one who had dropped the acorn. That made her feel partially culpable. She shivered, frightened, wondering how to extricate herself from the situation.

"Dad," she said, "surely you can see it was an accident? Not my fault?"

"There is no such thing as accidents," he replied, standing up. "All is foreshadowed, all is meaningful. Blaming me will get you nowhere, even if there might be an element of truth to your side of it. But *you* dropped the acorn, and that was your future tree, where your spirit will reside. Can't you see the consequences? What do you suppose the king will think of you?"

"Why don't you stay to help? I've been cursed."

He shook his head. "Missionary work. Good night, Alfreda."

Halfie watched him take her mum by the arm then lead her from the room.

The door shut.

Footsteps receding, then silence.

For an hour, she fretted. Badb was asleep – no use. There was only one thing she could think of that might calm her agitated mind.

Dressing, she crept to her door, then opened it. From the lounge came the sound of music on the stereo – rock music, with lots of strange keyboards and wailing guitars. In others words, parent noise. She tip-toed downstairs, heading for the back door in the kitchen, from where she slipped outside, to follow the wall around to the side of the yard. Ahead, fifty yards off, lay the barn; inside it a light shone. Some years ago it had been refitted for habitation; that was a bulb inside a posh lampshade.

She crept towards the barn, then peered through the nearest window. Inside she saw the Wise Woman sitting on a rocking chair: wrinkled, white-haired.

She darted back. She was not sure if this was going to work. The Wise Woman, as her dad would say, was persona non grata at the smallholding, a state of uneasy tension existing between the family and her. Halfie knew nothing about her origin, though it was obvious that some Faerie connection existed, since the Wise Woman, as her name suggested, was no ordinary mortal.

Halfie tried to calm her nerves. After a few moments, she took a deep breath and knocked on the door. It opened half a minute later.

"Halfie," said the Wise Woman. "What are you doing out?"

"Can I come in?" Halfie replied.

"Of course, dear. What's the matter?"

"I need to talk to you. For advice."

The Wise Woman stood motionless, studying her. Then, with a wry smile, she said, "Yes, that is what I do."

Halfie had been inside the barn on a few occasions, despite the family rule forbidding contact. Since arriving a few years ago the Wise Woman had been an anomaly; resident, yet banished. Persona non grata, yet approachable. Banned from speaking with Halfie, yet never punished when conversations happened. Derided, yet holding sufficient power to deny any chance of eviction.

The barn was warm, subdivided into chambers, with the main downstairs room bright and heated by a wood-burner. The Wise Woman threw in a couple of logs then settled on her rocking chair. Halfie sat in the chair opposite. The odour of mould rose to her nose. The clock ticked. Sap crackled inside the log burner.

"What was it you wanted?" asked the Wise Woman.

Halfie looked down at her lap. She felt frightened now. "I think I've been cursed by the Elf King," she said.

"Oh, really?" the Wise Woman replied.

Halfie glanced up. There was a hint of mockery in the tone of voice, albeit tempered with a kindly look. "Yes, really," Halfie said.

"Go on, dear."

"Mum took me to lunch by the Faerie spring, then said I had to choose elf or human. I had to do it by dusk."

17

The Wise Woman shifted in her chair and, from the expression on her face, Halfie knew she was struggling to contain a terse, angry response. "My dear," she said eventually, "that's a terrible thing they told you. Oh, dear… I knew nothing about it." She shook her head. "Just terrible. So, what happened? You chose?"

"The elf world. Mum. But Dad's just told me there's been an error, so the Elf King might curse me."

"Oh, he won't do that."

Halfie sat up, holding her breath. She said, "Really? You know?"

"Yes, I know. He won't."

"But Dad said they always punish mistakes in the wording."

The Wise Woman sighed, tapping her fingers against the arm of her chair. "That's what legends say, certainly. But legends don't necessarily reflect reality."

Halfie didn't understand this remark, so she waited for more.

The Wise Woman continued, "It's commonly held that Faerie Folk operate by the letter of the law. But country tales have them as whimsical, fey people, so, you see, there's nothing definite about it."

"Dad sounded pretty definite."

"And was he following what your mother told him?"

The question puzzled Halfie. "Of course. He is the Ambassador."

The Wise Woman chuckled. "Yes, doing missionary work in town on behalf of Snittonwood Shee."

Halfie frowned. "That's his job. I think he's very good at it."

"Indeed he is."

Now Halfie sensed something in the Wise Woman's tone that she had never detected before; and, strangest of all, it matched her own opinion of her dad. "Don't you like him?" she asked.

"I don't give out opinions on such matters."

Halfie glanced away. "Sorry."

"Don't apologise, dear. He is what he is. So, what are you going to do? Have a lovely Whit holiday? You're on half term from school, I suppose."

"Yes, for the week. Thank goodness."

The Wise Woman said, "Exams next year."

"I know. Don't remind me!"

"I suppose you and your friends are all trying to forget about them."

Halfie pondered this question. She tried not to think about school when she was on holiday at home.

"You *do* have a few friends, don't you? Girls always do."

Halfie shrugged. "One or two."

The Wise Woman pursed her lips. "Honestly, anyone would think that crow you keep is your only sounding board."

"Badb? Badb tells me the future. I think she must have escaped from Faerie, don't you?"

The Wise Woman leaned forward, her rocking chair creaking. "Do your school friends know about your mother?"

Pain welled up inside Halfie, and she tried to stop her face expressing it. She looked away, hoping to force her feelings back into her body. She gazed down at her lap. "Well, you know... some people think she's odd."

"Tell me, dearest. Tell the Wise Woman. You mustn't bottle up your feelings, otherwise they'll come out in strange ways."

"There's not much to say. Most people don't believe in elves. I researched it, and I think it's quite rare in England. But there *is* a shee in our wood – I've seen it. I know."

"Yes, a great mound in the ground, that's for certain."

"They stare at me a lot in school," Halfie continued, "and I know it's a Mum thing. It always is. They laugh. I know people gossip in villages, even in towns like Ludlow, but, well, with Dad doing his Faerie missionary work…"

"And do your friends want to know about your mother, do you think?"

"Not really. I think Billy might."

"Who's Billy?" asked the Wise Woman.

"You know, from Stone Farm next door."

"Oh, William Ordish's boy. Yes…"

"I don't really talk to him about Mum though," Halfie added. "Not properly."

"No…"

Halfie glanced up. The Wise Woman was staring at her, sympathy clear in her face. "What?" Halfie asked. "Don't you believe me?"

"I believe everything you say," came the reply. "I knew nothing about this choice today. What a shame. Perhaps I could have intervened. But you've been told now. You've done it. Too late. I suppose there was a ritual of some sort?"

"That's what went wrong. Dad tripped and dropped his lantern, which made me drop the sprouting acorn." She sat up, taking a deep breath. "So you see, it *wasn't* my fault, was it? Do you have any sway with the Elf King? Can you explain to him and make it better? I know you've got country lore, so you could, couldn't you?"

"I've got human lore," the Wise Woman replied with a sigh. "You mostly get that through age."

"But you could talk to the King?"

"I'm going to talk to *you*," the Wise Woman replied. "That's what matters. *You*. So, regardless of what your parents say about me and my ways, you come here from now on whenever you want to. I can see that today has frightened you, confused you. I'm not surprised. I'm not best pleased about it, to be honest. But I'll *listen* to you, and that's what matters. You need somebody to hear your side of the story. Make sure you come here in private so there's less by way of fuss. Night is good – in secret, yes?"

Halfie nodded.

"Go on then, dear. Back to bed."

"Thank you," said Halfie. "Shall I see you tomorrow? It's the Faerie Fayre on Bank Holiday Monday, so there'll be all sorts of things going on around here tomorrow…"

"Hmph. A riot, as usual. But you come and see me whenever you like. Because of today we'll make that our special bargain."

Halfie slipped away without replying, feeling at once chastened and supported. But her anxiety had faded; that she knew.

Back in her bedroom, she knelt before Badb.

"Oh Badb, I think I've got another ally."

The crow made no response.

"I've only had you up to now. But the Wise Woman was really nice to me. I mean, I know she has been before, but Mum and Dad are always so set against her. Things seem different now, with this curse and everything. So I might have to go behind their backs when I talk with the Wise Woman. Do you think that's bad?"

Badb gave a quiet caw.

"Yes, I don't think it can be too bad. It seems different now between me and the Wise Woman. Perhaps she'll use her special powers to help me."

CHAPTER 2

Halfie looked at a photograph of herself that stood on her bedside cabinet. It showed a girl with red hair; smiling, comfortable, free. That was well over two years ago, when she had turned thirteen. How different she felt now.

She took a mirror and checked her roots. Blond hair – the same as her dad's – showed through, telling her it was time to bring out the red dye again. Her mum had natural red hair, and insisted Halfie colour hers the same.

Downstairs, the atmosphere in the kitchen was tense. Her mum and dad sat together at the table, bowls of cereal before them, a kettle whistling on the Aga.

"Morning," she said.

Her mum glanced up at her, but said nothing. She looked melancholy.

Her dad looked at the grandfather clock, tutted, then said, "Morning, Halfie."

"Any news from the King?" Halfie asked.

"Yes," he replied.

His voice sounded dead. His expression told her nothing.

She felt her heart begin to beat fast. "Is it bad news?"

He nodded, biting his lip. "The King noticed the error. He is very unhappy about it, and after midnight ordered his herald to proclaim to all Snittonwood that you're under a curse."

"What curse?"

"Seven years' bad luck."

Halfie sat down. Her hands trembled. "But it wasn't my *fault.*"

Her mum looked up. "There are ways of lifting a Faerie curse," she said, "even one given out by the King."

"What ways? Tell me!"

"You can kill the curser. Of course, in this case that is impossible. Not only is he the King of Snittonwood Shee, you'd have to get past his elven guards, and it would be a miracle if you even saw them. Or, you can die and come back. Then the curse doesn't apply."

"But... you can't be serious—"

"It's not an option for you, of course," her mum said. "Technically you're still half-human. The mundane part of you would never come back after death."

Halfie felt sick hearing these desperate, impossible measures. "Aren't there any other ways?"

Her mum nodded. "You can apologise to the King."

"Yes! I'll do that."

"But in this case you can't. Because you only chose yesterday to walk into the Faerie world, you're still unformed. Most of the elves consider you to be beyond their reach – only human, lumpish, clumsy. They know you're my daughter, but they don't see your elven spirit. They will see it, Alfreda... but perhaps not for a while yet."

"Then, I'll promise to apologise, and do it when I'm an elf."

Her mum shook her head. "Far too vague. The King would never hear of such a thing. But there is one other option. Sometimes the elves will set somebody an impossible task, which goes by way of repayment for the ill deed. You could try that."

"If it's impossible, what's the point?"

Her dad said, "That's not the attitude to take. Your mother's trying to help you here, can't you see? Be grateful."

"I'm not ungrateful."

"Often," her dad continued, "elves value cleverness, wit, originality. That's certainly the case with the King of Snittonwood Shee. He considers himself the finest Faerie philosopher in south Shropshire. So if you accepted an impossible task, then circumvented it in some original, clever way, he might pardon you, thereby lifting the curse."

"And you'd help me with that?"

"Oh, no," her dad said.

"I would help you," said her mum. "As an elf, I could do the research for you. What do you think? Will you accept an impossible task?"

Halfie looked away. Anxiety filled her. Her entire *life* seemed impossible now, not just one task. Why was she being put in such an awful position? Because of the King's whim? Or had she really upset the balance of natural forces by dropping the acorn?

She shrugged, looking at her mum. She felt trapped, isolated. Then she remembered the Wise Woman. "Is there a deadline?"

"No, Alfreda. You've got seven years to think about it."

Halfie stared. No tenderness sounded in those words, no sympathy.

She glanced at her dad. "What do you think I should do?"

He stood up, his chair screeching on stone flags behind him. "I've got missionary work to do in Ludlow. You consider what we've told you, and we'll discuss it over supper."

"Will there be time? You'll be setting up the stage for the Fayre."

"There'll be a few minutes I expect. Rainbow Tom and the lads will do all the hard graft on stage. The bands and musicians will arrive this afternoon."

"Okay," Halfie said with a nod.

"Leave your mother alone. She's got to channel music from Snittonwood Shee to play on her flutes tomorrow."

Halfie looked at her mum, who already seemed to be channeling elven music. "I won't be a nuisance," she said.

"And get your roots done," he added. "I thought you were dying your hair last weekend?"

Halfie jumped, as if he had secretly observed her in her bedroom. "Yes, Dad. Sorry."

He strode away. Halfie studied her mum for a few moments, but their gazes did not meet. Still feeling nauseous, she stood up and walked away.

In her bedroom, she knelt before Badb. "What shall I do, Badb? I feel so nervous all the time, it's making me feel sick. Now I can't eat breakfast, and when I feel better again I'll be light-headed and starving. I don't know what to *do*."

Badb croaked a couple of times.

"Yes, it's got to be the Wise Woman. I'd better see her this morning, before people start arriving for the Fayre."

Half an hour later she went outside, finding her mum with the goats in their pen. "All right, Mum?" she called out, waving.

Her mum waved back. "Can you collect the eggs for me?"

"Yes, I will! In a moment."

"Then take those old hens in a cage to the wood for the foxes."

"Okay."

At the barn door she knocked; a few moments later the door opened, revealing the Wise Woman. "Hello, dear. Back already?"

"I need more advice."

"Of course. Come in. I just put the kettle on."

The Wise Woman led her into the main room, where Halfie sat down. In a tiny kitchen the Wise Woman made tea, bringing in a pot and a couple of cups on a tray.

"Not too early for a second cup," she said. "What did you have for breakfast?"

"Oh… nothing, really."

"Nothing?"

"I felt a bit sick," said Halfie.

"Why, dear? Did yesterday upset you?"

Halfie gazed at the Wise Woman for a few moments, pondering the swift accuracy of this guess. "Yes," she murmured. "And there's more. They told me this morning that the King's cursed me."

"Really."

Again the almost mocking tone, as if the Wise Woman did not believe. "Don't you take the King's proclamations seriously?" she asked. "Are you independent of Snittonwood Shee?"

"That depends what you mean," came the reply. "Listen to me now – because I *am* the Wise Woman. Will you?"

"All right."

"Drink your tea. Go on, right now. I want to see you drink."

Halfie, feeling a little better from the fresh air and the release of tension, sipped her tea.

"What about some honey on toast?" asked the Wise Woman.

"Um... maybe later."

"Now you just listen to me, dear. Elven curses aren't what they're cracked up to be. I know about these things. Your mother isn't the only elf authority around here, you know. It's actually fairly easy to lift them. If you know what you're doing."

"How?" Halfie asked.

"Well, let me see. You said you dropped the acorn?"

Halfie nodded.

"So all you've got to do is change that circumstance. Yourself. Change it seriously, and deliberately."

"Change it? How?"

"Well, all you have to do is..." The Wise Woman hesitated, as if for decisive thought. "... replant it."

"Replant it?"

"Then *feed* it and *water* it – the vital aspects. That's all, dear. It changes the circumstances, you see. It's like re-doing the ritual. Then everything will be back to normal again."

Halfie finished her tea. "You make it sound so easy."

"That's because it is. For me, anyway. We can do it this morning, get it over with, then the worry won't cloud your mind, will it? Are you ready for some breakfast now?"

"Honey on toast?"

Without replying the Wise Woman stood up and returned to the kitchen. Halfie followed her.

"How many slices?" asked the Wise Woman.

"Two will do. I've got to go back and dye my hair."

The Wise Woman gave a little grimace. "To red."

"Yes."

"Hmm… Why not do that here?"

"Here?" asked Halfie. "Why?"

"I'll help you. Dying your hair isn't easy. Stains, you know?"

"I can do it on my own, I always have."

"No," the Wise Woman insisted. "I want to help you. We'll do it together, once we've gone to Snittonwood and replanted the acorn. Will you be able to find it for me?"

"Oh, yes. I chose the spot myself."

"Good."

"But Mum said I've got to take the old hens to the wood for the foxes."

The Wise Woman said, "We'll take them together."

Halfie nodded, though she felt doubtful. She had never been with the Wise Woman except inside the barn. "My mum's in the yard. She'll see us."

"We'll do it in secret."

Halfie nodded. A dozen questions bubbled up in her mind. "Don't they like you?" she asked.

The Wise Woman thrust a plate at her, then gestured into the main room. "Away with you. Eat. Got to keep your strength up."

Sitting down, Halfie ate the toast then accepted a second cup of tea. But she still wanted an answer to her question. "They don't like you, do they?"

"Your father?"

Halfie shrugged. "Both of them, I think."

"I don't speak of such matters."

Halfie pondered. "Where did you live before you came here?"

29

"Near Ludlow."

"Were you married?"

"My husband died two or three years ago," the Wise Woman replied.

"I'm sorry."

The Wise Woman said nothing more as she gazed out of the window. Halfie thought back to her sudden appearance, also two or three years ago. That time seemed now to have been when her own life began to change, become difficult, complicated. Her dad's mood changed then too. He was always complaining about her being a teenager; yet now, in the barn, with the lore of the Wise Woman informing her, another explanation suggested itself for his irascibility.

"Did you have a fight with my dad when you came here?" she asked.

"I don't talk about it. Just *trust* me. I'm the Wise Woman. That means wise."

"All right. I really do trust you."

"Good. Ready to go out? We'll see where your mum is, then sneak into the chicken coops. Then we'll be off, quick as foxes themselves."

Halfie made a reconnaissance of the yard, declaring the coast to be clear. As fast as they could they caught the marked hens, stuffed them into a cage, then hid behind the pig sheds. Nothing happened. No noise.

"Mum must be indoors," said Halfie. "Probably with her tarot or something."

"Then we're free to move about. Come along."

They hurried along the western track, then up the bridleway to Snittonwood. Rooks croaked high in the canopy, and the breeze was light and warm; a beautiful May morning. On the wind, Halfie heard the bells of St Laurence's church.

Having released the hens and watched them run off, the Wise Woman turned to Halfie and said, "Show me the seedling."

Halfie took her to the glade. She felt nervous now, recalling what had happened on the previous evening. The solemn tone taken by her parents at breakfast returned to mind: this was a serious issue. But the Wise Woman made no comment, humming a tune as she followed.

Halfie cleared a few leaves and pointed to the tiny shoot. "This one," she said.

The Wise Woman knelt down, grumbling as her knees clicked. "Ouch. Old age, you know."

"What should I do?" Halfie asked.

"Crouch down by me. Roll your sleeves up please."

Halfie did as she was told.

"Now thrust the fingers of your left hand into the earth to pull up a clod with the acorn in it. Then transfer it to your right hand. Then replant it."

"Anywhere?" asked Halfie.

"Anywhere nearby."

Halfie dug a small hole, then lifted the seedling and replanted it. As she tamped the earth down a sense of relief swept over her. Tightness gripped her throat, and she choked, gave a little sob.

The Wise Woman handed her a tissue. "I know, dearest. It's been a horrible weekend. But it's over now. Blow your nose, will you?"

Halfie took the tissue, dabbed her eyes with it, then blew her nose. "Now I water the acorn?" she asked. "And feed it, you said. How?"

"With wood water. We'll find a puddle."

"It hasn't rained for a good few days."

Halfie

"There's always puddles in woods. I know these things."

"What if there isn't?" Halfie asked.

"I can smell water nearby, don't you worry."

They searched the deepest brakes for standing water, finding some beneath brambles.

"The more difficult the job, the more efficacious it is," the Wise Woman explained. "Like a sacrifice. Got some? Come along. The more effort you put into this, the more likely the King is to revoke the curse."

"Do you think he will?" Halfie asked, as she let water fall from her cupped hands onto the seedling. "I'm not sure it's possible."

The Wise Woman paused, gazing up into the branches, listening. "Yes, I'm certain of it now. The curse is lifted."

On impulse, Halfie hugged the Wise Woman, who hugged her back. Halfie disengaged, looking at the seedling then turning back, to see the Wise Woman patting a tissue to her eyes.

"Just a bit of woodland dirt, dear," she said. "I'm all right now."

Early that afternoon, as Halfie made herself a cheese and lettuce sandwich in the kitchen, she heard the sound of a distant door outdoors being knocked. With her dad in Ludlow, it had to be either her mum or the Wise Woman. Taking a big bite of the sandwich, she slipped outside into the shade at the rear of the house, from where it was a few steps until she stood at the house corner.

She glanced around, to see her mum standing at the barn door. The Wise Woman opened it as she watched.

It was not easy to hear the conversation, but from the opening exchanges she knew their mood was fractious. So she ran around the goat pens until she stood beside the end chicken coop, from where she was well placed to listen.

"I'm sorry, Jane," said the Wise Woman, "but you have no right to tell me where to go or what to do."

"Snittonwood is not yours," her mum replied. "You're banned from entering it."

"Nonsense. That's only you telling me. And you know very well what I think of your ideas."

"Do you have to be so rude? Aren't we all entitled to our own space, our own peace, our own ways? You're a traditionalist. You're not like me. You don't understand."

"You're telling *me* I don't understand. I couldn't have put it better myself. But nothing you say will make me budge. And you know why that is, Jane."

"You hold it over me every time we have to talk."

"Every time we *have* to talk? Oh, Jane... am I so awful to you?"

That made her mum hesitate. Waiting for the conversation to continue, Halfie realised how unusual it was for her mum to be so talkative. This must be a serious matter.

"Rules are rules," her mum said at length. "When you turned up here, well... what happened happened. I don't regret anything. But I told you even then that Snittonwood was for me and the elves, not for you. Not even for Duncan, though the elves allow him access because he's my husband."

"That wood belongs to the smallholding," the Wise Woman replied. "It's on the deeds. I can go in if I want to."

"You can't! That's the *point*. The elves are displeased."

"I hear they cursed Alfreda."

Her mum gasped. "What... you know about that?"

"Alfreda told me."

33

"Then... you went into the wood *with* her?"

In a prim voice the Wise Woman replied, "We went together. The curse is revoked."

"But you don't understand! The curse isn't affected at all. Only the King can change it."

"Oh, nonsense. I can't be doing with all this. We've discussed it a thousand times, and still you tell me the same thing."

Her mum gave a strange, hollow laugh. "Who are you to oppose the King? Don't you understand? He's a male monarch. You're nothing."

To this, there came the sound of the barn door being slammed.

But Halfie's mum was not finished. She hammered on the door and shouted, "I'll deal with you later! I won't have Snittonwood spoiled, and I won't have Alfreda hurt. Leave her alone!"

There came a muffled response which Halfie did not catch.

"I'll take all your attic stuff and throw it out! I will. You watch me."

Another muffled reply.

"Fine! Ignore me. I'll sort you out later. Wise Woman, eh? We'll see how wise you are against the elves. And I'm telling Duncan exactly what you've done."

Now Halfie crouched down behind the chicken coop as her mum strode by. Anxiety struck her. The Wise Woman would be no match for elves on the warpath. Perhaps her attempt at lifting the curse had made it worse.

Guilt overcame her. She felt her limbs go weak with fear. A king was a king, after all.

Not knowing what to do, and frightened that her mum would go looking for her, she ran around the eastern side of the house to the little door by the lavatory. Indoors, she hurried up the narrow staircase to the corridor outside her bedroom, then slipped inside.

Just in time. She launched herself onto her bed as footsteps sounded outside. Then the door opened.

"Halfie! Are you all right, darling?"

Halfie put on her best innocent expression. Years of practice at school had made it perfect. "Just having a lie-down, Mum."

Her mum sat down at the end of the bed, breathing deep and fast. "Did you go into Snittonwood with the Wise Woman?"

"Well, not inside exactly." Halfie made her drawl as nonchalant as possible. "Just to see the bluebells."

"Did she say anything about lifting the curse?"

"Well... she mumbled something, but I couldn't tell what it was. Why?"

"That curse can't be lifted by anybody other than the King. You do know that, don't you?"

Halfie had no reason to disbelieve her parents on the matter. She nodded.

"I'm afraid that wretched, interfering old woman has hurt you, lied to you. You've *got* to take this seriously. Your decision yesterday has set a whole chain of events going. Please be careful."

Halfie felt the return of her anxiety. "I will. You know that. Sorry, Mum."

There came the sound of a distant car horn.

Patting her forehead with one hand, her mum stood up. "That'll be Tom with the stage gear. I've got to go. Be a good girl and make some food, will you? I can't cope with today, it's too much. I'm supposed to be preparing my music. Why can't I hear it?"

"I'll do it, Mum. Don't worry about me. I don't mind helping."

"Be a good girl, that's all."

With that, her mum hurried away.

Halfie exhaled as she flopped back onto the bed. As the minutes passed she felt her heartbeat slow. The day's tension was suffocating her. She felt sick again.

Badb cawed once.

"Curse?" Halfie said. "Yes… I need to research them. Perhaps in the study."

Badb cawed a couple more times, then fluttered against the window pane. Halfie let her out, setting the catch firm so that the window would not close in a draught.

The study, directly below her bedroom, contained the collection of damp, mouldy books owned by her parents, of which many were esoteric volumes purchased wholesale by her dad when a shop in Glastonbury High Street closed down. Perhaps there she might find a clue about revoking curses.

Outside the study door, she listened to the house. Silence. At her side stood a great Indian bronze statue, its base dusty with incense ash. She pushed the door open, then listened again. Nothing. As usual, the study window was shuttered, making the room feel cold, unwelcoming, but she crept inside anyway then shut the door.

As far as she knew the books were arranged at random, but by luck it was only after a minute that she found a volume entitled *Nineteenth Century Faerie Lore.* This book she took to the enormous chair that stood by the fireplace.

Dust and mould rose in billows around her as she sat down. She coughed, then opened the book to find its chapter list, and soon she located what she wanted.

There were other ways to deal with Faerie curses.

Such a curse could be passed on, like a bad penny. Halfie read the appropriate section, discovering that she could pretend the curse was some sort of gift. That sounded promising, and she liked the notion. Then there was something called the power of love. Here, the text made little sense. Love between whom? The author was vague on the matter. But a third option was listed: an escape clause in the wording of the curse. Now Halfie felt hope, because her mum and dad both emphasised the importance of the letter of Faerie law. It seemed many elf decrees could be sidetracked by means of wordplay, puns, or alternative meanings. Halfie looked up, gazing at the ash-covered debris in the fireplace. This sounded encouraging, although she had never been told the precise wording of the King's curse. Yet surely her mum could find out?

She snapped the book shut. There was hope! Better make that food now.

As the sun descended in the west, Fayre people began arriving in numbers. Soon five VW vans stood in the yard, and a line of cars and motorbikes lined the track leading down to Woody End Lane. Already Rainbow Tom and his aides had constructed the pyramidal framework of the stage, and were tacking canvas onto it – Halfie, from her position atop a water butt, could see it in the lower of the two disputed fields. She jumped down, then returned to the kitchen.

Sometimes she enjoyed the Fayre, other times she did not. Sometimes she enjoyed the buzz, at other times she disliked the invasion of privacy. Her bedroom door was locked, the key on a thong around her neck.

There were five strangers in the kitchen eating sandwiches made by her; only crumbs left.

"Got any more cheese and pickle, darlin'?" asked one long-haired old woman, giving her a gap-toothed smile.

"Er... I'll make some," she replied.

"Good gal," said another. "Got any vino blanc?"

"In the cupboard maybe?" Halfie replied, not sure she had heard aright.

The old woman chuckled. "He means wine," she said.

"Oh. No. I don't know."

Turning her back on them she sliced bread and made a stack of sandwiches, which she took to the table.

"Cheers, darlin'. How's Jane these days?"

"Fine, thank you."

"Gonna join us tonight for a smoke and a jam?"

"Um... probably not."

They all laughed, and she took a step back, uncomfortable with what reminded her of school taunts.

"I've got to go now," she said. She tried to summon up some gravitas. "There *is* a smallholding to be run here."

A couple of whoops followed her as she departed, then more laughter. She halted by the corner of the house as a mixture of frustration and embarrassment rose inside her. This year, she knew, it was not going to be an enjoyable Fayre.

She strolled along the western track, halting at the bridleway. The two disputed fields were triangular, set edge to edge, with the Faerie spring in the northern field. The southern field held twenty people at least, with the stage at the western end. Four times that number would arrive tomorrow, causing vehicular havoc in the lane. Halfie looked beyond, to see two tiny figures in the distance. She knew at once who they were: William Ordish and Billy.

Halfie

She swallowed as a flutter of anticipation made her heartbeat race. William loathed the Fayre and usually made his point in some spiteful way. Last year he stacked manure next to the adjoining hedge. One year he spread discarded tractor oil along the lane track, though his attempt to set fire to it failed.

Halfie sighed, glancing back to the farmhouse, then at Snittonwood. She had three options: take part and try to enjoy, lock herself into her bedroom with the portable television, or escape them all inside Snittonwood.

With reluctance, she walked forward. Above all she wanted to see her mum.

By now Rainbow Tom had left the final structural adjustments to his aides, and was busy setting up two speaker stacks. It was not long until music began playing through them; not loud, but, nevertheless, suggestive of what was to come. Halfie began to relax. Though not musical, she loved watching her mum perform on stage, and that Fayre experience she always enjoyed. Her mum had a gift – everybody agreed. Flutes were her real voice, the music sourced in some spiritual realm inaccessible to most.

A man approached her; short, slim, with lank black hair tied into a ponytail. Sunlight reflected off his sweaty pate. His waistcoat – or what remained of it – was sewn with circular mirrors, and he held a cigarette in one hand. Then Halfie smelled that thick, sickly odour which meant it was a joint, not a cigarette.

"Hullo, sweetheart!" he said. "You remember me, don'tcha?"

Halfie did, though she could not recall the man's name. He stood beside her, gazing at the stage, then gave her a hug, side-to-side. Halfie pulled herself away and said, "I vaguely remember you."

"Ha ha! Sure you do. Brian Speed." He took her hand and shook it. "You're looking as pretty as usual. Love the red hair – must run in the family. Half term, is it? Nice." He took a drag of his joint then gave her a smile that exposed most of his yellow, crooked teeth.

"Yes, Mr Speed," Halfie murmured. "Do you know where Mum is?"

"Call me Brian. And no."

"I've got to go, then. I need to talk to her."

"See you later! Don't miss the jam. Come and sit by me, yeah?"

Halfie ignored him, trotting forward until she reached the stage. "Have you seen my mum?" she asked Rainbow Tom.

"All right, chuck!" he replied, grinning at her. "Nice to see you. I think she's over there behind the hedge, taking Slick Lizzie to see the spring."

"Thank you."

Halfie walked towards the gap in the hedge, where she found her mum and another woman.

Her mum stared at her. "What?" she asked.

"I just came to see if you were all right," Halfie said, aware of tension in the air. "Do you need anything?"

"I'm explaining something to a friend," her mum answered. "It's *personal*. What do you want?"

"Oh... I see. Sorry, Mum. I didn't mean to barge in."

"Has your father come back from town yet?"

"I don't know," said Halfie.

"Well go and find out. Tell him we need him here. There's a problem with the CD deck. Tell him to bring ours out of the front room."

"All right."

Halfie hurried away. Something felt wrong. Although used to being given the brush off by her parents, she had never before heard her mum say anything was personal in quite that way. It sounded weird. It cut her out of the conversation. It isolated her.

Again she felt that familiar mixture of nervousness and confusion which characterised so many of her recent years. Just hours before, her mum had been all quiet words and sympathy; now she was back to being remote and distracted.

Halfie halted, standing still. She needed to talk to somebody. But no Wise Woman nearby, and no Badb...

She told herself to calm down. It was an accidental slip of the tongue; her mum did not mean it, and she did have that other woman with her. It was an exciting day for her mum. Tomorrow would be the best day to ask about the wording of the curse.

Then she took a few deep breaths and gazed with yearning at Snittonwood.

"I'll go to the Fayre tomorrow," she told herself. "I'll feel better in the morning. And Badb will tell me what to do. She always does."

CHAPTER 3

A few hours after sunrise there were ten cars parked on the verge of Woody End Lane and forty people in the Fayre field.

Halfie rose early, having slept well, locked into her bedroom with earplugs in to stop her being woken up by the noise of strangers exploring the farmhouse. She let Badb out, went to the lavatory, then grabbed breakfast in the kitchen, ignoring as best she could the two ancient men smoking and drinking coffee there. Five minutes later she stood outside, dressed in jeans, a linen shirt and sandals, the sun low in the sky and already warming things up.

No music sounded, but the field was dotted with tents, a yurt, and groups of people sitting around, some with acoustic guitars. Halfie wandered amongst them, smiling at the few she recognised, avoiding the rest. Every dog was on a leash, tied to stakes hammered into the ground; unbreakable Fayre regulation because of the livestock. One man played a harmonium while another plucked in uninspired fashion at a painted sitar; elsewhere people smoked, or did tai chi.

Many of these people would have turned up last night. The Fayre was one day only, but nobody wanted to miss a second of it.

One of her jobs was to manage parking. She strolled down the track leading to the lane, cars and motor-bikes to her right, a fence to her left. Already beer cans and other debris littered the track, and this she picked up, putting it all into an old Co-op bag. But the lane itself was already half blocked. William Ordish would be on the warpath.

Even as she thought this, a figure stepped out from behind a van; then a second. It was William Ordish and Billy, William dangling a cigarette between the fingers of one hand, Billy looking crestfallen behind him.

William strode towards her, wagging a finger. Then he halted and pointed at the van. "*That* van's movin'," he said, "and that 'un too. *Now.*"

Halfie glanced at the vehicles, parked well onto the verge. "All right," she said, "but they look okay to me."

"It don't bloody matter what you think," he replied. "What matters is what *I* think." He coughed, then took a drag of his cigarette.

Though she was used to this sort of tirade, Halfie nevertheless felt irritated. "A car can easily get past," she said.

"Who said anythin' about cars? I can't get a tractor past, can I? Or a baler?"

"You're not baling," Halfie replied. She glanced over her shoulder. "And you don't have any fields down here."

"That ain't the *point*. Get these vans moved. Any other vans blockin' the lane, I'll bloody well drag 'em out meself, understand?"

Now Halfie felt the diatribe was going too far. Wounded pride rose inside her. "Is it because of the Fayre again?" she asked. "It's all perfectly legal–"

"It's bloody hippies blockin' this lane with their bloody vans and stuff! Get 'em moved. I won't tell you again. If you don't, I'll call the cops."

Now Halfie knew he was going too far. Despite the annual friction he had never once called the police, because cars and vans were always moved at his request and the lane was never so blocked a car could not pass by. But she felt frightened. His long, grizzled hair stood out like a halo as he lit a new cigarette from the butt of the old one.

At length, she glanced at Billy then said, "All right, but you never do call the police, Mr Ordish."

"First bloody time for everythin', gal. Get goin'. Quick. Get these vans *moved.*"

With that, he coughed again and stomped off.

Halfie looked at Billy. As she turned to walk away he ran forward, then handed her a small cardboard box. "Sorry 'bout that," he said.

She frowned at him. "You don't care either way."

He grimaced. "You'd be surprised. He had no call to talk to you like that."

Halfie raised the box. "What in this?"

"He's got a special plan for the Fayre later. A drone."

"A what?"

"You know – a little plane, flying. Radio-controlled."

Now Halfie understood. Billy was tipping her off! "Oh," she said. "Er... thank you." She smiled. "So, no manure this year."

"Just you shush a moment," he said, glancing over his shoulder. "I ain't got much time. I made him a custom controller for the drone in coding class at school – in the IT lab. This is a duplicate. Dad doesn't know I made it, or that you've got it. He's planning to use the drone to buzz the musicians when they're playing, see? To put them off. With this you can interfere, maybe send the drone away." Again he glanced over his shoulder, and now an expression of fear crossed his face. "But *don't* make it obvious. If Dad finds out, he'll likely whip me."

Shocked to hear this, Halfie felt her hands begin to tremble. "Gosh, Billy," she said, "I didn't realise he was that horrible."

"No. You probably didn't. Gotta go."

He turned and ran along the lane, catching up with his father then walking at his side back to Stone Farm. Halfie watched them until they went around a bend in the lane. She memorised the van's registration plate, then hurried along the track.

The music began at noon with a few acoustic sets. Amplification was low, and with the wind in the west there seemed little chance of sonic overspill onto Stone Farm property. Nevertheless, the rumour of old William Ordish and his tricks did concern a few festival-goers.

Over a hundred people had turned up this year, all of them dressed in multi-coloured clothes, most of them old, or middle-aged at best, with a few half-dressed children running around, their hair dreadlocked, feet unshod. The atmosphere was relaxed. Halfie's mum wandered around in a happy daze, often singing in the elvish tongue with wild exaggeration for her friends. Her dad meanwhile chatted to all and sundry, but she noticed he looked a little uncomfortable when her mum began singing. Nevertheless, Halfie began to unwind, sitting with a couple of old women to watch a solo singer, moving on to another pair for a chat, then returning to the farmhouse on her dad's orders to fetch sandwiches and crates of beer, a load she pulled along the western track in a converted pram.

Around mid-afternoon, Brian Speed hailed her, then approached. "How you doing, sweetheart? See your dad's got you working hard. Must be time for a break?"

"Yes, I think it is," Halfie replied. "I haven't had any lunch yet."

"Aha! Then let Brian help you out with that."

Halfie looked him up and down. He carried nothing. "I think I'll need more than a toffee or some chocolate," she said.

"Ah, but no. I've got something special. Faerie food."

Halfie frowned, watching him take a paper bag from his pocket.

"You know what this is, sweetheart?"

She replied, "What do you mean, Faerie food?"

He grinned, raising one hand into the air then moving it aside, as if to indicate the land around them. "This is a special place on a special day. This is the Faerie Fayre. Surely Jane's told you about Faerie food?"

Intrigued, Halfie nodded. "Yes, but it's quite hard to obtain."

"Not for me it isn't. Faerie food locks you into their ways, into their *world,* don'tcha know? It can make you see them… really *see* them."

Now Halfie felt more than intrigued. Having never seen an elf because of her half-elf nature, she wondered if this could be a way of pulling herself into Snittonwood Shee, which might then make revoking the curse easier. She said, "What does it taste like, Mr Speed?"

"Brian. Aha… it's lovely. But you've got to be of an age to eat it."

"Of an age?"

"You sixteen yet, sweetheart?" he asked.

"Not quite."

"But not far off, eh? When's your birthday?"

Halfie hesitated. She tended not to reveal information like this. "Soon," she replied.

He studied her for a few moments, as if thinking. Then he nodded. "I reckon you're of the age. I will let you eat some. Your mother's never let you have any of this, then?"

"Not yet, no."

"I see."

From the bag, he took a handful of mushrooms, which he held up. They were small, their triangular caps topped with a nipple-shaped protuberance. "Just mushrooms?" she said.

"Special mushrooms, sweetheart." He looked around the field, then added, "But we need somewhere quiet, away from the crowd to taste them. The elves don't like noise – not human, mundane noise."

"That's right," Halfie said, recalling some of her mum's lessons, and thinking of Snittonwood. "Where shall we go?"

He nodded to Woody End Lane. "Down there, where it's more peaceful. We'll sit quiet under the bushes, then eat. Okay?"

Halfie nodded, but felt uncertain. The curse meant bad luck. "I'm not sure I'd be allowed."

"Ah, it'll be fine. Nothing to worry about. We won't stray from folks seeing us, okay?"

They ambled down the track, then Brian led her to a grassed-over layby, above which hazel grew luxuriant. But now out of sight of the Fayre and with no traffic along the rutted, narrow lane, all Halfie could hear was the faintest hint of music and the twittering of hundreds of birds. She felt nervous again as she sat down.

"Do you really eat this food?" she asked.

"'Course I do. Not often, mind. Takes me into the Faerie world. Yeah, you've got to eat it, got to discover yourself. It's all within, Halfie, didn't you know? You've got to go inside, on an inner journey, 'cos there the elves want to help you."

He divided the mushrooms half and half, then passed one lot over. Then he stared at her. She could not be sure how or why, but somehow he managed to look into her eyes and at her body at the same time.

"I'm not sure I ought to eat these, Mr Speed. Dad might tell me off."

Studying the mushrooms he grinned and said, "It takes about twenty minutes for you to properly digest them. Chew them well, then swallow. We'll lie back and wait. After a while you'll feel yourself floating, and all the birdsong will sound different. Then... you and I'll take a journey together. A lovely, pleasant journey. It's so warm! Better take the waistcoat off, and mebbe shoes and socks too. You do as I do, sweetheart, follow Brian's lead, yeah? You don't need many clothes, too hot."

Halfie nodded, tempted by the lure of seeing the Faerie world but perturbed by Brian's sly manner. "Should we eat now? Perhaps supper time would be better."

He looked up, then stared over her shoulder. "What the–"

"What are you doing?" came a gruff voice.

Halfie spun around to see Billy a few yards away, a pad of paper in one hand and a pencil in the other. "Billy!" she cried.

"What's them?" he asked, pointing at the mushrooms.

"You get lost, boy," Brian replied in a harsh voice. "Sod off."

But Billy leaned over him and said, "You leave her be." With a swipe, he took most of the mushrooms, then snatched Halfie's. "Thought so," he said.

"Billy," Halfie said, "that's special food–"

"Oh, no it ain't," he replied, looking up and down the lane.

As Brian struggled to his feet Billy ran off, stopping at a huge cow pat, dropping the mushrooms on it then grinding them in. He turned around, a triumphant look on his face.

"No magic for you," he told Brian. "That's my neighbour, that is, so you leave her alone."

Stunned, Halfie stared as Brian approached Billy, fumed in silence, then grunted something. Brian returned to pick up his socks, shoes, and his waistcoat, then stalk off.

"That was close," said Billy, walking up to Halfie. "Lucky my dad told me to take all the parked vehicle registration numbers."

Halfie's shock departed, leaving her furious. "You *idiot*. That was Faerie food, and he was just about to let me have some!"

"No it weren't," Billy replied. "I seen them mushrooms before, your Fayre people usually bring them on a Bank Holiday Monday."

"What do you mean? You ruined everything."

He shook his head. "I saved you."

"*Saved* me? What from?"

"From that low-life dealer."

"You don't know anything. You're just a stupid boy."

He appeared unconcerned by her insult. "I'll tell you about it if you like," he said.

"Go *on* then."

He hesitated. "But you won't believe me, because you believe other things."

"*Tell* me, Billy Ordish. Tell me how *you* managed to *save* me."

His thick, black eyebrows descended as his expression darkened. He scratched the uncombed thatch of hair on his head, then looked away.

"See," Halfie said. "You can't."

"I can," he replied. "They were magic mushrooms, hippie stuff, and that man was gonna make you take them. They're drugs, Halfie, didn't you know? They're illegal. He was gonna force you to eat them."

"I know. I agreed. Faerie–"

"There ain't no such place!" he interrupted, angered. Scowling, he added, "It's just stuff people believe – what your mother believes. Those were what they call psych'logical active mushrooms – shrooms, hippies call them. They're dangerous."

Halfie stared at him, sensing his shock, his hurt, his anger. If nothing else he was speaking sincerely. And she knew Billy Ordish from school. He was not one of the bad lads. He was ordinary, polite – a thinky boy as some of the girls called him.

Yet still her anger and disappointment riled her. "You talk such bollocks," she said. "I bet you think you know it all."

"Only a farmer's boy, am I?" he replied. "I gave you that custom drone controller, though. That seems decent enough to me. I don't like to fight. It upsets me, seeing angry people. I don't like this now."

Disarmed by his speech, Halfie glanced away. She had never heard him talk like this. "You don't understand," she said, "because *my* mum's not yours. My mum knows things because she's an elf – secret things, things of country lore. She's taught me a lot of what she knows."

He shook his head. "That's not what I say. Nor do a few others."

She glared at him. "Say? At school?"

He nodded. "I try to see both sides though. I feel a bit sorry for you."

"*Sorry* for me? What right have you got to feel that?"

He shrugged, his cheeks turning pink. "Some people think your mother's a bit…"

"A bit what?"

"Strange."

"She's an *elf.* She's *special.* And that means I am too."

He glanced away, his expression disbelieving. "What exactly do you get?" he asked.

"Get?"

"For being an elf."

She hesitated, surprised by his question. "It feels wonderful," she said in a low voice. It felt odd telling him – embarrassing, almost. "I get to feel nature more, feel it with all my senses. When I look at a tree I see it from another plane, I sense its potential, its seeds, its saplings, and what that means to the planet. All those feelings come into my mind. My body too – a glorious shiver! This planet is special, Billy, and we should be able to feel that, but usually we can't. Elves are made by nature and nothing else. Not people, just nature. That's me now."

He studied her, biting his lower lip. "So, you're like a half-elf," he said. "Halfie. Is that what you believe?"

"It's a fact. I don't need to believe it."

"Facts are what's in books. I think you *believe* what you believe because you was told it. You ain't read it in no book."

"As a matter of fact, I did last night," Halfie retorted.

"Where did the book come from?"

"Glastonbury."

He snorted. "Glastonbury. We all know what people live there."

"Well you go on thinking that then. I haven't got time to talk with you any more."

He nodded, pensive. "Don't forget the drone controller," he said, a faint smile on his lips. "I gave you that honestly enough. You'll need it. My dad's fuming with your parents, he is, because they spoil every Whit week. Hopping furious, I'd say."

"*That* doesn't surprise me," Halfie replied. "Maybe we'll get you back."

"Half-elf? Can you cast a spell on me then?"

Halfie squashed her anger down so that her reply was coherent. "Listen, *you*. I'm going to tell you something, all right? On Saturday I had to choose between being an elf or a human, because my dad's human. I chose to be an elf, so maybe later on I *will* be able to cast a spell on you. A bad one."

She watched as his expression changed. His face turned pale and his eyes went round.

"What?" she said.

"They made you choose?" he murmured.

"Yes. Well, the Elf King did."

"But..." He shook his head, an expression of horror on his face. "Don't you see what's happening?"

"What do you mean?"

"They're getting divorced. That's why you had to choose – between your mum and your dad. Halfie... now I've got it. That happened to me when my folks got divorced. Dad made me and my bro' choose him. He wouldn't let me see my... even though... even though I wanted to."

"Getting divorced? No, they're not."

Billy nodded. "I bet they are. They make you choose, parents. They sidle up to you and tell you bad things about the other. All the grievances come out of the woodwork, they do, when parents get divorced."

"My parents are not getting divorced. It's all perfectly clear. The Elf King... Billy, where are you going?"

"Home."

"Don't go," said Halfie. "I haven't finished explaining yet. Stop!"

"Not likely," Billy said, glancing over his shoulder. "I'm sorry I spoke rude to you. I didn't mean to. You made me get annoyed a bit. Keep the drone controller – and use it. Otherwise my dad'll ruin the festival, and I don't think he should."

"Come back!"

But he was running away now, arms pumping, not looking back. She watched him until he disappeared around the bend in the lane.

In her bedroom, the door locked, Halfie knelt at Badb's side.

"Badb, what am I going to do?"

The crow croaked, then began pecking at seed on the iron perch.

Halfie continued, "The curse is still active, isn't it? Nothing's changed. That's why I had bad luck just now, with Billy spoiling the Faerie food. But, why should it have changed? Just because Billy doesn't believe and a few people at school think my mum's odd. I've known that for years, so it doesn't bother me. No... the curse is active all right. So I've got to do something to stop it."

Badb uttered a caw, then hopped away.

"I think the best bet is to pass it on, like a bad penny, as the book said. But who to? There's nobody I dislike enough to do that."

Badb cawed.

"Brian Speed? Yes... he was trying to help me, but he was ogling me too. I know it. I did feel uncomfortable then, I've got to admit. I wonder if he is a bad man? Billy called him a dealer, and I know what that is. Dealers get put in prison."

She glanced down at herself. Lacking any idea of how pretty she was, she looked in a mirror, then tried to recall any gossip about what the boys at school thought of her. But all she could think of was taunts, whispers and sidelong looks. Some of the boys shunned her. She had no proper friends, except Billy, who anyway was more of an acquaintance brought by being a neighbour.

"He thought he was trying to protect me," she mused. "He called me his neighbour, and defended me, even though he was wrong. So, at least he's sincere in what he's doing. And he gave me the controller, which he didn't have to do. Perhaps he is on my side... but no. He knows *nothing* about Faerie. Nothing."

Badb cawed a few times.

"Yes, we'll do it, Badb. We'll pass the curse on to Mr Speed. But how? I suppose it'll have to be via the seedling." She paused for thought. "I'll dig it up, put it in a pot and present it to him as a present," she said at length. "I'll pretend it's a gift, like the old book said, to make up for what Billy did. Then I'll be free." She sighed. "Free to be a proper elf."

Intending to walk to Snittonwood she kicked off her sandals and put proper shoes on, collecting the drone controller before going downstairs and picking up an empty plastic pot from the stack behind the house.

A shadow fell upon her, and she turned to see her dad. "Oh, hello. How's it going?"

"Very well indeed," he replied. "You coming back now? Rainbow Tom's band are on in a few minutes."

"Are they the ones with the girly dancers?"

Her dad grinned. "Ooh, yes."

"Um... maybe. I'll see." She hesitated, looking him in the eye. "Dad?"

"What?"

"You'd never divorce Mum, would you?"

He stared at her. "What the *hell?* Who said I would?"

"Nobody–"

"Somebody must've. Who?"

"Nobody did! I just wondered."

"Why?" He leaned forward. "*Why?*"

She shied away from him. "Because... of the choice."

"Choice?"

"Elf or human... you or Mum."

"We're not getting divorced, you stupid girl. What a mad idea! Blimey... talk about off-target. She was with the *King,* Alfreda, the King himself. On Saturday you had to choose, it's what all half-elves have to do. Divorced... I'd *never* leave Jane. I'm her Faerie Ambassador for chrissakes. Have you been smoking something you shouldn't?"

"You know I hate that stuff."

He glared at her, then grimaced. "Just get along and listen to the music. Have a beer. You shouldn't be inside the house in this glorious weather. Look at you – all skin and bone, and white as a Goth. You look like a match right out of a damn matchbox."

With that, he strode into the house.

At once Halfie felt nervousness settle upon her. Was going into Snittonwood the right thing to do? She hesitated as her heartbeat raced, but she knew she had to move on, and quickly. Approaching the stage, she managed to crawl unnoticed behind it, where she hid the drone controller in a discarded pizza box. She waited. Nobody came to fetch her out.

At last she hurried away, scared her dad might return, and soon she was out of sight in the big field east of the spring. Minutes later she found the seedling, dug it up, filled the pot with earth and replanted it. Then she carried the pot to the edge of the wood and looked out over the fields. Seeing a couple of backpackers walking up the bridleway she hung back, and as they passed she heard snippets of their conversation.

"... they get everywhere... ruining the countryside... every one a drug addict..."

Halfie stuck out her tongue at them, then hurried along hedges to the western track, from where she strolled into the Fayre field. Most of the festival-goers were standing around the stage as Rainbow Tom's band played, but there were a dozen other people lying, sitting or standing around – and one of them was Brian Speed. Seeing him brought back the memory of his leer, and she felt discomfiture again.

Slowly, she approached him and his friends. He noticed her, scowling, then looking away as he took a puff at his joint. A few yards away she halted, staring, silent, waiting for him to look at her.

He took his time. A minute passed before he turned to glance at her. "You still here?"

She tried to reply, but her tongue felt stuck against the roof of her mouth. She began trembling. She swallowed, but her mouth was bone dry.

"What?" he asked. "Come to do some gardening?"

"Not really. Um…"

"Um what?"

"Nothing, Mr Speed. Sorry."

She could not do it. She could not break through his disdain, even now, when he clearly loathed her and she felt nothing but unease. The curse could not be passed on. She was stuck with it.

She walked away.

In the yard, she hid the flower pot by a chicken coop, then paused, unsure what next to do. She felt as though a hundred paths lay before her, all heading into danger. She felt lost, alone.

"What's the matter, dear?"

She turned to see the Wise Woman in the barn doorway. She approached, saying, "Oh… nothing."

The Wise Woman looked down at her arms. "You're trembling. Again."

"I'm just a bit cold. The sun's going down."

The Wise Woman compressed her lips together, then reached out to touch her shoulder. "I'm not blind, Alfreda. You look unhappy. Unsettled. Won't you tell me?"

"Oh, it's just this curse thing. I don't want it."

"No… of course not. Listen, dear, you do look nervous. Anxious. Why?"

Halfie replied, "I don't know."

"You're nervous often, aren't you?"

"No, not nervous exactly. I've had quite a nice time today. Though I am a bit peckish now."

"Come in," the Wise Woman said. "We'll have tea. And I've got something to show you."

"What?"

"Inside first. Come along."

The Wise Woman led her into the barn, settling her in a chair. For a while all Halfie could hear was food being prepared in the kitchen, before the Wise Woman reappeared carrying a tray. On it Halfie saw sandwiches, scones and tea.

"What are you going to show me?" Halfie asked.

"Eat first."

They ate, finishing everything on the tray. Halfie realised she had eaten nothing except a few biscuits since breakfast. But somehow, she didn't mind that. She felt she should be the one to decide when and where to eat.

Then the Wise Woman said, "What do you know about breathing?"

"Breathing?"

"Yes."

Halfie had no idea what this question referred to. "We did respiration in biology last term."

"*Breathing*... in... out... taking your time. Thinking about it. Listening to your body."

"I don't know what you mean. Like tai chi?"

The Wise Woman stood up, gesturing for Halfie to follow. "Stand upright," she said, "like me."

Halfie did this.

"Now, Alfreda, what I want us to do is as follows. I want us to take a deep breath in over a count of three. Then I want us to hold it for a count of ten. Then gently breathe out over a count of five. Got that?"

Halfie frowned. "Who'll do the counting if we're holding our breaths?"

"I'll count down using my fingers, ten to one."

"All right."

"Ready?"

Halfie nodded.

Following the Wise Woman's lead, Halfie took in the deepest breath she could, held it during the countdown, then exhaled.

The Wise Woman said, "Got it?"

Halfie nodded again.

"We do that ten times. Remain silent. Ignore everything you hear outside. Just concentrate on deep, full breathing."

"Really, ten times?"

"Really ten times."

This they did. As the exercise progressed Halfie felt light-headed, but for the sake of the Wise Woman she continued.

"How do you feel now?" the Wise Woman asked when they finished.

Halfie sat down. "A bit dizzy."

"How do you feel in yourself?"

"I do feel a bit better I suppose. What's it all about?"

"It's a calming exercise," the Wise Woman replied. "*Don't* you go forgetting it – I do have the wisdom, after all. But I'm becoming worried about you, to tell the truth, so every time you feel your nerves coming on I want you to do that exercise. You'll find it will help. Do it calmly, and alone. Do it deliberately. Know the reason you're doing it."

"What reason?"

"I just told you. It's a well-known calming exercise. There's lots of them. In fact I'm going to teach you a few, because I think you need them."

A shudder passed up Halfie's spine. Feeling awkward, she said, "You mean, you think I'm ill?"

"Not ill. Just stressed."

"I'm not stressed, not a bit."

The Wise Woman grunted something. "I'll be the judge of that," she murmured.

Halfie did not want to upset the Wise Woman, so she nodded. "I didn't mean it badly," she said, "I just didn't realise you saw me like that. Are you really worried about me?"

"A little."

Halfie shrugged. "I can't think why."

"*That's* part of your problem."

Halfie frowned, waiting for more, but the Wise Woman seemed to think she had said enough on the topic.

"What'll you be doing next, Alfreda?" she asked. "Back to the festival?"

"Yes," Halfie replied. "Dad told me to."

"Told you?"

"Yes. Not horribly. Just told me."

"But you don't have to if you don't want to."

Halfie nodded. "I know." She hesitated. "But, there's no point annoying him if I can do otherwise. I wouldn't want to."

The Wise Woman leaned forward on the rocking chair, staring at her. "They're not your monarchs, you know."

The tone of the Wise Woman's voice and the look in her eyes transfixed Halfie. Now she felt uncomfortable. "I'd better go," she said. "Thank you for the tea, and the exercise, and the help. 'Bye."

Not waiting for a reply she slipped out of the barn, collecting the flower pot from beside the coop then hurrying into the field above the farmhouse. Ten minutes later the acorn was replanted.

Done. She stood up. Again she felt isolated. Who could help her? Nobody. She would have to help herself.

"I'll apologise to the King," she said. "Nobody can refuse a sincere apology."

She hurried back to the house. Once in her bedroom, she locked the door and took out a sheet of white A4 paper and an envelope. From her school bag she took a biro.

Bank Holiday Monday, May 28th.

Your Majesty, the Elf King –

This is Alfreda Chandler writing, daughter of Jane Chandler.

I was told that an error was made during the choosing ritual on Saturday. I am writing to you to express my sincere apologies for the offence caused.

Please accept this apology so that the curse can be revoked.

When I am accepted as a full elf, I will do everything you ask, like any loyal subject. You will find me honest, decent and true. I really want to be part of the Elven world.

Yours sincerely,

Alfreda Chandler.

Having written the letter, she folded the sheet twice then put it into the envelope. For a moment she wondered how she should address it, deciding in the end to explain to her mum what it was, then let her deliver it.

Apprehension flooded through her. She imagined what might happen when she met her mum in the festival field, what recriminations, what accusations.

No. Best not to imagine. Best to just do it.

She took a deep breath, then departed the house. The sun hung low; a marvellous sunset of orange and red. But something was bothering the musicians. As she watched, a small aeroplane swooped down across the stage, forcing Rainbow Tom to duck. Alarmed, she remembered Billy's drone controller, hidden behind the stage. As fast as possible she crossed the field, crawled behind the stage, then grabbed the pizza box and pulled out the controller. Moments later she sat hidden beneath the hedge, trying to work out the controls.

No time to think. She pressed a button, looking up at what she could see of the area around the stage. With a mosquito buzz the drone flew up, then across the stage, spiralling into the sky. Pulling one joystick left made it bank to the left, and the same with the right, so that after a few experiments she saw that her controller was overriding the other one. Holding her breath, she sent the drone across the hedge into Stone Farm property, and with a final twist of a joystick crashed it into the ground.

Success! She felt delight rise up, a tear in one eye. Triumph over enmity!

She whispered thanks to Billy, and swore never again to argue with him.

Together, she and Billy had rescued the Faerie Fayre from disruption.

The music continued. She crept around the side of the stage, seeing her mum at the back of the audience, a bamboo flute in each hand.

She caught her mum's gaze, then approached. "All right?"

"I'm on next. I can hear my music… can hear it."

"Good luck, Mum. Er, will you deliver this for me? Not now – tomorrow."

"Deliver?"

"It's for the Elf King," she explained. "That's why I haven't addressed the envelope."

"What?"

"An apology. To revoke the curse. I really mean it, it's not just any old letter."

"*Alfreda.* What are you doing? I'm about to go on stage and you're bothering me with *this?* I've told you all about the curse. We've discussed it. Now go away. What will be will be, and no note is going to change that."

And her mum walked away, gripping the flutes white-knuckled.

Halfie watched, appalled. Denial and anger: the last things she had expected.

She heard her mum's voice echo through her mind…

You've got to take this seriously. Your decision yesterday has set a whole chain of events going. Please be careful.

Rejection chilled her.

Yes, she had to be careful… yet she realised now she would get more help from a crow, an old woman and the boy next door than from her own family. That felt so wrong.

Halfie

CHAPTER 4

Halfie recalled something as her dreams vanished at dawn's break.

I'll take all your attic stuff and throw it out! I will. You watch me...

This threat, uttered by her mum in a voice not far off a tantrum, bothered her so much that on the morning after the Faerie Fayre she lay in bed and wondered what attic stuff could possibly have been referred to. Nobody went into the attic, which her dad described as half cobweb city and half-dead furniture parade, from which Halfie imagined a haunted place, never to be disturbed. But the thought would not fade. Her mum had threatened the Wise Woman, and it sounded personal. Why would the Wise Woman have stuff stored in the attic?

She turned over to glance at Badb, but the crow did not move, hunched over, feathers fluffed up. "You're quiet this morning," she said.

Badb made no reply.

"I'll have to answer my own question then."

Because everyone stores stuff in the attic.

64

Everybody kept junk, that was well known. Throwing things out was difficult, except when people moved house. Billy told a great story about his dad burning dresses, blouses and shoes the night before his mum moved out. Apparently a few weeks later a new partner moved into Stone Farm, with a new load of junk.

This being the morning after the Fayre, the smallholding would be quiet, a place of nursed hangovers, semi-stoned zombies and whining dogs. With the weather so warm and glorious, few, if any of the festival-goers would be inside the house. Still... if she was going to explore the attic, probably best to check.

Orange rays of sunlight made corridor wallpaper glow; rooms were vacant, silent, stuffy. The kitchen was empty, littered with beer cans, discarded food, ash and dog-ends. The place stank of stale smoke. But the house was silent. Not a murmur.

Back in her bedroom, she questioned Badb. "Shall I go now, while I've got the chance?"

Still Badb said nothing, nor even moved.

"Might as well," she whispered.

Snittonwood Farmhouse was not small: six bedrooms, three lavatories, two bathrooms, and any number of closets and chambers, not to mention extensive cellars. The attic, her dad said, ran from end to end and could itself encompass a small festival.

She prepared with care. She dressed in ripped jeans and a thick shirt, taking a woollen hat to protect her hair. She wore trainers with thick socks. In one hand she carried a torch, in the other the water spray she used to moisten her pot plants – this latter item her weapon against spiders. Then it was out into the corridor to pull the stepladder out of a closet and position it underneath the attic opening.

That opening was a semi-rotted board covering semi-rotted jambs, whose peeling paint showered down when she pushed the board aside. Cold air sank over her. She shivered, switching the torch on and pointing it up. No spiders.

Moments later she stood in the attic. All she could hear was noise outside: a few goats bleating, distant rooks, the squeak of the weathervane. No human voice disturbed the peace.

So began her exploration. Most of the stuff was indeed junk: ancient furniture, random cardboard boxes, a couple of metal-studded trunks, and any number of clothes hangers and shoe boxes. Disappointed, she traversed the attic from end to end, discovering nothing worth investigating.

She returned to the two trunks, finding one padlocked and one not. This latter she opened.

Clothes lay inside: vintage clothes, beautiful clothes. She plucked out a few, to find gauzy blouses, silk scarves, and a couple of lush, sequin-spattered dancing gowns. Yet they looked old-fashioned. Could these belong to the Wise Woman?

It seemed unlikely. She put her hand underneath the clothes to see if anything lay beneath, but it was garments all the way down.

The padlock on the second trunk had a four-digit lock, set to 3854. She studied it. Perhaps the code was something simple, like a default computer password: 1234. She raised the padlock and was about to set it when she stopped. Should she really try to guess the combination with nothing to go on? Again she studied the lock, thinking about its use, imagining somebody moving the cogs after snapping the padlock. Perhaps... perhaps that person had been careless.

Perhaps they had moved all four cogs at the same time. That *would* be something to go on.

It was worth a try, and better than 1234. She set the lock to 4965, but nothing – no click. 5076. Nothing.

When she set it to 6187 there was a click. She pulled the padlock open.

Jewel boxes lay inside.

There were not many – the trunk was three-quarters empty – but they were marked Liberty, Boodles and Hancocks. One was labelled in a Russian script.

She opened the top box to see a ruby necklace inside. It looked real, valuable. Other boxes held more jewellery, one a diamond brooch. The Russian box held an enamelled cigarette case.

One box stood out, however. It did not contain the best-looking piece, nor the most expensive, but she loved green gems, and the bracelet inside, created from silver-mounted emeralds, was too gorgeous to resist; and it fitted her slender wrist perfectly. She hesitated. She had not intended to keep anything. But an eerie sensation passed over her, as if she was being magically compelled. This bracelet was *special,* perhaps even of Faerie, and although her conscience twinged she could not bear to put the bracelet back when it felt so comfortable on her wrist. Something real and deep was calling to her through these green gemstones.

She padlocked the trunk shut and moved the cogs. Then she returned her attention to the other trunk. She lifted the top blouse, and in flickering torchlight saw a name sewn into the back of the collar: Nancy Sanders.

This was not a name she knew. Could it be the real name of the Wise Woman?

She felt she did not have enough evidence to know, though it seemed a possibility. Again she wondered why the Wise Woman might have belongings stored in the attic. Perhaps Nancy Sanders was the original owner of the smallholding. Yet she could hardly confront the old woman with such a claim, not after so much kindness.

With nothing left to explore she departed the attic, but standing beneath its opening she felt a pang of guilt as she glanced at the bracelet. She tugged her sleeve down to cover her wrist.

At noon she ventured out, finding a few hungover festival-goers wandering about. Half the cars had gone, though Woody End Lane still looked full from what she could see of van roofs peeking over the tops of hedges. Another pang of guilt rose up as she realised she had neglected her duties.

The lane was not blocked, though passing cars might struggle. She decided to leave it. Atop the lower field of Stone Farm she saw Billy in a tractor, so she waved to him. He waved back. She turned, but, hearing a hooting noise, turned back, to see Billy still waving at her. She waved again, but then, aware of something amiss, waited to see what he would do. He leapt out of the tractor and sprinted down the field to the lane hedge.

They spoke leaning against a gate, he on the field side, she in the lane.

"What do you want?" she asked.

"Did you use your drone controller?" he replied.

"Yes! Thanks very much."

"I thought so. Dad was fuming yesterday. And he had a right go at me about doing a shoddy job with the controller, though I think he was just embarrassed he'd crashed it."

"Well, that was a nice thing to do for me, Billy." She hesitating, trying to decide what effect her words were having. Not much. "You're the decent type," she added.

He smiled. "Maybe. But listen... are all those hippies going soon?"

"Usually what happens is they leave on the Tuesday apart from a handful of friends – half a dozen at most. People my mum knows from her young days. They sometimes stay the whole Whit week." She shrugged. "Rainbow Tom will stay an extra day to dismantle his stage and gear, but he'll be off tomorrow to another festival." She shrugged again. "I can always lock myself into my bedroom if it's too hectic in the house."

He pursed his lips, glancing over his shoulder at the Fayre field. "What do you reckon, then, to what happened?"

"What happened when?"

"With my dad."

Halfie said, "He was his usual self. We were expecting it."

"Ain't denying you were. What I meant was, it's a pity that stage has to be on that partic'lar field."

"It's a Faerie field," Halfie replied, "they both are. The spring feeds them. Not with water – with magic."

"And that's why your mum puts the stage there?" he asked.

"Of course."

He paused for thought, taking a grass stem to chew, leaning against the gate to study the two fields.

"What?" said Halfie, aware that she was missing his point.

"Be a shame if them fields turned out to be my dad's."

"Well, they won't. The elves wouldn't allow it. They'd stop it. They *own* the fields."

He looked surprised. "What, they'd stop the English law? You believe that?"

"Of course I do. They'd put a spell against you."

"Not me," he replied. "You mean, my dad."

Now Halfie hesitated, aware of an odd undercurrent in his voice. "I suppose so," she said, glancing away, "though I've never heard you speaking against him."

Billy looked at her, his expression blank. Then he gave a ghastly grin and said, "Not the sort of father you can go against."

Halfie felt more than she heard. She felt his pain, his exasperation, his confusion. "Is he... rough with you?" she asked.

"Sometimes."

He said it in a way that meant: often.

She did not know what to say. Though William Ordish's reputation for being a spiteful malcontent was known across Ludlow and its surrounds, she felt she had acquired via Billy a window into a shameful, unpleasant secret. It made her feel uncomfortable, as when her dad was rude to her, or peeved.

She could not look Billy in the eye now.

"You all right?" he asked.

She glanced at him, then nodded. "You?"

"S'pose so."

Silence fell over them.

Then Billy said, "Elves couldn't go against the full law."

"That won't happen anyway."

"What if the bridleway is the real boundary?"

She glanced at him. In overheard conversations, she had gathered that this was the gist of the Ordish complaint. "I don't think it can be, Billy. The elves don't follow our ways, our laws. They have their own paths, which we have to follow. The bridleway happens to go through our fields. It's not a boundary, not even an ancient one."

He nodded, then replied, "S'pose the elves could be forced, or bought off. You reckon that could happen?"

"No."

"Why not?"

"They don't pay attention to anything like that," she replied. "They're their own people – the country folk. They've got their own ways. I told you."

"You ever seen one?"

"Not yet."

"Because you're only half and half?"

She scowled, unhappy with the term. "I wouldn't put it like that."

He stood upright, nodding once. "I meant nothing by it," he said. "Honestly. I meant, you know... because you only recently chose to become an elf."

She sensed him making an effort to understand her. "It's not a belief," she said. "It's true. My mum knows, and my dad's the Faerie Ambassador."

"Yes... doing missionary work in Ludlow."

"I told you – that's his job."

"You reckon?"

"Yes," she replied. "Why?"

"Nothing."

"*What,* Billy? What are you saying?"

"Nothing."

Again she felt riled by his scepticism. "You'd better get back to your tractor," she said, turning away.

He reached out to grab her by the shoulder. "Wait. Don't forget what I said about them fields, Halfie. All right? No Faerie spring's gonna get in the way, nor even your elves… I mean, if there is a legal dispute."

"Well there *won't* be one," Halfie retorted, walking away.

At the bottom of the track she paused to look back. In the distance, she saw Billy inside his tractor cab. All seemed returned to normal.

Yet something nagged at the back of her mind. It was almost as if he had been trying to tell her something, to warn her, at first directly, in his clumsy way, then with more thought, more sensitivity. She felt uneasy. He was mundane, Billy Ordish – a lad of the human world, clad in mud and wellies. She was an elf – red-haired, slender, fey.

But for all his mundanity she felt sure now he was trying to help her, or, if not, to interfere for what he thought was the common good. And that felt disquieting.

Next morning she happened across her dad in the kitchen. Her mum was in Snittonwood, communing with the elves.

"Dad?"

He sent her an expression of dull defeat. "What?"

She hesitated. His mood seemed fair, if rather distant.

"Sorry," she said, "it's just a quick question."

"Go on, then."

"You know the disputed fields?"

"Yes."

She continued, "What if a full legal dispute comes up?"

He shook his head. "Old Ordish has been threatening that for years. But the spring stops him, and he knows it."

"Does he?"

"Of course."

Halfie pondered Snittonwood to the north of their smallholding. Stone Farm had its own woodland, also to the north. "Is there a Stonewood Shee?" she asked.

"Some say so. But elves are mighty territorial folk, and often they won't acknowledge other Faerie outposts."

"Is that what Mum told you?"

He hesitated. "I do know a few things myself, Halfie."

"Being the Ambassador."

"Exactly."

Halfie looked away, dropping a couple of slices of bread into the toaster then saying, "Did the Elf King himself invest you?"

"Not directly."

"Did you see him?"

He shook his head.

Halfie grasped for a lead. "Did you want to?"

"I didn't mind. I've got the document, transcribed by your mother."

"Where is it?"

He frowned. "If you want to look at it, well... maybe later. Not now, I've got a headache coming on. It's locked in a drawer somewhere in the study."

His nonchalant acceptance made her realise the document was insignificant. But there was still more she needed to know.

"William Ordish tried to stop the music last night," she said.

"I know. With a radio-controlled plane. What an idiot. We soon put paid to him."

"Who did?"

"We cast a spell to make him crash it," he said. "And it worked. He's a moron."

Perplexed, Halfie leaned on her elbows and looked away. The toast popped up. "Want some?"

"Only with aspirin on it," he grunted.

Halfie thought as she spread butter on the toast. They had cast a spell... yet she knew *she* had saved the Fayre. "But spells sometimes don't work," she said.

"True enough," he sighed. "But this time it did – we got the proof."

"Proof?"

"The crash. Ordish's face must've been black with rage. The stupid old coot. At least it wasn't manure this year – that really was annoying."

Halfie nodded. Still baffled, she said, "What if the spring doesn't stop Mr Ordish?"

"Why do you keep on about it? He's a coward, like all blustering troublemakers. We can safely ignore him. Anyway, so what? We can beat anybody."

"Well, what do the farmhouse deeds show?" she asked.

"That's none of your business!" Now he seemed vexed. Halfie turned away, preparing to flee, knowing she had prodded too far. "Anyway," he continued, "the deeds are very old, and the bridleway's new. Damn council regulations a few decades ago. Local politicians – all idiots, and all in the pockets of big business. What the hell do they know about country rights of way?"

He calmed down, wiping his mouth with a tissue.

Halfie made ready to run, but he said nothing more. He seemed sore-headed rather than angry with her.

At length he said, "All *you* need to focus on is the curse. Your mother will try to help you, but you're the one who's got to put in the work."

She nodded. "I will, Dad, you can rely on me."

"Yes, well, I hope I can. Elves are *so* damn particular."

Halfie hesitated as a thought occurred to her. "I hope I don't bring bad luck on the smallholding."

"Me too."

She looked at him, surprised. "You mean, that could happen?"

"Didn't we tell you? Seven years of bad luck. That covers you and everything around you."

"Then... if there's a dispute over the fields, that might be my fault."

He grimaced. "That *would* be your fault. Stop talking about the fields, I'm sick of it. I told you – Ordish is a coward and a dunce. He won't dare take me on."

"And Mum."

"*Me*. Leave your mother out of this. She's got enough on her plate already."

"Sorry, Dad."

"Haven't you got school work to do?"

She shook her head.

"Why not?"

"Nobody gave us any," she answered. "We had our end of topic exams, then that was it."

Her dad stood up, striding away. "Can't even trust the school to do its job properly." He slammed the kitchen door behind him.

Now Halfie felt anxious. The curse was real. The curse was active. It could even spread to her own family. She felt she had to believe her parents' warnings, so she hurried upstairs to consult Badb, but still the crow was quiet, and silent. She opened the window, but Badb did not move.

"I need help," she said, stroking black feathers. "Bad luck is on the way, I can *feel* it."

Nothing.

She sat back. Perhaps a quick visit to the Wise Woman…

Knowing her mum was in Snittonwood, and seeing her dad walking back to the Fayre fields, she hurried across the yard to knock at the barn door. A few moments later the Wise Woman opened it.

"Hello, dear. Time for a morning cuppa?"

"Er… yes, thank you."

"Come in, then."

She followed the Wise Woman inside, then sat in her usual seat.

"Do you like herbal tea?" the Wise Woman asked, poking her head through the kitchen doorway.

Halfie was familiar with the vast range of herbal teas stocked by her mum. "What sort have you got?" she asked.

"Chamomile."

"Okay. That'll do."

A few minutes later the Wise Woman returned carrying a tray, on which stood a teapot and two cups. "You sounded quite dismissive of it," she said.

"Of what?"

"Of chamomile tea."

Halfie said, "Not really."

"They sell it at Myriad Organics in Ludlow, you know. I think it could be good for you."

"Good for me? How?"

"Country lore. Wise Woman knowledge. It's called the Mother of the Gut."

"That sounds vile," Halfie said.

"Listen to me. I'm serious. It's been known for centuries that chamomile is good for things like sickness caused by nerves."

Now Halfie thought she grasped what the Wise Woman was talking about. "You mean, me?"

"Who else? Do pay attention, dear. I want you to begin drinking this regularly."

"Why? What does it do?"

"It's particularly good for gastric irritation," said the Wise Woman. "It's an anti-inflammatory. It works on dyspepsia, stomach ulcers and the colic."

"But I don't have those."

"Don't you?"

Halfie shrugged. "Well, I don't think so."

"Then you don't *know*. I suspect you do have dyspepsia, of a sort anyway. You've been suffering from a lot of anxiety recently, and that can affect a delicate stomach. You struggle to eat sometimes. Look how thin you are. You've told me any number of times that you feel sick, or nauseous, or that you're not hungry. I know the signs, so don't go denying it."

Halfie could not argue with this. If country women of wisdom knew anything, it was herb lore. "How often should I drink it?" she asked.

"Once a day will be enough. It's particularly good for nervous tension which brings dyspepsia. That's you, I'm certain. It's nothing to be ashamed of. Some people are more prone to it, some less. In some people it's their heart that's affected, not their stomach. Then they get a heart attack because of stress."

"Do you really think I've got stress?"

The Wise Woman nodded. "I think you've got *far* too much to think about at the moment, something which shouldn't be bothering a tender teenager one year away from her GCSE exams."

Halfie nodded, glancing away. The Wise Woman meant the elven curse.

"Chamomile can also soothe a painful period," the Wise Woman continued. "You might like to remember that – I know you started a couple of years ago. So, drink a well-steeped cup in the evening. It's a mild sedative, so it'll help you sleep too."

"All right, I will. I'll raid Mum's stock, then buy some more at Myriad."

"Well make sure you do. Get the best brand, the most expensive one."

"I will."

Halfie sat forward to pour the last of the tea into her cup, but as she did there came a gasp. She looked up to see the Wise Woman staring at her hand.

"Where did you get *that?*" the Wise Woman asked, pointing.

Halfie quailed. The Wise Woman looked appalled. "What?" she asked.

"That bracelet."

The emerald bracelet had ridden down her wrist, emerging from the long sleeve of her blouse. "Um…"

The Wise Woman stood up, her face red with anger. "*Where?*"

Halfie froze. Stunned, she stared.

"*Answer* me."

"Er…"

"Did Jane give it to you?"

"No!" Halfie said, standing up. Her limbs trembled and all she wanted to do was run. "Nobody did," she said. "I'm sorry, is it yours? I didn't know – honestly."

"How could you have just found it? You thieved it!"

"But… but… no, I *didn't*. I just found it."

"Where?"

"In... in..." Halfie sighed, then collapsed back into the chair. "But I didn't *know*. I just found it, and it called out to me. I felt Faerie pulling me, I really did."

"You found it in the attic? Locked up?"

Halfie glanced up, horrified. "Are you Nancy?"

"Come here, girl. *Here*. This instant."

Halfie dared not move, so after a few moments the Wise Woman strode forward and grabbed her hand, pulling the bracelet off. Then the Wise Woman stepped backward, clutching her neck with one twitching hand.

"Jane must have given it to you," she said. "Those things were locked—"

"*No*," Halfie cried. "No, *honestly,* I swear. I overheard you arguing with Mum, and Mum mentioned things in the attic. So, well... I had a look."

"It was locked away."

"Only with a padlock. I guessed the combination."

The Wise Woman choked. "Guessed? Impossible."

"I *did*. I truly did. It was easy—"

"This is *not* for you, nothing in the attic belongs to you. You'll leave it alone."

"Oh, I will," said Halfie, "I promise. I didn't mean to—"

"Well, you *did*. Now get out of here."

"But it's magic, I'm sure."

The Wise Woman uttered a single laugh. "There's no such thing."

Halfie leapt up and ran to the door, but, fumbling at the catch, she risked glancing back. The Wise Woman stared at her, face red, gasping for breath, clutching the bracelet to her mouth as if kissing it.

"Bad luck," Halfie wailed. "It's happening—"

Halfie

"Nonsense," the Wise Woman shouted. "You can just stop all that as well. It's stuff and nonsense. There is no curse, there *never* was. I'll make Jane regret this for the rest of her days."

Halfie fled.

CHAPTER 5

William Ordish visited the smallholding on Friday morning to make his declaration. He wore a grease-stained jacket over a vest, black trousers, and walking boots with red laces. He held a dog-end in one hand and an unlit cigarette in the other. It so happened that Halfie and her dad were in the yard, clearing away wood used to repair pig pens, so they saw him stomping up the track from the lane.

"Uh-oh," her dad said.

"Shall I go and get Mum?"

"No."

Halfie hesitated, wondering if she should depart, but before William entered the yard her mum turned the farmhouse corner and saw them all.

"What's going on here?" she asked, as William arrived and lit his cigarette.

"I got a bone to pick with you two Chandlers," he replied, gesturing at her. "An' this time I got the maps to prove it."

Halfie shrank back as her dad took a step forward. "You'll deal with me," he said. "What maps are you talking about?"

William gestured again, whirling his hand like a windmill. "See all this? This ain't no farm, not like mine."

"That's why we refer to it as a smallholding," came the reply.

"I always known you had too much land–"

"Too much? What do you mean, too much? Is this about those two fields again?"

"That it is," William replied. "And, like I says, this time I got the maps to prove it."

Halfie glanced aside to see her dad gave a sneer. "I'd like to see *those*," he said. "Drawn by your own fair hand, I expect."

William rummaged in his pockets, bringing out a scroll of what appeared to be photocopied papers. "You ain't got no cause to mock me this time, Duncan Chandler. I done me research. As I always suspected, the bridleway yonder is the original boundary 'tween my big farm and your itty-bitty plot of land. Them two fields is mine. And now I got the evidence I'm gonna take you to court – get 'em back, see? Unless you hand 'em over, that is – 'cos you'd better."

"You won't win any court case, William Ordish. I've done my research too. The bridleway is only a few decades old, made by the local council–"

"You shush yer mouth! I lived at Stone Farm all my life, and there was always a track there before the bridleway. Public right of way, as was. Them council nobs just upgraded it to a bridleway so as horses and whatnot could go up and down. Now, you see here. You're new folk, you two. My family's always been here. We know what's ours, and we'll have it. If you don't give them fields back to me I'm takin' you to court."

"Threats don't scare me."

"Like as not," William replied with a scowl. "Seems nothin' scares him with drugs for brains."

Halfie's dad leaned forward and snatched the scroll, opening it to view the map. After a while, he said, "I've got a brain. These are only old picturesque maps, made by country squires in the nineteenth century. They're not legal, or even evidence."

"Yes, they bloody well are."

"They're visual representations, pictures, paintings. They're semi-imaginary." He thrust the scroll back. "Take them away. If you bring a court case, I'll defend it – and win."

"Hah! No, you bloody well won't."

At this, Halfie's mum stepped forward, raising her hands as if for calm. "Mr Ordish," she began. "William... please. Let's not become rude. This is all about a little bit of mess made by my kin, isn't it? Beer cans... pizza boxes. Some sound overspill from the stage."

"Kin? What's kin?"

"The elven folk. You've always disliked the Faerie Fayre, and–"

"Don't you *see,* woman?" William retorted. "You're a bloody hippie and he's a bloody hippie and your gal is too, and every bloody man or woman who came here on Monday was a hippie too. This elf business is nonsense."

"No it isn't. This is all about the spring. You want the spring because the brook runs into your fields. You want what it can offer. But you have your own wood – Stonewood. Snittonwood and its shee are ours, and the spring is too."

"Jane Chandler, I'm tellin' you this right now. No lawyer in the world'll believe your hippie crap. If I gotta take you to court to get what's mine, I will. Now see sense, will yer? You ain't got a hope of winnin'. I want what's mine. Give it me. If you do, we'll say no more about it. You can have your bloody festival in some other field – eastwards, like, well away from my land."

"But we can't. It has to be near the elven spring."

William threw up his hands with a shout. "Gagh! Right – don't say I didn't warn you. Expect to hear from my lawyers."

"We'll do that," Halfie's dad said. "We'll defend ourselves and win. You'll have to pay a lot of money for lawyers, and my guess is you don't want to. That's why you've held off for so long."

"Says you."

"Yes! Says me. Now get off my property."

William glared at him. "*Your* property, is it?"

He stormed out of the yard, his hair as wild as a thorn bush. Halfie heard a diminishing stream of curses as he strode down the track.

She looked at her mum, who stood silent, white-faced.

"You all right, Mum?"

But her mum said nothing. She seemed in shock.

"Leave us be for a moment," her dad told her.

Frightened, Halfie ran around the farmhouse, hesitating by the kitchen door, listening, then walking indoors. She shut the door.

"You okay, love?"

She turned around to see Slick Lizzie, the last person from the Fayre staying at the farmhouse. Sitting at the table, Lizzie wore tie-dyed trousers and a silk waistcoat, her feet bare, a cup of herbal tea in one hand.

Halfie nodded at her, though she could not change the expression of horror on her face. The curse...

"What's the matter?" Lizzie asked.

"The neighbour. He's taking us to court. Mum looks white as a sheet."

Lizzie studied her, sympathy on her face. "I've known your mother for over twenty years," she said. "And..."

Halfie held her breath, sensitive to what she felt might be a revelation. But Lizzie deflated, sinking into her chair, placing the cup on the table.

"Perhaps not," she murmured.

"What?" Halfie asked, running up to her. "Do you know something?"

Lizzie looked at her again, and now Halfie received a clear impression of empathy. "Not really. Things change."

"What things?"

"It's difficult to explain."

"Try me," Halfie said. "Why won't you tell me?"

"Your mother... she... some people get sucked in too deep, in our culture."

"Your culture? You mean, elven?"

"The alternative. The counter-culture. The underground. It's had all sorts of names over the years. And some parts of it are quite dangerous."

"What parts?"

Lizzie shook her head. "Your mother was always away with the fairies."

Halfie nodded. "We call it Faerie."

"I mean... she was prone. To being imaginative."

"You mean, musical?"

Lizzie smiled. "Rainbow Tom knows every band on the festival circuit, and he says for all the talented musicians he's worked with, only Jane has the gift. She is very special. But she was tempted. She went too far."

"Too far into what?"

"The whole Faerie thing. She believed."

"Of course," said Halfie. "We all do. Snittonwood Shee *is* in Snittonwood. I realise it's unusual, but nobody could deny that."

Lizzie shrugged. "Some could."

"You mean… nonbelievers?"

Lizzie hesitated. "Have you done that at school in R.E.?"

"Not really."

Lizzie leaned forward, putting a hand on Halfie's arm. "Listen to me before I go. Take great care of your mum – she's fragile – but don't forget yourself in the process. I remember when you were born, and growing up. In some ways they weren't the best of parents." She sighed. "I suppose I shouldn't have said that. I hope you don't mind. I mean, your father… I don't suppose he ever imagined being a parent."

Halfie did not know what to think. "Well, my dad has got a temper."

"Yes, that's the kind of thing I mean. And I do know them both very well, so I'm not speaking entirely out of turn. Halfie, all I'm saying is this. Keep a sense of proportion. Look at the wide world and see how varied it is. Then put yourself first when you need to."

Halfie understood less of this declaration, but she did sense the significance of it. "I won't forget what you've told me," she said, "though some of it I don't really…"

"No," Lizzie sighed. "I'm sorry."

"Will you tell me more?"

Lizzie studied her for a few moments. "Do you think you'll maybe have children?"

Abashed, and surprised at the personal nature of the question, Halfie looked away. "I honestly haven't thought about it."

"No."

"Have you got any?"

Lizzie shook her head. "Some women know they don't want to. But the pressure is very strong to be a mother. Yet... I always knew my path lay elsewhere. Jane was like that. Then, she had you."

Hearing this, Halfie felt she could at last see a glimmer of what Lizzie meant; but it felt dangerous. Too painful to consider. Too ferocious.

"She had you," Lizzie continued, "and that changed her... a little."

"It would though."

"It will change her some more I hope, as you get older. Make the effort to find out who you really are... Alfreda." Lizzie stood up, stretching. "I'd better see if our car will start. We haven't used it since Monday, and with some VWs that's not good."

"Wait," Halfie said. "What do you mean, who you really are?"

"Just don't be who people *tell* you to be."

Now Halfie was baffled. "All right," she said.

Lizzie studied her. "Do you have a middle name?"

"Maeve."

"Maeve," Lizzie said with a smile. "What a lovely name. Alfreda sounds so old fashioned!"

Halfie nodded. "I suppose so."

"Goodbye... Maeve. 'Til next Whit."

"'Bye. Drive carefully."

Lizzie turned away and departed the kitchen. At once Halfie knew she needed to see Badb: there were things to say, to express, to feel. But upstairs Badb lay on her side, quite still.

Halfie froze, staring. Her skin crawled. Then she inched forward, eyes wide, until, at the corrugated iron dais, she reached out to touch Badb.

Badb did not move. Badb was dead.

Halfie stared for a long time.

Then she stepped back.

All she could feel was numb isolation. She had *wanted* Badb – to speak with, to listen, to be there for her. Now the Wise Woman was gone, and Badb too.

She stood in Snittonwood at dusk, alone.

She listened. She strained every sinew in her body: leaning, turning her head, shutting her eyes, concentrating. But she heard no hint of elven voices, no shimmer of elven music played on silver harps and flower petals. Badb was silent and the elves were too.

She was not an elf yet. The curse ran true. She was trapped; half mundane.

By a deep hole in the earth she knelt. Badb lay wrapped inside a cloth of green raw silk. She had brushed the feathers with a paintbrush, and cleaned the beak and talons with soapy water.

Inside the hole she laid Badb, half a metre down. She pulled back the silk wrapping for a final peek. Badb seemed to be sleeping; she could not view it any other way. Then she took a piece of red sandstone and laid it over dead Badb. Protection from woodland beasts.

She filled the hole to half its depth, then placed another, larger stone inside: double protection. Then she filled the hole, leaving a small dip in which she planted a seedling – she knew not what sort. That it would be a tree was all she cared about.

Trees… they swayed about her. She listened. Sometimes they sounded like the sea… certain species, with certain leaf shapes. Could that be the real elf music?

She waited. Feelings would well up, she knew. Soon.

The sun set. Evening light faded.

Tears trickled down her cheeks.

"Goodbye, Badb. Thank you. I won't forget you."

She strolled to the edge of the wood, hands in pockets. Clouds earlier in the day had leaned in from the west, suggesting rain to come; the end of the glorious weather. The curse again. Deep, broad, natural symbols mirroring her bad luck, emphasising it, articulating it.

She trudged back along hedges to the bridleway, which she followed to the spring field. There she turned in, walking across the grass until the ground became boggy, her shoes squelching in waterlogged earth.

All this turmoil over a simple spring. Why couldn't people leave it alone?

She knelt down, dipped her hands into the clear centre of the spring – a basin little broader than her hand – and lifted up enough to drink. The ritual action cleared her mind. Glancing up at the twinkling yellow lights of Stone Farm she flicked a two-fingered V, then turned away and hurried along the western track.

In the kitchen she found her mum, sitting alone.

She halted, trying to sense her mum's mood.

She said nothing: waited.

Her mum looked up, melancholy in her face. "Hello, Halfie. Did you feed the goats?"

"Er… this afternoon."

"Good."

"You all right, Mum?"

"Slick Lizzie left a present for you." Her mum indicated a large wicker picnic hamper.

"Oh… right."

"Who's M?"

"M?" said Halfie.

"It's labelled M. Who are you supposed to give it to?"

Halfie walked across the kitchen to examine the hamper, upon which a re-used envelope had been taped, labelled M.

"Er," she said, "I think that's the original owner. Lizzie did say this was for me?"

"Yes, she did."

"I'll take it upstairs then."

"All right."

Halfie glanced back. "You look… sad, Mum."

"I'm so worried about your curse."

Halfie did not like this emphasis on *your*. She turned away, sitting on a stool beside the empty, cold wood-burner. "I want to have it removed," she said.

Her mum was in a distracted frame of mind – no reply.

"Mum, I'm sorry about that letter," she said in a meek voice.

"What letter?"

Halfie hesitated, wanting to reach the important issue. "Won't you tell me the full wording of the curse? Because I read that often…" She paused for thought, knowing she must get this correct. "… often a Faerie curse can be dealt with through an escape clause in the words – a pun, a double meaning, you know the kind of thing."

"The King is such a stern monarch. He will have carefully considered every sentence."

Halfie asked, "But does the curse exist anywhere, written down?"

"I heard it as he uttered it. It won't be proclaimed again."

"Then... it *could* be written down. For me to read later. Please?"

Her mum turned a cold gaze upon her. "Do see sense, Alfreda. Do you imagine the elves know how to write? They don't. Theirs is a spoken, sometimes sung culture. I hear their music on the Snittonwood breeze. It keeps me alive. It's why I play it on my flutes, to sustain me, to feed me. I'd never survive otherwise. I'm sure I'd starve. Oh, yes... I'd starve."

Halfie shuddered, disturbed by these unexpected references. She drew breath to make a soothing comment, but then held it. Her mum was so black-and-white. She would simply return time and again to her own thoughts; that was always her way.

But now a new line of enquiry suggested itself. "How long have you known the elves here?" she asked.

"Since the day we arrived."

Halfie said, "You must know the elf scribe very well then."

"The what?"

"The... herald."

Her mum nodded.

Halfie continued, "Couldn't you get him to proclaim the curse again? Then you could write it down exactly."

"An impossible task," her mum cried, sitting up. She gave a strangled wail, then sat back.

"To have it proclaimed again?" Halfie whispered.

Her mum leaned forward, resting her head on her arms. "You've got to undertake an impossible task," she murmured, "that's the only way to have the curse revoked. Oh, it's hopeless… hopeless…"

In desperation, and seeing the state of her mother, Halfie felt sudden courage. "It *can't* be," she said. "There's always an escape clause, you know that. Dad'll know it too. It's how the elves work – by words. Words will save us, Mum."

No reply.

Halfie continued, "I read some of the books in the study about Faerie lore. I know what I'm talking about. It's true though, isn't it? I *do* know how serious this is, whatever you might think. I know the elves are out there, thinking about me, annoyed at the insult. I *know* all that, Mum, honestly. So I want to get out of the curse their way, and that means using their words to revoke it. You've got to write it down for me. *Please.* I need that."

"I'll try," her mum muttered, not moving.

"Can't you do it now?"

No reply.

"Strike while the iron's hot, Mum? Let's do it. Before horrible Mr Ordish comes back and–"

"*Don't* you mention that man's name in my house," her mum cried, sitting up. "Never again. And for goodness' sake… don't mention iron."

Halfie shrank back. Elves abhorred iron. "Sorry," she murmured.

"That farmer is the enemy of Snittonwood Shee. The rumour is, the elves of Stonewood Shee are massing for battle."

Halfie stared. There was an irrational edge to this claim. "You heard that? How?"

"In the air. Elf speech… elf songs… martial songs. Can't you hear it?"

Halfie shook her head. Something in her mum's manner made her feel that the claim was foolish at best. "Surely not war," she said.

"The farmer is their mundane agent. He and Stonewood Shee will ruin us if we let them, so we've got to resist."

Halfie said, "Agent? Mum, I don't think that could possibly be true. But anyway, Dad will resist in court."

Her mum gave a wild laugh. "That's just the mundane side of it! Halfie, can't you see what's going on here? It's a battle for the spring, for Snittonwood Shee, for *me*. He hates me because I'm an elf. He's got me in his sights."

"Who has? Mr...?"

Her mum did not hear the question, or ignored it. "They'll fight over me, the Stonewood elves, until they've destroyed me. But I won't let them. Together we'll stand our ground, protect our smallholding, the wood, the fields. This is our land. We're tied to it by magic, by nature, by earth forces. All that old man's got is his deeds. Paper! It's nothing. Ink and dead trees. That's for ordinary folk. But we're not ordinary, we're special. That's why we live out here in the middle of nowhere. We're different. So we'll use different methods to fight back."

Halfie stood up, now too frightened to stay. "Okay, Mum. I hear what you're saying. Time for bed. Um... sleep well."

"I won't sleep tonight."

Halfie crept away then hurried upstairs. With the bedroom door shut, she glanced around her room, realising that, at last, the house was empty of strangers. She took the key from around her neck. Best to lock herself in anyway.

She stood motionless, silent. There was no Badb to reassure her.

She began taking deep breaths.

Halfie

On the Saturday, Halfie wandered along Woody End Lane, completing her Fayre task, which was to collect any rubbish left lying around; but nothing remained except a couple of cans and a stack of cigarette ends. Grey clouds swept over western skies, threatening rain, but the forecast for Sunday was much better. Halfie hoped the last day of the holiday would be sunny and warm – something positive to take back to school.

She was not looking forward to going back to school.

At the top of the adjacent field she saw William and Billy, but she dared not wave at them. For a few minutes she watched the pair as they walked up and down a hedge, until William pointed at Billy then strode off.

Taking her opportunity, she waved at Billy. Without hesitation he hurried down the slope, stopping at the gate.

"Hello, Halfie."

"How are you?" she asked.

He glanced over his shoulder, a look of irritation on his face. "Got told off again."

"What for?"

"Ah... nothing. What you up to?"

"Tidying. But there's almost nothing been chucked down here." She hesitated, wondering how to broach the topic of the legal dispute. "I'm sorry about..."

He nodded. "Yes. That."

Without hope, she said, "It's not really anything to do with us, is it? We're just hangers-on."

He nodded again. "You got that right."

"And you did help me on Monday. I know you mean well."

"Changed your mind about me, then?"

She scowled, but then found it impossible to repress a grin. "Maybe. You were trying to warn me before, weren't you?"

"About the…"

"Yes, that."

"My dad told me he come over to yours yesterday," Billy said, "but he didn't get nowhere."

"You can say that again. My dad'll fight it in court."

"Yes…"

"You and me won't fight though, will we?"

He shook his head. "S'pose not."

Halfie glanced back at the lane. "I'm glad they're all gone," she said.

"Too noisy was it, your place?"

She studied his face, uncertain as to his meaning. "You don't mind a bit of music, do you? Just for one day."

"It don't bother me none. But my dad, he loathes it. Keeps a grudge, he does."

Halfie nodded, thinking of what her mother had said the previous evening. She felt she needed reassurance, certainty. "Whatever happens, Billy," she said, "you and I mustn't fight."

"No." He glanced away, then looked back. "'Cos you ain't got nobody else, have you?"

Halfie felt her eyes mist and her throat tighten, but she forced the emotion back. She did not want Billy to know about her isolation – about losing Badb, about the rift with the Wise Woman. "I never had a brother or sister," she said.

"I got the kid bro', but I might as well not have. Daft bugger."

"Dave? He's all right."

"No he ain't," Billy grunted. "Anyway, I'm not here to talk about him."

"Oh. Did you want to say something else?"

"Just that I set up a new document for IT at school, for you and me, like. I'm gonna keep a record of what my dad does with this dispute. You do the same. Then we can share it if we need to. Compare notes."

"Billy! That's kind. You really don't want this to go ahead, do you?"

"It's stupid," he said. "But my dad's a bad sort. He'll do you over if you put a foot wrong. He don't care none – and that's not my way, though I gotta hide it from him else he tan me one. So, you see, I wanted to warn you."

"Again."

He nodded. "I can't do much 'cos I'm only his son, but I'll do what I can. I don't believe in your elves or any of that kinda stuff, but I see right enough you're upset, and worried about the law. And that ain't fair."

Halfie stood listening, realising to her surprise that he was sincere in everything he said. She had earlier guessed about his reluctance to follow his father, but this was different. This was a deeper, hidden Billy emerging.

"Listen," she said, "have you got much work to do on the farm tomorrow?"

"Mebbe 'til noon."

"Shall we have an end of holiday picnic?"

"Where?" he asked.

Thinking of the picnic hamper, Halfie turned to gaze at Snittonwood. "I got a present yesterday," she said, "and it's full of leftovers from the Fayre. Good ones, nothing off. Posh food."

"Hippie food?"

"No! Decent stuff. Shall we take it to... Stonewood? Tomorrow, one o'clock."

He hesitated, looking her over. "What's the weather forecast?"

"Surely you know?"

"No."

"Sunny. Warm."

"That'll be high pressure," he mused. "Well, I don't see why not."

"Oh, Billy! Show a bit of enthusiasm."

"Okay. I'll come."

"Will you be able to sneak away from your dad?" she asked.

"Pretty easy, I reckon." He paused, then nodded with more vigour. "Let's meet by the hedge at the top field on my side, just under Stonewood eaves. There's a thin bit of hawthorn you can squeeze through. You can't see that hedge from the farmhouse nor any of the lower fields, so we should be in the clear. Yes... it'll be nice. Reckon you're not ready for school."

"No. You?"

"Not really. Rather stay here." He glanced over his shoulder. "Better go. One o'clock tomorrow, or thereabouts then."

She smiled as he turned to leave.

Stonewood... and she was an elf.

An opportunity to listen.

CHAPTER 6

alfie waited for almost half an hour before Billy turned up, a time in which she became agitated. She could hear vehicles at Stone Farm, but could not see them. She could hear the faintest echo of voices, but saw no people. As the minutes ticked by she began to regret asking Billy. Most girls at school thought him a no-hoper.

Then, as the wind carried the sound of St Laurence's bells striking the half hour, she saw him running along a hedge. She sighed, relieved, but could not let go of her irritation. All that worrying for nothing.

"You're late," she said as he came within earshot.

He did not reply until he stood beside her. After a few deep breaths, he replied, "Sorry about that. Dad wanted me to move some extra loads of manure. Anyway, it's harvest coming up, and he thinks it'll be early this year. Fine weather." He took a final deep breath, exhaled, then added, "I need some food now. Hungry."

Halfie felt her anxiety begin to fade. "Well," she said, "at least you made it."

"Is that the hamper?"

"Yes."

"It's a big 'un."

Halfie wanted to scorn this obvious remark, but she did not have the heart to. He was here, that was what mattered. "Well... where shall we go?"

"It's so warm already. Let's go in the shade."

Halfie nodded. "If we get too cool, we can sit in the sun."

He laughed. "That's science!" He seemed in a good mood, which Halfie appreciated. Too often when the name Ordish came up everyone felt apprehensive, or solemn.

"Do you want to do science for A Level?" she asked.

He pointed to a glade just inside the wood. "I want to drive racing cars," he said.

"Yes... Lucy Rees said that, but I didn't believe her."

He glanced at her as he led the way into the glade. "Lucy Rees? Does she like me?"

Halfie chuckled. "No! She just mentioned it one time."

"Why didn't you believe her? Mum said I was driving soon as I was out of the pram."

Halfie hesitated as he sat down on a mossy log. "Your real mum?" she asked.

He looked unconcerned by her question. "Yes. Not the step one."

She sat down beside him, placing the hamper between them. Expecting to see evidence of Stonewood elves, she checked for figures between the trees, slender elven forms with red hair, but she saw nothing.

"I can't believe we're back to school tomorrow," she said. "Already."

"I know. But, summer soon."

Halfie nodded, wanting to listen for the Stonewood elves – the noise of swords clashing, of the martial songs her mum mentioned.

"What you heard?" he asked.

Halfie looked up again into the canopy. Trees swayed in the breeze, making the light shimmer above her. She had heard the term forest bathing – this was it. She felt calm, now; at last. "Just the trees," she murmured.

"Can I open it?" he asked, tapping the hamper lid.

"Please do." He rummaged around inside the hamper as she surveyed the land between Stone Farm and Ludlow. "It looks so tranquil," she said. "So lovely."

Already he held a bagel in one hand, a big bite taken out of it. "What?" he asked.

"So *lovely*. The beautiful River Teme, the Whitcliffe rocks with all their fossils. Don't you think so?"

He nodded. "'Course. I like it 'round here."

She glanced at him. "Are you taking over the farm, then? I mean… when the time comes."

"'Course," he said, chewing. "Well, most probably. And have cars. You not eating?"

"I'm not hungry yet."

He finished his bagel, then studied her. She turned to glance at him, finding his gaze keen and direct.

"What?" she asked.

"I noticed that about you. You don't like to eat, do you?"

She felt insulted by this question. It made her heart beat a little faster. "I'm not a big eater, that's all."

He shut the hamper lid. "Do you mind talking about it?"

"Maybe. I don't know. Why?"

"You must be the thinnest girl in school. You know some teachers are worried about you?"

"Worried? Nonsense. Anyway, they have strict guidelines about what to do – my dad told me. He knows. He's DBS-checked – you have to be when you work with children. He said…"

Billy waited, then said, "What did he say?"

"That if they had a concern, they'd have to do something about it by law."

"And… nobody has?"

Halfie turned to face him. "How do *you* know any of this? You don't know what teachers are saying, nobody does, it's confidential. I think you're guessing."

"No, no, it ain't like that," he said, looking surprised. "But, you see, my stepmum, she'll occasionally work at the community hospital, and she told me…"

"What?"

"That some girls have eating problems," he concluded.

"You mean, anorexia?"

He shrugged. "I can't remember what it was called. Mebbe I read about it."

Now Halfie felt the conversation had gone right off the rails. "We're here to discuss other things," she said. "Anorexia is an illness, they told us in PSHE. I'm not ill."

"No," he agreed.

Again Halfie turned away, this time to put him out of view. Billy was boy standard at school: cars, sport, work, with farming an addition if he felt like talking. She had little idea he knew about such things as eating problems, still less that he thought he had noticed it in her. It felt a bit early in the day to be flouncing off, though.

"Do you watch me?" she asked.

"You're my neighbour."

"I don't like it that you think I've got an eating dis–"

"I never said you had," he interrupted. "No way. I just said, you mebbe don't like to eat."

"I'm amazed you'd ever bring that up in conversation."

"Well… you are my neighbour. I do see quite a bit of you."

Not an unreasonable point, Halfie thought, though she still felt uncomfortable; and baffled. But she wanted to move the conversation to important subjects. "You don't believe a single thing about elves, do you?"

He opened the hamper again, taking out a bar of chocolate and a can of Italian lemonade. "No," he replied.

"They're here now, listening to us. To me especially."

"Can you see them?"

"Not yet," she said. She glanced around the glade; still no sign of company. "But this is the problem, Billy. The elves on your farm and those on mine are enemies. Mum is terribly worried about it."

"Yes… your mum."

Halfie continued, "I have been cursed by the King of Snittonwood Shee, because of an accident with a ritual. And I'm getting some bad luck, and it might even be spreading to my family. So I've got to do something about it."

"How can I help?"

Halfie pondered this question. Why would a nonbeliever want to help her?

She sighed. "Give me a piece of chocolate – just one."

He snapped two squares off, broke the piece in two, then handed one over.

Halfie said, "You've done a lot already, and I'm really grateful – the drone controller, and the shared document. But, is there any way you could influence your dad to stop this legal case?"

"You don't know my dad," he replied. "There never was a man holding more of a grudge."

Halfie felt sorry for him – she always did – and sensed an opportunity to probe, as he had probed. "Is that why your real mum left?"

"Yes."

"And what about your stepmum?"

"What about her?"

"Well..." Halfie did not know how to phrase her question. Divorce was an unknown quantity to her. In the end she managed to say, "I s'pose... you know, she must see something... positive in him. To stay with him."

He glanced at her, expression gloomy. "P'raps, yes."

"So you think your dad will carry on with the case against us?"

"He'll do whatever he can to get those fields."

Halfie sighed. "I was hoping you'd be able to..."

He shook his head. "He don't see no sense, except farming sense, which is all he knows. He sees two fields that should be part of his farm."

"Do you hate him?"

Billy looked away, and for a long time silence covered the glade. Halfie peeked into the hamper and withdrew a packet of shortbread biscuits, which she unwrapped as quietly as she could. As she ate, he continued thinking.

"Sort of," he replied some minutes later. "Do you know Philip Larkin?"

"No. Is he local?"

Billy gave a reluctant laugh, the corners of his mouth turning up. But soon they dropped again. "He's a well-known poet. He said a very famous quote about all this."

"What quote?"

"They f..."

But he turned silent again.

At length he sat up and said, "Man hands on misery to man. It deepens like a coastal shelf. Get out as early as you can, and don't have any kids yourself."

Halfie sat entranced. That Billy Ordish of all people could remember something so ephemeral as a line of poetry amazed her. "I didn't realise you liked poetry," she murmured.

"I don't," he replied. "It was in English class, and it really struck me."

She nodded, understanding at once. "Because of your dad."

"Yes," he said in a dejected tone of voice. "And I can't escape." He looked at her. "You must feel the same."

"Well, my dad has his ways, and he's often short with me—"

"No, I meant about your mum."

"What about her?"

He returned to studying the field outside the glade. At length he said, "You must hear some terrible stuff about her."

"At school?"

He nodded.

"Well... yes." Halfie did not know how to reply. She did not feel bullied at school. She ignored all the taunts thrown at her. Teasing bounced off her. Of course, she never forgot a single word of what was said.

"Don't it bother you?" he asked.

"I ignore it."

He sat up again and looked at her. "You see, *that's* what I do with my dad. But my stepmum said it ain't a good thing to do, 'specially when you're young."

"Why not?"

"It messes you up inside. And they told us about that in school, so it must be right."

"Sarky. What do you mean?"

He shrugged. "You're not s'posed to bottle things up, I heard."

Halfie felt uncomfortable with this observation, yet moments later recalled a similar piece of advice, acquired from a teacher – random, or so it seemed at the time. But she could not recall the circumstances. Perhaps after all there were people at school concerned for her. At last she drew a deep breath and said, "I do know my beliefs are unusual. Faerie lore is country lore, and very rare. But it's no different to any other normal belief. It's spirituality. Aren't you spiritual sometimes?"

"No."

His denial was definite. He was mundane.

She pursed her lips. "Then," she said, in what she hoped was a common-sense tone, "there's not much point us discussing it."

"Okay."

That reply felt unsatisfactory. She said, "Is your dad a Christian?"

"No idea."

"No *idea?* You must have! Does he go to church?"

He laughed. "Do any, these days?"

"*Billy.* I asked you a serious question."

"He won't go in no church."

"Then," said Halfie, "perhaps he really is unspiritual. That's his loss."

"Mebbe 'tis."

"But you're missing out on so much. The magic of the trees. The wonder of nature."

He shrugged. "It's science that powers a racing car. Science makes aeroplanes fly."

"You're teasing me now."

"Not really. Just telling it how it is. I don't go in for magic."

Halfie sat back, at once perplexed and annoyed. His blunt sincerity was a thing to behold. But his mention of cars and aeroplanes reminded her of something.

"Billy?"

He turned to look at her.

"Can I ask your opinion on something?"

He gave her a broad smile, then plucked an apple from the hamper. "'Course!"

"I'm not agreeing with you at all, but I want to tell you something, then ask you. You know that radio controller you gave me?"

"Uh-huh."

"I used it to crash the aeroplane."

"I know!" he said. "Very good, that was."

"The thing is, my dad told me a spell had been cast to down the drone. And he really thought the spell had been successful."

"Well, it weren't."

Halfie nodded. "So... that's what I wondered."

"What's the question then?"

"How can him and me both know for certain different things about what happened?"

Billy frowned at her, throwing the half-eaten apple into the undergrowth. From the hamper he took another can of Italian lemonade, opening it with a hiss. "You should try some of this. Have some more chocolate?"

"Only if you answer my question."

"Hold your horses, I was gonna. But chocolate first." He broke a whole bar in half and gave her one piece. Then he took a second can and opened it for her.

"Go on then," she said, taking a sip.

"I s'pose it's pretty obvious. The radio controller controlled the drone – we know that for sure. The spell is something you believe in if you believe in elves. That ain't known for sure, except by them who believe it." He shrugged. "I always go for the obvious explanation."

"Then, according to you, my dad's wrong?"

"'Fraid so."

Halfie sat back. This dilemma had been growing in her mind for a day or two. Instances of spells being proven not to work were almost non-existent: always there was some latitude, or alternative interpretations. Yet here, in her own family, there was now proof of mundane forces at work. She *had* controlled the drone. That fact she knew, for all that she had used the controller like an amateur. The timing was too close, the link too obvious.

To be certain, she said, "What if... we showed that the radio controller doesn't work? Perhaps it was broken. That would count as a scientific explanation."

"Don't work? I could prove that wrong in ten seconds."

"Yes... you could. Maybe..." She hesitated as a shudder of nervousness passed up her spine. "Maybe..."

He turned, waiting, expression expectant. "Go on."

"Maybe you should prove it."

"Okay. I'll tell you at school tomorrow."

"No. I need to see it proven with my own eyes."

He considered this. "You're right. You *do*. Otherwise, it's only hearsay."

She nodded. She felt queasy now, as if going against her parents' wishes. "But keep it to yourself," she said. "Don't tell a soul."

"All right. I promise."

"Thank you."

"But what I don't get," he added, "is why you believe all this elf stuff. I reckon it's all out of legends, or novels."

"Because it's true, Billy. It's in my family. It's *personal.*"

He nodded. "It's that all right."

Halfie felt slighted. "You'll never understand because you're mundane. That word means of the ordinary world."

"Oh, ta."

She ignored his sarcasm. "My mum is an elf. She *knows.* I'd ask her own mum – I mean, my Nana – but she died when I was tiny, my mum told me."

"So we're back to your mum again."

"What are you trying to say? That she's wrong as well as me?"

"Reckon I am," he replied.

"Well *you're* wrong."

He glanced at her. "I s'pose we would need a pretty big experiment to prove her wrong, 'specially if she's the source of it all."

"*No,* Billy! I won't let you."

"I was only saying. Keep your knickers on. I ain't doing no experi–"

"Exactly! You are *not.*"

"Blimey," he muttered. "Sorry I spoke."

"How could you do it?" she said. "You have to be an elf to see the elves."

"That's handy."

Annoyed, Halfie stood up. "If you hurt my mum again, I'm going. My mum is out of bounds. Leave her alone."

He shrugged. "All right then. That don't bother me."

Halfie sat down, pouting. "She's special. She's different, that's all. You're not supposed to make fun of people because they're different."

"I wasn't."

"Rainbow Tom knows all the festival bands, and he says she's the only one with a true gift for music. That gift came from Faerie, Billy. From *Faerie*. It's obvious. It explains everything."

"Well, if Rainbow Tom says that…"

His face remained deadpan; she detected no sarcasm. She said, "You can be a real downer sometimes. I'm glad *you* didn't get invited to the Fayre."

"An Ordish? See sense."

She looked away, wondering what time it was. She had quite lost track of the real world outside Stonewood. "I'm beginning to regret coming here now."

"I'm not."

"What?"

"I don't regret it," he said. "I quite like talking to you. We're neighbours, after all. Gotta look after each other."

"Well that's very *nice* of you, but neighbours are supposed to be polite."

"And honest when they gotta be."

"Are you going to do that controller test still?" she asked.

"Still? Nobody told me not to."

She hesitated, frowning. "Just bring it in tomorrow. We'll test it at lunch break."

"Okay."

Halfie

Halfie watched him as he rummaged in the hamper for something new to eat. She tried to analyse her feelings, her thoughts. She had assumed the conversation was going to be easy: her and a boy. But no. He was not much like her preconception of him. The poetry thing floored her. His grasp of life at school surprised her. His speculation about bottling up emotions disconcerted her. In fact, he was much more like she was than an ordinary boy. But was that just him, or everyone? Had she underestimated what other people guessed about her, *knew* about her? Was she under a kind of friendly local surveillance?

She shivered. He glanced up and said, "You cold? Aww, c'mon. Let's park ourselves in the sun. Reckon I need a few rays too."

"You do talk funny, Billy," she giggled as he carried the hamper into the field.

He settled on a knoll soft with moss. "It's dry here," he said.

She sighed, sitting down and looking back at the trees. "Aren't they just gorgeous, swaying like that in the sun, all together... like a crowd of people, except green and whispering."

"Is that from a poetry book?" he asked.

"No! That's me. Don't you like trees?"

He pondered this question. "They have their uses, I s'pose. You can pop 'em in the wood chipper and–"

"Billy. That's mundane talk. Think art. Think art class at school. Look at the trees and tell me what you feel."

He did as she asked, then said, "What do you feel?"

"What I told you," she replied. "They're not just trees, not just wood for people to abuse. Trees have sensitive spirits. If you're lucky you can sense that spirit by walking amongst them. Do you know what forest bathing is?"

110

"No, thank goodness."

She hesitated, embarrassed at his crass utterance. She thought about giving up on him, but that did not feel right either. She needed to be a missionary for the elves, like her dad. After a while she said, "It's Japanese, I think. You should try it. I know you understand the land, but maybe you don't feel... or *see* it quite the way I do. But you could change that."

"How?"

"By opening up your senses. Listen... watch... feel. Concentrate on the feel of the breeze, on the swaying of the trees. Have you noticed that some leaves rustle like surf?"

"Well," he murmured, "I have actually. Reckon it's linden trees do that. Just like at the seaside."

She sat back, astonished. "Really? Then you... you thought the same as me. Lindens. That's weird."

"Why?"

"I don't know. Because... I'm different to everybody else, I suppose."

"You were *told* you were different," he said.

"What do you mean?"

"It's not the same as being different."

For a while, she could not imagine what he meant. Then, some moments later, she thought she could guess. But his notion was so unexpected she wanted to hear more of what he thought, so she said, "I'm not sure what you mean by that. Will you tell me?"

He shrugged, and she watched as his cheeks turned a deeper shade of pink. "Well... tricky to explain." For a few moments, he thought, before continuing, "My dad always told me I was a useless runt, and that I'd come to no good. Mostly then he'd add that I had to follow his way. I sometimes think that's why I've got his name."

"Got his name?"

"We're both William."

Halfie had never thought of this before. William...
Billy... they were separate in her mind, because the
individuals were so different. But Billy of course *was*
William. Suddenly attuned to his plight she said, "That's
actually quite cruel if you think about it."

He stared at her. "Cruel... yes. You're right. What a
thing to do – name a kid after yourself. He only wants me
to become a chip off the old block. Thing is, I'm not sure I
am."

Perturbed by this awful vision, Halfie shuddered. "I'm
sorry," she said. "I've had this all wrong up to now. But
you're correct. He told you that you were the same as him,
but you're not. You're different, I see that now. Billy, I'm
really sorry. You must have had a horrible time of it."

He nodded, saying nothing.

"I didn't mean to put you down about trees," she said. "I
was a bit uppity, I think. Sorry."

"That's all right."

"Then... what were you trying to say about me?"

He shrugged again. "That your mum and dad told you
what you are."

"But they know me."

He grimaced. "Yes. They do. But I can tell you
now, that don't mean they got it right."

She nodded, seeing his point at once. "And you think
they've moulded me, like your dad moulded you?"

He nodded.

Halfie sat back. This felt like a revelation to her, yet,
because she could now see her own situation via his, she
sensed the truth in what he said. But it was an unpalatable
truth. She shook her head, wondering how to argue against

him… and she could not. The feeling was there, the drive to oppose him, but there were no words. Not a one.

She choked as emotion welled up, a tear rolling from the corner of each eye.

"Did I say summat wrong?" he asked. "I didn't mean to."

"It's all right. It's just me. I didn't expect you to say that. I don't know what to think now."

"About…?"

Again, Halfie could not articulate the feeling of being *changed* inside. It terrified her. She jumped to her feet then hurried down to the corner of Stonewood, so that she could see her own farmhouse.

"Where you going?" Billy called after her. "Don't leave."

"I'll come back," she replied, waving in his direction. For a few minutes she studied the farmhouse, then Snittonwood, then the fields. Then she returned.

"What was that all about?" he asked.

"I don't know. It came over me all of a sudden. I had to see my own place."

He nodded, gazing at her. "Right enough," he said. "Home. Important, that is."

"I suppose it is. You scared me, telling me all this stuff about families. I knew mine was different, but I didn't expect yours to be similar."

"Everybody's is," he replied. "You just never saw that before. But I did. I heard mates at school saying awful things about their folks. Horrible things. Sometimes the school steps in – like what you were saying before about teachers having concerns. But mostly it's mates, having a bad time with their folks and saying nothing."

She looked at him. "That's not really how girls do it," she said.

He gave a half-hearted laugh. "'Spect not."

"A shame," she added.

He twisted his lips into something akin to a grin, but she sensed his sorrow.

"Is it helping that you've got me to talk to?" she asked.

He nodded, then sniffed. "Yes," he said at length. "Thanks. It's nice to speak things on my mind. My stepmum's all right, but she's not my real mum, and, obviously, I can't say anything to dad."

She felt a little closer to him now. "Do you think I'm wrong for not knowing much about other people's lives?" she asked.

"Not really. We live so far out in the sticks, don't we? Shropshire Hills and that. And I reckon you never fitted in to school, even in a place as small as Ludlow."

"Did you?"

He nodded. "But that doesn't always help a lad, does it?"

She did not know the answer to this question, but she shook her head anyway. "I need to do more of what you do," she murmured. "Watch more, listen more. Be an observer. Not be... in myself quite so much."

"That'll help. Then you'll find out everyone's life is pretty miserable."

"That's too... down for me."

"Well, it's a point of view. And it's mine."

She nodded. "We can agree to disagree, can't we?"

He nodded, smiling this time with warmth. "Don't do no harm. I helped you, and you'd help me, if I needed it."

"I would."

He looked away, taking a sip from his can.

After a while, she said, "Have you got a middle name?"

"No. Just his."

Her heart skipped a beat in response to his terse assessment. "Mine's Maeve."

"That's nice. Where's it from?"

"It's Irish. I had a pet crow with a similar sounding name. The real Irish people spell mine M-a-d-b."

"Are your folks Irish, then?" he asked.

Halfie considered. "Dad isn't. But Mum..."

"They say they're a very musical race. Not that I know about music."

She glanced at him. "Mum says it's not something you should *know* about. It's all about what's inside you, coming out in music, playing it or listening to it."

"And what do you reckon's inside her?"

She gazed into his eyes. It was an impossible question. At last she blinked, took a deep breath, and sighed. "The truth is, I don't really know."

"Do you want to?"

She shrugged, then gave a mournful smile. "I think you've put me off finding out, Billy."

"Well... that wasn't my intention, honestly."

"I know. I believe you. But, still..."

"I hope I ain't given you too much to think about," he added. "You did invite me up here for a chat."

She nodded. "It's been lovely. I'm so glad I did it."

"Me too. Thanks. You're a good listener. I didn't know that before."

"You are too. Oh... I can't believe I'm saying that to a boy!"

"No." He shrugged. "Maybe I'm not cut out for racing cars then."

She laughed. "Don't worry about me, honestly. There's nothing wrong with thinking. And I know now I can count on you for help."

"That you can." He stood up. "C'mon, then. Better get back, the both of us."

He carried the hamper to the gap in the hedge, allowed her to push through, then handed it back.

"Nice lunch," he said.

"I'll bring the leftovers to school tomorrow. See you then!"

"'Bye."

Halfie walked away, telling herself not to look back, but after a dozen steps she could not resist. He strode away, hands in his pockets, his mop of hair flat in the heat of the sun. She watched until he was out of sight, then walked back to the edge of the wood, where she listened. There was no sound of impending battle; all she could hear was rustling linden leaves.

Returning home without news or insight felt disappointing. Where were the Stonewood elves?

CHAPTER 7

Halfie woke up. For the first time in years she did not feel the dread of returning to school. She pulled the duvet aside and sat up, glancing over to see that her alarm was due to beep in five minutes. So she had slept well. Why, though? Was it because of yesterday's chat in Stonewood? Billy had said it himself: *You're not s'posed to bottle things up.* It was the talking cure. Not that she was cured of anything, but perhaps talking had helped.

In the kitchen she made herself a slice of toast, listened for signs of her parents – nothing – then packed her bag and walked down the track, then Woody End Lane to the Ludlow Road, where she waited for the bus. She put in a pair of ear buds so she did not have to talk with anybody.

At school, it was straight into the usual whirl of activity, academic and social. The hours sped by. At lunch she found Billy, who was waiting for her in the corner of the school yard.

"Hello," he said. "I brought the drone and controller, though we ain't allowed to use them here, so we'll have to dive away out of sight."

"How about the little playing field by the hedge?"

117

Halfie

Concealed from prying eyes, Billy checked then activated the drone, while Halfie took the controller. Moments later she was flying it. A minute later Billy put it back in his bag.

"Well?" he said.

"It could have been broken, then mended – like an intermittent fault."

"Balance of probability," he replied.

"What?"

"If we can't prove it one way or the other – I mean, we can't go back in time, can we? – we have to go on balances. I know perfectly well this controller is solid. It worked last week."

Halfie bit her lip. "So you're saying my dad and his friends got it wrong on balance of–"

"Probability."

She nodded. She felt reassured, yet unsure. The incident still niggled: her dad's confident certainty of the spell's success, his casual interpretation of what happened. But she knew different from him, and now had proved it. He was wrong. That felt strange...

"What you thinking?" he asked.

"I don't want him to be wrong. His work is so important."

Billy shrugged. "What do you know about his work?"

She frowned. "You do ask some odd questions sometimes."

"Okay. You going to the canteen now?"

"No, I..."

"You don't like going in when it's full, do you?"

She glanced at him, but looked away at once. "Well... I don't like it when it's busy."

"Don't you like people watching you eat?"

"Oh, Billy, please *stop* it! I'm not anorexic. I just prefer a bit of peace and quiet."

"When you're eating," he said.

"Why have you become my inquisitor all of a sudden? These are very personal questions you're asking, and I'm beginning to get suspicious. Are you working for a teacher?"

He stared. "You gotta be joking! I was asking for me. I noticed it ages ago. You don't like the canteen when it's full, or even half full. You leave lunch to the last possible moment. I always wondered why that was."

"Then you must dislike it too, because you're often there when I'm there."

He shrugged again. "Don't let's argue about it."

She scowled. "You showed me that you care before. There's no need to go over the top now. You're a good neighbour – that's it."

"I know. I was only asking."

"Well don't."

He walked away without replying. Halfie sank back into despondency. Now she had irritated him, and that was never her intention. She wondered what to do. Best to send him a conciliatory email.

He had IT club after school, so she did not see him on the bus. She strolled up the track at home wondering what mood her mum would be in, but in the kitchen she found her dad sitting whey-faced at the table.

"You're home early," she said.

He looked up, then glanced at his watch. "Er... yes."

"Where's Mum?"

"In Snittonwood, I think. I... only just got here. I haven't seen her."

"Okay. Has she made anything for supper?"

He sighed, then stood up and with poor grace checked the various pots standing on the Aga. "No," he said, before sitting down again.

Halfie hurried away, aware of his bad mood. She changed into old clothes then went outside via the side entrance. A car drove up the track, gravel crunching beneath its tyres, then parked in the yard. A man got out whom she did not recognise; short, with a pot belly, and round spectacles to match his round face.

In a posh voice he said, "I do believe you must be Alfreda. I am looking for Mr and Mrs Chandler, are they in?"

"Dad is," she replied. "Who shall I say it is?"

"Colin Wright."

She hesitated. "And what shall I say it's about?"

"I'm your father's lawyer."

"Oh! All right." Halfie ran back to the house, opening the kitchen door to say, "Dad, a man's just arrived, says he's your lawyer."

"Bring him in."

Halfie did as she was asked, then stepped back to observe the opening conversation.

Her dad reached out to shake Colin's hand. "Duncan Chandler. Pleased to meet you."

"Colin Wright. Will your wife be joining us, Mr Chandler?"

"Duncan." He turned to Halfie and said, "Go find her. In the wood, I expect."

Halfie ran off, sprinting up the bridleway, meeting her mum where it skirted Snittonwood. "Mum!" she called out. "The lawyer's here. Dad says come back."

"Oh, no…"

They observed one another for a few moments, silent, awkward, before Halfie said, "I'll go back with you. How's your day been?"

"Not good, Alfreda. Oh… the solicitor…"

Halfie fretted, wanting to get back to listen to the conversation but paralyzed by her mum's tone of voice. And her mum looked pale, as if tired. Her hair was uncombed.

She took her mum's hand and said, "Come on, Mum. It'll be all right. Lawyers must know what they're doing, they're professionals."

"No they don't… they're notorious… all they want is the money."

Something about her mum's moaning voice scared Halfie. She withdrew her hand, looking back down the bridleway. "But Dad said to fetch you."

Her mum shrugged. "If I must," she said, gazing with longing into the wood, then sighing and walking forwards. Seeing that her mum was even more distracted than usual, Halfie walked a couple of steps in front, looking out for stones and holes in the path, as if guiding a blind person. It felt so wrong.

At the house, nervousness began to overwhelm her. In secret, she took a few deep breaths, before leading her mum into the kitchen.

Colin stood up, smiling. "Ah, Mrs Chandler. Good to see you. Smallholding ticking over nicely?"

"Yes."

"Duncan has already covered the basics of the problem."

But her mum made no effort to reply, instead staring out of the window by the sink.

Halfie glanced at her dad. "Go upstairs," he told her, "get on with your homework."

"All right."

She was tempted to listen behind the door, but knew she could not – too risky. So she went to her room and, in desultory fashion, answered a few chemistry questions. Then she heard footsteps on the patio outside her window. She looked through the window to see her mum walking around the house, her hair blowing in the wind, hands clasped together.

More time passed: fifteen minutes. She heard the click of the downstairs lavatory door, then the unmistakable sound of her dad winding up the grandfather clock. She opened her door and crept along the corridor to the top of the stairs.

The toilet flushed, then the door opened. She heard her dad speak first.

"Thanks for coming over at such short notice."

"No difficulty there. Business is slow. This is an unusual case. May I ask, is your wife quite well?"

"What do you mean?"

Halfie held her breath as Colin hesitated. Then he said, "To me, she appeared somewhat distant, even, perhaps, a little unwell."

"It's just her way."

"And the girl?"

"The girl?" her dad said.

"Your daughter."

"What about her?"

"Is she quite well?" asked Colin.

"I don't know what you mean."

Again Colin hesitated. "Most likely the horror of returning to school," he said. "It has been quite the most glorious Whit week, hasn't it?"

Before her dad could reply the front doorbell rang. Halfie heard footsteps, then the sound of the door being opened. "Billy!" said her dad. "What the hell are you doing here?"

Halfie could not catch Billy's reply. Scared, heartbeat racing, she ran downstairs to see him handing over a sheaf of papers. Her dad turned around to frown at her.

"I heard the doorbell go," she explained. "Billy! What's the matter?"

He gestured at the papers. "Photocopies of my dad's maps," he replied. "But he don't know I got them. You better keep quiet about it, else..."

Her dad stared at him. "*You're* bringing these?"

"Dad!" Halfie cried, running forward. "He's on our side."

"He's a–"

"*No,* Dad!" Halfie interrupted, determined to clarify the confusion. "He doesn't want this case to go ahead any more than we do. He's *helping* us. Aren't you, Billy?"

"I am that," Billy replied.

Her dad turned back. "Why?"

Billy gestured into the house. "She just told you."

"But you're... a..."

Hearing this, Colin stepped forward. "Are you from Stone Farm?" he asked Billy.

"I'm William Ordish's son."

"And you..."

"Think this case is daft, mister."

Colin nodded. "I see."

"I know my dad better'n anybody," Billy continued. "He won't give in. I don't see why he needs them fields, except out of spite. He holds a grudge terrible, my dad. So, in secret, I took his maps and photocopied them." He stared at Halfie's dad. "At the *library*."

Halfie watched her dad's face turn red. "Get out, Ordish," he growled. "Stay out of my hair or take the consequences. This case has *nothing* to do with you. Out!"

Billy turned and walked away.

"But, dad," Halfie said.

He pointed at the stairs, fury in his face. "Upstairs! Not another word!"

Halfie turned and hurried up the stairs. She paused at her door, to hear muffled goodbyes then the front door shutting. Would her dad come up to castigate her?

He did not.

A few moments later she heard him outside, calling, "Jane! Jane! Where are you?"

Halfie knew the answer to that one: Snittonwood.

At school that week she endured the usual taunts about her mother, which she ignored. But something had changed during Whit, some subtle alteration in her mindset that gave her access to something she had never felt before: courage. Perhaps it was the knowledge that she had an ally in Billy, perhaps it was seeing her dad in a different light – a more realistic light – or perhaps it was just the process of growing up, but she knew she was a different person to the one who had gone home a fortnight before. Perhaps, then, it was time to stop ignoring the taunts.

Thinking about Billy and his situation, she realised he had been forced to grow up early. Too early, perhaps. He was her age. Could the same thing have happened to her because of being born a half-elf: growing up too early? She knew of no other girl or boy in her situation, having to look after herself because of isolation and a semi-absent mother, while at the same time helping out with the smallholding. And she had no sibling, like Billy's younger brother David. Had she lost part of her childhood, as Billy had?

Don't ever tell people at school that your middle name is Maeve, she thought. Madb: don't tell them that. They'll laugh and chop it up into Mad Bird.

Her only other friend at school was Lucy Rees, but Lucy was beginning to drift away into another group of girls. Halfie knew that Lucy would never talk about her own parents because of the possibility of Halfie then speaking about hers; and that was a subject to avoid. Lucy knew any number of methods of changing the subject from parents or family. Lucy was embarrassed when once Halfie tried to explain what it was like being an elf. So Halfie had learned to appear aloof, separate, so that she would not be associated even by implication with her mother. Yet that took a terrible toll on her, as she now knew from talking with Billy.

She dug deep. She needed even more courage. The legal tussle over the fields would be public knowledge soon enough, and then the boys would ask her if she was going to put a spell on Stone Farm, or call up an elf army. There would be any amount of laddish speculation about what her wand was made of.

On the Friday of the first week back she found a tattered copy of *Lord Of The Rings* in a plastic bag hanging from her locker handle. Big joke... Sour-faced, she threw away the bag and took the book to the school library, where she donated it.

On the following Saturday morning she found her dad in the kitchen, stirring a pot of porridge. She hesitated. This was not their usual breakfast. Glancing at the packet, she saw it was the Co-op's economy range; the cheapest possible.

"Did you buy this?" she asked.

"Yes."

Cool weather had drifted down from northern latitudes, and the draughty house was uncomfortable. She warmed her hands on the Aga. "Why porridge?" she asked. "I didn't know you liked it."

"It's okay."

Halfie thought she could guess the reason for economy brands. "Is it because having a solicitor is so expensive?"

Her dad hesitated. "Yes."

"And is that to do with the curse?"

He nodded. "Yes," he said. "It's dragging us down, inch by inch."

Halfie looked down at the Aga, perturbed by her dad's tone of voice. "I don't know what to do about the curse," she said. "There only seems to be one option, the impossible task, but I still don't know what that might be. Can't Mum ask the King what it is I've got to do?"

He let out a cry of exasperation. "That's what she *is* doing, Alfreda." Thrusting the wooden spoon into her hand he added, "Stir this, and don't you dare let it burn. I've got books to find."

With that, he stomped away.

Only a minute later Halfie heard the kitchen door open. She turned to see her mum looking wide-eyed and frightened, the odour of wet leaves following her into the room, a trail of muddy footprints on the floor.

"Mum, what's happened?"

"Alfreda... oh, it's all gone wrong."

Halfie hurried over, helping her mum to the kitchen table then shutting the door. "What's happened?" she asked, returning to sit beside her.

"I met the Elven King. I saw him, Alfreda, so tall and glowing, so noble. He spoke to me about the curse, but his speech came over all garbled."

"Speech?"

"I was trying to write down the words of the curse."

Halfie held her breath, waiting. "And?"

"The wind blew his words away – bad luck. My ears were so cold. Then he got angry with me, told me to leave him. I tried to explain that I was defending the spring for him, but then he began shouting, and... oh..."

Halfie shuddered. "What did he say? You've got to tell me."

"That we're sure to lose the fields and it will be impossible to get them back."

"Impossible?"

Her mum nodded, pushing back hair in which twigs were entangled.

"But," Halfie continued, "we will win the case, won't we? That's mundane work. It's up to Mr Wright."

Her mum stared at her, eyes wide. "What if we don't? What if I lose the spring... oh, no..."

Halfie swallowed, anxiety rising within her. "That won't happen, Mum."

"No. *You'll* get it back. You'll defend us alongside Colin."

Halfie felt the weight of expectation upon her shoulders: sudden awful pressure. "Then, are you saying that's what I've got to do? The impossible task?"

Her mum nodded, but she might as well have been nodding at a ghost. Detecting an odour of burning, Halfie took the wooden spoon and began stirring the porridge again. Despite the dismay she felt at her mum's appearance, she sensed hope. At last she had something defined to do: a plan.

To restore the atmosphere she said, "Fetch me the honey, Mum. We'll put a load in to sweeten this. It'll be good, and so healthy. It'll strengthen us all."

"But we've run out."

"Okay. Well, I'll pop into Ludlow later and get some from the market."

"What will you use for money?"

Halfie hesitated. Again she felt the burden upon her. "Yours. Or Dad's."

"Do you have any cash?"

Halfie sensed the conversation drifting into a strange area. "A few quid," she replied. "Why?"

"You buy it, then."

Halfie did not answer. Instead, she rummaged through cupboards, finding at the back of one an ancient jar of local honey, its label peeling off. "Here we are," she said. "This must come from Pearl Farm down the lane. I recognise the handwriting."

"Are you going to put it in?"

Halfie nodded, spooning out the oozing, half crystallised honey into the porridge, which looked ready to eat. She glanced around the kitchen. "Do you reckon Dad's ready for a bit of breakfast?"

"I've no idea."

Halfie grabbed three dishes, then put the pot on a cork mat in the centre of the kitchen table. "I'll go get him," she said. "We'll have breakfast together. We don't eat together often enough. We've got to support one another."

She hurried away, but slowed to a stroll as she approached the half-open study door. The sound of books thunking on shelves... he was in there, doing something.

She slipped into the room – shutters closed as usual – to see him at a bookshelf. "Breakfast," she said, in as bright a voice as she could manage.

He turned. "Oh, thanks."

"Yes, I've finished all the prep – it's ready. You coming now?"

"In a minute."

"What are you looking for?" she asked.

"I'm sure we had some rare nineteenth-century esoteric books here."

Halfie hesitated. "You mean, to research the court case?"

He glanced at her. "Er... yes. The spring, you know?"

She nodded. "The spring." When he did not move, she added, "See you in the kitchen."

"Okay. Thanks."

His mood seemed fair. In the kitchen she dished up two bowls of porridge, but while she ate hers with gusto, her mum only picked at hers. "Don't you like it?" Halfie asked.

"Modern food is so full of chemicals."

"Chemicals?"

"Bad chemicals made by multi-national corporations. There's evil in this world, Halfie, terrible evil, and people just can't see it. Our food is poisoned."

Halfie said, "All food?"

"No. Not natural food, not local. Not ours. But we need to stop shopping at the Co-op. We need to buy farm local, so there's no chemicals, no artificial preservatives, colouring. Why do they need to colour food anyway?"

Halfie shrugged. "To sell it better."

"To sell *more,*" her mum said, with sudden passion. "They only care about their profits, their shareholders, they don't care about the victims, about the *land.*"

"What victims?"

"You and me! Ordinary people, Halfie, who go to the supermarket to buy poisoned food, treated with chemicals to make it addictive, so there's more money, more profits..."

Halfie had heard this sort of diatribe before, but something about her mum's manner disconcerted her. "So... we won't be shopping at the Co-op any more?"

"No. I'm banning it."

"But the Co-op are ethical."

"*No.*"

Halfie looked down at her porridge. "Okay..."

"If I hear you've been there, even with your school friends for sweets, the curse will be redoubled. The Elf King knows what's going on, Halfie. I tell him. If you want to secure your life as an elf you've got to eat like they do, and that means *natural.* No more caffeine. No more refined sugar. No more preservatives. No more throwing away money we don't have."

Halfie wanted to ignore her mum's changed attitude to the wording of elven curses, but she could not. So much hung on that wording; so much fear. "How can the Elf King redouble the curse?" she asked in frustration. "That would totally change his words."

"He *rules,* Alfreda. He is our monarch – you and me."

Halfie said nothing for a while, looking away, struggling with the feeling that something was wrong. "Where will we get food from then?" she asked. "We can't live off our own stock, it's not enough, you know that."

"Local farms. We live in a rural community, don't we? Honey, like you said, from Stone Farm."

"Pearl Farm."

"Bread too," her mum continued, "and butter, which most farms sell. Vegetables – only farm vegetables from now on, plus any we can grow. We could dig up the front lawn to make a permaculture patch. And we'll have to manage our own livestock better. No more selling. We need to eat. They're our animals, after all. More eggs... maybe we should get some geese to go with the hens. Geese can be eaten."

Halfie stared. This did not sound practical. She realised that what before had seemed foolish or wild was now verging on unhinged, as if her mum was fighting some kind of inner turmoil. But all she could think of doing was emphasising the practicalities, so she said, "What about loo roll?"

"We'll make our own."

"What about washing up liquid? Soap?"

"You can make soap from soapwort leaves. Saponaria officinalis."

Halfie bit her lip. Some products would be impossible to make. This was definitely irrational. Her hands trembled; she placed them on her lap, out of sight. Thinking of herbs made her think of the Wise Woman, but that rift remained.

Disquieted and bemused, she murmured, "I suppose ancient women managed without tampons."

"They did," her mum replied in a matter-of-fact voice. "Or made them out of sphagnum moss."

"I'll go and feed the goats," Halfie said, getting to her feet.

"Collect the eggs too. I'll make scrambled eggs for lunch."

131

"That's all right, I'll make it."

Her mum nodded, looking in disgust at the cupboards. She stood up, opened the nearest one and began pulling out packets of food. Soon, many of those lay in the bin.

Halfie fled, the unexpected incident scaring her. Making soap from leaves was fantasy. Something had *happened*.

She glanced across the fields at Stone Farm. Relations with Billy were crucial now. If she was going to complete the Elf King's task, she would need all his help. Thank goodness he was a decent lad: honest, genuine. Those photocopied maps were a good beginning, but she would need more.

She looked at the barn. She thought of being courageous.

After dealing with the goats and taking the eggs into the kitchen she returned to the yard, standing awhile in sunshine to warm herself up. The yard remained quiet – the barn too. Yet she wanted to knock on the door.

She had to do it: be brave.

Knocking on the door, she took a series of deep breaths to calm herself.

The door opened. "Oh... hello."

Halfie smiled. "I'm so sorry to bother you, but–"

"Oh, don't you worry about that, dear. Come in. It's nice to see you."

Relieved, Halfie followed the Wise Woman into the barn, sitting on her usual seat, the Wise Woman in her rocking chair.

At once the Wise Woman said, "I believe I've got an apology to make about what happened. I over-reacted a little, I think. I'm sorry, dear."

"But there's nothing to apologise for!" Halfie replied, astonished. "You were right. It wasn't my jewellery, and, honestly, I *was* sorry – I'm still sorry."

"You didn't know what it meant to me," the Wise Woman continued, as if she had not heard a word. "You weren't to know. You didn't know anything, in fact. So I apologise, and let's make that an end to it."

"All... right. But..."

The Wise Woman smiled. "Things aren't looking too good for the Chandler family, are they? I'm glad you came to see me, we need to discuss options."

"What do you mean? William Ordish?"

"With what's happened to your father."

Halfie shook her head. "What's happened?"

The Wise Woman leaned forward. "Hasn't he told you?"

"No."

She frowned. "That's so typical! Sweep it under the carpet, as usual." For a few moments she thought, before glancing at Halfie.

"What's happened?" Halfie asked in a meek voice.

"I suppose... I'll have to be the one who tells you."

"What?"

The Wise Woman said, "He's been sacked."

Halfie gasped. "From being a missionary? But... how could he be?"

"From being a *librarian*."

Again Halfie shook her head. "He doesn't work in a library. He's the missionary for Snittonwood Shee."

"No, dear. That's what he told you. And a few others. Doubtless though he did try to do what he calls missionary work. In fact, I suspect that's why the council sacked him."

"Council? Sacked?"

"He was employed by the local council at Ludlow Library."

"But... I would have known," said Halfie. "I would've been told."

"People did try to tell you. Including, as I understand it, at school. But you couldn't hear them."

Halfie frowned, unable to comprehend. "Couldn't *hear* them?"

"Not in the literal sense, dear. You couldn't hear what people were saying for the same reason your dad can't, because you believe."

"Believe?"

"In what Jane tells you," said the Wise Woman. "He, because he believes it, you because you don't know anything else. You were brought up believing."

Halfie sat up. She felt danger surrounding her, its focus the barn. "You're trying to drag me away from the elves," she said. "You told me – there was no curse, you said. I haven't forgotten that. Stuff and nonsense, you called it. Then you told me you'd make my mum regret it for the rest of her days."

"I know what I said, dear, and I spoke in the heat of the moment. I have apologised. But facts are facts. You, however, are a believer in the overall story."

"But there *is* a curse. I've had terrible bad luck ever since the King put it on me."

"All circumstance," the Wise Woman said. "And there is no King."

"But..."

"Your mother's told you everything. It all comes from her."

"Of course. She's an elf."

The Wise Woman shook her head. "No, dear. I'm sorry." She sighed. "You had to find out eventually. People are becoming concerned for you."

"No, they're not. They just don't understand."

The Wise Woman pursed her lips. "It'll take a while for it to sink in," she said. "But your father not telling you what happened, that's wrong. So let's go and find him, shall we?"

"What for?"

"To present the facts to him."

Halfie stood up, but she felt torn. Not only did she sense an almighty row brewing, which she wanted to avoid at all costs, she felt again that vertiginous uncertainty provoked by Billy's comments.

"Do we have to go now?" she asked.

"Follow me, dear. I'll be calm, don't worry. I don't get angry very often." She smiled, then added, "I am the Wise Woman, after all. But women aren't supposed to get angry, are they? Perhaps if they did the world would be wiser."

"I don't know what you mean. My dad gets angry."

The Wise Woman nodded, sorrow on her face.

"In fact, he'll completely blow up," Halfie said, hoping the Wise Woman would be put off. "He's got a temper."

The Wise Woman opened the barn door. "I know."

They found him surveying stacks of books placed on the kitchen table, his back to them. Halfie stepped inside, but the Wise Woman remained at the doorway.

Halfie cleared her throat. Her dad turned around, glared at the Wise Woman then said, "What's going on?"

"I won't come in, Duncan," said the Wise Woman. "I know how strict you are on that point."

"What the hell are you doing here?"

"I just discovered you haven't told your daughter of your new circumstances."

He jerked upright, his eyes round, his expression apprehensive. "I don't know what you mean," he replied.

"Yes, you do. Are you going to tell her or shall I?"

"It's *private*. Stop meddling. Haven't we told you often enough?"

"How do you suppose I found out, Duncan?"

He shook his head. "Gossip? Biddies at the old peoples' home? Because that's where you belong. Now get out, before I throw you out."

"I'm not in," the Wise Woman observed. "So. Duncan. You were sacked from Ludlow Library today. What was the given reason?"

"Shut up! Get *out*."

He ran to the door, growling with rage. Halfie sprang aside, but the Wise Woman stood her ground.

"Go ahead and shut this door," she said. "I can still shout. I can still see you through the glass."

"*No,* no!" Halfie wailed. "Stop it, please. Dad, is it true? What's going on?"

He whirled around, stared at her, then sagged against the door. "For chrissakes," he muttered. "Can't you just leave me alone?"

"Dad!" Halfie insisted. "What's going *on? *Why won't you tell me?"

He did not reply for a while. Then he stood up, tottered forward and sat in a chair at the table, his back to her. "To protect you," he replied.

Halfie glanced at the door, to see the Wise Woman gesturing at her before walking away. Heart thumping, she approached her dad. "But I didn't know you had a second job in Ludlow."

"I know. We thought it best not to tell you."

"Why?"

"I *said.* To protect you."

Now Halfie recalled Billy's parting shot about photocopying maps at the library. Even he knew! Yet... how could *she* not have known?

"I don't understand," she said. "What's so secret about having a second job?"

"It interfered with my missionary work."

"Then... you were sacked because you're a missionary?"

"Yes," he answered. "Abuse of privilege they said. And some more."

Halfie shivered. "Will you get another job?"

"I don't know if I can."

Halfie took a step back, gazing around the kitchen. Memories returned... pieces of the jigsaw fitting into place. Her mum's words about the smallholding. "Won't we have any money?" she asked.

He shrugged, then leaned forwards so that his head rested on his arms.

Halfie thought she knew now why her mum had spoken about food in such strange terms. The money was going to run out. It was the curse again. "What about the court case?" she asked.

"Unless Colin works on a no win, no fee basis," came the reply, "we're sunk."

"Sunk?"

He said nothing more.

The finality of the situation struck Halfie then. Sunk. Doomed. Accursed.

Halfie lay in bed, unable to sleep.

Halfie

Night lay thick and cool around the farmhouse: distant owls called to each other, a vixen screamed in the adjacent field. But worry made Halfie's thoughts circle round and round, from one disaster to the next: the court case, an angry William Ordish, her mum's strange behaviour, the Wise Woman making a scene with her dad, her dad's anger, him being sacked, the lack of money, no funds for the court case... and so it went on. And what could she do? She had the weight of the curse to bear on her shoulders.

She heard a noise outside. Sitting up, she looked out, but saw nothing in the distance. She jumped out of bed and peered down, seeing a light on the patio below.

It was her mum, dressed only in a bra and knickers, barefoot, carrying a lantern. Halfie stared, not sure what to do.

The alarm clock said one in the morning. Dad would most likely be asleep.

She crept downstairs to the kitchen in time to see her mum pad by. But her mum did not look unhappy. In fact, she looked content.

Halfie decided not to interrupt. She ran down the corridor to the study, where her dad's binoculars lay in their rotting leather case. Moments later she stood at the kitchen door, and through the binoculars followed the lantern's progress up the bridleway. After a minute or so her mum appeared to begin dancing, twirling around as she stepped forward, swinging the lantern on an outstretched arm. In this way, her mum progressed all the way up to Snittonwood.

Halfie opened the back door. Night lay silent, dense, cool. From distant woods she heard murmurs of noise. From Snittonwood she heard nothing, as if the elves had smothered the place in mystery.

Halfie

Into that mystery her mum vanished, the lantern flickering behind tree trunks, then fading.

Ordinarily, Halfie would have been reassured by the sight, even soothed; a supernatural security lay at the heart of the wood, rooted in the shee. But now the manner of her mum's approach, her lack of clothes and her odd behaviour brought different thoughts to mind. New thoughts, uncomfortable thoughts. For the first time she had observed irrationality in her mum. Then again, perhaps it was not the first time. Perhaps she had been fooling herself about her mum.

CHAPTER 8

When Halfie returned home from school on Monday afternoon she found stacks of objects all over the kitchen, amongst them her dad, on his knees. He wore paint-splotched jeans and a Gong T-shirt, his hair greasy and uncombed. She had not seen him for the latter part of the weekend, though she had heard a lot of noise in the study.

"What you up to, Dad?"

He glanced at her, but there was no menace in his gaze. "Stuff to sell," he replied.

Halfie tried to keep calm. She put her hands in her pockets and leaned against the door jamb. "Oh, right, selling. All those books."

"We never read these," he said, patting the nearest stack. Dust billowed into the air. "Luckily they're in pretty good condition, no sun fading."

"They smell a bit mouldy though."

"That's second-hand bookshop smell, so it won't matter. No... some of these esoteric volumes are worth good money. I'll sell them to a dealer I know in Hay-on-Wye."

Halfie shivered to hear the word. "A book dealer," she said.

He nodded. "An antiquarian. He'll give me a good price. He's got whole screeds of customers wanting this kind of thing."

Halfie tried to smile. "That'll come in useful then."

He glanced at her. "Exactly."

She shrugged. "Will you try to get another job as well?"

"I don't know yet. Can you stop asking me that? It's stressful enough as it is."

Halfie glanced away. "Where's Mum?"

"Up in the wood."

Again Halfie felt the clutch of fear upon her heart. "I saw her last night," she said in a low voice.

"Saw her?"

"Going up there at one in the morning. Is she all right, Dad? She seems super distracted at the moment. What are the elves saying to her?"

"She's very worried about the curse," he replied. "We've got to win this court case. If we don't..."

"But we will. I'll make sure Billy's on-side. He'll help us, and that will be my contribution... and the impossible task. Then the King will let us go back to normal."

He nodded, then got back on his knees. "Hopefully."

Halfie waited for more, but he did not speak. She said, "What's for tea?"

He popped his head over a stack of books. "Whatever you're making us."

Halfie dumped her bag in her bedroom, changed into old clothes, then descended, but, glancing back down the corridor to the study, she saw all the Indian bronzes lined up on the floor. She halted. Those bronzes were beloved of her mum. Surely they were not for sale too? She poked her head into each of the downstairs rooms, to see, in the centre of every room, a small stack of items: ornaments, antiques, oddments. Yet, just as much had been left on the shelves, including items Halfie knew to be of value.

In the kitchen she ransacked the cupboards for food, but little remained from her mum's reorganisation. She checked the fridge. "How about scrambled eggs on toast?" she asked.

"Sure."

They had plenty of eggs, so she set to work, wondering how to broach the topic of antiques. "How are you deciding what stuff to sell and what to keep?" she asked.

"We'll probably sell the lot."

"Everything you and Mum own."

"Yes."

Halfie pondered. Why leave some objects on the shelves? "That seems sensible," she said. "But Mum won't let her bronzes go."

"She'll have to, I'm afraid."

"What did she say?"

"I haven't mentioned it yet."

Halfie shivered. "Has she been in the wood... all day then?"

"Speaking with elves," he said, "trying to renegotiate the curse. But it seems hopeless. They want their impossible task."

"The court case," Halfie said. "I'll help win it."

He glanced at her, grimacing. "Colin Wright had better win it."

"Won't he need paying?"

"I'll negotiate with him when he comes back in a week or so. I'll get a no win, no fee deal, don't worry. Old Ordish will have to pay him, and our damages too."

"When will the case begin?"

He sighed, as if fed up with her questioning. "In a few weeks, Halfie, okay? Early July, perhaps. Colin needs time to check documents, prepare himself."

"All right. Sorry. I only wondered."

He stood up, knees cracking. "Too old for this game. Right, you nearly ready? I'll go and fetch your mother. Don't put any sauce or anything processed out, she's off that sort of thing."

"I can't," Halfie replied, "she's thrown it all away."

"Good. Pure poison. We've got to eat natural from now on. Our own. It's what she wants."

Halfie nodded, watching him depart. Again she shivered, but this time it was because of what he said. It was almost as if he was parroting her. Yet he was the Ambassador of Snittonwood Shee, the conduit of the elves in the wider community of south Shropshire. Still... the way he echoed everything her mum said made Halfie feel agitated now, not reassured. Billy's hints and suggestions were beginning to affect her.

"I wish I knew what to *do*," she whispered to herself.

Billy was an outsider. She had always thought that outsiders knew nothing, because they weren't inside. Now she was beginning to wonder if his outside view allowed him insight she could not grasp.

She took a deep breath. Something inside her was changing, as if her thoughts were moving by themselves, configuring themselves in order to make revelations. She sobbed, then wiped away a tear. The burden was heavy.

When her mum and dad returned she put the toast in and laid the table. Her mum looked pale, chilled, as if all the warmth had been sucked out of her by the cool trees of the wood. Her dad looked dejected.

143

"Scrambled eggs," she told her mum. "Our eggs, and the last of the bread from the market baker – hand made. And some butter."

"Where's the butter from?" her mum asked, sitting down.

"Pearl Farm," Halfie lied, glancing at her dad.

But he didn't notice. Halfie sat down, glad she had won a little victory. Perhaps this was the way forward: lies and deception.

"Dad's been sorting out the antiques," she said, "which to sell and which to keep. There's a lot in the sell pile. Statues."

"Quiet, Halfie," her dad growled.

"It doesn't matter anyway," her mum said.

"What doesn't matter?"

"It's only things, and things don't matter." She gestured at the kitchen door. "What matters is out there... pure, natural, whole, green. That's where I need to live."

When Halfie came home on Tuesday she found the Wise Woman in the yard. She noticed at once that the Wise Woman was flustered.

"What's the matter?" she asked.

"Will you come indoors with me?" the Wise Woman replied. "I don't want to go in on my own."

Halfie glanced at the farmhouse. "In there?"

"Yes, dear."

Halfie hesitated. The subject of why the Wise Woman was banned from the house could never be mentioned. When the Wise Woman had arrived a few years ago Halfie once asked about the banishment, to receive a ferocious reply telling her to mind her own business. Since then – nothing.

She glanced around the yard. It appeared peaceful enough. "Er…"

"Won't you? For me?"

"I need to ask you a difficult question first," she replied.

The Wise Woman's expression changed from concerned to piqued. "Go on, then."

"Why did they ban you?"

The Wise Woman said nothing, gazing at the house.

"They're in there now, aren't they?" Halfie continued. "What did you fight about?"

"I can't tell you, dearest. I'm sorry. Not just yet, anyway. It's personal. But I find myself needing aid right now, and you're the only one I can rely on. I… looked in a few windows this afternoon."

"And…?"

"I saw things piled up."

"Dad's selling stuff to make money," Halfie said, "because he lost his job."

"I know." The Wise Woman paused for thought. "We'd better make sure he's selling the correct things, hadn't we?"

Halfie said nothing as thoughts assailed her. Could the antiques passed over by her dad belong to the Wise Woman? If so… how could that be? Then she recalled the emerald bracelet, realising that the stash of clothes and jewellery in the attic told their own, equally perplexing story.

Realising she had no choice she said, "I'll help you, but Dad can be stubborn at times. He looked upset last night."

"I can't say I'm surprised."

"Well… you go in first, and I'll do what I can. But I don't know what."

The Wise Woman said, "Just stand by me."

"All right."

The Wise Woman smiled at her. "Deep breaths first, Alfreda, remember?"

Halfie studied the old woman, heartbeat racing. "I'm also Maeve," she said.

"Yes. Your middle name."

"I don't mind being called that sometimes."

The Wise Woman looked at her, though her expression remained unreadable. "Is that so?" she murmured at length.

Halfie nodded, and they did the breathing exercise for a few moments. Then the Wise Woman walked towards the kitchen door.

Following, Halfie balled her hands into fists in a vain attempt to transfer her nervousness to a place where it could be controlled. Her body felt tight, like a fully wound clock spring. She wanted to run away but she could not. Trapped again. At least this time she was with somebody she thought she could trust; a kindly soul.

At the back door, the Wise Woman peered inside. Halfie saw her mum and dad sitting beside piles of books at the kitchen table. The Wise Woman rapped once on a pane of glass then walked indoors.

"Hello, Jane," she said. "Hello, Duncan."

He jumped to his feet. "What do you want?"

"I want to speak with you both," the Wise Woman replied, as Halfie took up a position beside her. "I was walking around the yard this morning when I happened to see some things piled up in the sitting room. I need to check them."

Halfie glanced up as her dad looked at her. "Go to your room," he said.

"*No,*" the Wise Woman said. "She's staying here. This concerns her."

"You're banned from this home," he told the Wise Woman.

"Not this time, Duncan. This time I need to see what's going on."

Halfie shrank back as her dad said, "You'll not interfere with *anything,* understand? Halfie! Go to your room."

Halfie froze. She wanted to stay put and flee – both at the same time. But, either way, fright paralyzed her. Then the Wise Woman put an arm around her shoulders and said, "She's staying right here, and none of your bullying is going to change that."

"Then," said Halfie's mum, "*I'm* leaving. Good*bye.*"

With that, she sprang up and ran through the kitchen doorway.

Halfie's dad scowled. "Well done," he said. "Now you've upset her."

"Upset her, have I?" the Wise Woman replied, without a trace of concern. "That was me, was it?"

He appeared disarmed by her confidence, by her immediate answer. "What are you here for?" he asked.

"To check what's been moved. I gather you're selling a few items, Duncan. I wouldn't put it past *you* to sell other things too."

His cheeks turned red as he took a deep breath, then exhaled. Struggling to control his anger, he said, "Slander me all you like. These are my books, for chrissakes. All the things I'm considering selling are ours."

"Well, I'm going to check – room by room."

"Then *I'll* come with you. I wouldn't want a thief in the house."

"That *is* slander."

He laughed – wild and furious. "Who cares? You're here now, ruining everything with your interference, as

147

usual. You were banished by the elves. What's Halfie going to–"

"She'll think what she *wants* to think!" the Wise Woman interrupted, in as loud a voice as Halfie had heard. "Perhaps today will do her some *good*. Because I've not seen much good in this house for quite a while now."

"No?" he sneered. "Says you."

The Wise Woman looked across at Halfie. "Come along, dear. I believe I just won the argument. We've got things to check."

Halfie felt herself trembling, and a strong desire to go for a wee came over her. "Um... I just need to go to the loo."

"All right. I'll wait for you."

Halfie ran to the downstairs lavatory. The sensation was sudden and intense, though before she had not needed to go. But this felt different. This felt like she was about to wet herself in front of them.

She leaned forward, head in hands, trying to force back the sobs – she did not want the Wise Woman to know she was upset. After a minute she flushed the toilet and walked out; not calm, but controlled.

Without a word the Wise Woman entered the nearest room, Halfie and her dad following. The experience was excruciating. Halfie felt insignificant and endangered, caught between this new, assertive version of the Wise Woman and her seething, foul-tempered dad. She wanted to be anywhere but here.

The Wise Woman examined the pile of ornaments on the floor, then cast her gaze about the room, walking to the mantlepiece to caress some of the pottery there. Halfie watched, astonished. It was obvious to her that these were objects the Wise Woman knew, and cared about. They *were* hers. Yet... how?

"Everything seems sound here," the Wise Woman murmured.

"*Good,*" Halfie's dad replied in a voice dripping sarcasm.

"Do put a sock in it, Duncan."

In the next three rooms the situation was the same. Then they arrived at the study. Halfie watched as her dad strode to the doorway and turned around. "There's nothing of yours in here."

"That's a decision for *me* to make," she replied.

For a moment they glared at one another, and Halfie felt sure the Wise Woman would give way. But then her dad buckled, glancing at the line of Indian bronzes. "Be quick then," he muttered.

Halfie followed the Wise Woman into the study. The room had been emptied of books – two dozen dusty, cobwebbed shelves all pale and barren – but there was a pile of antiques and other ornaments on the floor. The Wise Woman studied them, then leaned down to pick up a statue of a seated figure carved out of pale stone, its base flecked with the remains of gold paint.

"That's Jane's," Halfie's dad said.

"This was my husband's," the Wise Woman replied. Her voice was soft, as if expressing the pain of old memories.

"That's Jane's alabaster Buddha," Halfie's dad insisted. "Put it back."

The Wise Woman turned to face him. "This is *mine,*" she said. "Barry got it when he was on tour with the naval cadets in Vietnam."

"It's Jane's. It's one of her Buddhas. She collects them."

"She didn't collect *this* one."

"It's not yours!"

The Wise Woman glared at him, then took a step forward. "Are you going to snatch it away from me?"

Halfie shrank back. She was daring him! And he was hesitating...

He replied, "If you take it, I'll tell Jane, and then you'll be responsible for what happens."

The Wise Woman chortled. "I don't think *you* of all people are in a position to give lectures about responsibility. Out of my way. I've got upstairs to check."

He stepped aside. Head bowed, making herself as small as possible, Halfie followed. She dared not catch her dad's glance now.

Upstairs there were nine rooms to visit. Halfie said nothing, wishing for the nightmare to be over, but at last the Wise Woman pronounced herself satisfied and, clutching the Buddha, led the way downstairs.

In the kitchen, she again put her arm around Halfie's shoulders as she spoke. "Duncan, you will do exactly as I say in this matter. All the things on floors are yours. That, I accept. I'm pleased you've assessed their ownership accurately. All the other valuable things though belong to me. If I find one single item of mine moved from where it is now I swear I'll dob you in to the police as a thief. Understand?"

He glared at her, his mouth working, though without words.

She nodded once at him. "I'll take that as a yes. Come along, dearest."

Halfie followed her out of the house, then into the yard, but already she felt weak from anxiety. "He's going to kill me," she whispered.

The Wise Woman halted, sorrow in her face. "We'll let him stew in his anger for a while," she replied. "But I'm afraid we had to do that. We had to make a stand. You were *so* courageous – I'm proud of you. Listen... I've got a suggestion."

"What?"

"I think it would be best for you to stay with me for a couple of nights, just while those two sort themselves out. You've had enough stress for one day."

Halfie found herself wanting the toilet again. "Well... if you think so. But Dad won't let you keep me."

"Oh, he will. I don't believe he wants you in the house at the moment. He and Jane have things to discuss, to sort out, and they're best left to it."

Halfie stared as some of Billy's words passed through her mind. "Are they... getting... divorced?"

"No!" the Wise Woman said, hugging her. "Not at all. But this has been a tough time for them. They'll calm down by the weekend, don't worry."

Halfie struggled to break free. "I need a wee," she said, running for the barn door. She felt the hot, burning sensation again.

Afterwards, in the barn's main room, she found the Wise Woman waiting for her. "Sit down, dear. I've put some chamomile tea on."

"Thank you," Halfie replied. "I don't think I should drink too much though."

The Wise Woman studied her. "Is that so... Perhaps some passiflora or valerian."

Halfie had never heard these names. "What are they?"

"Herbs to counteract nervous tension irritating the bladder."

Halfie shifted in her seat, uncomfortable with this return to the focus on nerves and stress. "It's nothing, really," she said.

"On the contrary," the Wise Woman replied, "it very much *is* something. You should always listen to your body, dear. It's the same as for feelings, and emotions. They come to make themselves heard."

Halfie said nothing.

"Dandelion tea with a bit of lemon and honey is perfect for your sort of problem," the Wise Woman continued. "I'll make some later."

"I haven't got a problem," Halfie said.

"Don't deny it, dear. We all have things happen to us. Bottling it up or ignoring it only makes it worse."

Halfie said nothing, thinking of Billy. Were these two in league? But, no... that was a flight of fancy. She said, "I'll take some tea, then." She looked around the barn. "Where will I sleep? You've only got four rooms."

"I'll sleep where I always do, in the mezzanine. You'll be nice and comfortable on the old sofa over there."

Halfie glanced back, feeling doubtful.

"Dear," the Wise Woman said after a pause. "May I tell you something, in all honesty?"

Halfie felt a sense of foreboding. "Well..."

"I've been on this planet now for almost seventy years. I've learned a few things. One of those things is this. You don't have to love your parents."

Halfie stared, not sure she had heard aright.

"Does that shock you? It would. You're young, so it's quite all right. But you're under no obligation to love them. You didn't ask to be made, did you? You had no say in whether or not your parents were ready for you."

"I don't know," Halfie replied.

"Of course," the Wise Woman continued, "it's exactly the opposite the other way around. Parents should always love their children. But that doesn't always happen. Sometimes, in fact, I wonder if it's quite a rare thing."

Still, Halfie said nothing.

"I look at it this way. Parents should love their children, or, at the very least, learn to love them. But, so often, they leave it too late. You, on the other hand, were brought into this world with no say in the matter, no say in who your mother and father were, where they lived, or anything. And over the years they put things into you, as parents do."

"But... I *do* have to love them. How can you say that?"

"Because loving and knowing are the same thing, dear. If your parents truly know you, they love you. If they don't, they don't. But *you* don't get to truly know your parents until much later in life, and then, as is the way with such choices, you can love them or not, as the case may be."

Halfie shook her head. "But it's my *mum*."

The Wise Woman smiled. "So it is. And you don't know her yet, truth to tell. Your love is the automatic child's variety. But that's really attachment, you see. You're almost sixteen. Soon you'll be breaking away. That'll be very good for you, although it's going to be very painful too. I needed to tell you that, dearest. You'll understand in time."

Halfie looked away, dumbfounded. She had never heard anything so harsh.

This, however, was the Wise Woman.

Two uneventful weeks passed. One day in the fifth week of term Colin Wright visited the farmhouse a couple of hours after Halfie returned from school.

Halfie

Life at the smallholding had settled into a routine of wary, uneasy peace. The Wise Woman made herself scarce. Halfie's dad said very little, while her mum spent as much time as possible in Snittonwood. Halfie, meanwhile, returned to living in her bedroom.

The lawyer drove up in his battered car, parking in the yard then knocking on the front door. Halfie opened it, turning to lead him into the kitchen, but before she could he tapped her on the shoulder.

"Wait just a moment," he said.

Halfie watched as he rummaged inside his briefcase. He took out a large manilla envelope, which he handed to her.

"These are for you," he said. "I would be grateful if you could read them later, and on your own."

"What's inside?"

"Some leaflets. They are merely informative documents that I felt the need to give you. We lawyers... we get to learn secret things, things in corporations, things in public life, things in families. My experience is that family secrets are always the most shocking." He gestured at the envelope. "Hence, that. Read the leaflets or dispose of them as you see fit. But they are for *you,* not anyone else." And he raised a forefinger to his lips.

Halfie glanced down at the envelope. "Thank you," she said. "Dad's in the kitchen."

"I will accompany myself there," he replied with a grin. "No need for you to trouble yourself."

"All right then."

She let him depart, then went upstairs. Not feeling like opening the envelope just yet, she crept to the top of the stairs to listen. By chance the interior door was ajar, but the two voices remained inaudible. Not daring to descend in case her dad caught her, she waited. Now though she was curious about the contents of the envelope, which she sensed must have an importance beyond mere leaflets.

Colin stayed for an hour. At last, with the hall clock chiming seven, she heard the dual squeaking of chairs that meant they were standing up. She tensed, readying herself for flight. As they walked to the front door she overheard their conversation.

"Thank you very much, Colin," her dad said as he opened the front door.

"Well," Colin replied, "it does seem the best thing for me to do. This is an unusual case, and one that concerns me. But I am confident we shall win, since William Ordish can have very little by way of a case. It will come down to a matter of interpretation, and there, I think, we shall have the upper hand."

"No win, no fee?" said her dad. "You're certain?"

"No need to ask again, Duncan. No win, no fee. But we will win, and then perhaps it will be the Ordish family selling accoutrements, not you."

"Good. I need that. Jane…"

"Yes, yes, no need to repeat the circumstances," Colin said. "It is all rather trying. You have my sympathies. I hope it all works out in the end."

"Me too."

"On that note, I must depart. Good evening."

"'Bye, Colin."

Halfie crept back into her bedroom, shutting the door then pressing her ear against it, sure her dad would come upstairs to say something. Her heart thumped, loud and fast. But he returned to the kitchen; then, silence.

She breathed a sigh of relief, then took the envelope and opened it.

A sheaf of leaflets fell out, scattering over the floor. She read the title of the nearest one.

Mental Health & You. A Community Guide.

Halfie stared, horrified.

Colin Wright thought she was mentally ill!

It was the Friday of the penultimate week of term. Summer beckoned all at the school.

At home, Halfie wandered up and down the hedge between the smallholding and Stone Farm, waiting for Billy, who had sent her an enigmatic email earlier in the day. But he was already half an hour late. She sighed. He was not the greatest timekeeper, and he did have his dad on his back.

At last, as the sun sank into horizon haze, he appeared, glancing over his shoulder as he ran up to a great oak tree in the hedge.

"What's the matter?" she asked, as soon as he was in earshot.

"Ah," he replied, a black look on his face, "Dad again, telling me off."

Halfie nodded, feeling concerned. "Can I help?"

"No. Don't worry."

"What do you want me for?"

"Needed to tell you summat," he replied.

"What?" She wondered why he could not just have told her in the email.

He hesitated. "It's pretty personal."

"For you, or me?"

"Well… you. And you don't always like that."

Halfie hesitated. Perhaps this was more school gossip. She shrugged, then said, "You'd better tell me if it's that important."

Halfie

Again he glanced over his shoulder, before squeezing under the hedge and sitting between tree roots. Halfie sat beside him, gazing at the farmhouse as he settled himself, then at the spring, not far away. She could hear the music of the bubbling brook.

"You seem flustered," she said.

For a while he said nothing as he studied the smallholding, before turning his attention to Snittonwood. Then he said, "I seen your mum in there at all hours."

"Yes," Halfie replied, "she's communing with elves. She's trying to acquire spells for me to counteract your dad with. I might have to cast spells, you see. The case is starting soon."

"I know."

"Well? What's the big news?"

"That's it – your mum."

"What about her?" asked Halfie.

He grimaced, looking away. He seemed perturbed, even alarmed. "I don't know how to tell you. A few at school have tried, but…"

"Tell me what?"

"About your mum."

"What about her?" asked Halfie.

"See, it's tricky. But my mate James – James Bowen, you know? With the curly brown hair – he knows Francis Wright at the private school near Leominster. For football, like, not anything else."

"Who?"

Billy shrugged. "Colin Wright's son."

Now Halfie felt a tingle of fear pass up her spine. She shifted, feeling uncomfortable in the arms of the tree roots. "What about him?" she asked.

"Francis told James something, that he knew. About your mum."

"*Tell* me, Billy!"

Billy took a deep breath. "That Francis' dad thinks your mum is mentally ill."

Halfie sat staring. Then she laughed. Relief poured through her. "*No,* Billy!" she said, patting him on the arm. "You've got it completely the wrong way around. He thinks *I'm* mentally ill."

Billy turned, shock on his face. Then he shook his head.

"Yes, Billy! And I can tell you why I know. I can *prove* it. A couple of weeks ago Colin came to see my Dad to finalise the case details. He passed me an envelope, secretly – and told me to keep it quiet. The envelope was full of hospital leaflets about mental illness." She laughed again. Suddenly she felt her laughter acquire a new note, as if some potent fuel deep inside her had kicked in. She choked, laughed, then with an effort forced the emotion down. That was close... She had almost become feverish.

He looked at her, disquiet on his face.

She slapped her collar bones, coughing again, then patting her cheeks. "Have I gone all red? I don't know what came over me. I felt so funny. Hyper! Sorry, Billy, I wasn't laughing at you, I never would. But... it's me he thinks has gone mental."

Billy studied her, his expression neutral. Then he shook his head again. "No, Halfie," he said in a voice low and solemn. "No. This is what I felt I had to tell you, 'cos nobody else would, and, anyway, they'd only cock it up. It had to be me. I been wondering for days how to do it. Your mum really is mentally ill. There's no such thing as–"

"No! *Don't* start that again. I've got the proof, I've got it still, the leaflets, and the envelope too." She gasped for

158

breath. "It'll have his fingerprints on it!" she said. "We'll dust it, like scientists. He gave the envelope to *me*. Don't you believe me?"

"'Course I do," he replied. "But Francis overheard it all, told James his dad gave them to you for you to know about your mum. And... a few people do know about your mum now."

"Know?"

"In Ludlow. Town gossip, like. Beginning to get around, that she's getting worse."

"Worse?"

He nodded. "And that your dad got the sack, and that you're selling antiques to get a bit of cash flow."

Halfie looked away. "*No,*" she said, shaking her head. "Just no, Billy. You've got it all wrong, and those boys have too. It was *me*. Colin Wright thinks I'm strange."

In the same serious voice he replied, "He may well think that, but he thinks your mum is stranger. Mebbe he's got to do something about it."

"Do something?"

Billy chewed his lip. "Like... the social, or whatever."

Halfie could not imagine what he was referring to. "The social?"

But before he could reply she heard a noise from behind the tree, a thunking against the ground. Boots – and then a voice.

"Billy! Is that you? Billy, come 'ere, boy."

Halfie scrambled to her feet, looking around the tree to see William Ordish.

"Billy, it's your dad," she said.

Billy stood by her side, patting his hair down. "Hiya, Dad. I was just–"

"You bloody shut it, boy!" William waved a finger at Halfie. "As for *you* – you stay away from my son, and my land. Who d'you bloody think you are, tryin' to twist my son away from me? I know what you're doin' right enough – gettin' yer girl's claws into him, 'cos of my court case. Billy! *Here.* Now."

Billy squeezed through the hedge, but stood well away from his father.

"And you tell this to that oaf of a father of your'n," William said, still shaking his finger at her. "From now on, *no* contact. Nothin'. Not you, not your bloody father, your mother – not to me, nor me boys. Absolutely *nothin'.* Got it? And if you does try any funny tricks… there won't just be hell to pay, there'll be bloody *me* to pay. Now scram!"

Halfie turned, but, as she did, she glanced at Billy. Though his expression was grim he winked at her, just once, before trotting away.

CHAPTER 9

Returning to school for the last week of term, Halfie
heard news about Billy. There had been a minor
accident at Stone Farm involving a tractor. Billy
had been injured and taken to the community hospital out-
patients, meaning he would be off school until the new year
in September. For a couple of hours Halfie fretted about
him, wondering how to get more details – she had emailed
him but received no reply – until she realised the truth.
There had been no accident. It was William Ordish
controlling his son.

She spoke with Lucy Rees about it, and Lucy was
sympathetic; rumour of William Ordish's lamentable
parenting was well known. But Lucy, preparing for a
summer of boys and idle gossip, and reluctant to speak
about anything relating to Halfie, was sympathetic only up
to a point. Soon Halfie realised she was, as ever, alone
when it came to her home life.

During the evening she considered her options. Noticing
in the front room bin a sheaf of old letters she plucked out
an NFU envelope in good condition, the logo clear on the
front. She discarded the pamphlet inside. Next day she

printed out Billy's name and address on a sheet of white paper and stuck it over the Snittonwood address. Then she wrote Billy a letter, popping the envelope into the Stone Farm mailbox on her way home. It looked genuine, albeit a little unusual because of the reused envelope, but hopefully William would not notice that.

On Wednesday evening she waited at the grassed over lay-by on Woody End Lane. As dusk fell she saw Billy tramping along, eating an apple.

She ran forward. "Did your dad see it?" she asked.

He shook his head. "That's why I'm here. Nice plan! Clever. How are you?"

"All right. You look... uninjured."

"My dad was hopping furious. He fetched me a couple of belts 'round the ear, I can tell you. Told me you were a harpy. I had to look that up in the dictionary."

Halfie felt her spirits sink. "Oh, Billy... it's so *wrong*. All this awfulness because of one man."

"We'll keep on meeting up, don't worry. One thing I'll say about my dad is his regular habits. Best place for us to talk in private is up by the woods around one to two-ish. He won't never let things get in the way of lunch, even farm stuff. Same for supper. So we'll say half one, by Stonewood corner?"

"Yes, that'll be fine, once we're on holiday."

Billy glanced down the lane. "I'd better get back in a minute. But listen. You print out that shared document by tomorrow at the latest. Colin Wright might need the information."

Halfie nodded. "I will. You can rely on me."

"And don't tell anyone at school from now on about your mum, your dad, the legals or anything."

Halfie hesitated. "Why not?"

"There's talk. You don't want to feed it."

"What talk?"

"About you and your family," he answered. "I told you before – town gossip."

Halfie nodded, glancing up the track. "Does everyone think she's mentally ill?"

"Pretty much." He shrugged.

Halfie sighed. How could she counter these rumours?

"I saw her again last night as I was putting out a few salt licks," he said. "She were dressed... not in much, like. 'Course, it was warm. She held an orange lantern in one hand and a white one in the other."

"A silver one," Halfie said.

"Silver?"

"It came from the elven smiths of the shee."

He studied her, then looked away. "Reckon it came from India," he said.

"India? Why do you say that?"

"You know. Your al-ter-nat-ive culture." He pronounced the word with care. "Lots of people since the 1960s have gone to India, my stepmum told me about it... like, when I asked her. I think she watched an American telly programme about it."

"Why did you ask?"

"Because of knowing what people your parents go with. Hippies. Or maybe I saw the programme. Ain't you wondered about that? I heard it's quite a drug scene."

Halfie felt perturbed by the direction of the conversation, but Billy's recent revelations made her keep quiet. Besides, she wanted to know what he thought. He had insight she never guessed possible. "I remember you getting annoyed about that." She glanced around the lay-by. "Right here."

"That bastard dealer."

She stared, amazed at the change in his tone of voice. "You sound shocked."

"Dealers is bad people. Even I know that."

Halfie nodded, recalling the incident with Brian Speed. "Hippie stuff, you called it," she mused. "Brian was going to make me eat the mushrooms. But it was actually Faerie food. Illegal drugs, you told me."

"That's right," he said. "And some drugs can affect you. Permanently."

She looked at him, feeling anxiety rising. She swallowed, then said, "Go on."

"Well... psych'logical drugs can harm you. We learned about them in PSHE."

Halfie nodded. She remembered that lesson, yet at the time it had seemed a world away. "Are you really worried for me?" she asked.

He nodded. "I need to make you *see,* otherwise something bad might happen to you. Your parents might... neglect you. I don't mean to make it sound bad, Halfie, honestly. Neglect is an official word that the social people use – my stepmum said. She knows because of her hospital training, I think. Summat like that. Maybe I read it somewhere. I'm sorry, I can't keep it in any more. You've *got* to find out what your mum's really like. I don't see who else is gonna tell you if not me."

"Everybody at school has, according to your account."

"That's laughing at you, not *telling* you."

Halfie felt the return of her indignation, albeit weak. "Just because the lantern came from India doesn't mean it's not magical," she said.

He shrugged. "You can put a bit of magic into it," he said, "make it special for your own sake. But it ain't proper special. It's Indian silver, I bet."

"It's Faerie silver."

He glanced over his shoulder. "I really got to go. Saturday, half-past one, okay?"

With a sullen expression on her face, Halfie nodded. "S'pose so."

"'Bye."

He ran off. Annoyed – at him, but also because she felt tense again – she walked along the lane. At the foot of the track she took a series of deep breaths, then looked at the land westward. In twilight the rolling countryside dipped and rose, shadowed deep green by Mortimer Forest. Sheep bleated, birds sang, and it was warm again: no breeze, no clouds. Tranquil, beautiful… magical. She felt a little more relaxed.

She found her mum and dad in the kitchen. All the books and other oddments had gone, to be replaced with what appeared to be a random assortment of items: wooden bowls, a box of apples, bread, and a selection of cutlery. On a chair she saw a bedroll and a pillow.

"What's going on?" she asked her mum.

"I'm going to live in Snittonwood," came the reply.

Halfie glanced at her dad, but his expression gave nothing away. "Why?" she asked.

"Why not?" her dad replied.

Halfie ignored him, irritated by his manner. "Why, Mum?"

"To escape all this," her mum said, gesturing at the kitchen. "All this manufacture, all this concrete and steel."

Halfie glanced aside. "It's stone," she said. "That's natural, isn't it?"

"Cement binds the blocks."

Desperate to counter her mum, she said, "I think it's *lime* actually. We did that in history – the Middle Ages. They used dung too."

"It's cement," her dad said, "and your mother's sensitive to it. She's got to live in natural surroundings for a while."

Halfie nodded, not knowing what to say. She felt two opposing wishes, of her old self and of her self now, one wanting everything back to normal, one wanting the truth. But what was the truth? Now her mouth felt dry, and her heartbeat raced. "I... don't like to see you like this," she told her mum.

"What do you mean?"

"Upset."

"I'm not upset, I'm very happy. Snittonwood will sustain me. The elves know me. It's only the curse holding us back, and you'll sort that out."

Halfie tried to keep her expression neutral, but it was difficult. She felt something welling up inside her, that she knew her parents must not see. "I've got to go," she said. "It's bedtime."

Upstairs, she flung herself on her bed; but no tears came. A sick horror crept over her, a suffocating paralysis. She felt exhausted from keeping her feelings locked away. That drained her. Yet, now that she was alone, she could not weep.

And she needed the toilet again. The sudden burning sensation was back.

For a while afterwards she lay in sleepless immobility, as one half of her craved security and the other craved resolution. Billy had made her feel like this, she realised: Billy and the Wise Woman. Yet those two individuals were her only friends.

Halfie

How could they be telling the truth? Faerie was real –
that was known. Faerie was ancient, like the Church, and
ancient things never died. Besides, she only had to take in
the wonder of the landscape to feel Faerie magic:
Bringewood, the High Vinnalls, Monstay Rough. That
supernatural power was articulated by twilight, founded in
soil, fuelled by the breeze and the sun. It was as obvious as
the sun itself.

She *felt* that natural wonder with every sense of her
body. How could it be false, the invention of hippies?

Billy must be wrong. But perhaps her mum could
enlighten her further.

She sat up. Night covered the smallholding, and the
house was quiet. The alarm clock told her half an hour
remained before midnight. After a visit to the lavatory, she
dressed in a thick jumper and put on socks and her old
trainers.

Outside, night sounds floated by. She hurried along the
western track then made up the bridleway, listening for
noise as she approached Snittonwood. At the edge of the
wood she heard the unmistakable sound of a bamboo flute.

For a while, she stood undecided. She wanted to learn,
yet she was frightened of what she might learn. Then a
new, turbulent thought moved inside her: go now, it said.
Ask your mum.

Inside a glade her mum danced, bending like a silver
birch before the breeze, first to her left, then to her right, as
if performing elven ballet. She played one of her
Indonesian suling flutes, all breath and glissando notes.
This was the gift everyone remarked upon, and for a while
Halfie soaked it in. Then, when the music stopped, she
stepped forward.

"Halfie!"

"Hello, Mum. Sorry I startled you."

"The elves sense you…"

Halfie glanced around the glade. "Yes, they do. But I came to talk with you. Do you mind?"

"No. Sit down on this log."

Halfie did as she was told, noticing a part-made shelter of wood at the edge of the glade, inside it the bedroll, the pillow, and most of the other items. "Are you really going to live here?" she asked.

"I must. The world scratches me, Alfreda, it irritates my skin. You should stop using cosmetics, they're not natural. Besides, they're tested on animals, and that's deliberate cruelty sanctioned by multinational corporations."

"Not our cosmetics. Ours are cruelty-free."

"It's all the same," her mum replied. "In the elder days women used kohl and red ochre. That's what we should be using. Kohl will magnify your eyes, make you look sexy to boys."

Halfie shivered. Such talk lay entirely out of normal conversation.

"Did I say something, Alfreda? Don't be surprised. We're *women*. We're linked to the land in a way men aren't. We *know,* don't we? You know. You've had your period for years, haven't you? That's the moon speaking to you. It's no accident that the moon and our periods change once a month."

Halfie felt glad of the darkness now; she sensed the heat of embarrassment in her face. "Mum," she said, "never mind all that—"

"Oh, but it's important! Men have ruled us for five thousand years. Men have trampled us down with their violence. Men have constrained us, bound us, spoiled us. It's a terrible, *terrible* world out there, Alfreda, especially

168

for us. The only thing we can do is reforge our links with the world – with nature, the moon, the seasons. The eightfold wheel of the year, not that useless Christian calendar. No more Easter and Christmas for me. Besides, they were stolen from the elves, from the Tuatha Dé Danann, millennia ago... millennia... stolen from us by men."

Halfie listened, in sorrow, yet also with comprehension. She was not too young to see the way of the world. William Ordish could be a bully because he was a man holding power. Yet... his son was so different. How could she persuade her mum of that fact?

At length she said, "You sound like you're withdrawing from the world, Mum."

"Not withdrawing, that's too negative. I'm sinking into the *real* world, the world of land, of magic, beauty, love, peace. The shee is my home, not a house made of brick and metal. This should be your home too. Your father's perfectly capable of looking after the farm. Why don't you come and live with me here? As soon as the curse is lifted you'll be an elf in the eyes of the King, and then the shee and the entire wood can become your home."

"I... don't think I'm ready for that yet."

"Perhaps not."

Halfie struggled for a way into the questions she wanted to ask. "Mum... did you realise you were an elf right from the beginning?"

"I didn't think about it until I was a teenager. Then the world went sour around me. I needed answers. In due course, I realised what I was. I'd been travelling, and the things I saw, heard about and read opened my eyes. Arriving back in Britain I happened to meet your father. You came along at the end of that year."

Halfie caught a glimpse of a long-concealed past. "What about *your* mother?"

"An elf, of course. They both were."

"Are they here now?"

"No."

"Do you ever see them?"

"No."

"Do you... want to?"

"Not really."

A sense of rugged finality lingered over these replies, and Halfie realised the subject could not be opened. She sighed. "Well," she said, "what shall I do about all the people who can't see the elves?"

"Ignore them. They're mundane."

"But Dad's mundane."

"He's your father," her mum replied in a firm voice. "Besides, he understands."

Halfie nodded. In her mind she heard voices: *he believes, he believes.*

"I suppose he does understand," she said.

"He's been a wonderful support to me. Such a kind man, and gracious. No wonder the King chose him to be Ambassador. He does wonderful work in town. He'll be rewarded one day, I know it. And he'll have deserved it."

Halfie nodded again, but she felt torn. She could tell now how little her mum saw of the real man, his tempers, lies and casual insensitivity hardly known to her. Or perhaps she knew, and chose to ignore. A sudden sense of isolation struck her then, almost horror, as she saw him through her mum's eyes, then her own. Those two men were sundered: one real, one unreal. Tears trickled down her cheeks. *She* knew her real dad. Her mum knew only a phantasm. That, now, was clear. And she would have to live alone in the house with the real man, while her mum entertained someone long since let loose.

After a pause, she said, "Do you still love me, even with the curse?"

"Of course! I'm so glad you came home to talk to me, woman to woman. I can't remember us doing that before. It must be a full moon."

Halfie smiled. She sat up, expecting her mum to walk over and give her a hug, but her mum looked elsewhere, turning the flute in her hands.

Halfie peered up into susurrous darkness. She heard no elf music, no elf voices. She felt no warmth. Only sorrow filled her.

Over the first weekend of the summer holiday, Halfie developed a routine. Twice a day she would carry bags of food up to the wood, pausing at the spring to collect water, which, on her mum's command, she carried in a wooden bowl. This was not easy. She had to develop a method of hanging the bags on her shoulder while holding the bowl in both hands. On the second day, her mum told her to ditch plastic bags and only use linen ones.

Halfie struggled to find food her mum would accept. Nuts were fine: peanut butter was not. Local bread was fine: pasta was not. Anything made with their own eggs or local vegetables was fine: cheese was not, unless it was goat's cheese from a farm. Honey was acceptable but jam rejected.

The key was how natural, how unprocessed the food was. If Halfie could demonstrate or otherwise convince her mum that the food was untouched by modern hands, it was accepted. All other cases were instances of poisoning. When Halfie talked about lessons in fairtrade ethics that she had taken in geography, her mum told her that was corporate propaganda by a conservative elite, refusing to give way. Halfie found she lacked the energy to argue the point. Her spirits sank hour by hour.

By Monday, her mum began to look pale, ragged, unclean. She had stopped combing her hair because plastic combs created negative ions. Halfie, in a flash of inspiration, asked the Wise Woman for an antique bone comb, which her mum later agreed to use. Halfie mentioned nothing about its origin. The next day there was a pile of rejected clothes at the edge of the glade, her mum dressed in knickers and a slip, her bare feet black with woodland dirt. Desperate, Halfie waited until her dad was away in the livestock sheds before raiding their bedroom, gathering every garment labelled 100% cotton and taking it up to the wood. Her Mum, at first suspicious, was soon pleased, trying on several garments before settling on shorts and a cardigan.

"What about shoes, Mum?"

"Leather, taken from defenceless animals. Or spoiled by plastic."

Halfie pondered this. "What about sandals made of rushes?"

"I haven't got any."

"No, but I have."

Her Mum began to pay more attention. "What size are you?"

"Six. You are too, give or take a half."

"Bring them to me, I'll have a look at them."

Halfie smiled. Her mum could be reasoned with. There was some hope.

Halfie

On Wednesday, William Ordish strode up the track to the yard.

Halfie had been cleaning out the pig pens – she was sweaty and dirty. But her dad walked around the house just in time to stop the old man.

"What are you doing here?" he grunted.

William grinned at him, then took a drag at his cigarette. Halfie knew there was something wrong – she distrusted that expression. "Got a li'l offer for you, as it happens," he said.

"An offer? You mean, the fields?"

"Case ain't started yet, has it?" William continued. "Sometimes, folks settle outa court."

Halfie moved closer to hear better. "Well, I'm not settling," her dad said.

"Ain't yer? Not heard me offer yet."

"What offer?"

Again William gave the grin, showing snaggle teeth stained orange. He lit a new cigarette. "I heard you folks had a bit of a cash flow problem. Mayhap I can help there."

Halfie's dad spread his arms out in a gesture of bafflement. "With cash, I suppose. What are you going to do, just hand it over?"

"Thought I might buy them fields, I did. Give you a tidy sum. Proper price, not knock-down. What they be worth, see? With us both being men of the world, an' all."

Halfie stared. The cunning of the man! He had heard about her dad being sacked, about antiques being sold, and he was setting himself up to exploit the situation. She knew her dad would reject the notion out of hand.

But he said, "What price, Ordish?"

"*No,* Dad!" Halfie cried. "What about Mum?"

"Shush, you," he said, waving her away. "Get back to work."

Halfie took a few steps away, but found herself too fascinated by the discussion to leave.

William said, "So, yer gonna consider it, Chandler?"

"Maybe. What price?"

"Reckon they're just under an acre, so I'll make it a straight three thou'."

"Three thousand?" Halfie's dad said. "You've got to be joking!"

"Why not? That'll last yer 'til autumn when you'll have a proper job."

"It's a ridiculous suggestion."

William scowled. "All right... four thou'. My last offer."

"Equally as ridiculous."

Now William looked angry. "Yer a fool to ignore this," he said. "What you gonna do, eat fillets o' fresh air? You ain't got the nous to run this place and make it feed all three of you, not for the full year anyhow."

"We'll do what we please. You'd better go, Ordish. I can smell your bullshit from here."

"Four'n half thou'!" William cried. "My top offer. Take it or face the consequences."

"We *are* facing the consequences. I'll fight you in court, and win. That you've come here to offer money just proves to me that you know you'll lose. Get off my land, Ordish. You're a crook and an idiot."

"Gagh!" William cried, throwing his dog-end away. "Then I'll see yer in court, and no fancy solicitor's gonna save yer."

With that, he stomped down the track, muttering to himself.

Halfie ran up to her dad. "You would have done it if he'd offered you enough!" she said.

"What? Go away. I was just seeing what he'd do. It's called bluffing."

"You were *serious*," Halfie insisted. "I felt it in what you said."

"You felt nothing. An act, that's all. I thought you had pigs to muck out?"

Halfie staggered back. She did not trust him: *could* not trust him.

"What?" he said, glaring at her.

"You would have sold her out."

"*What* did I just tell you?" he said. He pointed at the nearest shed. "Get back to work."

Halfie shook her head, trying to control her anger. But she could not. "You're a liar," she said.

"You *what?*"

"You're lying to me right now. I can feel it. You would have gone for it if he'd offered you enough. I *know*."

"You know nothing," he retorted. "This is none of your business."

"It *is*. I *live* here. Why can't I have a say in anything?"

He growled an incoherent reply, then took a rake and raised it. "Get to work, or else."

She fell back, but then a voice cried out.

"Duncan! Put that *down*. If you touch her I'll run you off this smallholding myself."

It was the Wise Woman, standing in the doorway of the barn. Halfie stared. Her dad calmed, as if remembering who and where he was. But his mood changed in an instant. "I wasn't serious," he said. "Just angry. You know I didn't mean it."

"Get away from her. Now."

Halfie

Halfie watched as her dad looked from her to the Wise Woman and back. Then he told the Wise Woman, "I'll deal with you later, when all this has blown over."

Halfie watched him depart. She ran to the Wise Woman. "He did what you told him to!" she said, astonished.

"He did. I do hold some aces, dear."

"Did you do magic on him?"

The Wise Woman's face fell, disappointment clear upon it. "I thought you'd been told there's no such thing."

Halfie hesitated. She did not know what to think. "But... why..."

"Because I hold power here," came the reply. "You'll find out. Soon, I'm afraid. I sense imminent crisis."

"The court case?"

"Something like that."

Halfie considered her seething father. "I think I'd better stay with you again for a few days."

"You're going to," the Wise Woman said, "because I've got a visitor coming later this evening who wants to speak with us."

"Who?"

"Never you mind. Finish the pigs, then I'll accompany you to your bedroom to fetch a few things. We'll get nice and cosy in the barn. Your father won't miss *that* message."

The day sped by as Halfie finished her tasks then went with the Wise Woman to her bedroom. She heard her dad clattering pots and pans in the kitchen. Minutes later they were outdoors again, and Halfie felt free.

The Wise Woman glanced at her as they strolled across the yard, hens scattering this way and that. "Anxious, dear?"

Halfie shook her head.

"Don't deny it. Remember what I said before. You had a horrible time just now, and that leaves a mark. Accept it: Deal with it. Then move on."

"Is that wisdom?" Halfie asked.

"It certainly is. Now, what shall we have for tea?"

"Um, what about veg stew?"

Later on, Colin Wright parked his car outside the barn. The Wise Woman let him in and the three of them sat in the main room. A fine smell of chamomile tea wafted in, along with a hint of freshly baked scones.

"Good evening to you both," Colin began.

Halfie looked at him with suspicion. His spectacles twinkled in low sunlight shining through a window, his paunch flopping over his trouser belt. But he seemed at ease; even affable. "What have you come here for?" she asked, as the Wise Woman went into the kitchen.

"To speak about your mother."

Halfie had guessed this, so she was able to control her expression, betraying nothing. "Oh, really? What about her?"

"Did you read the leaflets I gave you?"

"I read a couple. But they didn't seem terribly relevant to me."

Colin glanced at the Wise Woman, returning with a tray. "Believe me, I have the deepest sympathy for you and your family. A very difficult time."

"Well, you don't have to have," Halfie replied. "We're doing okay here."

"Alfreda... I wish to present to you an alternative explanation for your mother's behaviour. It will upset you, but there is no way around that."

"There is. You could not tell me."

He nodded. "Yes, but some people in public life have certain obligations to meet. For instance, you're at school, aren't you?"

"You know I am."

The Wise Woman said, "That was a rhetorical question, dear. Just listen to what the man has to say."

Colin sipped his tea, then continued, "If at school a teacher has concerns about the welfare of a pupil, they have a legal duty to report that. It's part of something called safeguarding. Every school by law has to have at least one Designated Safeguarding Lead, and a deputy too. Usually that's the head, or the deputy head, but it can be any suitable person. Sometimes, a pupil will make a disclosure to a teacher about the circumstances of their life. That has to be acted upon immediately. At other times, a teacher may get a general feeling that all is not well. For instance, a pupil may have poor hygiene, appear thin, or unkempt, or even have bruises or other symptoms. By *law,* Alfreda, that has to be acted upon without delay."

"What's this got to do with me?"

"There is a feeling amongst a small number of people – tiny, Alfreda, really very tiny – that your mother's behaviour is becoming erratic, distressing, perhaps even perilous... to you, for instance. You are legally a minor, so certain people – your teachers, the DSL I mentioned, and others – have to consider your welfare."

"I'm fine."

"I expect you feel fine in yourself. You would say that, I think. But others are not so blasé. Some others, myself included, are very worried about your mother's mental state. We consider her to be mentally unstable. What do you think about that possibility, may I ask?"

Halfie

Halfie looked down at her lap. "Well," she said at length, "a couple of my friends have mentioned it. But they don't understand. Nobody does... except my dad."

"We must leave him out of this for now," Colin replied. "You are a minor. In some cases, children have to be helped by the state if their family cannot cope with looking after them. I know all about your father's situation. He was sacked by the local council for abuse of privilege. He was using the library and its resources for his own ends, not for the ends of the public he was employed to serve. He was, in a nutshell, sacked for not doing his job."

"But he's Snittonwood's Ambassador."

"No, Alfreda. He is the husband of Jane Chandler, who is mentally unstable, but whom he believes to be an elf. You believe that too, I have been given to understand. I am here to tell you all this, informally, you understand, and to explain to you that, in some cases, the authorities have to step in to save individuals from themselves." He hesitated, glancing at the Wise Woman. "That however, for you, is not yet in the offing. By great good fortune you have a friend here who is entirely trustworthy. That makes a considerable difference. But if she, I, or anybody else in a position of authority comes to suspect that your safety is being compromised by the behaviour of your mother, your father, or both of them combined, we will have to step in. It will be for your own good, Alfreda. And... I truly am sorry. As I remarked when I handed you the envelope, my experience of working with families is that their secrets are always the most shocking. Your case meets that criterion."

Halfie did not look up. Again she felt forces inside her battling for supremacy: the old and the new, the child and herself now... her parents' daughter and the friend of these people, and of Billy.

They all agreed, it seemed. There was no such thing as elves. Yet they *had* to be wrong. How could she discard everything she had lived for? Why should she?

She looked up and said, "What do you want me to do?"

"Keep yourself safe. Rely on those you can trust. Then take the time to consider everything you've been told. There is precedence for the situation you find yourself in. Some children are brought up in religious cults, and, when they come out into the real world, they have to be... it is called deprogramming."

Halfie leapt to her feet. "Cults? No! It's *not* like that. It's good, and natural, and all about the land. You just don't realise because you're mundane."

Colin shook his head. "Not true. But I will say this. If you can break free yourself, albeit supported by those who care for you, that will be the best outcome... for your sanity."

"I knew it!" Halfie exclaimed. "You think *I'm* mad. You think I've got it from my mum!"

But his face betrayed no emotion as he studied her. "You got something from your mother, Alfreda, but it was something she put into you. Doubtless that was without malice, but it was certainly without wisdom. I am sorry I have had to tell you this." He sighed, glancing away. "The truth has a way of breaking free. That, in essence, is the meaning of my job. I cannot say it is ever easy."

CHAPTER 10

Halfie knocked on the barn door. It opened a few moments later, to reveal the Wise Woman in an apron.

"I'm going up to the wood to talk to Mum," said Halfie. "Would you like to come?"

The Wise Woman considered this question for a while before shaking her head. "As you can see, I'm busy cleaning. No, I think for now it would be better if you went alone. What are you going to talk to her about?"

Halfie felt glum, and she decided to show it. "I don't know."

"There there, dear. It would be best if you went alone. Perhaps later..."

Halfie nodded. "I'd like that. I'm sure it would help."

Alone and disappointed, Halfie trudged up the bridleway, picking a few flowers as she went so that she had a posy to present to her mum. But as she approached the wood, nervousness returned. She did not know what she might find. What made everything worse was that she no longer felt able to see her mum through the old Halfie's eyes – the simple view of a child. Now she saw her mum in a new way, a pragmatic way.

The real world, from which she had been insulated for most of her life, was beginning to intrude. Even at school, life had been easy and wrapped in cotton wool. Now there were characters like Colin Wright to deal with. Yet for all that she was trying to disregard the complexities of the world, it had a way of moulding her, and she did not know from where she would get new strength to resist it.

She sighed. Her sixteenth birthday was near, and she dreaded it. But perhaps this was all part of growing up. Her mum had once warned her about the rigours of adolescence, albeit without any mention of the turmoil she now felt. That had been a conversation about travel and excitement and finding yourself. Not once did her mum mention stress, confusion or anguish.

Standing at the corner of the wood, she thought of Billy and his clumsy, though sincere attempts to put his view across. Perhaps she had sailed through five years of school by ignoring everything that assailed her. Perhaps people had been trying to reach her all that time, yet had failed because the insulation created by life at Snittonwood was too thick. Perhaps that insulation was beginning to wear thin.

She swallowed. Time for the deep breathing exercise again.

After a few minutes, she walked to the glade where before she had spoken with her mum. The shelter remained, much improved with the addition of moss and other materials in the roof. She studied it with admiration. That was rainproof for sure. Inside she saw the bed roll and the pillow, alongside a mess of other items.

She stood up. "Mum? Where are you?"

Halfie

There came a rustle in the undergrowth from the direction of the shee mound, and her mum appeared. She looked gaunt, pale and dirty, though she was at least wearing sensible clothes.

"Mum," Halfie said, approaching, "you need a wash." Hesitating, she added, "Won't you come back home for a bath?"

"Tap water is full of fluoride," her mum replied. "And chlorine. Those are both dangerous chemicals."

For a moment Halfie felt like agreeing. She had heard this before, and believed it. But some spark rose inside her to make her reconsider. "Well," she said, "I'm sure it's all been tested by scientists, otherwise it would be a health hazard."

Her mum walked to the moss-covered log, where she sat. "Scientists would say that, because they're in the pay of corporations."

Halfie sat beside her. Her mum's reply reminded her of her dad's, as if he parroted her and she parroted whoever had told her: a game of hippie whispers. "Where did you read that?" she asked.

"It's well known in the Faerie community. Why do you think they only drink rainwater?"

"And spring water."

"No, Alfreda. Didn't you know? That water is contaminated by agricultural run-off. All the chemicals used by Ordish on his fields seep into the ground, then into the spring."

Halfie said, "But you drank spring water in the bowl. I brought it for you."

"That was a mistake. Now I drink rainwater. So long as it hasn't touched the ground, the elves consider it pure."

Halfie

Halfie looked away. The temptation to give in was strong, but still the spark burned inside her. "We were told in chemistry about halogen additives – that's the chemical word for fluorine and chlorine."

"Is it?"

"They add fluoride to water to stop tooth decay," Halfie continued. "Sodium fluoride they put in toothpaste, and it's perfectly safe. It's all been tested. There'd be a national scandal if it was unsafe, and... there hasn't been."

"Not yet. The underground is still fighting corporate lies."

"Chlorine they put in water to stop diseases. Mum, I'm pretty sure that's been known for decades. I think it's why there's no cholera or dysentery any more."

"I don't doubt you mean well," her mum replied, "but you're too young to understand the ways of the world. Men don't care about public health, they care about profits. If it suits them to put chlorine in the water, they will, regardless of the consequences."

Halfie fretted. How could she make her case without alienating her mum? "Well," she said, "what about this underground group doing the fighting? They drink tap water, and they brush their teeth." She glanced at her mum's mouth, but her lips were closed. "Are you brushing your teeth?"

"With salt."

"Salt?"

"Rock salt, the old fashioned way," her mum said. "Pure and simple."

Halfie hesitated. The principle of the saline mouthwash was known to her. "I still think you should follow the example of your underground friends. I bet they use toothpaste. Why don't you pop down to the house and

phone one of your friends? Maybe… Lizzie. She was nice.
She gave me the hamper."

"I already know the dangers of fluoride, Alfreda. I've
done the research."

Halfie leaned forward, elbows on knees. At length she
said, "What about tap water? They must drink tap water. If
they can, why can't you?"

"They're tempted. They're impure."

Halfie sighed. She felt on a losing streak now. Birds
sang all around them and the air felt warm, if a little
muggy. Noon was approaching.

"Why are you so dead set against men, Mum?" she
asked.

"Men rule through violence, intimidation and fraud.
Their world is the world outside, and I reject it utterly."

"That seems a little… harsh. There must be some good
men. Dad."

"He's different. The King made him Ambassador
because he accepts his feminine side."

Halfie knew this to be nonsense, yet she could think of
no way of opposing it. Her status as their daughter
disallowed any subtle rejoinder, and telling her mum the
truth was not an option. After a while she said, "What
about Billy Ordish?"

"The son of his father."

"What about Colin Wright?" She pondered Billy's
shared document, now sent to the solicitor. "He's working
for free, and he's really sympathetic."

"A functionary of the legal system," her mum replied.
"Corrupt. A liar."

"But he'll help us win the case."

"*You'll* win the case. Your Faerie strength will shine
through."

Halfie

"What if it doesn't?" Halfie insisted. "You and Dad both admit spells don't always work."

"Have *faith* in yourself. The fields belong to the elves of Snittonwood. That magic won't go astray."

"Why can't *they* save their fields?"

"Because they can't act in the mundane world, where Ordish lives, so we have to do that work for them. It's why they need a representative – your father."

Halfie looked away. Her mum had an answer for everything.

Then her mum said, "Why are you so argumentative today? Is it PMT?"

"Mum! Don't be daft. I was just asking, that's all."

"Don't ever lose your faith, Alfreda. That's what supports us."

"I know."

After a while her mum gave a little moan, then said, "The world out there is an awful place, Alfreda. You'll have seen a little bit of that in town and at school. But I've travelled the world, and I've seen hideous things, that, actually, I'd like to forget. Things in India... in Turkey... in London. Nobody *cares* any more. Everybody walks around in their plastic clothes carrying plastic bags full of consumer tat. Nobody sees the land... except Faerie folk. We're so lucky to have this little haven. Without it, I don't know what I'd do. It's a sanctuary of peace in a world of hell. Don't ever be seduced by the world, Alfreda, you'll wither and die. People will exploit you, corporations will lie to you, politicians will ignore you, and all the time they'll be fighting wars and dominating the poor and the weak. You and I can't oppose that. Our task is to reject it and create a little bit of paradise – to lead by example. That's the joy and the beauty of living in Faerie. My elf senses show me green perfection. I see it, I hear it, I smell and taste it every day. I touch a leaf and my skin tingles. *You* know what I mean, don't you Alfreda? You feel that magic in nature. It's all around us here."

Halfie nodded. That, she could not deny.

Halfie did not now enter the farmhouse unless she knew her dad was outdoors, but she could not avoid him around the smallholding. Warily, if politely, they circled one another, doing all the jobs that needed doing; livestock, feed, clean and repair.

In the yard one day she found him whistling as he moved sacks. Taking the opportunity to approach him, she said, "You seem well today, Dad."

"Colin told me the case is due to come up next week."

Halfie felt apprehensive, though she sensed his relief. "Good!" she said.

"Then we can get on with winning it."

"And get Mum back."

He glanced at her. "Yes... this whole fields business has upset her a lot."

"I think she's sensitive that way. I mean... about the land."

"Well, I think we all are in this household."

His willingness to talk encouraged her. "Don't you miss her?"

"Sometimes. Why?"

"I just wondered."

He glanced at her, but did not seem displeased.

Emboldened, she said, "You know my friend Lucy Rees at school?"

"Vaguely."

"She's fifteen and she's just got a baby brother. She said it must have been an accident."

"That happens."

"Wouldn't you like to have had another one? A boy."

Now he halted, looking at her. "What's that got to do with you?"

Nettled by his sudden change in mood – which seemed more like rejection than any normal question – she replied, "I might have liked a brother, or a sister."

"Are you complaining about being an only child? That seems rather selfish to me."

Now irritated, she made no comment, wondering how far she dared go. Then she said, "Maybe I was an accident, like Lucy's brother."

"Nah," he said, picking up a sack.

"But Mum said I came along not long after you met."

He halted. "Did she now? *That* bit of the story she seems to have mis-remembered. I thought you were mucking out the pigs?"

"I am."

"Well, get on with it then."

Halfie watched as he strode away. As usual, his gruff insensitivity had killed the important part of the conversation. As he disappeared into a livestock shed she felt sudden nausea well up, but she did not feel as though she was going to be sick. This was nausea at *him*.

The Wise Woman had spoken true. It was all right to be averse to your parents – one, anyway.

Seeing that he was busy, she hurried to the kitchen door and went inside. She felt hungry; not eating a school meal had its drawbacks. But the cupboards were as good as empty, just half a packet of muesli and some tins of chopped tomatoes remaining. The fridge contained one dish of butter. Only crumbs in the bread bin.

Having eaten with the Wise Woman for some time, this aspect of life had passed her by. Then she heard a car drawing up into the yard, so she went outside to see who it was. It was a van labelled: *Jim Taylor, Slaughterman.*

Though familiar with the purpose of livestock, this aspect of smallholding life always caused her difficulty. Taking old hens up to the wood for the foxes was feasible because she never saw what happened next, though, of course, she could imagine it. But imagination was sanitised: and blood stank. Her dad felt no such ambivalence. She knew he entertained no compunctions about the slaughter of livestock.

Hurrying away, she entered the barn, calling out, "Only me."

"I'm up here," came the reply from the mezzanine.

Halfie ascended the rickety wooden steps to see the Wise Woman sitting on her bed amidst an assortment of oddments – mostly jewellery. "What are you doing?" she asked.

"It seemed to me that the time had come for me to make my contribution," the Wise Woman replied.

Halfie did not understand. "To what?"

"The smallholding."

Now Halfie realised. "You're not selling those?"

"I'm having them valued later on. Dear! Don't look so appalled. I never wear any of this. You must have noticed I rarely go out. There aren't the occasions any more to wear beads and baubles."

"But this is yours. You shouldn't be paying for anything anyway."

"Why not?"

Halfie glanced around the barn. This had been a working part of the smallholding before the Wise Woman's arrival. Stuck for a reasonable reply, she said, "But why should you? You don't pay rent, do you?"

"No," came the prim reply.

"Well, then."

"I must pay something. I'm coming to realise how bad your parents' cash flow crisis might be. I have food enough for myself, but not for you and me both, at least, not for long – even with my pension."

Halfie thought about what would be happening outside. "Jim's come in his van."

"I saw him."

"We know what that means."

"It's what pigs are for, as well you know."

The Wise Woman seemed to have little sympathy on this matter. Halfie nodded, but said nothing.

"Dearest, it was like this after the war. Years of rationing, with people growing their own, butchering their own. You're a country girl, I know you understand." She hesitated. "But perhaps in your current mood it's a bit of a shock."

"Oh, I know what the animals are for."

The Wise Woman smiled. "At least there your father knows his business. Times are hard and we have to be practical. Duncan has got some common sense in that department, thank goodness."

Halfie said, "Do you think we're going to run out of food?"

"Not with a stack of salted pork, no. But I am worried about all the other things which need paying for. What about toilet roll? Soap. Buying local is all well and good if you have the money, but your father seems unwilling to find a new job."

Halfie agreed with this assessment. "I don't see why."

"He's worried about your mother. I suppose we should make at least a bit of an allowance for that."

"I asked him if he missed Mum."

"Oh. What did he say?"

"He pretty much cut me dead," Halfie answered.

The Wise Woman nodded. "He's far from perfect, that's for certain."

Halfie sighed, glancing away.

"What, dear?"

Halfie turned back to reply, "You and Billy are giving me a lot to think about."

"That's all for the good. In the long run, anyway."

"But it's so *difficult*. And so painful. I wasn't expecting that."

"No. I imagine not. But I'm afraid none of us has any choice."

Halfie glanced at the sparkling array on the bed. "Are you really going to sell this – for our sake?"

"Wouldn't you?"

"But why would you? You don't have any responsibility towards us."

The Wise Woman looked at her, mouth shut. No reply came.

Halfie shrugged, then descended to the main room.

"Where are you going?" the Wise Woman called down.

"Might as well help Dad."

Halfie stepped outside into the yard. Jim Taylor stood by the main pig shed, washing down the yard with a hose. Halfie saw the water run vivid pink into the drains.

Halfie

Jim glanced up at her, his expression neutral. "Nice day for it," he said.

They met at one-thirty, Halfie and Billy alone, on a day threatening thunderstorms.

"First hammerheads of the season," Billy observed.

Halfie was in no mood for small talk. "I need your advice," she said.

At once he sat upright, his face serious. "'Course," he replied.

"Everybody except me and my dad says my mum is ill. I... I don't know what to think now."

"You reckon we're all wrong, then?"

"That's the problem," she said. "I appreciate that you're all doing what you think is the best for me, and that includes Colin Wright. But how can it be the best?"

"It's more'n a difference of opinion to you."

Halfie nodded. "Trouble is, I can feel myself changing. And I don't *want* to change, Billy. It's frightening. I want my old life back."

"A new life might be better for us both."

"*You* might think that for yourself, but I can't. You've got a horrible father. I've got an elf mother. It's completely different."

"Is it?" he said.

"There you go again! Assuming."

He shrugged. "We spoke about that before. We did the test. We proved it."

"This is *different*. How can I give up what I know? I'd have to give my mum up too. Don't you see that's impossible?"

Halfie

He nodded, tapping his fingers against his knee. "I ain't got the answer," he said, "but I'll tell you a story. Mebbe it'll help, then again, mebbe not."

"Go on then. What's it about?"

"My dad."

"Is it a nasty story? Because if so, I don't want to hear it."

Billy paused for thought, then said, "Some time ago, I reckon about a week or so before I was due to go up to secondary school, I had a bit of an illness. The doctor didn't know what it was. I had a rash, I was off my food, and even found it quite tricky to drink. They said it might be an allergic reaction, but then they said not. Then they thought I might've been bit by something – them horseflies reg'lar saw their way into you – but they couldn't find any wound or owt. Then they thought I might've got Weil's disease out of the brook, but then, no, not that. So it went on for a few days. Anyhow, by the time September come along, I was in a bad way. Thin, and very tired. So my dad began talking to me, trying to find out what it was ailing me. Mum had left by then, you see. He'd come upstairs with me at bedtime, which he'd never done before, to try to get it out of me. Not horrible, like – not at all. But fair, quick-spoken, not taking any shilly-shallying for an answer. Seemed he really needed to know what the thing was, and he'd decided to find out himself. And... you know what?"

"What?"

"I got to enjoy it. Saw a different side to him, I did. And then the illness faded. By the time it came to the first day of big school, I was, well, half-starved you might say, and still a bit tired, but I was all right."

"What's that got to do with me?" asked Halfie.

193

He shrugged. "Well... you know your own mind, and all..."

"What's that supposed to mean?"

"I ain't never heard you say a good word about my dad. What if he helped me while I was ill, made me recover, by paying me a bit of attention?"

"I've never heard *you* say a good word if it comes to that," said Halfie.

"No... likely you ain't. But that don't mean no good word's been said."

Halfie did not reply, gazing at him.

"Like you told me before," he continued, "my stepmum, you said, she must have a reason to stay with him. Remember that?"

Halfie nodded.

"She must see something positive in him, you said – like she's seen a reason to stay, another side of him."

Halfie answered, "And you said, p'raps she has."

"There you go," said Billy. "If I completely give up my dad, I give up what he did for me then."

"I don't think I can bear seeing my mum in the woods for much longer, Billy. It's tearing me up. But, if I accept what people are telling me, I've got to give her up – and Faerie too. I don't know what to *do*."

"Mebbe you could try to separate the good from the not so good?"

"How do you mean?"

"My dad's got a fearsome reputation 'round Ludlow, and mostly that's well-deserved. We all seen him in one of his spiteful rages. But my dad, and what he does... I try to separate them. I don't like the bad stuff while liking the good stuff, though, to be fair, there's precious little of that."

"And," Halfie said, "you can do that?"

"Separate what they do to you from who they are?" He shrugged. "I dunno. It's only this year I been thinking about it, what with A Level choices and that. Plus... I've got my stepmum to rely on."

Halfie pondered this. She had never seen Billy's stepmum. "You never talk about her – hardly ever."

"No. Bad times."

"The divorce."

He nodded. "And my dad got in with my stepmum pretty sharp after the separation."

"Too sharp?"

Billy shrugged. "I don't wanna talk about that."

Halfie gazed at him. In another way he was like her! Some things cut too deep. "No," she said. "But I do understand. Too painful."

He nodded, looking down.

"So what I've got to try to do," Halfie murmured, "is separate my mum's behaviour at the moment from her as a person."

"Reckon you could do that?"

"I don't know. That behaviour includes my behaviour. I *chose* to be an elf."

"Can I say something?" he asked.

"Of course."

"But you won't like it. You might be angry."

"Um..." Halfie sighed. "I know you mean well, Billy. Oh... go on, then."

"Where's your elf ears? Your mum too."

"Elves don't have pointy ears."

"They do in all the pictures," he said.

"It's just pictures. My mum told me all about that. It's called cultural representation. Elves look that way for artistic reasons, not because they really do have pointy ears."

He glanced up, as if over her head. "You got the hair for it though."

"Have you been *researching* this?"

He looked surprised. "'Course."

"Why?"

"It's important."

"To you?"

"I gotta know what's what," he replied, looking indignant. "I gotta get me facts right for your sake. 'Course I been researching it! Legends and that. Red hair, I know about that one."

"My mother's got red hair."

He nodded. "Pretty common in Ireland, I read."

"What do you mean?"

"That's what they call genetics."

"Anybody from Faerie has red hair," Halfie said. "It's their mark."

"But yours is dyed."

"No it's not."

He bit his lower lip. "Girls at school say it is."

Halfie looked away, glowering. He had her there. Denying it would be wrong. "It's dyed at the *moment,* a little bit, yes, but that's because I only recently chose Faerie. It'll grow red, you wait."

He looked away.

"What?" she asked.

"Don't reckon it will, Halfie. Genetics don't lie."

"Well, we'll wait and see. Want to bet on it?"

He glanced across. "A tenner?"

She stared at him. "You *would* bet?"

"How can I lose?"

"But…"

He looked away again, a mournful expression on his face. Halfie pondered what she had heard, realising that the certainty he felt about her mum not being an elf was secure enough for him to wager ten pounds. She felt trapped. Sincerely, with self-effacing candour, he had routed her again. Two worlds colliding, herself their battleground.

At length she said, "Let's forget the bet. Thanks for the advice, I honestly do appreciate it."

"I know."

"Well… we'd better get back. If your dad finds us together again, you'll catch it hot."

Billy stood up. "I would that."

"Thank you for helping me with my mum. I am very worried."

He gave her a peculiar, almost pained look. "Don't you get it? You're helping me as much as I'm helping you."

"How?"

"To see my dad for what he is. You see him like I don't. That helps me."

"But your dad isn't… mentally unstable."

"No," he replied, "but he ain't normal either. If I can see him like you see him, that'll help me to separate the man from the nastiness."

"And you really want to do that?" she asked.

"Mebbe."

"But you already know what his reputation is. Why do you need my view?"

"I'm trying to work him *out,* Halfie. Not saying it's easy…"

Halfie studied him. She sensed nothing of manipulation, of fraud. "Then," she mused, "perhaps… perhaps… I could do the same thing with my mum."

"It would definitely help. Like me, you're sucked in too deep. We only just realised the both of us what's going on. In a family... I s'pose you never can see it from the outside. But I'm beginning to reckon that'll help. It's why I like talking to you. I don't mind admitting I need a hand, I ain't proud. You could be more like that."

"I'm not proud either."

"Well..."

"You think I am?"

"Not that exactly," he said. "But you're so sure of Faerie. And nobody else 'round these parts believes in it. Mebbe that's summat worth considering."

Halfie felt a little insulted. "Then I will consider it. But if I don't like it, I'll stop considering it."

"Sounds fair enough to me. You gotta do it yourself."

As he spoke, words uttered by Colin Wright floated through her mind: *If you can break free yourself, albeit supported by those who care for you, that will be the best outcome... for your sanity.*

She glanced at Billy. He was trying to help. But she would have to make the final decision – break free herself, if that was what happened. That was her right, though it might also be her downfall.

Yet again she faced her dilemma. To see herself as others saw her was to lose something of profound value. She was not ready for such trauma. But she understood now, with dread in her heart, that events were pushing her in one direction only.

CHAPTER 11

The first week of the summer holiday drifted by without further bad luck from the curse, and Halfie began to relax. Her compulsion to go to the lavatory receded, her dad settled into a pattern of brusque requests about smallholding jobs, and the Wise Woman fed, comforted and talked to her. She met Billy every day. He began bringing her small boxes of food, which he said were leftovers, but after a while she realised they were more than that. Billy had heard about the cash flow crisis. He might have seen Jim's van. He had drawn the appropriate conclusion.

Halfie did not know what to think. It seemed wrong accepting handouts, yet what else could she do? Theirs was a family with no income: perilous. They had a small stock of food, but it would not last forever; and she had five more weeks to manage without the assistance of a school meal.

One day she thanked Billy, then said, "Why are you giving me these?"

"To help."

"Don't you need it?"

He shook his head.

"Does your dad know?"

"'Course not."

"Then your stepmum does."

He hesitated. "Well…"

"Was it her idea?"

"No. Mine. She agreed."

"Then you're both in league against your dad."

Again he shrugged. "No need to shove it down my throat."

"I just meant… that's risky."

"It's like I told you," he replied. "I *want* to be different to him. My stepmum's all right. We get on pretty well, and she knows what's going on over here – and she sympathises. She likes you."

"She's never met me." Halfie glanced down at the box. "I'm grateful, though."

"I know."

"Your family's as split as mine is."

He asked, "How's your mum?"

"Well… I'm really worried, Billy. Yesterday I found a tenner, so I bought some hand-made bread and farm honey, and took it to her. She rejected the honey because she said it exploits bees. That's not normal, is it?"

He raised his eyebrows. "Not at all. Bees do what bees do naturally, they make it from pollen. No… so she meant, in a hive?"

"Yes."

"But in the wild they just make hives in old trees and things. A wooden hive's the same. Was the honey shop-bought?"

"No, I got it from Pearl Farm," she said. "I've been going there lately."

"Halfie... your mum's getting worse. I'm guessing she's been in Snittonwood for quite a few days now. She's missing a lot of... you know. Home comforts."

Halfie sighed. "She's dirty and smelly, and her hair's a mess. She won't even use the bone comb I gave her."

"This sounds bad to me. If she goes below a certain point..."

"What do you mean?"

"You and your dad'll have to step in. I mean, you can't let her starve."

Halfie said, "You mean, force feed her?"

"Persuade her out of the wood. Give her somewhere to live near the house – one of them fancy round tents your hippie friends had for their festival."

"A yurt?"

"Yes! She'd live in one of them, wouldn't she?"

Halfie shrugged, unconvinced. "If it was made of natural products."

"But I think they are."

"I'll see what I can do. I suppose you're right. She can't live in the wood forever, even as an elf. She has to have..."

"Help."

Halfie nodded. "Oh, Billy, what am I going to *do?* If me and Dad force her, she'll..."

"She'll resist."

Halfie glanced up at him, tears in her eyes. "What if she won't come?"

"There's always other help. The social people."

Halfie looked away. Tears trickled down her cheeks. "I couldn't bear that."

He coughed, and when he spoke his voice was thick. "I'm really sorry, Halfie. It's a horrible thing to go through. But I'll help, and I heard the Wise Woman is looking after you. You've got to try to persuade your mum out – that's the first step."

"Yes. Thank you, Billy. I suppose you're right."

"Unfortunately."

"Perhaps… perhaps the elves are rejecting her and she's not telling me. I'm wondering if they're getting fed up with her. Perhaps she's trying to protect me."

"She's telling you as it is," he said, "exactly how she sees it. You need to listen to her carefully."

"I am. She's rejecting the world. She *hates* the world."

He nodded, pursing his lips.

"It's impossible to convince her," Halfie continued. "She's got a reply to everything. She's got it all worked out in her mind. But… it's so extreme."

"You were right. That's not normal. You've got to take the lead now."

"I *tried* to, Billy. I tried to inject a few of your thoughts into the conversation. She called me argumentative."

"Hah!" he said, grimacing. "Sounds like my dad. Classic dad reply, that is."

Halfie nodded. "They do it to cut us dead. My dad does it too."

"Means they don't wanna hear any more 'cos it's dangerous territory. Your mum and my dad are the same like that, though for completely different reasons. I know my dad knows he's wrong when he cuts me off."

Halfie sighed. "My mum doesn't know wrong from right any more."

He stood up. "No…" He glanced towards Stone Farm. "Sorry, Halfie, I gotta scram. Visit your mum when you can, try to persuade her to set up camp outside the farmhouse – maybe in your old orchard. We'll pay for the yurt if you can't."

Halfie

"No, Billy! A yurt would be really expensive. A natural one, anyway."

"What matters? A bit of cash or your mum?"

She looked away, again reluctant to accept his generosity. "It's too much to ask," she said.

"You didn't ask. It was my idea."

"But... why..."

He gave a laugh, though it sounded more like a grunt. "To help. Don't you believe I feel sorry for you?"

"I know you do."

"Good. 'Cos it *ain't* just me, Halfie. There's a few folks worried about you, and wanting you to be all right."

With that he strode away, leaving Halfie to ponder his final words.

For a while she stood amongst the nettles, studying the box in her hands. She opened it to find packets of nuts, some dried fruit, and slices of rye bread wrapped in paper. She looked up. All natural food. Billy was listening, he was really helping.

She decided she must visit her mum now.

In Snittonwood the air was cool and flower-scented. Birds fluttered amongst the undergrowth. But as she approached the glade she smelled less pleasant odours. In the distance between trees the sun illuminated the mound that was the elves' shee, throwing the ditch surrounding it into relief.

"Mum?" she called out.

Her mum struggled from inside the bed roll, standing up, swaying, then steadying herself against a tree.

"You all right, Mum? It's getting on for two, were you asleep?"

She looked like a scarecrow now – skinny, bedraggled, her hair a tangled mess like a red storm cloud. Algae stains covered her clothes, and her bare feet were dark with filth.

She yawned and said, "I'm hungry."

Halfie glanced down at food remains strewn across the glade. As she watched, a grey squirrel carried some of it away. "Didn't you eat what I brought you?"

"Poisoned."

"Not all of it."

"Yes."

Halfie felt sudden hot anger welling up. "No, Mum! Don't you think I *checked* before I brought it up? Is that what you think I am, a poisoner?"

For a few moments her mum stared at her, before looking away, dejected. "I can't eat bad food. What have you got there? More of the same?"

There was a gleam in her mum's eyes now that Halfie had never seen before. A gleam of delirium. "Mum," she said, "you've got to take your food more seriously. Why don't you put me in charge of it? I think you're listening too closely to the elves, and not enough to me. I wouldn't poison you, you know that."

"Other people would, using you as their conduit–"

"*No,* Mum. That's not *true.* You've got to listen to me today. I can see you're getting thin, and I think you're getting weak too. You're sleeping in, and when you got up you were dizzy and had to lean against that tree. So that tells me you're not eating enough. Let *me* be in charge of your food. I care about it, and you, you know that. I'll *help.*"

Her mum looked at her, expression blank.

"Are you drinking?" Halfie asked.

"Water from the heavens, filtered by the elves' canopy."

204

Halfie knelt down to pick up the white mug her mum used. It was empty. Frustrated, she went to the nearest clean puddle, dipping it in to fill it. As she did she noticed the name on the bottom.

"Look, Mum, this is one hundred percent natural – just clay and glaze. And look! It's from the Stonehenge range. You like Stonehenge, don't you?"

Warily, her mum took the mug, raised it to glance at the bottom, then drank. "Have you got nuts?" she asked.

Halfie handed over the box. "This is all natural too. No wrapping, except ordinary paper. Look – nuts and dried fruit, nothing artificial at all. And some homemade bread."

"Who made it?"

"It's from Stone Farm."

Her mum threw it away. "Muck," she said. She sniffed a handful of nuts, then began chewing.

Halfie watched. Desolation began to fill her. The scene was pathetic: this pale, dishevelled woman whom she was beginning to lose amidst a barrier of invective and freakish behaviour.

"Have the elves rejected you?" she asked.

"No! Alfreda, how *dare* you say that?"

"But *Mum*... look at you. If the elves are looking after you, why are you so skinny? Look at your hair, what does the King think about that? And, Mum... you smell a bit. What happened to that soap I brought, the stuff made from soapwort?"

"Used it," came the reply.

"What if I brought you some cruelty-free natural soap?" said Halfie.

"Where from? The moon? All soap exploits animals."

"Then... I'll make you a big lot from soapwort. You *can't* say no to that. You mustn't. You've got to clean yourself."

"The elves never use–"

"Yes they *do,* Mum!" Now Halfie felt desperate. "They *do.* I *know.* They use herbs, and rainwater, and they use it to clean themselves. Elves have bodies, Mum, like we do. Of course they clean themselves, and they do a very good job of it. So you're going to do what they do. I'll make it today. Right now."

Halfie stood up, but her mum showed no enthusiasm.

"I'll be back later," Halfie said in her firmest voice.

"If you like."

"Or... why don't you come back to the farmhouse for a while?"

"No."

Halfie refilled the mug, handed it over, then strode away. She felt anger, despair, wretchedness. Tears dripped off her chin as she walked. This was not right. Even if the elves were caring for her mum, they were making a mess of it.

She halted with a gasp. *If*... What was she thinking? If...

"No!" she cried. "They are in the wood. I'm *sure* of it. That's their home."

She walked on, heart thumping.

All she sensed in the wood now was her mum.

In the yard she saw her dad beside the goat pens, fetching buckets of feed. Balling her hands into fists she walked over, heedless now of her anxiety.

"Dad," she said, "I need to talk to you. It's *urgent.*"

He turned to face her, dull-eyed. "What about?"

"Mum. She's skinny, and doing weird things, and I think the elves aren't looking after her properly. So we've got to do something."

"We are."

"Well... we've got to do more. Can't you see she's faint from hunger?"

"Nonsense. She's eating the food you give her," he replied.

"What? Don't you care that she looks a mess? What about her hair? Have you ever seen it like that before?"

"Don't talk to me like that–"

"I *will,* Dad! I've *got* to now." She paused, choking as she forced despair back inside her body. "Don't crowd me out, Dad, *please.* I've seen what I've seen, and it's *wrong.* She might be getting ill. Why aren't you doing more to help?"

"I've got the smallholding to look after and the case to prepare for."

"Mr Wright's doing the case, not you. And you've got plenty of time in the evenings. Why aren't you up in the wood–"

"I *am,* Alfreda! And I told you not to talk to me like that. I am there with her... But you live with the Wise Woman now, so you don't see me come and go. She's my wife, isn't she?"

"Then why aren't you *doing* anything?"

"I am! I am, and don't you dare tell me I'm not. We talk all the time, your mother and me. The elves are angered because of the curse, and your mother's being made to suffer for it. *I'm* doing everything I can to speak with them–"

"You? What are they saying to you?"

"I just told you," he said. "It's seven years of the curse. But we're almost at the end of waiting for the case to begin, so you leave it to *us*, Alfreda. Things are getting delicate. So, you take her food to the wood, and all her other things, and leave the negotiations to us. You're too young to understand them."

"But Mum said I've got to make my contribution, so the curse—"

"Just *listen*. You're doing enough by believing. What the elves can't stand is disloyalty. That's the nature of the impossible task, isn't it? It's your contribution. I thought your mother told you that. When we win the case, all will be proven as the King demanded, and then everything will go back to normal."

With that, he turned away, threw the buckets he was carrying to the ground and stalked off into the house. She heard the kitchen door slam.

On the following day, the Wise Woman told Halfie she needed help inside the farmhouse. Expecting another fight, Halfie at once felt apprehensive, but the Wise Woman patted her on the shoulder and smiled.

"Not to worry, dear," she said. "We're going in to rescue a few items, that's all."

"Like, antiques?"

"Indeed."

The Wise Woman led the way indoors. Halfie listened out for her dad at the kitchen door, but heard nothing.

"He's digging up early spuds in the garden," the Wise Woman said.

Halfie nodded. "We didn't plant enough."

"*He* didn't plant enough."

"Well… he wasn't to know what was going to happen."

"Don't make excuses for him, dear."

This seemed a little harsh, even given her dad's excesses, but she let it pass. "What antiques are we collecting?" she asked as they made for the main staircase.

"Every last one."

"To take back to the barn?"

"At first."

Halfie shuddered. "Then sell."

"They're mine, so I can do what I like with them."

"But…"

The Wise Woman halted in the middle of the staircase. "Don't you like being helped?"

"Not at everybody else's cost."

"What other way is there?"

"But," Halfie said, "I can't do anything in return."

"Why do you need to?"

"To make it fair."

"Life isn't about fairness," the Wise Woman said. "It's about doing what's necessary at the appropriate time. That's what friends are for. My goodness… you would have been hopeless during the war, dear. Everybody had to help one another then, mucking in and doing what was appropriate. Some people miss those times."

"The war?"

"The *times*. Not the fighting, of course, that's men's wretched business."

Halfie nodded as the Wise Woman began climbing again. "You sound like my mum," she said.

"About men? There your mother and I sing from the same sheet, though for completely different reasons. Your mother likes nothing more than quoting Simone de Beauvoir, or Rosalind Miles, or whoever the latest hot author is. I said what I said because of the stupidity and childishness of most of the men I know."

"Even your Barry?"

"Even my Barry."

Now they stood underneath the attic entrance. The Wise Woman clapped her hands together.

"We've got an attic to clear."

Halfie watched the Wise Woman size up the area. This old woman, she realised, must have bonds of obligation with her family. Was it possible she was related?

She held her breath as the thought struck her. That possibility had never before occurred to her. And yet... if reality was as people told her, there must be a tie of duty here. And that could only mean family.

Suddenly, she was trembling again.

"Come along, dear, don't look so frightened. There weren't any spiders last time, were there?"

Halfie swallowed. "Um... only dead ones."

"There you go, then. Where's the stepladder?"

Halfie pulled it out of the closet and set it up. "Shall I go up for you?" she asked.

"That is the general idea. You don't think I can climb up there with these knees?"

Halfie clambered up the ladder, opened the hatch, then climbed into the attic.

"Have you got enough light, dear? You should find those two chests up there."

Halfie looked around. On her previous visit it had been twilight outside. Now sunbeams shone in through cracks in the walls, and through one gap in the roof tiles.

"There's a big hole up here," she said. "The rain's got in and made all the dust covers mouldy."

"If your dad did any repairs around here that wouldn't have happened."

Halfie thought it best not to reply, so she hauled the two chests to the hatch, then, inch by inch, let them drop to the stepladder platform. The Wise Woman grabbed the first by its handle, then the second, and soon they were safe.

"Anything else up there, dear?" she asked.

"Just junk. What about the rooms?"

"Them next."

Halfie climbed down, but hesitated on the bottom rung. "Are you Nancy?"

The Wise Woman replied, "I don't think that matters just now."

Halfie felt she had to know the truth. "Well, may I call you Nancy then?"

"Can I call you Maeve?"

This unexpected reply floored her. "Er..."

Without a word the Wise Woman turned around and entered the nearest room, collecting a number of ornaments, putting them on a porcelain dish, then walking to the next room, which was the main bedroom. Halfie hesitated.

"What's the matter?" the Wise Woman asked.

"Mum and Dad don't allow me in there."

"Those days are over, dear. This is far more important. Come along."

Halfie had been inside only a few times, the most recent to gather clothes for her mum – an act of desperation. She quailed. Now all this seemed wrong, like theft. Yet she knew of no reason to argue. She followed, tip-toeing inside to watch the Wise Woman gather a few pottery figures.

"You carry these, dear, they're Staffordshire, and valuable. Don't drop them."

"I won't."

The Wise Woman glanced around, then picked up a cardigan. "Hold them in this."

"I think that's Mum's—"

"It doesn't *matter.*"

Halfie did as she was told. Of course, the Wise Woman was correct. It did not matter any more.

For a few moments the Wise Woman surveyed the room, clicking her tongue against her teeth. Halfie also looked around. The room smelled of old incense, and there were joss stick holders and piles of ash everywhere. On a sideboard stood half a dozen framed photographs, which the Wise Woman approached, picking them up one by one, then putting them back.

Again she made the tsk-tsk sound.

Halfie approached. "Are those old family photos?"

The Wise Woman pointed to a couple. "Your mother and father in Turkey, the year after you were born. Here's one of your mother when she was a teen."

Halfie looked. Her mum appeared a bit like herself: the same pointed chin, the same big blue eyes.

Then the Wise Woman muttered under her breath and raised the final picture. Turning it around, she undid the clips with a fingernail, pulled out the photograph and tore it to pieces. Halfie leapt back as, looking around, the Wise Woman searched the room, hurried across to a box of matches, struck one, then set light to the fragments, dropping them onto an incense holder when the flames leapt up.

Shocked, Halfie stared. This was sacrilege.

The Wise Woman glanced at her. "Do close your mouth, dear."

"But…"

Halfie

"I regret nothing, just like your mother. Remember?"

"But that photo was…"

The Wise Woman approached her, anger in her face. "Do *you* know who it was?"

"No."

"An American man called Timothy Leary. Before your time, dear."

"Who is he?" Halfie asked.

"A dangerous, dangerous man."

"Is he related?"

"No. Thank goodness. Now let's go back downstairs."

Halfie shook her head. "But… Dad'll go absolutely–"

"No he *won't,* dear."

Halfie felt afraid now, not least because she was complicit in the crime. "He will!" she cried. "Oh, he'll go berserk. You can't–"

"I can dear, and I have. Didn't I tell you? I hold power here."

Halfie felt her heart begin to beat fast and strong. Desperation fuelled her now. "You're related, aren't you? You're Nancy… you're not the Wise Woman."

"I *am* the Wise Woman and I *am* Nancy. Can't I be both?"

"Who are you?" asked Halfie. "Are you family?"

"What did I say about that before?"

"That…"

"That *now* is not the time!" The Wise Woman paused to take a few breaths, then sagged. "I'm sorry, dearest, truly I am. But you'll have to wait a little longer. There is a reason I can't tell you now."

"What–"

"I can't *tell* you. But you will be told, and most likely by me. Soon, I'm afraid."

"Soon? Is it to do with Mum?"

But no reply came to this query, and moments later the Wise Woman swept out of the room and clattered downstairs. Disconsolate and frightened, Halfie followed.

They spent a silent ten minutes collecting antiques from ground floor rooms before depositing their haul on the kitchen table. The Wise Woman found a few empty boxes, dropped the jewelled ornaments in, then wrapped the delicate ones in old tea towels.

"Now we depart," she told Halfie.

Halfie glanced up at her, then looked away. She felt fatigued and defeated.

"You look unhappy, dear. Sullen, even."

"You've made everything worse. Dad will–"

"*No.* He will *not.*"

"*Why* not?" Halfie shouted.

"Because to outsmart me he reveals himself. And that, at the moment, he is trying not to do."

Halfie sprang to the kitchen door. "You can take all that stuff to the barn yourself. *I've* got jobs to do."

The Wise Woman nodded, smiling. "Tea at five-thirty. It's pork and wedges."

Halfie did not reply. She went outside and was about to slam the door, but as she grasped the handle she thought of her dad doing that same thing. She froze. She was not like him. She shut the door quietly, though it exasperated her to do it.

Halfie lay awake as stars wheeled over her bed – she saw them through the barn skylight, minute by minute, hour by hour, never faltering, marking numinous time. Sleep lurked far away. All she could see was the angry face of the Wise Woman, the angry face of her father. Now she too had been driven to rage. Would the curse stop at nothing? She thought of Billy, the closest thing to a friend that she had. Would Billy succumb to the curse too, spoiled because he wanted to help her? Perhaps she should do something about that. Billy was decent. Billy should never have got mixed up in Faerie affairs, whose rules were grim and precise, whose vengeance was faultless, whose methods were honed through passing centuries from their origins in deep history.

And Billy should never have got mixed up with this family, whose affairs were a torment, whose rules were cryptic, whose vengeance was inexorable, whose methods were forged by misfortune in the furnace of fury. Again, tears fell down her cheeks.

In the morning she got up early so she did not have to take breakfast with the Wise Woman. As the sun ascended she finished all the smallholding jobs which needed doing, then waited for her dad to appear, doing her deep breathing exercises and walking around the yard, then up and down the track to keep herself active. Around nine he stumbled out of the kitchen, bleary-eyed.

She approached him at once. "Morning, Dad! I've cleared up all the old bags and stuff, and mucked out the pigs. They weren't too bad, actually. The goats are fed and the eggs collected. And there were some old dip chemicals lying around, so I've locked them away in the tool shed."

"Er... right. Good."

"How are you?"

"Okay," he replied, shrugging.

"It's a beautiful day. Have you had breakfast?"

"Some eggs on toast."

"Shall we go up to see Mum together?" she asked. "We haven't done that for ages."

"Er… all right then."

She smiled at him, then strolled to the gate at the western track. He followed. She expected him to broach the topic of missing antiques, but he did not. "When does the case begin?" she asked.

"Why?"

"I noticed Mr Wright sent you a letter yesterday."

Her dad said, "Yes, he did. It begins the day after tomorrow."

"How long will it last?"

"Couple of days maybe. Could be just one."

"And when we win, then Mr Wright will be paid?"

Now he hesitated, leaning against the gate as if to stop it from being opened. "Yes," he replied.

"Let's tell Mum the good news, then."

Again he paused for thought. "Okay."

Halfie opened the gate and waved him through with a smile, determined to avoid all deviation from her plan. They walked side by side along the track. To make small talk she said, "We had a great Faerie Fayre this year, didn't we?"

"Yes, it was good."

"I thought Mum was brilliant on her flutes."

Her dad smiled, though it was faint. "She always is."

"Do you think she's a genius?"

"Er… could be."

"Why don't you try to get her a record deal?"

"It's not that sort of genius," he said.

"On an indie label, I meant. Rainbow Tom told me last year there's one based in Glastonbury for hippie bands – Magick High Records."

Her dad said, "That was last year."

"Then, it's folded?"

216

"Er… no."

"Well then. Ask her. See what she says."

Now they were walking up the bridleway. He glanced aside at her and said, "You're up bright and early today. What have you been doing?"

She sensed his bemusement. "I told you."

He glanced back at the smallholding. "Yes…"

"Cheer up, Dad! It's a lovely day. Let's enjoy it, see Mum, talk to her. Perhaps she's lonely without you."

"Maybe," he replied, "but that's not really any of your concern."

"Nor Nancy's."

He halted. "What?"

Now she could see he was having doubts about her. She beamed at him, gesturing at the wood nearby. "I asked her what her real name is. The wood's almost here. You don't mind, do you?"

"She *told* you?"

"Didn't seem bothered."

He stared at her. "Not bothered? Really?"

"No. Why?"

He looked along the bridleway and seemed about to walk back, but Halfie grabbed him by the hand.

"Come on," she said, "the wood's nearly here."

He pulled away, clearly suspicious. "Okay, but not for long. I've got things to attend to."

Amongst tall trees, they walked until they reached the glade. Flies buzzed around rotting food and the bed roll. Seeing no sign of her mum, Halfie put her hands to her mouth and called out. "Mum! It's only me. Where are you?"

From between bushes, a bedraggled figure emerged.

Halfie glanced at her mum, then looked at her dad. The expression on his face told him everything she needed to know.

"Dad, you *lied* to me," she said.

Her dad dragged his gaze away, glancing at her. "What?"

"You told me a complete lie. You said you've been coming up here, but I didn't think you had. You haven't seen her for days, have you?"

He stared at her mum, taking a few steps forward then halting.

"Look at her, Dad! I don't think the elves are caring for her. *We've* got to. Talk to her, explain to her what's happening."

"But, the elves…"

"*No*, Dad. They're *not* looking after her. Look at her hair! And can you smell her?"

He continued staring.

"*Please,* Dad. Look at the state she's in. There's something wrong. I had to show you somehow, I had to *do* something."

He blinked. "Jane…"

Halfie looked at her mum, but the eyes were glazed over, the expression dead. Her mum seemed some dreadful ghoul of woodland lore, a witch, a harridan, with detritus-covered tangled hair, teeth gone yellow and the stink of a sunken marsh. Halfie looked away, unable to bear any more.

Again her dad whispered, "Jane…"

"The curse, Duncan," she replied.

"Yes," he said at once, "it's the curse. It's acting on you now. Damn it all! But don't worry, darling, the case is set for the day after tomorrow at Ludlow Magistrates Court.

We'll win it. Halfie's been doing her best, haven't you Halfie?"

He tapped her on the shoulder to elicit a reply, and she muttered, "Yes."

"Jane, keep strong for me. But... you do look a bit scrawny. Are you being fed properly?"

"Nuts and rainwater, like the thrushes of lore."

"Good. Halfie will bring more if you need it."

He turned away, glancing into the canopy.

"Dad!" Halfie cried. "Where are you *going?*"

"Back to the farmhouse. Your mother looks a bit the worse for wear. I'll cook her something to eat–"

"That's what *I've* been doing!"

He said, "Only packet food. I think she needs something more substantial."

Halfie gestured at her mum. "She won't eat it! Don't you *understand?* She just won't, and you cooking it won't make any difference."

"Well, *I* think it will."

He hurried out of the glade.

Halfie jumped as a twig snapped behind her. She spun around to find her mum just a few feet away. Staring into those barren eyes, she squealed and backed away.

Her mum said, "You are barred from eating human food from this moment."

"What?"

"No more poison! Not for me or you. You're my only kin here, Alfreda, we must live together, in harmony. Your dad can't cook anyway. Do you hear me?"

"Um... Mum," Halfie said, "I really think there's something wrong with you. Are you sure the elves know what they're doing?"

"The elves have known for millennia. They're born of the earth, made from the stuff of the earth. They feel the track of the sun and the moon."

Halfie stepped back, unable to bear her mum's proximity. The shock of her dad's departure was beginning to fade, allowing deeper despair to return.

"Mum, I think there's something *wrong* with you," she insisted. "I think the elves must've made a mistake."

Her mum nodded. "Wrong? With the world! And it's almost got you in its clutches. But if you eat well and stay with me in Snittonwood, you'll be like me, and then we'll be happy together. That's what I've always wanted, Alfreda, for you to be happy and in tune with the land... just like me."

She stumbled forward, but Halfie sprinted away, arms pumping, gasping for breath, leaping over holes and tree roots, until she was halfway down the bridleway and almost beside her dad.

She paused, looking back.

No sign of her mum.

She was not sure now whether or not the case would be heard soon enough.

She bit her lip, unable to think of anything to say to her dad.

But her mum was not going to starve just yet, though she looked in a bad state. She uttered a forlorn cry of despair, wishing the seconds by, the minutes, the hours, so that the case could be heard and her torment end.

Her dad trudged on. Standing motionless, she let him go.

She waited for him to reach the farmhouse before continuing down the bridleway. The sun beat down on her – a hot summer day. Heat haze made distant fields shimmer. Behind her the wood shimmered too, as if marking an elven barrier.

Again she felt surging despair rise inside her. Not knowing how to counter it she knelt down and compressed herself into a ball, as if by physical force she could contain all her feelings, forcing them back into the pit from where they came. But they were strong. They demanded to be heard.

After a few moments she fell over, weeping, and she knew not how long it lasted.

CHAPTER 12

A broad smile animated Billy's face when they met the day after the confrontation in Snittonwood, but Halfie's solemn demeanour soon wiped it off.

"What's the matter?" he asked, handing her the usual cardboard box of food.

She struggled to speak. Having decided not to show her feelings, she spent some time looking across the fields and battling with herself, his obvious sympathy causing emotion after emotion to rise up. Above all, she did not want them to overwhelm her. That, she felt, would be counterproductive.

"I can see you're upset about something," he said at length.

"Billy, please stop being nice to me, it makes it worse."

He frowned. "Don't see how it could."

"Well *try*. Please. I don't mean to be rude, it's just that things are very difficult at the moment. If you could just…"

He shrugged, looking away, though he did not seem irritated. Then the slightly moon-faced look appeared on his face, which she had learned meant he was deep in thought. She also looked away, allowing herself time to regain her composure.

"You seemed in a good mood when you arrived," she said.

"Yes. Had a bit of good news."

"Tell me."

"Sure? It's about the case."

Halfie sat up. "Oh. What?"

He glanced across at her, then extracted an apple from his pocket and took a bite. "Reckon old Wrighty the solicitor is gonna win."

Halfie stared. "How do you know?"

"I don't. It's a hunch."

"But you must have some reason for telling me."

He nodded. "I'd not give you false hope, no."

"Then, what's happened?"

"I overheard a phone call my dad made last night. He must've thought I was in bed, but I'd had a bath, and was drying off. He's been in a fuss all week, hardly knowing if he's coming or going. He's losing it, I'm telling you."

"Losing it?" Halfie said.

"Getting fretful about the case. This morning, my stepmum told me he thinks he might lose."

Halfie felt her heart beat fast. "Really?"

He nodded, and the smile returned. "She warned me to keep quiet though. We mustn't aggravate him, she said. I said amen to that, I can tell you."

"You would," Halfie agreed. "And it sounds good news, which we need."

"I don't know who my dad was speaking with, but he sounded down. He mentioned maps. I wonder if me passing those old papers to your dad made a difference?"

Halfie shrugged, not knowing what to say.

"How's your mum?" Billy asked.

"Not great."

"Is she eating?"

Halfie nodded. "Some things, yes, but not enough. She'll survive, I suppose."

"Are you gonna tell her?"

"Your news? No. She's a bit delicate at the moment."

"Did you try to get her back to the farmhouse?" he asked.

"She refused. I knew she would. We've got to wait until tomorrow, when the case is heard."

"Okay. Well, I'm off now."

Halfie sat up. "Already?"

"Don't want to rock the boat today. Besides, spraying to do."

Halfie glanced across the field. "Mum says it's wrong to spray chemicals."

"'Course it ain't. How else do you keep pests down?"

"She said people are growing everything on too large a scale. It's called monoculture."

"What culture?" he asked, frowning.

"Monoculture – planting one thing in artificial conditions. It's growing a single crop in huge fields–"

"Don't tell me my business," he interrupted. "We both know your mum talks elf nonsense."

"We don't *both* know, Billy."

He looked at her, and she sensed the atmosphere change. He was a farmer's boy, after all, for all that he had leapt in with the traditional argument.

"What's the matter?" she asked.

"I honestly thought you were coming out of it," he replied.

"Out of what?"

Halfie

"The elf stuff."

She gazed at him. "Are the elves really so wrong to you?"

"Not wrong," he replied. He gave her a look of bafflement. "Just loopy."

Halfie felt insulted. "Thank you very much. But anyway, monoculture isn't elf stuff, it's called environmental thinking. It's science, and it's getting quite popular."

Without further word, he turned and walked away.

Feeling hurt, Halfie glanced back at Snittonwood. She needed to see her mum again.

Inside the wood all was calm: sunlight streaming down in golden columns, dust motes flickering through the air, birds calling, leaves rustling. The glade was silent and empty, so she crept on to the mound itself, thirty yards or so further on. As she did, her mum appeared from behind it. Dressed in clean white clothes, she spun around, dancing, whirling, a flute in one hand and a feather-clad stick in the other. Halfie watched for a few moments, entranced, as if seeing for the first time the awesome passion of the elves – their direct contact with the land, articulated in dance.

And her mum looked better. The hair was still a haystack and her feet were black with mud, but she had colour in her cheeks, and renewed energy.

When she saw Halfie, she halted.

"Hello, Mum," Halfie said.

Her mum looked at her, bright-eyed, active, pondering... yet it seemed without recognition.

"You all right, Mum?" Halfie added.

"Who are you, visitant from the mundane world?"

"It's me."

225

"This is Snittonwood Shee, noted in lore," her mum replied. "Stay away, or we shall place a malison upon you. Here resides King Lune of Erin, travelled in aeons past from the ancient isle, come hither on thistledown boats with his host at his side. And they carried a halbert, and a recurve, and a single young meadowlark."

Halfie listened, aware that her mum was in a trance. But this had happened before, so she did not feel worried. In fact, the light in her mum's eyes gave her hope.

"Get back, visitant," her mum continued. "Slay you we shall, if your feet touch this shee, which is sacred to my King. See my wand of birds' clothes, it will gouge out your orbs, that you never again see the sun."

Halfie took a few steps back. "It's *me*, Mum. Alfreda."

"Who is this Alfreda of lore?" came the immediate reply. "She is named *alf freda*... elf counsel, elf strength, good counsel, yet she is a yellow-haired wanton with nought to do for us. Begone."

Now Halfie sensed more amiss than wholesome. Not a word of normal language had been uttered: no greeting, no comment. This trance was dangerous. Feeling frightened, she turned around and ran away.

At the farmhouse she paced around the yard, part of her wanting to speak with her dad, part of her not daring. In the end he made the decision for her, emerging from a shed with buckets in his hands.

"Can you see to the goats' water trough, Halfie?" he asked. "Almost empty."

He seemed in reasonable mood. "All right," she replied. "Er, Dad, I've just seen Mum in the wood. She was dancing around the shee."

"Yes, I gave her something to ingest last night."

"To ingest?"

He glanced at her, without kindliness. "Something more wholesome than nuts, something to perk her up a bit. You've got a problem with that?"

Halfie hesitated. Something about his use of the word ingest concerned her. "You mean, you gave her something to eat?" she said. "Some supper."

He shook his head. "Same thing, isn't it?"

She watched him walk off.

Somehow, she was not sure it was the same thing.

She had heard that word before. It was a Faerie Fayre word.

In the barn, Halfie and the Wise Woman sat in their usual places. Halfie glanced up at her, looking through her lashes, pretending to read the magazine on her lap. A pact had been agreed. The Wise Woman was to be Nancy, and she was to be Maeve.

But it was weird. The atmosphere between them remained convivial, yet somehow redolent of the tension they had experienced in the bedroom.

"Nancy?" Halfie said.

She looked up from her crochet hoop and smiled. "Yes, dear?"

"What do you remember of hippies?"

"Why do you ask?"

Halfie said, "I just wondered. I was thinking about some of the people at the Faerie Fayre."

"Hippies have been around for a while I suppose," Nancy replied, "though I don't believe I was paying much attention when the Summer of Love happened."

"Did you like all that stuff?"

"Some of it. The bringing of women into better visibility. The anti-war sentiment. I approved of that."

"What didn't you approve of?" asked Halfie.

"The drugs."

There was a pause. "Why?" Halfie asked.

"Because I found out they're very dangerous. I've lost friends, you know. It's a great relief to me that you've had enough common sense to reject that side of things. I do understand they're tempting, especially for teenagers, who are testing every boundary they can."

Thinking of the day Billy rescued her, Halfie said, "Not me."

"Good."

"And I've met a few dealers."

Nancy looked up. "At the Fayre, you mean?"

"Yes. Do you know Brian Speed?"

Nancy chuckled. "Is that his real name?"

"Uh... I suppose it must be."

"How ironic. No, I don't know Mr Speed, though I believe I can imagine what kind of man he is."

"Why do you think people take drugs?" Halfie asked.

Now Nancy hesitated, looking up again from her crochet work. "Is there a reason for this line of enquiry?"

Halfie glanced away. She wanted to appear confident, yet she required vital information, and that made her feel nervous. "There is," she said in a firm voice. "I want to know. I *need* to know, to keep safe."

"Well... in my opinion, it's all about holes."

"Holes?"

"Drugs fill a hole, dear, exactly the same as drink or cigarettes. Drugs take people away from what's missing inside them, things they can't face, because they don't have the strength, or the insight. Alcohol and tobacco are drugs anyway."

Halfie nodded. "But didn't you used to smoke?"

"We all did back in my day. My Barry did."

"Why did you stop?"

Nancy gazed up at the ceiling, lost in memories. After a while she said, "We decided to quit at the same time, really. We both seemed to know it was the right thing to do. We were crabby for months, and it wasn't easy... but we had each other, which made all the difference." She sighed. "For all his faults, he was a thoughtful man. Not much of a hole in him."

"Did he drink?"

"An occasional pint at the Cart and Salamander."

"Did he know about drugs?" asked Halfie.

"We none of us did, dear. Apparently drugs arrived in the 'sixties."

"And the 'seventies. The free festivals."

"Yes... your mother went to enough of *them.*"

Halfie said, "Did she tell you that?"

"At great length."

There came another pause in the conversation. Then Halfie said, "Has my mum ever told you she took drugs?"

Now Nancy stopped crocheting. "I believe she might have."

"And Dad."

"And Duncan." Nancy paused, and the concern vanished from her face. "He encouraged her. He was the real druggie back in those days. She fell into it. It could have been different. But he's a proselytizer – an evangelist. He believes all that acid crap spouted by Timothy Leary."

"That's why you don't like dad, isn't it? I thought so."

"It's more that I don't trust your father, dear. He has some good points. If we are going to speak of such things let's at least be accurate."

"All right. Sorry."

"No need to apologise." She took up her crochet hoop again.

Halfie sat back. She had the information she needed.

But she felt sick. Something had changed inside her – a truth born.

"I'm going out for a stroll," she told Nancy. "Won't be long."

"Mind how you go. It's getting dark."

Halfie slipped out of the barn then walked up to the yard. In the farmhouse, a single light shone from the main bedroom. Distant noise from traffic on the A49 arrived reverberated by hill and field. The air was cool, soft.

Halfie leaned against the gate to the western track as she wept. She gazed up at Snittonwood through a mist of tears, each tree limned with faint moonlight, roots sunk into nocturnal shadow. Somewhere up there her mum danced, in a trance, such as Halfie had observed before. She guessed now the true meaning of such trances.

Again she wept, and this time she knew she must not bottle up her feelings. They must come out, that she gain the courage to do what she next had to do.

It was the day of the court case: sunny, breezy, blue sky and high cloud.

Halfie waited until her dad was at work in the sheds before entering the house and heading upstairs for the bedroom. She walked in now without compunction. The room smelled of incense. On the sideboard lay a colourful sheet of what looked like blotting paper.

She ignored her dad's junk to search the chest of drawers, and soon she found what she wanted, a linen scarf, cream-coloured with the faintest printed decoration, its label declaring: 100% linen. This best matched the clothes her mum currently wore. She took it away, returning to the barn, where she stowed it amongst her belongings. Then she visited the tool shed to raid her dad's gadget box. At the bottom, orange with rust, lay a reel of wire: steel.

She raised it in trembling hands. In chemistry she had learned that steel was just a different form of iron.

Iron...

She wiped away a tear. She had to do this herself. The decision had been made – hers and hers alone – and she would not now turn back. This was the final test.

Back at the barn, she commandeered Nancy's sewing machine, unpicked the two main seams of the scarf, laid a paired length of wire inside them, then sewed them up again. It was not perfect, and it meant the scarf had firmer edges, but it was the best she could do.

Then she walked outdoors, breathing deep, trying to calm herself, carrying the scarf in her right hand. Billy would be proud of her for doing this experiment.

The bridleway felt like the final walk of doom. Hot summer weather oppressed her now, her teeming thoughts roiling around her mind. She gripped the scarf tight. She wiped the sweat off her brow, then loosened her blouse.

In the wood, she paused to listen, but she heard no sound of her mum. Sudden fright took her: what if she had collapsed?

She ran forward, through the glade – empty – then to the mound.

There stood her mum, motionless, arms at her sides, still dressed all in white, gazing at the mound. For a while Halfie waited, to see if her mum would hear her, perhaps turn. She took a few steps forward, stepping on a twig. It cracked.

Nothing.

Halfie began to feel frightened again. She headed off to the side, then towards the mound, so that her mum would not jump at her appearance.

When Halfie came into view, her mum turned her head to look.

"Hello, Alfreda."

Her voice sounded composed. Yet her skin was pale, her cheeks algae-stained, and her eyes looked glazed over again.

"I brought you a new scarf to wear," Halfie said. "It's the same colour as what you're wearing now, and all made of natural unbleached linen."

Her mum reached out. "Thank you. Yes, I remember this one…"

She took it in one hand. Halfie stared, arm outstretched, frozen.

Her mum took the scarf, handled it, then draped it around her neck.

Halfie staggered back.

"What's the matter, Alfreda?"

Halfie just stared: the experiment performed, the result clear.

No denizen of Faerie could stand iron. That was well known.

Halfie's dad sprinted out of the front doorway of the farmhouse. Part way along the track, Halfie stopped to watch, the sun descending behind her. Then he jumped in the air, flinging his arms out wide.

She ran up, then heard the news.

"I won!"

Though she had known the chances because of Billy's hint, she still wondered if she had misheard.

"Really?" she asked, hurrying towards him. "How do you know?"

He took her in his arms and hugged her. "I won!"

She struggled free, pushing him away. "How do you *know?*"

"Colin just telephoned! Very late session."

Halfie watched as he capered around her. When was he going to say *she* helped?

"Thank goodness I called Colin in," he continued. "I knew he was the best. You know sometimes. Hah! My goodness... I *won.*"

Halfie glanced aside as Nancy emerged from the barn. "Duncan?" she said.

He turned to face her. "We've won the court case," he said. "I've told Halfie."

Nancy approached. "It's confirmed?" she asked. "*Without* doubt?"

He nodded. "Colin just telephoned me from Shrewsbury. He told me straight. It was old maps that proved it, that there always was an ancient right of way *crossing* our land, *through* it, not between two separate pieces of property. Old Ordish was wrong, however far back his damn family goes."

"Don't crow, Duncan. Still... I am pleased."

"We'd better hurry up and tell Mum," said Halfie. "She needs to know straight away–"

"Wait," Nancy said, taking her by the arm. "*Not* just yet."

Halfie turned to stare. "What? Why?"

"We need to... perform a... rite of thanks first."

"A what?" Duncan said.

"The Wise Woman speaks," she replied, glaring at him. "A rite. I demand it."

He shrugged, calming, and again Halfie sensed the hold she had over him in times of difficulty. Could this be... her son?

"If you like," he said. "My rite is going to be opening that bottle of red wine I kept aside. Ha ha! I thought it might come in handy, and damn me, if I wasn't right."

He ran off into the house.

Halfie turned to Nancy and said, "What's going on?"

"Just for a few moments, dear. Be patient. I have something to do first."

"What?"

"Something private and important. Just a couple of phone calls. Then we'll formally enter the farmhouse and speak with your father."

The way she said this made it sound like a solemn endeavour. Knowing her mum was not in imminent danger, Halfie said, "All right. But I want to tell her soon. Anyway, evening's coming on."

Nancy glanced up at the sky. "Rain on the way overnight," she said. She smiled, and yet, to Halfie's eyes, it lacked all warmth. Something felt wrong. "Not the kind of night your mother should be outdoors," she added.

"But she's managing," Halfie said. "The shelter is waterproof, in fact, it's really well-made. You'll see it when you come up to the wood. You are coming, aren't you?"

"I expect we'll all go."

Halfie tried to look pleased. "A triumphal march!" she said.

But Nancy just looked melancholy and turned away. "Go and see if your father's still sober," she said without looking around.

Now worried, Halfie ran into the house, where she found her dad slouched on a kitchen chair, an empty glass and a part-empty bottle of wine in front of him.

She sat opposite him, her smile radiant. "The curse, Dad! The King's sure to revoke it now."

He nodded. "Yes. I think we did it – the impossible task. And, chrissakes... it *was* as good as impossible."

"Though without Billy we might not have done it."

He shook his head. "*You* did it. You kept the faith."

Halfie felt the warmth depart her body. Before her mind's eye she saw her mum wearing the iron-tainted scarf. "I suppose... I... I must have," she said.

He did not notice her change of mood as he poured another glass of wine. "At last. A bit of success. Perhaps we'll see out the year after all."

"What do you mean?"

"It was always touch and go," he said. "But you must have given the vital input, Alfreda. Jane said you would."

"Did she?"

He nodded. "And she was right."

Halfie fidgeted. "Can we go now to tell her?"

"Better wait for the old woman."

Halfie glanced over her shoulder. "Dad..."

"What?"

"Is she family?"

He jerked upright. "Eh?"

"Is she your family?"

He stood up, looking angry. "Don't be ridiculous. She is *not* mine – that's categorical."

"Sorry, I only wondered. You looked like you were..."

235

"Were what?"

"You know. Giving in to her."

He smacked the glass upon the table. "More damn flights of fancy," he grunted. He glanced outside. "Getting dark, now. Come on, enough chat – let's go, old woman or not."

They walked outside, heading for the gate at the end of the western track, but in the twilight Halfie saw three people in the nearest Stone Farm field. She could not be sure, but they seemed to be carrying something.

"What's going on over there?" she asked.

Her dad gave an incoherent cry, then stood on the gate. "What the…?"

Halfie felt fear enfold her. "What can you see?"

"Looks like they've come down from the spring."

"You mean, the bridleway?"

"They're going back across Ordish's field," he said.

"Who are they?"

"I don't know. There's not much light left."

She said, "Shall I get your binoculars?"

"Er… yes! Good girl. I think they're still in the study."

Halfie sprinted along the track as fast as she could, skidded into the kitchen, found the binoculars, then ran back. Her dad remained in his position on the gate, leaning his shins against the top bar. He took the binoculars off her and raised them to his eyes.

Halfie studied what she could see of Stone Farm. In the gloom, she saw buildings, the tops of trees, and most of the great silo at the end of the main yard. But the buildings appeared to be jumping in her sight as if leaping between two positions, one dark, one illuminated blue.

"What is it?" she asked.

"I think there's a police car there," he replied. "I see flashing blue lights."

"Police? Oh, no... not Billy."

"Billy?"

"He *helped* us!" she said. "If his dad finds that out..."

"Shush now, Halfie. Their farm track runs towards our land, easily visible. I'll see what's happening, don't worry. If it is Billy, we'll just have to go and find out."

Amazed at her dad's charity, Halfie said, "All right. Together."

"Together," he agreed.

He watched for a few more moments.

"Anything?" she asked.

"I see old Ordish, I'm sure. I recognise his hair. There's the glow of a cigarette... yes, and there's Billy, running back to the house."

"Billy? He's all right?"

"He's perfectly all right. But wait... he's coming this way now."

"Are the police going?" she asked.

"Yes... I can see them on the track now... wait! Oh no... *no*. It's a damn ambulance!"

He leapt off the gate, throwing the binoculars aside then staring at Snittonwood.

"No!" he cried at the top of his voice. "Not *that*."

Halfie shrank back, terrified.

"*Nancy!*" her dad yelled as he began running back down the track. "I'll damn well kill you for this!"

Halfie fell back upon the ground as her legs gave way.

For a few moments all she could see was the sky whirling around her. She smelled something sour in her nose, as if she had been hit. She blinked, took a few deep breaths, managed to stand up.

Behind her came the faint sound of shouting.

She turned to see Billy running towards her across the field.

"Halfie!" he yelled.

She only just heard his voice in the distance, but she sensed his urgency.

She ran as fast as she could along the track, then down the southern arm of the bridleway, watching him squeeze through the hedge.

She slowed, to shout, "Billy! What's going on?"

He continued running, and now she could hear his breath coming hoarse. "Halfie," he cried as he neared, "come back! *Now.*"

"Back where?"

"To our farm."

She halted. "Why?"

"They took your mum away in an ambulance!"

CHAPTER 13

A t the edge of Stone Farm's huge central yard they halted, both out of breath, Halfie leaning against a wall as she gasped. Billy took a few hoarse breaths, then grabbed her and dragged her behind a shed.

"My dad at the upstairs window," he said.

"Looking for you?" she replied.

He nodded.

She clutched him, saying, "What am I going to *do?* It's the end. She's ill–"

"I don't reckon so Halfie," he said, taking her by the shoulders. "Quiet, please! He might have the window open. No, I don't reckon it was that sort of ambulance."

Halfie stared at him, uncomprehending.

"I'm guessing I know where she is," he continued, "and I'm going to take you there. Shrewsbury."

"How?"

"In the car."

"But you're not seventeen, you can't drive–"

"Can't drive?" he interrupted. "I'm a farm boy! I could drive before I went to secondary school."

"But... isn't it illegal?"

"Mebbe, but it's getting dark. Besides, this is an emergency."

Halfie let go of him, aware now that she had gripped him tight. "What car?" she asked. "Won't your dad see?"

"I'll use the old Citroën down by the water tank," he said. "It's my dad's own car, but there's no choice. We can get away without being seen, straight onto the track leading down to the lane. The family car's in the garage – too risky."

"But you might be heard."

"I'll take that risk."

She followed him around livestock sheds to the track, where, beside a cubic tank, she saw a battered car with its canvas roof down. Billy jumped into the driver's seat and reached down. "Key," he said. "Dad used it last week. Hop in."

She sat beside him, brushing away dried bird droppings and the remains of nests, then fumbling for the seat belt.

"It ain't got none," he told her. "Old, like I said. Just hold tight."

"Oh, Billy, please take care. I'm not sure…"

"We'll be all right," he said. "This ain't the first time I've driven this old clunker." He glanced up. "There's a bit of a moon, I won't put the headlights on just yet."

He turned the key, and the engine coughed, then failed.

"Huh," he said. "Try again."

The second and third time the engine failed, but it sounded livelier. Halfie crossed her fingers. When he tried a fourth time the engine caught. He revved, then released the handbrake.

"Hold firm," he said.

Moments later they were careening down the track, the car bouncing in all directions as Billy negotiated potholes, then headed for the lane. The five-barred gate was open: he sped through, leaving a cloud of dust and a slew of gravel. Then onto the lane, at speed.

"Where is she?" Halfie asked, raising her voice over the wind.

"Shush now," he shouted back. "Gotta concentrate. We won't be long getting there, forty-five minutes max. Not the community hospital here, the special hospital in Shrewsbury, right?"

Halfie did not know what he meant, but she grasped the importance of him attending to the road. She gripped the door handle with her left hand and the edge of the seat with her right. Soon Billy was at the main A49 junction, turning right towards Shrewsbury.

The road was quiet, few cars around. The minutes ticked by as they passed through Craven Arms, Church Stretton, then Dorrington. At the edge of Shrewsbury they drove along the old A5, passing through at thirty then turning into a secluded lane, where they slowed. Halfie frowned. She knew Shrewsbury well – this was a residential area.

As he slowed to a crawl she said, "Is that somebody's mansion?"

He halted at the roadside, pulling up the handbrake. "No," he said, taking her hand in his. "Sorry, Halfie, this is the time for me to tell you." He pointed at a tall building. "You know what that is, don't you?"

Halfie looked. The place seemed forbidding. Yellow-lit glass doors at the front suggested a block of flats. "No," she said.

"It's Shelton Hospital."

Stunned, Halfie appraised the building.

"The secure mental hospital," he added.

"But…"

"Your mum's been sectioned, which is why I pelted over to fetch you straight away."

"Been what?" Halfie asked in a daze.

He leapt out of the car, ran around the front, then opened the door and helped her out onto the pavement. Guiding her forwards he said, "It's when somebody's taken away for their own safety."

"But..."

"Just follow me. Likely you'll be a bit shocked, but I'll help you."

He led her to the glass doors, which opened automatically. Inside stood a desk and more glass doors, these thick, covered with posters, and closed. At the desk sat a middle-aged woman wearing a blue overall, her blonde hair pinned up in a bun.

"Oh, hello, Sandy," Billy said, strolling over.

"Billy! What on earth are you doing here?"

Billy stepped back to pull Halfie to his side. "This is Jane Chandler's daughter. We came as quickly as we could."

Sandy looked at Halfie with round eyes. "Oh..."

"So, can we get the formalities over with?" He leaned forward to pick up a pen from the desk.

"Well... Billy, this isn't..."

"Did she just arrive in the ambulance?" Billy asked. "There were three men with her, I noticed."

"Yes... but..."

"But what?" he asked. "Can't we visit?"

"Visiting hours are almost finishing."

"But this is different, ain't it? Her mum only just came in."

Halfie, still numb, watched as a number of expressions passed across Sandy's face. Then she picked up a telephone and said, "I'll find out for you, Billy."

There followed a quick phone call. Billy glanced at Sandy, then at Halfie. He winked. "D'you know Sandy? She lives in Ludlow. You okay?"

Halfie did nothing, said nothing, felt nothing.

"I'll send you through," Sandy said, putting the telephone down and picking up a couple of badges. She walked to the inner doors and pressed a series of buttons. "This is a secure unit," she said, writing on the badges then handing them over. "You're visitors. You must remain quiet. You're here at your own risk."

"Okay," Billy said, fixing one badge to Halfie's collar.

Sandy looked at Halfie. "Take care, won't you? Let me know if I can help when you come back. We have leaflets."

Halfie shook her head. "I already saw them," she murmured.

Sandy stared at her as Billy led her through the open doorway and into a long, reverberant corridor. The doors snapped shut behind them. At the end lay a large room filled with tables and chairs, half a dozen people sitting or standing around. The place was calm. To the left lay an illuminated courtyard garden full of green plants. Before her, at the far side of the room, there was an office in which three people stood.

One of the men saw them and hurried out. He wore a clinical uniform.

"Who are you?" he asked.

"We're here for Jane Chandler," Billy replied, tapping his badge. "Visitors. Immediate family. Sandy sent us through. I know her well enough, from Ludlow."

The man frowned. "You shouldn't have been let in. I gather the patient arrived in distress."

Halfie sobbed, leaning against Billy. At once Billy said, "Yeah, but this is her daughter, and she's been looking after her mum. Won't it calm Mrs Chandler down?"

The man glanced over his shoulder. "It's a new admission, I don't know the details, so..."

"I'm just doing what the family wants," Billy said. "We're here now, and Halfie – I mean, Alfreda, sorry – she'll definitely calm her mum down."

The man sighed. "Okay then." Glancing at his wristwatch he added, "We've just about got ten minutes. D'you want to follow me?"

He led them past the office into a dim corridor with doors down one side.

Then they turned a corner, and Halfie stared.

"Nancy!"

She stood alone in front of a closed door. She turned, and Halfie saw her face wet with tears. Running forward, Halfie hurled herself into Nancy, clutching her; and Nancy hugged back.

"I'm sorry, Maeve," she said. "It had to be done. But how did you get here?"

Halfie pointed at Billy, hanging back. Already the hospital man was walking away.

Nancy gave a great sigh, then gestured at the door. "She's in there. They've just this moment sedated her."

"But... you..."

"I'm Nancy Culpepper," she said. "Jane is my daughter."

Halfie stepped back, and for a few moments could not move, speak or even breathe. At last she choked, "You're my nana."

"Yes, dear."

"But…"

Nancy hugged her again. "Don't ask those questions yet," she said. "They'll be for later."

Halfie glanced at the door. "Is Mum really inside?"

Nancy nodded.

"And… is she alive?"

"Oh, yes. That's why she's here – because she's alive, and we all want to keep her alive."

Halfie nodded. "Billy said she'd been…"

"Sectioned. Doctors are allowed to do that by law if a person is thought likely to endanger themselves, or others. I asked for a Section 2, as is my right." She sighed again. "It's not an easy thing to accomplish, actually. I had to pull a few strings. You need two doctors to sign it off for a start. Luckily I know them both. But the nurse psychologist who initiated and managed the thing was helpful and sympathetic."

"Then, you…?"

"Yes, dear. I had to. No choice."

Halfie shuddered. "Then she really is loopy, not an elf. And I'm not an elf. And… I suppose you're not an elf either."

"No."

"But I thought I was."

"You and your parents did," Nancy said.

"But–"

"No more questions. This isn't the time or place." She hesitated. "Dearest… I think you'd better have a look at your mum. They come round to check patients every fifteen minutes, and we'll have to be gone by then. But there's a little peephole in the door for the doctors. I want you to be brave and have a look through."

Halfie hesitated.

"Will you do that for me?" Nancy asked. "I think you should."

"What will I see?"

"Your mum. She's alone in there, there's nobody else."

"All right."

Nancy pulled a square of plastic aside in the middle of the door to reveal a pane of wire-reinforced glass. Halfie looked through.

Her mum lay upon a bed, on her back, eyes shut, her blanket fallen to the floor, one arm hanging down. She wore white trousers and a white top, a red band around one wrist.

Her face was as white as her garments.

Halfie stared, then fell back. With a scream she ran down the corridor.

Dark night pierced by sodium glow. The noise of traffic on the main road nearby. Cool night air, whirling head...

Halfie was not sure where she was. Minutes had passed with only vague sensations. She remembered running into a glass door, hurting herself. Then voices... then a struggle.

"Maeve?"

She whirled around. Nancy emerged from the main doors, Billy close behind.

"Maeve, come here. We need to talk."

Halfie began to remember. She must have lost control for a while – gone hysterical. It was all too much for her.

She turned around, trying to rid her mind of the image of her mum lying insensate on her back, but she could not. She knelt down, hugging herself.

Then Nancy hauled her to her feet and led her to a bench, where they sat side by side. Halfie felt something warm around her shoulders – a cardigan. Billy stood before her, but at a distance, as if uncertain of his position or role. He jangled the car keys, looking up at the hospital building.

"Don't do that, Billy," Nancy said. "Go and talk with your friend at the desk."

"Sandy? Okay."

"I'll thank you properly in a moment. Right now, we two need peace and quiet."

He hurried away, and Halfie heard the swish and clunk of the main doors.

After a while, Nancy put her arm around her and said, "What are you thinking, Maeve?"

"I can't stop seeing Mum lying sedated."

"It is a shock."

Halfie glanced up. "You *told* me to look!"

"You needed to see the reality of it. There's no hiding any more."

Halfie looked away. "Where's Dad?"

"I expect he'll be here any minute. Don't be angry with him when he arrives."

"He said he'd kill you for… what you did."

"He'll have a job," Nancy laughed. "They rarely make them as tough as me."

Halfie made no reply. It sounded like boasting, and she was not impressed.

"You have to be tough, Maeve, if you're a woman. You have to present a smile to the world all the time – women are supposed to. But you have to endure a lot. You'll find that out as life hacks away at you, bit by bit. Then you'll begin to discover inner strength you didn't know you had. In fact, you're discovering it now. But your father is a weak, ineffectual man, I'm sorry to say. He has little by way of inner strength and a lot by way of external distractions. I did make such observations to Jane, but she was in love, and she ignored me – called me interfering."

Halfie still felt angry. "Perhaps you are," she muttered.

"Well, at my age, you often know what's for the best because of experience. Don't be harsh on yourself, dear, or on me. I saw this coming months ago, which is why I made preparations weeks ago, and why the sectioning went smoothly. Sometimes it doesn't. Sometimes people hurt themselves. There was always a chance that Jane would do something irrational based on her beliefs, something fatal."

"*Irrational?* She loves the elves, and totally believes in them!"

Nancy looked at her. "That is precisely what I mean."

"Then *I'm* irrational."

"Would you say that of a Christian?"

"No," said Halfie.

"But it's the same thing – a deeply held belief. Yet some beliefs are weirder than others, and some beliefs come from tainted sources, not from wise men or ancient scripture. I'm an agnostic, myself."

Halfie replied, "I'm an elf, and therefore you are too."

"Nobody thinks that except you, Jane and your father."

"You're trying to persuade me out of my belief! I *know* it!"

Nancy looked surprised. "Indeed I am. I'm your nana, aren't I? I love you. I always have."

Then Halfie wept, as Nancy hugged her. All the pain of the day came out, washing fear away, cleansing her of despair. Then she felt warmth beside her and a deep ache inside.

"There, there dear. Let it all out."

And Halfie did.

Halfie

At length, she felt her tears subside. She looked up and said, "I think it's gone for now. Thanks, Nana."

Nancy glanced up, alert. "I hear a car parking," she said. "This might be your father. Have *strength*. We're together, you and me. You can always depend on me."

Footsteps sounded, as of somebody running, before her dad appeared around a corner.

"Nancy!" he cried, halting. "You're here!"

"Where have you been?" she replied. "Your daughter's been here fully fifteen minutes."

"*Looking* for her! And you."

Nancy nodded. "Well, I suppose that's not an unreasonable explanation. You'd better go inside and speak to the nurse. It's gone visiting hours, but for you I expect they'll make an exception. Jane's all right. She's sedated, though."

He grunted something, then pointed at Nancy. "I'll deal with you later."

"You will do no such thing, because *I* will be dealing with *you*. Get inside, Duncan, before they close up for the night. And tell Billy to come out."

He hurried away, passing into the hospital. Billy appeared moments later.

"We'll go home now," Nancy said. "There's nothing more to be done here."

"But Dad," Halfie said.

Nancy shook her head. "We'll be keeping well out of his way for a while. Besides, this will affect him deeply. I'm not insensitive to that. He'll need support too." She glanced at Halfie. "But not from you. You've done quite enough of that sort of thing for them."

"We'd better call for a taxi," Halfie said.

"We already have a chauffeur," Nancy replied. "There's room for me in the back?" she asked Billy.

"Reckon so, Mrs... I don't know your real name."

"Culpepper." She grinned. "Rather ironically, that means false pepperer, or herbalist."

Billy nodded, his expression suggesting ignorance.

In the battered Citroën they drove home, Halfie praying no police would stop them, Nancy telling her that was ridiculous. At the five-barred gate Billy slowed to a crawl, then, headlights off, inched the car up the track to the tank. They got out, speaking in whispers, Billy checking that the car stood in exactly the same place.

Then a lamp shone out from somewhere at the edge of the yard. A distant voice called out, "Billy? Is that you?"

Billy ducked. "Get down! He'll see you."

Nancy bent down as best she could. "Your father?" she asked.

"Yes. Oh, no... he's coming down the track."

"At quite a rate by the sound of it," Nancy replied. "I can't run, Billy."

"Hide somewhere!" he whispered. "I'll try to put him off."

But it was too late. William's voice sounded clear in the night as he shouted, "Who's that! Halt!"

Nancy grumbled, then took Halfie's arm. "Leave this to me," she whispered.

Billy lurked nearby, swearing under his breath.

"It's only me, Mr Ordish," Nancy said. "We got lost in the lane in the darkness. We're leaving now."

"I thought I heard my old Citroën and I wanna know why," he replied, throwing a dog-end aside. "Billy! What the bloody hell you doin' with these two on my property?"

"Nothing, Dad."

"Did you take my private car?"

Billy hesitated. "No. Well... only to get some chips."

"Fuckin' *chips?* What have I *told* you about my Citroën? I'll fuckin' kill you if you've damaged it, or anything inside it."

"Dad! Please..."

"You fuckin' liar! That's *my* car, an' I told you never to touch it. *Never.* Now get away from them two troublemakers while I see what you done to it."

"We haven't done anything to it!" Billy cried. "I just drove it, then drove it back. Honestly."

But William ignored the protestations, surveying the car inside and out with his lamp. After a few moments he cursed, then turned to face them. "You'll not get away with this, boy. That's *my* car, my own, an' I told you never to mess with it. I didn't raise no fuckin' liar–"

"Wait, wait!" Nancy said, raising her arms. "Mr Ordish, is this language entirely necessary? We–"

"Don't you tell me how to deal with me own flesh and blood," he replied. "You fuckin' witch!"

"Dad," Billy said, "there was an *emergency–*"

"I know exactly what happened. And across my land too! That's bloody typical of newcomers, that is, no respect for country ways. Couldn't deal with the loony on your own property, eh, witch?"

"That's quite enough," Nancy replied. "Come along, dear, we're going." She glanced at Billy. Halfie did too, seeing terror on his face. Then Nancy said, "Billy... why don't you come along for a nightcap?"

"Don't you *dare,* boy!" William said. "You'll come straight indoors with me and tell me what you done with my private car. Then there'll be an accountin'."

Billy turned to Nancy and said, "I'll come with you, Mrs Culpepper, if I may."

William stared, mouth open.

Nancy grabbed his arm and strode away, but William jumped forward and shouted, "You'll do no such thing, boy. Oi, you! Leave him be."

Nancy turned. "How will you stop me?" she asked. "With force? Is that how you dealt with your wife, Mr Ordish?"

"What?"

Nancy turned, walking away.

William stood still, gasping for breath.

As they reached the lane Halfie glanced back, to see a tiny speck of orange glowing in the night. But it was motionless.

"How did you know about my mum being hit, Mrs Culpepper?" Billy asked.

"I didn't. I made an educated guess based on the evidence. Was I right?"

"I... don't honestly know. But..."

Nodding, Nancy said, "But I probably was right."

The three of them sat inside the barn: Nancy on her rocking chair, Halfie in her usual chair, Billy on a wooden stool. Tea and scones lay on the table before them. Halfie sipped chamomile, steeped in a separate pot.

"It's not much of a supper," Nancy said, "but it's all I've got at the moment. I haven't been to the Co-op for days."

Halfie glanced at her. She said, "It's fine."

"What will you do?" Nancy asked Billy.

He shrugged, glum-faced. "Can't stay here."

"Well... not in the barn, no. But you can't go back."

"You don't need to help me."

"But we do," Halfie said. "You helped me, didn't you? And look what happened." She glanced at Nancy, then added, "It's what friends are for."

He shrugged again, mute.

Nancy asked, "Has your father ever struck you?"

A third shrug. "Hard to know how to define it," he said.

Nancy raised her eyebrows. "That's all the answer I need. So, we'll be wanting a plan for you."

"He can't go into the farmhouse," said Halfie. "Dad would throw a fit."

"But there's a tent indoors, isn't there? Quite a big one, as I recall."

"Yes! In the cupboard under the stairs. I could get it for you Billy, and you could pitch it on the grass outside the barn."

He gazed at her. "S'pose I could."

"Will your dad come over to fetch you?" Halfie asked. "He might see the tent."

Billy pondered. "Not if we pitch it out of sight from the road and the farm."

"Why was he so angry about a stupid old car?"

"You know what he's like."

Nancy leaned forward. "You don't need to be afraid, Billy. I can't guarantee success, and it depends what he does, but at least your father won't dare touch *me*. And I can be a witch if I need to be."

"I'm sorry he said such things to you. I know you ain't no witch."

"There's no harm done," came the breezy reply. "Besides, why are you apologising? Now then, I said I was going to properly thank you, and I will. You did a courageous thing, Billy, for which we are both very thankful. A remarkable thing, some might say."

253

Billy said, "It's no bother."

"Regardless of that, you must accept what praise is due. I don't hold with people doing false modesty."

"No, Mrs Culpepper."

"And call me Nancy."

Halfie glanced up. After a pause she said, "I'll be Maeve."

Nancy looked at her. "Do you mind that now, dear?"

Halfie shook her head, but became aware of Billy watching her.

Nancy continued, "You know, having such a pretty second name could be a saving grace in times to come. This is a watershed moment. You're not a girl any more, not with the things you've had to see lately. I know we've still got some work to do regarding what you believe, but, perhaps… what if you took on the name? I'm told being a teenager is all about identity. I don't think there's any particular harm in you shedding your first name – which your parents gave you for a specific reason, a *selfish* reason – and taking on your second name. Then the young woman might find it easier to be somebody different from the girl. Do you see what I mean?"

Halfie gave the meekest nod she could.

"It doesn't mean you have to abandon Alfreda. Just that Alfreda would be in the past. You've learned a terrific amount this year, so perhaps it's time to recognise that. Maeve… and it acknowledges your Irish heritage, which is important. So you see, there'd be a root in the past after all."

"Mum and Dad won't let me do it."

Nancy laughed. "*Let* you? Those days are over. Besides, in two years you can do what you like. Why not begin now? It'll be like growing in a new direction… towards a new light. That sounds plausible, doesn't it, dear? Quite organic, I'd venture to say."

Despite the persuasiveness of Nancy's argument, Halfie felt uncertain. Though the evidence was stacked against her she still felt leaving Faerie might be impossible, inside her mind at least. It felt tangible to her – a presence in her head.

Yet that name stuck in her throat: Alfreda. It sounded clumsy now, ancient, even foreign. Obsolete, anyway.

"Maeve will be nice," she said, making an effort to sound positive.

"I like it too," said Billy.

Nancy studied him. "You feel you've betrayed your father, don't you?"

He looked up. "My dad? Um... mebbe a little."

"While I'm dispensing wisdom, let me give you some advice. I am still the Wise Woman after all."

Billy nodded, grinning. "Reckon you are. Ain't heard you say a duff word yet."

Nancy continued, "I spoke to Maeve recently about this. You don't have to love your parents, I told her. You're under no obligation to love them Billy, or even like them. You didn't ask to be made."

"I s'pose not," he replied.

"And it's the opposite the other way around, but that doesn't often happen." She shrugged. "I don't know about your exact family circumstances, of course. I'm speaking generally in case I'm of help to you."

Halfie said nothing, looking down in embarrassment.

"Billy, you were brought into the world with no say in the matter, no say in who your mother and father were, or anything like that. And over the years, as I emphasised to Maeve, they put things into you. They force things in."

"I do miss my mum," Billy murmured.

"I'm sure she misses you. If I knew where she was, I'd write to her, tell her what a fine young man her Billy's growing into."

Halfie shook her head. "Nancy! No..."

Nancy smiled. "Don't be embarrassed. I know the British don't like speaking about such things. But, you see, by heritage I'm not British, so I don't care."

"Are you Irish?" Halfie asked.

Nancy nodded. "By culture, not by anything formal. Barry was Welsh. He wanted Jane to be called Siân, but I injudiciously disagreed. I regret that now. So there's a lot of Celtic in you, dearest."

Halfie sighed. "I'd better go fetch that tent in case Dad comes back in a rage."

"He'll come back defeated," Nancy said. Her voice was solemn, quiet. "He'll come back depressed and taken aback," she added. "You'll have to keep an eye on him. He'll be vulnerable, and as I told you before he doesn't have what you and I've got inside us to give him strength."

"What will he do?"

"Let's wait and see. There's Jane to think of first. We'll have to check visiting times. Will you come along with us, Billy?"

"Oh, I don't think it's my place to, Mrs..."

Nancy said, "I think it is."

"Well... let's see what happens with me dad. I've got the farm to think of. It's the hay harvest soon, and I can't let that pass by. I'm needed."

"You certainly are," said Nancy.

CHAPTER 14

Halfie set up a table and three chairs behind the barn, out of view of the farmhouse and of the patch of grass upon which Billy's tent stood. The view looked south-west, across Woody End Lane to Mortimer Forest on the hills above Ludlow. To the right lay Stone Farm, but as yet, even though morning was well under way, the place lay quiet. No cars troubled deep silence. Birds twittered, the sky was blue, the day already warm. A perfect time and place for breakfast.

Now that the immediate crisis was over, Halfie found herself suffering again with the need to go to the lavatory. It was not a pain, nor even discomfort, more a sensation of urgency – that she had to get to a toilet quick; that something embarrassing might happen. She had spoken to nobody about the condition. Deep down she knew Nancy would describe it as a stress symptom, perhaps a mark of anxiety, but as yet she did not want to have that conversation, even with her nana.

Indistinct within her, buried at depth, she sensed something unwilling to give up the past, that manifested as an enclosure, a wrapping that she made for herself. It blocked her feelings and stilled her tongue, yet she needed it, for all that her conscious mind knew bottling things up was perilous.

They ate fruit salad, Greek yoghurt and toast, admiring the landscape, speaking little. At length, when Nancy went into the barn to make another pot of tea, Halfie glanced at Billy and said, "How did you sleep?"

"Okay."

"You're not happy, are you?"

He dragged his gaze from Stone Farm. "Are you surprised?"

"Not really."

"No... we had a bit of a day of it yesterday." He shrugged, then put his hands in his pockets. "I see Dad moved the Citroën from by the water tank. Probably locked it away in a shed. Not that anyone would nick that battered wreck. I'm amazed it started at all."

Halfie leaned forward. "That's not important. You'd better get in touch with your stepmum to tell her you're safe."

"Dad will have told her where I am. It can wait."

"She'll want to hear your voice."

He glanced away. "Oh, really," he grunted. "Reckon she loves me that much, do you?"

Embarrassed by his tone, Halfie murmured, "Well, you can use our phone if you like. Nancy's got an extension in the barn."

He gazed up at the green-stained thatched roof. "Nice barn, that is," he said. "Why was it converted?"

"I can answer that Billy," said Nancy, returning with the tea tray. She sat down, gave the pot a swirl, then continued, "I arrived here about three years ago. At the time, the barn was being used for bales of straw and tractor storage."

"That's why the yard's full of tractor bits," said Halfie.

"My Barry had died the previous year from lung cancer, so, for complicated reasons, I had a bit of cash. I decided to move here and convert the barn into a residence."

Halfie listened, curious. Though she knew this story, Nancy's use of *decided to* made her seem the dominant partner in the event. Yet her parents must have had something to say. "Didn't Mum and Dad object?" she asked.

"Oh no, dear. They agreed. Besides, they'd banned me from the house, even though there's loads of room inside, so the barn was the only option."

"But... I don't understand how you can just come here, but then they ban you."

"Well, I didn't mind living in the barn. I didn't want to crowd their space. I like my independence."

This did not answer Halfie's question. Then Billy said, "I remember this barn being done up. Reckon I was... twelve. My dad told me it was gonna be a drug den and get raided by the police. I reckon he was quite looking forward to making that phone call. Then you, Mrs... then you turned up. He was disappointed."

Halfie said, "What was the exact reason they banned you, Nana?"

"To keep me away from you."

Halfie sat back. This had been said before. "You could have lived in Ludlow and still looked out for me."

"I didn't wish to. Not there."

Halfie gazed at her. Nancy gazed back. A new tension filled the air.

"What, dear?" Nancy asked.

"It doesn't *feel* right to me."

Nancy looked away, sipping her tea. "Haven't you wondered," she said after a pause, "what the source of my power here is?"

"Of course – you know I have! It must be from the land, like women of old – crones, enchantresses, sirens, Faerie fortune tellers."

"No, dear. I own Snittonwood Farm, lock, stock and barrel."

Halfie looked in mute astonishment at her.

"I'm surprised you didn't realise," Nancy added.

Billy cleared his throat and said, "My dad guessed."

Nancy nodded once at him.

"But," Billy continued, "he's kept it to himself. I dunno why. I guessed too, but I'd never tell nobody."

"It's a final ace for your father to play in his battle with Duncan," Nancy told him. "I thought your father was going to play that ace by revealing the truth during the court case, so I made preparations for that eventuality. But for some reason he kept quiet. I'll be honest, that does worry me a little."

"He plays a long game, my dad."

"Yes... thank you for the warning, Billy. Still, now that I've revealed all, he can't play the family off against me, or Maeve." She turned to look at Halfie. "Well, now you know, dear."

Halfie shook her head. "But *how?* And why?"

"My father bought this place outright. I came along a few years later. I grew up here. In fact... I knew William at that time – he's five years younger than me. Stone Farm has been in the Ordish family for generations though, and my father was mocked as new money from the city – and Irish with it. There was a generational gap, too. When William took over the running of Stone Farm he was young, twenty-three. His father died early – as mine did. But for those couple of years when my father and William owned these two places, they were at daggers drawn. Did you know that, Billy?"

Billy shook his head. "No, I didn't. Do you know more?"

"Oh, yes. Much more. I left here to go to work in London. Later I worked in Fishguard, where I met Barry. I was an only child, so, when my mum died, I inherited Snittonwood Farm. For a while I rented it out, but that never properly worked. I never found tenants willing to make a go of the place. Time passed by, as it does... Then, when Jane married Duncan, we drew up a formal arrangement whereby they would live here permanently and have control over it. I was still in Fishguard, you see." She paused, gazing at the sky, then continued, "I did know about Jane's love of the alternative culture, I knew about the Windsor Free Festival, and the Psilly Fayre near Aberystwyth, and I should have been more careful. But I thought they would both calm down as they went into their thirties, grow out of the hippie culture. And you had come along, Maeve, so I assumed that would be the shock they needed to make something better of their lives." She sighed. "But I let it slide. Barry needed constant care, and I lived so far away, in Fishguard. I'm not a confident driver, it should be said. I only visited when you were a babe in arms, dear, though I got plenty of letters and photos. I think you were in nursery school when I last saw you. But I didn't realise what was going *on* here. Then, three years ago, the Christmas after Barry died, I stayed for a fortnight. That was when I grasped how bad things were."

"Bad?" Halfie said. "But I vaguely remember you coming. Mum said you were a family friend. She said you'd not visited for eight years."

Nancy grimaced. "True enough. Barry needed a lot of care, and he lingered on the edge for ages. Awful times. I didn't travel anywhere much, let alone as far as Ludlow. I was shocked, though, when I arrived. I saw something terrible. They refused to acknowledge who I was. No first names. That was when I decided I had to come back permanently." She hesitated. "There was an appalling row, of course. I told them a few home truths. They denied them all. Duncan told me not to interfere, Jane told me I knew nothing. The whole shee thing, Faerie and everything else was firmly in place – and the Faerie Fayre. My heart sank when I heard about that, and all the drifters and dropouts who turned up. By that point I'd heard of acid and all the rest of it, you see. So I gave them an ultimatum. I *would* live here, in the place I owned. They *would* give way. Duncan tried to fend me off with the legal agreement, but I called his bluff. Though it was written down, I didn't think it would stand up to scrutiny, and, anyway, I was the rightful owner of the place."

"And you still are?" Halfie asked.

"Of course."

"Then... why the Wise Woman?"

"Because of you, dearest. Why do you think?"

Halfie shrugged. "I don't know."

"I could see your parents believed in Faerie like a religion. But you did too, and you were a child, only just in secondary school. So I devised the Wise Woman persona, so you wouldn't run from me, so I'd fit in, so I could live here as easily as possible. I had to get to you through what you believed, not by force or anything like that. I had to be crafty. I had to be subtle."

Halfie said, "You had to be wise."

"Duncan told me he'd do everything he could to frustrate me. He knew perfectly well that you would be a point of strife. I told him straight I'd have the barn converted to live in. He calmed down a bit then. Up until that point, we'd only discussed me living in the farmhouse, and that really vexed him. But, I have to say... although it was Duncan doing all the talking and fighting, it was Jane who told me I was banned from the farmhouse. I was horrified. I felt I hardly knew her. But it seemed to me that my plan might work. The barn would be comfortable, I'd be living at the place I owned, and I'd be near you. So they agreed, and I agreed. It was a stalemate."

"And," Halfie said, "is that why you waited until the court case was won before having Mum sent to hospital?"

"Yes, dear. I knew sending her in before the decision could break her mentally. She might go under. So I waited. It's why I couldn't tell you all this until the case was decided. I'm sorry. That must have hurt you terribly, but, you see, I had no choice. My hands were tied by the strength of their belief in Faerie, and yours."

Halfie nodded, feeling sad. "I do see," she said. "And it does hurt."

"I'm truly sorry."

Halfie sighed. "Once, Faerie answered all my questions and made everything run smoothly. Now everything is much more complicated."

"I'm afraid that's the real world butting in. It does that, you know, regardless of what people want."

"So everyone keeps telling me."

She glanced at Billy, but, embarrassed, he looked away.

Halfie

Nancy said, "More tea, Billy?"

He pushed his cup forward. "Thank you, Mrs…"

Silence fell. Halfie pondered all she had learned, but still one point lay unresolved. She said, "What I don't understand is how I missed all this, yet you and Billy saw it. I'm not stupid. It seems I'm the daft one, overlooking every single clue."

Nancy gave a great sigh. "As I told you, I'm an agnostic. But we all believe things, dear, because we all need a framework to live in. In Britain and Ireland, that's traditionally been Christianity, like my parents. But your mum and dad, they were different. Barry and I never told Jane she had to be like us, or be a Christian, or anything. We left her to her own devices. I still think that's the right way to bring up a child. But you… they put things *into* you. That's why you're suffering now, that's why you just said Faerie used to explain things and now it doesn't."

"Why?"

"Because Faerie is not real. The world outside is real. It runs by its own rules, and nothing you, your mum and dad, Billy, me, or anybody else can do will change that. *We* defer to *it*."

"But… what if I don't want that?"

"You have no choice. Nobody does. It's a crucial lesson in life."

Halfie looked away. She sensed now that the deep core in her heart was a kernel of Faerie, lingering, secret, dormant. But she also knew Nancy would never give up, not now she had declared her hand; and that rankled. For all the talk of love and family one thing stood out, and that was struggle: Duncan versus Nancy, Nancy versus Jane, herself versus the world.

Who would win?

Next morning Halfie went to see her dad, finding him in the hall, having just put down the telephone receiver.

"Who was that?" she asked.

"Just Colin."

She hesitated. It seemed a peculiar answer. "You're not still talking with him, are you?"

"Obviously, yes. What do you want?"

"Um... I wondered if you were going to see Mum this morning or in the evening."

Grumbling, he strode into the kitchen, to sit at a chair in front of a half-eaten slice of toast. Halfie followed. "This evening," he said. "You coming?"

Halfie glanced at documents lying on the table. "Probably," she said in her lightest tones. She picked up a photograph. "What's this?"

"Came in the post this morning. Just that. No letter, nothing."

Halfie studied the photograph. It was large and looked old, the paper foxed and battered. Though it was in colour, the colours were faded, lacking yellows and greens. Yet the image was striking, showing a silver object made of many pieces, all joined into what appeared to be a bulky necklace. She put it down.

"I'll see you later then," she said.

He glanced up. "Will you?"

"Have you heard from Shelton Hospital?"

"Not a peep. You?"

She ignored his jibe, departing the kitchen and hurrying to the barn, where she met Nancy and Billy. "Dad's going to Shelton this evening," she said.

Halfie

Nancy glanced at her watch. "Then we should go there now. There's a bus in twenty minutes. Think we could walk to the main road by then?"

"If you can," Billy replied, "we can."

"Come along, then. Jane may be conscious."

At the hospital they met a nurse outside the office, who, after checking notes on a clipboard, said, "She's still heavily sedated. We're bringing in a medical orderly later to check her bloods. There's evidence of infection."

"Infection?" Nancy said. "Where? Bad?"

"No, not bad. Internal. She's been eating poorly for some time, and that's knocked her immune system for six. But nothing serious."

They all peered through the glass pane in the door, then departed in sombre mood. Halfie, expecting her mum to be awake, even active, was disappointed at the lack of progress. But it had only been half a day since she had been brought in.

She spent the rest of the day with Billy, tidying up as much of the smallholding as she could – her dad did not seem to have done anything since the sectioning, except basic livestock feeding. She felt a ghost of sorrow for him; this was his wife, after all. Billy meanwhile seemed perturbed by the lack of activity at his home. He told her that, having expected his dad to make an almighty row, he felt put out by the lack of a commotion. It was the calm that bothered him.

Next morning Halfie again went to see her dad, finding him in the kitchen. He looked pale and exhausted, his hair greasy, wearing the same old clothes as the previous day. A hint of pity rose to trouble her.

"It's not nice, is it, Dad?"

He glanced at her. "Not *alone*, no."

Halfie

Presuming this to be a reference to visiting times, she said nothing, feeling guilty and looking aside. "Nancy insisted on going early," she said.

He slammed his tea mug onto the table. "She's good at that."

Halfie glanced down to see a new envelope and a new photograph. "Another one?" she asked.

"This morning."

She picked up the photograph to find that this time it was a photocopy. Yet the image was of the same object, taken further away. The original photograph lay where it had yesterday, its envelope also. Halfie checked, to see that both envelopes were postmarked Ludlow.

"Can I have these?" she said.

"Do what you like with them. I really don't have time to be dealing with other people's post."

"Wasn't it addressed to you though?"

He swore under his breath. "I opened it because it arrived, okay?"

Halfie slipped away, sitting alone in the barn to study the photographs. Something about the object and the fact that two solitary images had been posted made an alarm go off at the back of her mind. Though she had no evidence, this felt deliberate.

Fetching Nancy's magnifying glass, she studied the first photograph. The object looked to be solid silver, a substantial necklace with clear evidence of dirt upon it, as if dug up from the ground. The photographer had laid it on a carpet of dead leaves to get the image. The photocopy showed the object upon the same woodland floor, with, in one corner, a hint of land beyond. Halfie studied this section but was unable to make out what it was. Yet now she felt troubled. She recognised that land – or thought she

267

did. But with so little to go on she could come to no conclusion.

She looked up, gaze defocused. Somebody was *doing* something here. She felt her heart beat a little faster as apprehension took hold of her.

During the day she did everything she could to ensure the smooth running of the smallholding, helped by Billy. He, meanwhile, said nothing about the standoff between himself and his father, though he had been persuaded to phone his stepmum upon seeing his dad in a tractor on Stone Farm's lower fields.

Next morning Halfie woke when her alarm went off – she slapped its switch down, not wanting to wake Nancy. Grabbing a quick breakfast she went outside, fetched a few odd jobs, then sat on a log partway down the track to do them. Half an hour later the postman arrived.

"I'll take those," she said.

"Ta, love," he replied, handing over a sheaf of letters.

As she had expected, there was a third A4 envelope, brown manilla like the other two, addressed to her dad and postmarked Ludlow. Stuffing the other letters in the front door letterbox, she returned to the barn and with trembling hands opened the envelope.

It was a second photocopy of a third image, this time the silver object from some distance, as if the photographer had wanted context for it. Hands trembling, she took the magnifying glass and studied the further land, to see a hillock.

She held her breath. There could be no doubt now. That was the shee at Snittonwood.

For a moment she felt her mind seethe with conflicting emotions: fear, awe. She grasped, with dismay, that somebody was carrying out a plan, and she felt frightened

268

by that possibility. But she felt awed by the beauty and size of the silver necklace.

Astonishment gripped her at the sight of the photograph of the shee mound, which had stood hidden from view on private property for decades. Who outside the family could have taken such photographs? Could the mound be something other than the home of the elves? Yet, if it was, who could possibly have the knowledge and motive to send such significant photographs?

She shuddered.

Again she held her breath, looking up. The photographs had arrived in succession, not hand delivered, addressed to her dad and without accompanying letters; all of them postmarked Ludlow. She sensed a hand behind such events – a local hand, a rough hand. Though she dared not admit any name to herself, she could not help but think of Stone Farm. Perhaps, then, she had an explanation for the calm there.

Next morning she told Billy she wanted to go into Ludlow alone with Nancy. He shrugged and told her that was fine. Still he had heard nothing from his dad, his stepmum describing the atmosphere at Stone Farm as calm and relaxed.

Neither Billy, Halfie nor Nancy believed that was the case inside William's head. In that vindictive mind anything could be happening.

Halfie felt the return of her anxiety and the return of her symptoms. She drank as little as she could and did two sets of deep breathing exercises. They helped a little.

On the bus she was quiet, staring out of the window.

"Penny for your thoughts?" Nancy said as the bus departed Ludlow.

"Oh, nothing."

"And nothing is why Billy's not with us?"

Halfie shrugged, unwilling to catch Nancy's gaze.

"Please do tell me, dear. Noncommunication is such a hazardous thing."

Halfie was tempted to tell Nancy that she would have to wait, that now was not the right time, but such a response felt immature, even rude. For all the pain Halfie felt, the part of it relating to Nancy's deeds was not deliberate. At length she said, "I'm worried about William Ordish."

"Why?"

"He's up to something."

"We all agree there," Nancy murmured. "That's old news."

"He's up to something new."

"Tell me why you think that."

Halfie wondered how to broach the subject. "You tell me about William when you knew him."

"Very well, dear. Well... he was quite a difficult boy. Quite solitary, I recall, and perhaps a little twisted. He didn't make friends easily. His father was a bit of a tyrant if all the rumours are correct. I knew him up to about his mid-teens, I think, and later heard that he'd taken over running Stone Farm. But he was rather young for such a responsibility. He married late. I don't think he truly likes women." She hesitated. "Mind you, few men do."

Halfie glanced aside at her.

Nancy sighed, then said, "Billy's remarked to both of us on the significance of William naming his eldest son after himself. That's the sort of thing men do. We wouldn't do anything so selfish and silly, of course, but they revel in it. Chip off the old block and all that. Load of nonsense if you ask me."

"What was he like with your dad?"

"Loathed him. Thought my dad was muscling in on country ways. And of course we all know what the British think of the Irish. Like I told you, for those couple of years when he had Stone Farm and my dad had Snittonwood Farm they fought like cat and dog. William tried a court case even then, you know… over forty years ago now. My, how time flies."

Halfie sat up, looking at Nancy. "A *court* case? What about?"

"Over the woods. Stonewood and Snittonwood were once one big wood, but at some point trees were chopped down and the gap made – the bridleway runs along the eastern edge of the gap, adjacent to Snittonwood."

"Then… what was the case about?"

Nancy said, "William tried to claim part of Snittonwood."

"The western part?"

"Well, yes, of course."

"That's where the shee is."

Nancy said nothing for a while, then turned to take Halfie by the hand. Looking her in the eye she said, "I'd quite forgotten about that case, dear. I was in London, far away, having the time of my life. But you think it's important, don't you?"

"Er…"

"You *do,* Maeve. I can tell. Why?"

Halfie exhaled, still unwilling to talk.

"You must speak, dear. We can have no secrets."

Halfie nodded, feeling disconsolate. "I know. And I didn't want to keep it secret, not forever anyway. But I suppose I've got to tell."

"What is it then?"

"I think I know why William wanted access to that part of the wood."

They walked into Shelton Hospital in silence, looked for a few minutes at the sedated form of Halfie's mum, then walked out again. The nurse in charge told them: no change.

"No change is better than deterioration," Nancy said.

But it was small comfort. Halfie felt battered by events. "Nana," she said, "I want to be alone for a while. It's all too much for me. Would you mind if I got the later bus home?"

Nancy twisted her lips, sighed, then took her handbag and withdrew some coins. "All right. If you like. There, that'll cover the fare and a bar of chocolate or something. But only a small bar. It's pork tonight, with potato wedges."

"Thanks. If I'm a bit late, I'll reheat it in the oven."

Halfie watched Nancy walk to the bus stop, then strode the other way, heading for the main road, where she caught a bus into Shrewsbury town centre. She knew where she needed to be next: the main library just down from Castle Street.

At the library she walked into the main chamber, checking labels on the ends of shelves for the history section. There, she headed into a dusty corner to find ancient history. It was the work of a few moments to select three tomes covering ancient Britain. Happy, she walked to the nearest table.

The books made their revelations in due course. In a photographic history describing art and archaeological objects, she found a long section covering Celtic Britain. Partway through, she stopped turning pages. Depicted on a black velvet background she saw a number of Celtic finds, all of them silver apart from a single golden torc of wound gold wire. But the silver objects bore a resemblance to the necklace of the shee – not exact, but noticeable.

She swallowed, gazing up.

Her mind expanded with sudden realisation.

Irish was Celtic. She was part Irish. Celtic treasure had been found at the shee.

Then words spoken by her mum passed into her mind, as clear as the day they were uttered: *The only thing we can do is reforge our links with the world – with nature, the Moon, the seasons. The eightfold wheel of the year, not that useless Christian calendar. No more Easter and Christmas for me. Besides, they were stolen from the elves, from the Tuatha Dé Danann, millennia ago... millennia... stolen from us by vile men.*

She read on. The Celts were a spiritual people who lived in Britain before the arrival of Christianity. They were an ancient people, pushed without mercy to the hinterlands of Wales and Cornwall by marauding English warriors. They were a people who valued women. They were a people who made beautiful things and knew the Tuatha Dé Danann. They buried their dead with reverence, and made sacrifices of precious things into bodies of water.

Questions dropped into her mind without delay. A silver Celtic necklace was surely evidence for the purpose of the shee. Was it possible that her mum had known all along about the Celtic connection? Their smallholding was nowhere near Ireland, but it was close to Wales, another Celtic nation. What if Nancy had missed the clues? Her mother, sensitive to such matters, could have picked them up.

She felt that a pattern was emerging. What if this was evidence that the elves did exist? The shee was real, after all. It could be their home. There could be a King. Her mum could have been right all along, and suffered torment as a consequence.

She stood up. Sudden anger burned inside her – then fell away.

Steady... She had to play this with slow, careful confidence. She stood on uncertain ground. It was she, after all, who had conducted the steel wire experiment. But, regardless of the truth, it was time to go home now.

On the bus, a hundred plans came and went. In the end, as she hurried along Woody End Lane in warm twilight, she decided that her dad was the best person to begin with, and was perhaps the only one she could talk openly to. Billy would not believe. Nancy would not believe, then would act against her. Her dad on the other hand might say something to indicate what he really believed.

She walked the length of the track up to the yard, slipping aside to follow the western track, then the bridleway. A couple of ramblers bade her good evening as they headed south, and she grinned at them, returning the compliment. She felt like jumping in the air and kicking her heels together.

Inside Snittonwood she halted at the glade. Her mum's belongings had been left scattered around, most of it stained by dew and woodland debris. Rotting food lay here and there, but not much. The shelter itself looked in good shape.

She crept on to the shee. There it stood: the hill, the home, the place of the Aos Sidhe, people of the Faerie mound, who were the remnant in this world of the ancient Tuatha Dé Danann. It felt so real! Evidence, as it might be called. Yet against that stood other evidence, which she could not forget; and not just the opinions of other locals. Iron was iron, after all.

Yet she felt alive and free now, not transfixed by bad luck, not battered by events, not weighed down by the expectations of family and friends. There was hope here of finding something special. Could that be elves? She did not know – yet.

Excitement bubbled up inside her. After a while she skipped back to the bridleway, then sauntered down it as the sun set into swathes of misty orange. She revelled in her solitary experience. The world outside could go away, leave her alone, allow her to sink into nature. It *would* do that, because if it did not she would force its hand.

At the upper field, she halted. There, the spring sent forth a brook into the farm adjacent. That spring had been disputed by an ignorant man who thought he could own nature. He was a malevolent fool.

Again she thought of the photographs. She did not doubt now that William Ordish had sent them, though what that implied about the whereabouts of the necklace she did not know. But she would find out. And then she would do some disputing of her own.

He was a cunning opponent, though. He had sent one genuine photograph then a couple of photocopies, the first to show authenticity, the other two to make his point. She would have to be canny.

She leaned against the stile, gazing at the water.

A flicker caught her gaze.

She looked, then stared. Above the water she saw a flying form, part insect, part human.

It was an elf.

Halfie

She clasped her hands together against her mouth as she watched. Delight took her. Captivated, she felt as though she was being shown an ancient secret – the true nature of the world. As the elf fluttered across the water she realised the spring must be its home. It hovered above marsh marigolds with their butter-yellow flowers, flitting from bloom to bloom, sunlight reflecting off its gauze wings separating into rainbow colours.

She blinked, and saw a dragonfly catching mosquitoes and midges. Or was it? She could not be sure.

But then there were more of them: three, half a dozen, a dozen. They multiplied before her eyes, dancing across their territory, guarding the spring, or so it seemed. And, considering that water, Halfie thought again about the Celts. They dropped valuable items into water as part of their rituals. Perhaps therefore it was no surprise that William had chosen these two fields to dispute ownership of. He either guessed or knew what might lie underground.

CHAPTER 15

The visit to Shelton Hospital the next day gave Halfie and Nancy a surprise. Halfie's mum was awake, alert and in fair spirits.

It was eleven in the morning and they had an hour for their visit. Nancy, Halfie and her mum sat in the warm courtyard garden, with just one other couple nearby.

"How are you?" Halfie asked her mum.

"I'm not sure. A bit woozy. They've told me some of what happened, but a lot of it I don't remember."

Nancy nodded. "Tell us what they said."

"That I had a psychotic episode."

"Had?"

Halfie stiffened, hearing a sharpness to Nancy's voice.

"Yes," her mum continued. "They explained the legal situation, that they're allowed to detain me and even forcibly treat me if I'm a danger to myself. They've been giving me drugs intravenously for some infection or other, and to calm me."

"But you're not a danger, are you?" Halfie said, putting as much confidence as she could into her voice.

"I never was."

"You were starving yourself in the woods," Nancy said. "That's not like an overdose or anything, no, but it is still dangerous."

Halfie watched as her mum studied Nancy's face. "Have you come to get me out?" she said.

"I don't know," Nancy replied. "That's up to the doctors here."

"Yes... but I feel different."

"How, Mum?" Halfie asked.

"I don't know. I feel more... in my own shoes." She glanced down at a pair of hospital slippers. "In my own body," she added.

Halfie nodded. Perhaps this had been a single episode after all. "I heard that most people only have one occurrence," she said. "You'll be all right now, Mum. You could come home, I expect."

"Wait a moment," Nancy said, laying a hand on her arm. "Your mother's still under medical supervision, and she'll have to undergo formal assessment before they release her. Anyway, where did you hear about single occurrences?"

Halfie turned to point at the male doctor. "He told me last time we were here."

Nancy glanced at the man, and her expression suggested she would check the truth of Halfie's statement as soon as possible. Halfie realised her mum's freedom might be hard-fought.

In her lightest tones, Halfie told her mum, "Now we've won the court case you can go back to being with Dad, and everything will be okay."

"I hope so, Alfreda, I really do."

Halfie flinched to hear the name spoken aloud. She glanced aside at Nancy, to find their gazes lock. "Er," she said, "Mum, call me Halfie for now."

"All right."

Nancy looked irritated, fidgeting in her seat. She stood up and said, "I need to speak to the doctors in private. You two remain here."

"All right, Nana."

Halfie watched Nancy leave, then turned to look at her mum.

"Yes, I know who she is," she said. "Nana told me everything."

"Oh."

Halfie took her hand. "No, Mum, it's all right, I've got fantastic news. I've seen the elves at last."

"Really? Where?"

"Over the spring."

But her mum seemed worried. "Not at the shee? Is it safe? It must *always* be kept safe, because that's their true home, the source of their power, their life."

"Mum, listen to me. They tried to convince me that Faerie didn't exist, and for a while I believed that. Then something really weird happened, which I can't tell you about yet. I need to find out the truth. Oh... it's complicated, so much has happened, things I've been told. Anyway, when you come home, I'll try to show you. Then we've got some planning to do."

"Planning?"

"You and me. Against William Ordish."

Her mum sat back, and Halfie wondered if she had pushed too far.

"Don't worry yourself, Mum," she said. "I know what I'm doing. Take it easy, and do everything you can to convince the doctors you're safe. You will come back to the farmhouse, won't you?"

"I haven't really thought about it."

"Then *act,* Mum. Pretend... because they won't release you if they think you're going back to the woods. We'll give you proper food, don't worry, but it'll have to be at the farmhouse. Nana will be watching you like a hawk, and any hint of... well, you know."

Her mum nodded. "I see what you mean. Thank you. That's good advice."

"Nana refuses to believe she's an elf, she thinks she's mundane. Did she do the same to you as you did to me?"

"Do what?"

"Give you the choice of elf or human – like you did to me at Whit."

"No," her mum replied with a smile. "I chose myself."

"Didn't the King mind?"

"It was his idea."

Halfie nodded, compelled by hope to believe that something, if not everything, about the shee might be true. "I hope I meet him. Do you see him as tall like Dad, or small like the spring elves?"

"Tall."

Halfie glanced away to see Nancy returning. "Keep this secret," she whispered, "between us only."

Her mum nodded.

Nancy approached, then sat down. "It seems they are satisfied with your progress," she said. "But you'll need a lot of monitoring after you leave."

Halfie heard the tenor of that remark. "After? Then she is leaving?"

"Not today. If all goes as the doctors hope, perhaps by Friday."

Halfie nodded. That was three days away.

Halfie

Back at home, Halfie fussed around Nancy in the barn then made excuses to leave: work to do on the smallholding. She hurried across the yard to the farmhouse, finding her dad sitting in the kitchen.

"Mum's looking well this morning!" she said. "The doctor said she might be coming home in a few days."

He nodded, and he too looked to be in a better mood. "Yes, they had her come around from the sedatives late yesterday. I was with her."

"It's good news, isn't it?"

"Very."

"And, Dad… I've got some fantastic news for you."

He scowled. "What?"

"No, really! I saw elves yesterday, over the spring. I honestly did!"

He sat up. "That *is* good news… yes, very good." He smiled: authentic and happy. "I'm pleased to hear it."

"I knew you would be. Um, any more manilla envelopes today?"

"No. Why?"

"I just wondered."

He surveyed the piles of paper covering the kitchen table. "Where are they? I'd quite like to have a look at them again."

"I took them into the barn for safekeeping."

He nodded, then glanced away. "I suppose we'd better get the house ready for your mother. There's quite a lot of cleaning to do."

"Leave that to me."

"Thanks."

Halfie returned to the yard, seeing Billy by his tent. Excited, she ran up to him, but then hesitated. Billy was decent – a friend now, without doubt, not just a neighbour. Best not to tell him about the elves.

"You all right, Billy?"

"Yes."

"What are you going to do today?"

Mournfully he looked across the way to Stone Farm. "Dunno. But I'll have to go back some time. Can't have this rift stay open. It's... daft."

Halfie felt sympathy for him. His situation was not dissimilar to her own: a parent astray, tension, anger, difficult times. She said, "They know where you are, so that's one helpful thing. The fuss will die down soon."

"Yes, but the hay harvest..."

"I bet your dad'll swallow his pride and ask you to come back for that."

"Demand it, more like," he muttered.

"Well, tell him to speak politely to you. Make a stand. That's what I did."

"You made a stand? When?"

Halfie grinned. "Oh, Billy... I'm bursting to tell you, and I know I can trust you."

"Trust me with what?"

"The most incredible thing! I know why your dad brought the case over the spring fields. And I found out that he did something similar, forty years ago, over Snittonwood."

Billy frowned. "Similar?"

"There was Celtic treasure under the shee."

"The–"

"The *mound,* I meant – in the wood. It's just a mound." She paused for thought, then added, "The Celts used to sacrifice precious objects in water, so there's likely buried treasure in the spring field too. Your dad wants it! I had to tell Nancy on the bus what I knew, but everything from now on I'm keeping secret."

"Treasure?" he said. "That's gotta be nonsense."

"I can prove it."

"How?"

"With photographs.."

He looked baffled. "Go on, then."

Halfie slipped into the barn, retrieved the envelopes, then returned. "Into the tent," she said, pointing at it. "These are top secret."

Inside, he studied the photographs.

"Only your dad could have sent these," she told him. "He's intimidating my dad, taunting him. *This* is why he never revealed that he'd guessed my nana owns Snittonwood Farm. It was part of a final card to play… and now he's playing it, hoping to bypass my nana's influence. He thinks we can't guess because the photos were sent anonymously, but I guessed straight away. Don't you see? It's part of a new campaign against my dad. He's got *more* plans against him. It's slow, careful, thought out in detail. He wants to play mind tricks now, make my dad paranoid, frightened. It's not a legal thing any more. He's hoping my dad's too addled to stand up for himself with everything that's going on – hitting him when he's down. He's *still* hoping to buy those two fields. I bet he's planning to make a bigger offer. Don't you think so?"

Billy frowned, yet he also looked frightened. "But that must mean my dad's got the treasure in the photograph."

"Obviously he found it, or keeps it."

"It must be in the farm somewhere."

"Yes!" Halfie said. "And together, we could take it back."

He stared at her. "That's…"

"Difficult, yes. But you know your farmhouse inside out."

"Wouldn't it be theft?"

Halfie thrust the original photograph under his nose. "Billy! *This* one was obviously taken at the time, a year or two before Nancy's father died. *That's* what those two fought over. I bet your dad was snooping around and found it under the mound – stole it right then. It's the only reason I can think of for the order in which these photographs were sent."

Billy bit his lip, studying the photograph, then the two other copies. "I wonder if he's planning to use me as a pawn in his game?"

"You?"

"He still ain't ordered me back. That's *odd*. That ain't how he does things. But... it ties in with your story. He wants as many aces as he can get, and he'll play them all. He could accuse your dad of child-snatching or summat." He paused, looking up, then added, "I never thought the fields case was anything other than spite, but now it looks different."

"Can you guess where in your house the necklace is hidden?"

He shook his head. "I'll think about it. We ain't gotta safe or owt."

"Oh, please do think, Billy. It belongs to Nancy, if anyone, though I expect she'd give it to me. Perhaps it's Celtic treasure. I read somewhere that you have to declare it to the government or someone."

"You do. They showed all that on the telly. It's to do with archaeology."

"How does it work?" she asked.

"The landowner and the finder get to share the value when the treasure's bought by a museum or whoever. Or you can keep it. I don't know the details to be honest."

"There you are!" Halfie exclaimed. "Proof positive. That's what your dad wants. What if there's more beneath the spring?"

Billy sighed, a pained expression on his face. "That's what he's after. Must be. If he owned the land he'd get the full value. Could be millions."

"We've got to stop him."

He nodded, though without enthusiasm. "This makes things ten times worser for me though."

"*I'll* help you, Billy," she said, leaning towards him. Lowering her voice she said, "We're friends, aren't we? Nancy understands some things, but not everything, and she'll interfere if she can. So this must be our secret. Do you agree?"

"S'pose so."

"Shake on it?"

He shook her hand, again without enthusiasm. "You gonna tell your dad?" he asked.

"Not yet."

"But the photos were sent to him. He might know already."

"He thought they were misdirected post," she replied, "if he even noticed them. I took them away. No, I only realised the truth when I examined the third one with a magnifying glass. Your dad is goading, taunting, as part of his build-up. He's as sly as a fox, and he'll make his move only when he's ready, when he's got my dad bewildered. Then he'll pounce, make an offer my dad can't refuse. What if he offers the silver necklace in return for the two fields? Remember – he believes my dad is a drug-addled hippie waster. That's why we've got to get the necklace back as soon as we can."

Billy shook his head, his face pale. "I'm telling you, Halfie, I don't like this. It's *really* scary."

"I know," she said.

"Not like me. My dad's not one to be obstructed. He'll go absolutely berserk if he finds out what we're doing." He shuddered. "You heard the swears he used just over a crummy old car. It'll be the end of me for sure."

"No it *won't*. We'll survive. Perhaps your dad will bust a gut or something. Twisted, my Nana called him."

"Bust a gut? Mine! *That's* what I'm worried about."

Halfie said, "Well, he can't do anything to you while you're here."

"But for how much longer–"

"I know, I know – the hay harvest." She tapped the photograph. "*This* is more important. This is urgent."

He nodded, his face glum.

"You shook on it, Billy."

"That I did," he replied.

Halfie crept into Snittonwood as twilight began. The place was quiet, dim, closeted in green and grey. The sun had just set and she felt magic hour falling upon her.

But the glade was still a mess. Taking a black bin bag from her pocket she began clearing away all the plastic and other detritus. A few bits of rotting food remained, but they were seeping back into the soil and could be left. Then, holding her nose with her left hand, she took the bedroll and pillow and stuffed them into a second bin bag. Dropping the bags beside the bridleway, she returned to the glade and began dismantling the shelter. As she did, she found one of her mum's bamboo flutes.

She hesitated. Surely the elves of the shee would wish to see her now?

Tidying completed, shelter dispersed, she washed her hands in a puddle, dried them on her jeans, then took the flute and walked forward to the shee.

She studied it with two pairs of eyes: her elvish gaze, seeing the enchantment of the place, and her real gaze, seeing the mound for what it was.

Taking a few steps back, she tried to assess where the third photograph had been taken. There: her best guess. She placed her hands to the ground, expecting to feel warmth, a shock, some sudden sensation... but nothing.

She stood up. The elves were not helping her. Slowly, with care, she circumnavigated the mound, observing in its steep slope a couple of dips, large holes as if made by badgers... or men. She hesitated. It was so difficult to know how to proceed.

"Are you there?" she called out. "Your Majesty? Anybody?"

No sound except birds twittering and rustles in the undergrowth.

"It's me, Alfreda Chandler. The curse is over now."

Nothing.

"Will you talk to me? I saw a few of you a while back, above the spring."

Silence.

Feeling anxious, she began twisting the flute in her hands. She glanced down at it. A beautiful instrument painted red, it had six finger holes between which a dragon of some sort had been painted. Around the blowing end a strip of bamboo had been tied, creating the mouthpiece. Her mum called it a *suling,* and for some years Halfie had presumed Sue Ling to be the seller. But apparently the flute came from Bali.

Her mum heard elf music, that she knew. But could *she* now play this flute? Was the magic in the instrument itself, waiting for her to discover it, as her mum had?

She placed the three middle fingers of each hand over the holes, using the pads of her fingers rather than the tips, as she had observed her mum do. Then she raised the flute to her lips, pressed them over the bamboo strip, and blew.

A gorgeous, breathy note sounded. She stopped. The note reverberated around the shee glade then faded. Delighted, she tried again, blowing with more confidence, more force, then raising one finger and another. To her amazement the instrument was easy to play; she could even bend notes by moving her fingers slowly.

It was almost too easy, in fact.

Her heart thumped. No. The flautist gift must run in the family.

"I'm playing this for you," she called out, before trying more and higher notes.

After a while she stopped, listening.

Still nothing. No response, no call, no echoing music floating out between the trees. Just nothing.

She sagged. Hoping she would hear something, she felt rejected. She walked away, collecting the bin bags and trudging down the bridleway.

At the stile by the spring she halted. Nothing there either: no elves, no sunshine, no feeling of mystery. It all seemed so different.

She leaned against the stile as disappointment turned to dejection, and a sob escaped her, to drift away into the mundane world.

A psychotic episode, her mum's days of instability had been called. Perhaps she too had suffered such a thing, one diminished, far less intense, in response to the shock of the sectioning and the thrill of the book discovery. Had Nancy herself not said: *You mustn't bottle up your feelings, you know, otherwise they'll come out in strange ways.*

Billy too. Even Billy had said it – a boy.

Strange ways, dangerous ways. It dawned on her that she might have copied this trait of concealing thoughts and feelings – copied it from her mum, who so rarely showed hers. That might even be the message of her dependence on Badb.

What had seemed certain now lay in doubt.

Again.

On the Thursday she went to the hospital with Nancy and Billy, to discover her mum well and rested. They spoke with her for a full hour, and Halfie noticed Nancy asking penetrating questions, as if aware that the following day would be crucial. She herself felt tired. Life was so difficult, home so uncomfortable. The absurd notion of pitching a tent on Stone Farm came to mind, just so she could escape her troubles for a while – or perhaps it should be Pearl Farm, which she visited at least twice a week to buy food with Nancy's money.

She would have to go again, in the afternoon, to fill the cupboards with natural food.

At the end of the hour Nancy took Billy aside. Her mum held her hand and whispered, "Is your father all right, do you think?"

Halfie nodded.

Her mum looked concerned. "He was distant yesterday."

"He's got an awful lot on his mind. He seems fragile, Mum."

"He spoke about the smallholding. He's been trying to find an entitlement document."

Halfie froze. Words of Nancy's drifted through her mind: *we drew up a formal arrangement whereby they would live here permanently.*

She said, "Entitlement? But you can live there, can't you?"

"Yes, I believe we can."

Now Halfie recalled the telephone call Colin made to her dad. It would be just the sort of stupid thing her dad might try, wresting control of the smallholding from Nancy. What if having lawful control over the farm meant being the beneficiary of anything found on it? She bent over, gripping her hands together, wondering what she could do.

"I wouldn't worry about it, Mum," she said. "You come home tomorrow, and everything will be ready for you."

"Thank you, Alfreda. That's good of you."

The thanks were given in a muted voice. Halfie glanced to where Nancy and Billy stood chatting with one of the nurses. "I'll ask Dad about the document," she said. "I'll put his mind at rest."

"Thank you."

Outside, at the bus stop, Halfie gave Billy a few coins to buy some chocolate. When he was out of earshot she said, "Nana, I've got something to tell you."

"What?"

"I think Dad's looking for the agreement document that you made when they took over running the smallholding. And there was at least one phone call with Colin Wright. Do you think he might be trying to get control?"

She frowned, then looked aside. "Interesting news."

"Well?"

Nancy shrugged. "Why would he still be speaking with Colin Wright?"

"Exactly!"

She paused for thought. "Your father is still seething about what I did, that I do know. He's looking for retaliation, perhaps."

Halfie nodded. "You could see why, though…"

"Revenge is for kids, dear, not adults."

"Well… either way, I thought you ought to know. Couldn't you draw up a new agreement, make it all official?"

"I might have to," Nancy replied, "although, if it came to it, even if he found the document I think I'd be judged the owner. My dad passed the place on to me. That arrangement we three wrote was drawn up for ourselves." She hesitated. "I did give them both right of permanent residence though, and control. I never thought it might be used against me. It could be a legal grey area."

"I'm glad I told you then."

"Yes…" She gave Halfie a penetrating look. "Then of course there's the necklace to consider."

"But he doesn't know about it."

"He saw the photographs though – the first two, anyway."

Halfie looked through the window, trying to recall the circumstances. "Yes… he did. But at the time he seemed so distracted. He'll have forgotten."

"He might have realised afterwards. Have you discussed the photos with him?"

"Um… I'm afraid so. He asked me, and I had to say I took them for safekeeping."

"Then he'll have been reminded. Keep a lid on it for now. We're only guessing, so don't panic." She sighed. "It looks like that wretched necklace is doing malicious work."

Struck by her choice of words, Halfie shivered. "Perhaps it's cursed."

"Nothing is cursed, dear. I thought we'd decided that one?"

"Suppose so."

Billy returned, and a few minutes later their bus arrived. They chatted about inconsequential things until alighting, then strolled down Woody End Lane. Billy paused to look up the track of Stone Farm, before heaving a sigh and moving on.

Halfie felt sorry for him. In sympathy, she put her arm around his shoulders and drew him towards her; just for a moment. "Don't worry, it'll sort itself out. He can't hate you forever."

"He can."

"Well, you're safe with us."

"I shouldn't be with you. I got my own home."

Halfie released him. "It's only for a while."

He offered no reply, his face gloomy. Halfie felt irritated, as if he had rejected her. She hurried forward to walk alongside Nancy.

At the barn, Nancy fumbled in her handbag for the door key. Turning it, she hesitated, then frowned. "I must've left it unlocked," she said.

Halfie glanced aside, but thought nothing of it. Common countryside practice was to leave doors unlocked more often than locked.

"You make sure you stay close this afternoon," Nancy added as she walked in.

"In the barn?"

"Yes. We've got something to check."

"What?" Halfie asked.

"Aha."

Halfie felt a twinge of concern, but Nancy spoke with levity, not solemnity. Shrugging, she sat on her chair, thinking about the events of the morning. Then she noticed that the three manilla envelopes were missing.

At two o'clock Halfie heard the noise of an approaching vehicle. Outdoors she saw a dark van coming up the track, a white-haired man driving it. He parked on the grass verge then jumped out.

"Maeve Chandler?" he asked.

Halfie stiffened, perturbed by the fact that he knew her new name. "Er... who do you want?" she answered.

"Mrs Culpepper."

"Um... I'll go fetch her. Who shall I say it is?"

"Frank Griffiths."

"And what's it concerning?"

He smiled. "The archaeology."

Nervousness rose up inside Halfie in response to this answer, a premonition of events to come, yet without a rejoinder she had no option but to fetch Nancy. Her nana beamed when she heard Halfie calling.

Standing close, the trio exchanged glances, before Nancy reached out to shake Frank's hand. "Thanks for coming. You've met my delightful granddaughter?" She turned and shouted, "Billy! Come here a moment."

"Lovely day," Frank replied. "So, what's all the secrecy, Mrs Culpepper?"

"Nancy. And, yes, it has been secret for a while... well, that's not the right word. It's been *missed,* I think you'll say."

"All very intriguing. Who's this then?"

Nancy replied, "This is Billy Ordish, an intelligent, resourceful young man who I'm looking after for a few days."

Frank shook Billy's hand. "Glad to meet you. Okay, so what next? Do we need Mr Chandler too?"

Nancy pointed to the western track. "No. Follow me, please."

She led the way without further comment. Halfie felt her spirits sink, aware of the significance of Nancy not explaining who Mr Griffiths was, and realising what might soon happen. At her side Billy sent her questioning glances, but she ignored them, then, when he persisted, she shrugged, hands outstretched, eyes round.

They strolled up the bridleway, Nancy explaining about the ownership of the fields, the history of the right of way, then the two woods.

"And we're going into that one?" Frank said, pointing at Snittonwood.

Halfie could hold back no longer. "Are you *sure, Nana?*"

"I'm certain, dear. This is going to be fascinating for all concerned."

Now Halfie felt defiled. This was sacred ground, not fit for the mundane feet of dumb outsiders. She halted, battling with herself. On the one hand, her younger self wished everyone as far away as possible; yet she could hardly go against the wishes of the woman who owned the property. Besides... was it even sacred?

"Nana!" she said. "I'm not sure this is right. It's Mum's hallowed ground. This man won't understand."

"He'll understand all right," came her reply. "I'm sorry, dear, but it really is for the best."

Trapped, Halfie followed. Billy hung back as if embarrassed to be witnessing such circumstances. Inside the wood, Nancy oriented herself, struck out for the glade, then made her way toward the mound. Mute, Halfie followed.

Frank gasped when he saw the mound. "My god!" he said. "Another one."

"Another what?" Nancy asked.

"Another Celtic burial mound. So unusual. But this one looks in far better condition than the ones we know about in England and Wales." He clapped his hands together. "This stretches the territory we've been exploring by miles. Remarkable! Do you realise there will most likely be grave goods here? Most Celtic burial mounds are much diminished by erosion and agricultural practice, but this one looks well preserved. I say, Mrs Culpepper, you've done Shropshire a great service. Thank you so much."

Halfie stepped forward. "Who are you?" she asked. "Are you from the government?"

"I'm the local Chief Archaeological Officer," he replied. "We've been excavating areas west of here for decades. This is quite a discovery. Of national importance, I'd say. Celtic burial practices changed as Roman influence increased, so mounds aren't common. This discovery could change a lot."

"Change... but why? Is it yours? You don't own this land."

"I know," he said. "This is private property, I quite understand."

"Indeed," Nancy remarked. "*I* own it."

"And will you allow us to excavate it?" Frank asked.

"No," Nancy said.

Halfie held her breath.

"No?" said Frank. "Why not?"

"I mean, no, not immediately. In fact, you might have to wait a few years. But in the end… yes."

Halfie felt her eyes mist over as she grasped the importance of Nancy's declaration. The delay was for her sake. Though Nancy did not believe in the existence of the shee elves, she did understand the consequences of their home being wrenched away at short notice. And she had uttered not a single word about the necklace.

Halfie murmured, "Oh, Nana," as she wiped her eyes with the back of her hand.

"I know, dear. It is a bit of a shock for you. But that's what this hillock is, an ancient site, which the whole country should come to know about. In due time, that is. In *your* time. You'll know when it's right."

Frank drew breath to speak, but Nancy raised a hand and shook her head.

Frank said nothing, exhaling.

They waited.

At length Halfie said, "Thank you, Nana. I suppose you're right. Everything feels different now." She glanced at Frank. "I expect you know what you're talking about."

"In the Celtic world," he replied, "yes. May I…?"

"Look around?" Nancy said. "Of course."

Halfie watched as Frank explored the mound. He became more excited as he did, and when he disappeared behind it they heard exclamations of wonder, and once what sounded like a whoop. When he reappeared he was grinning.

"This is marvellous," he said. "All I can see of damage is a really big badger sett entrance. If this bit of wood goes back to before Medieval times, the mound could even be untouched by local people. Stunning!" And he laughed, running up to them.

Nancy smiled. "I told you it would be good," she said.

He laughed again, turning to view the mound, but Halfie felt her energy drain away. "Could I be left alone, please?" she asked.

Nancy nodded at Frank then led him away, Billy following. Halfie stood alone for a while as the enchantment of the mound dwindled, and her inner thought with it. Birds sung, and they were marvellous; but magical no more.

A twig cracked, and she turned to see Billy.

"It ain't all over yet," he said.

"No," she replied. "Nana understood. But I'll need time. And... how will I tell Mum? What if it sends her into another episode?"

"I don't see why it should. That man said this was a place of national importance. Mebbe that'll help her with the shock a bit."

"My mum *believes* in the elves. My dad does."

"What about you? You said everything feels different."

Halfie shook her head as tears trickled down her cheeks. "The elves are gone. I know it, though it's hard to bear."

He stood beside her, putting his arm around her shoulders and drawing her towards him; just for a moment. Then he said, "Reckon it had to happen in the end. There's just no cause for anything else. At least the elves and Faerie make good tales. They live on like that, don't they? My mum used to tell me such tales."

"Did she really?"

"Oh, yes. And I liked them. But, you know... in the end you gotta tighten your belt and start dealing with school and jobs and stuff."

Halfie

Smiling, she nodded. "Yes... though goodness knows what I'll do. You'll run the farm, I expect."

He let her go, taking one step aside. "Mebbe," he said. His voice lacked all warmth. "We'll see when the time comes."

"Won't you?" she asked.

"Dunno. Cars, mebbe."

"Perhaps it'll be years yet before the necklace is uncovered," she said. "Did you notice Nana said nothing about it? That must have been deliberate. It'll be hidden in some out of the way place on your farm, made with cunning. That's your dad's way."

"It is that."

"Will you look for it when you go back home?"

"Not likely. Dad'll suspect. He's quick like that – cunning, as you mentioned."

She said, "Perhaps he'll bequeath you a map with an X on it."

He laughed. "Reckon not, Halfie. He's a grasping old skinflint."

"Or a puzzle box, or a key!"

Billy shook his head, then froze, staring at the ground. Halfie watched. He stood motionless.

"What?" she asked.

He looked up. "A *key?* Ah... I reckon I know exactly where that necklace is."

CHAPTER 16

They sat inside the tent, a cardboard box on the ground between them. Billy rested on a stack of pillows, Halfie sat cross-legged.

"All right," she said, "now absolutely nobody can hear us. Nancy's in the barn and Dad's mucking out. Where do think the necklace is?"

He shook his head. "I hope I'm right, Halfie. It came to me sudden, like, in Snittonwood. I been thinking for days about my dad going berserk when he spotted us putting the old Citroën back. I mean, it was his private car, and there was a cast-iron rule about never using it, but still…"

"And?" Halfie said, hardly able to keep her excitement contained.

"The language he used was something shocking. I'm not sure I ever heard him use such swears. It really got to me. For days I been wondering why."

Halfie began to feel disappointed. "But he was furious, Billy. It's hardly surprising."

"He wasn't just furious. I sensed something more. He was frightened."

"Frightened?"

Halfie

"Yes," Billy said. "I heard it in his voice. Didn't you?"

"No."

"Well, you don't know him like I do. Anyhow, when you said a key up there in the wood, my mind turned to thinking about the car key. And then I *had* it, in a flash. The necklace is stored in the Citroën."

Halfie sat up. "Are you sure? It was outdoors. Anybody could look and take it."

He shook his head. "Not that wreck. It's a *Citroën,* ain't it? Nobody'd even notice it sat there, unwashed, unloved, even with the key in the dash. That's the *point.* That's the cunning. That's the reason he made the house rule for nobody to touch it. That's why he always called it his private car, and hardly used it."

"But... we drove it to Shrewsbury and back."

"Exactly! *That's* why he was scared as well as angry. He had a narrow escape. I bet you the necklace is hidden beneath stuff in the boot, which *is* locked."

"But... *he* must've driven it out as well. You said he did use it."

"Yes, when the main car was in for a service," Billy replied. "But don't you see? That's the devious skill of it. Nobody'd look twice at that rustbucket, even parked in the middle of Ludlow... even by the *market.* Would you?"

Now Halfie began to see merit in Billy's idea. "Then, what if you're right? We could actually retrieve my necklace."

"And that's another thing," he said. "Dad moved it away from the water tank as soon as he could after I drove it. Proof positive."

"Where do you think it is?"

"Put away in an outbuilding."

"Which?" Halfie asked. "You've got loads."

"That's the problem. We'll have to find out."

"But won't he have moved the necklace out of the car by now?"

"That's a possibility," Billy conceded. "I dunno. My guess is that he doesn't want it in the house because of me and Dave. Too risky for him – could be accidentally found. So he stored it where nobody'd look. Reckon he'll stick to his original plan, but move the car away and pretend to be annoyed still."

Halfie nodded. "I think you could be right. What now, then?"

"A night-time venture."

Halfie bit her lip, considering options. "My mum's coming home tomorrow morning. I'm not sure how things are going to be."

"So?"

"Let's wait until she's settled down first, then do it."

"Shall I have a nose around, try to locate it?"

Halfie felt nervous now. So much rested on their success, and they might only have one chance to make the raid. "No. Much too risky. He mustn't see you back at the farm."

"Good point. At the weekend, then, mebbe. Weather's gonna stay fine."

Halfie nodded. "Billy... this could be the moment I've been waiting for. The end of a lot of troubles, for me and Nancy. I do hope you're right and the necklace is in that car. It would be a dream come true to feel it around my neck."

He reached out with one hand. "Wanna bet that it's inside the Citroën?"

Halfie

The gesture felt inappropriate – mercenary, almost, as if mocking ancient history – but she realised it signified his confidence. "This is serious, Billy."

"That it is. But you know I'm right."

She nodded. "It does make sense."

He relaxed, leaning back. "Will you get to keep the necklace?" he asked. "It might be wanted by the government. You know, saved for the nation."

She tried to smile, but worry now consumed her. "My dad knows something's up. He's taken the photos and he's checking out smallholding legals. What if he tries to claim it? For Mum, perhaps. He might want to present it to her... a gift from Faerie..." She buried her face in her hands, suddenly horrified. "Oh, they won't *understand*. They'll see the necklace as magical, not as treasure trove."

"Does your dad know Mr Griffiths was here?"

Halfie wiped her eyes. "He'll know," she said, "and he'll be angry. Another reason for him to try and establish control of the smallholding. It could be a legal grey area, Nancy said, even though she owns it. They're close family, after all."

"Then we gotta find that necklace this weekend," Billy said, "hide the thing ourselves. Then *we've* got an ace card to play."

She nodded, sighing. "Yes, Billy. Thank you. It got to me all of a sudden."

"Don't worry yourself, I don't mind a few tears, do I?"

"You've been such a good friend to me. I owe you a lot."

"Likewise."

Halfie's dad drove to Shrewsbury to fetch her mum at eleven o'clock, following a telephone call from Shelton

Hospital. At the smallholding, the atmosphere became solemn and tense. Even knowing that the release forms had been signed, Halfie could not imagine what state her mum would be in. All she could think of was those white hospital garments and the red wristband.

When they heard the car rolling along Woody End Lane, Nancy tapped Billy on the shoulder and said, "You'd better hide yourself for an hour or so. An Ordish in plain sight might not be a good idea."

"Understood," Billy replied. "Let me know when the coast is clear."

"We will." She grabbed him by the arm and said, "And, thank you."

He nodded once, gave a wan smile, then ducked into his tent.

"What shall we say the tent is for if Mum wants to know?" Halfie asked.

"I'll tell her it's for you to sleep outside because it's too warm in the barn."

"All right."

Nancy led Halfie into the yard as the car drew up. Halfie could see her mum in the back: face pale and gaunt, gaze down, swaying from side to side as the car slowed and turned. Somehow, that light rocking motion made her feel anxious. When the pair stepped out she saw that her mum looked as fragile as a dead winter leaf.

Without delay Nancy moved forward and said, "You're back! How are you feeling, Jane?"

Halfie watched and waited. For a few moments her mum did not seem to recognise anybody, but then she said, "They told me I'm no longer a danger to myself. I don't know what they meant by that."

Halfie's dad strode around the front of the car, taking her mum's arm and holding it close. "She's fine," he said. "I've been debriefed, so I know what to do. There'll be doctors' visits and regular appointments for therapy – I mean, talking therapy, not medical. You two don't need to do anything, it's all been taken care of."

This blanket dismissal made Halfie feel wretched. It seemed to her that her mum was struggling to stand up unsupported. With a tear rolling down one cheek she said, "Will you be eating with us, Mum?"

Her mum shook her head, gaze empty. "I don't know where I'll be."

Halfie quailed, reaching for Nancy's hand. Her dad scowled and led her mum away.

Nancy squeezed Halfie's hand. "That wasn't too promising," she murmured. "She looks awfully weak."

"She *must* get better," Halfie replied. "The hospital wouldn't let her go if they were worried."

"That's true enough, but some patients become good actors in order to be released. I hope Jane's not fooled the doctors into believing she's back to normal."

Halfie looked away, remembering the advice she had given her mum about acting. How could everything go so wrong in just a few days?

"Are you worried, Nana?"

"Very. Jane looks wretched. But I'll watch those two, even if Duncan confronts me about it. Farmhouse ban or whatever, that's my *daughter*."

"I'll support you," Halfie said. Guilt surged through her. "You watch them like a hawk, Nana. Shall we go inside the farmhouse now?"

"No. Give them time. We'll choose our moment. But, yes, we should do it together. If we present a united front…" She sighed, shaking her head. "It'll create a split, but how else can we do it? Duncan's on one side and we're on the other. It didn't have to be this way."

They stayed away from the farmhouse for the rest of the day, Halfie working around the smallholding, Billy with friends in town, Nancy inside the barn. As evening fell Nancy led Halfie to the kitchen door, motivated by the odour of food.

In the kitchen, Halfie saw her dad cooking on the Aga. Her mum sat on a chair, and she looked better, if still pale.

Nancy walked in and said, "It's only us."

Duncan grimaced, but said nothing. Halfie realised at once that power lay balanced, both sides with grievances but also restraints. She sat next to her mum and said, "How are you feeling?"

"Hungry."

Halfie glanced at her dad. As if in reply to her unspoken question he said, "Our chicken and Pearl Farm veg. Should be nice."

Halfie nodded, trying to relax. It felt so unnatural with all four of them in the same room, possibly soon to eat together.

"What did you make of those photos, Alfreda?" her dad asked.

Halfie glanced at Nancy. "What photos?" she replied.

"The three I was sent."

"Oh… just somebody's holiday snaps I expect. Perhaps somebody thought a previous tenant still lived here."

He frowned at her. "What do you know about previous tenants?"

Halfie hesitated. "Well… there must have been some before you and Mum came."

Her dad sent a look of anger at Nancy then turned to continue stirring his pots. At length he said, "I'm not sure I want Billy Ordish on our property. Why are you letting him stay here, Nancy?"

"He's had a set-to with his father," Nancy replied.

"So?"

"It's common decency, Duncan. Helping a neighbour. I'm not going to be lectured by you on that topic."

"The boy's a mischief. He'll have his grubby mitts on Halfie next. Get rid of him."

"No."

Expecting her dad to become angry Halfie tensed herself for flight, but he carried on stirring, bending down to check the oven, then standing straight.

"Will you two be eating with us?" he asked.

"Yes," Nancy replied.

"Good," he said.

Halfie exchanged glances with Nancy.

He continued, "I'm not sure old Ordish next door is quite finished with us. Something tells me he's up to something, and I think it's to do with our property. The two fields again, or maybe even the wood itself."

"Do you?" Nancy replied in a bored voice.

"Yes, I do. What do you know about that?"

"Nothing."

"Not so wise, then?"

"I don't much care about it," Nancy said. "We both know what would happen if there was a legal *dispute.* About *ownership.*"

He remained silent, and Halfie sensed that he knew he had pushed far enough. But he was staking his ground. He was going to attempt to alter management of the smallholding by establishing the validity of the original agreement. For all that Nancy owned the place, her parents had run it for a decade and a half, giving them a stake in whatever might emerge from the shee. All her dad wanted was that stake.

He said, "Tenants have rights if they've been gifted control of a property, especially if they've lived in that property for a long time. It was all done in writing. Just so you know, Nancy."

Nancy uttered a laugh of contempt. "I don't think the law in that regard is as grey as you believe."

He made no reply to that, but Halfie shivered, sure now that he had guessed about the shee, the necklace and the reason for Frank Griffiths' visit – which so far he had not mentioned.

Taking a tray from the oven, he set it on the table. "Roast chicken?" he said.

Saturday passed without incident, but Halfie became ever more concerned about her mum. She would wander around the smallholding in bare feet, never speaking, gazing at the sky, then disappearing back into the house. She did not visit the wood. This in itself spoke to Halfie of something perilous active in her mind.

As dusk fell, Billy returned from another sojourn in Ludlow. They sat inside the tent and planned the night's deed.

"This is what I reckon we should do," he said. "Dad goes to bed pretty late, but he makes sure all the important farm jobs are done for the sake of a bit of a lie-in. So if we go to bed early and get a good few hours' kip, we can set our alarms for, say, four o'clock and be up and alert long before he is."

"And your stepmum."

"Eh?"

"Your stepmum," Halfie said.

"Oh... yes. And Dave. Now, I've narrowed it down to three sheds that he might've stored the Citroën in – everything else is too full of farm gear or junk. They're not locked, but I reckon the one with the car might be. Padlocked, most likely."

"How can we get in then?" she asked.

"Each one has windows. If locked, that's our only chance. In town today I bought a glass cutter from the Bull Ring hardware shop." He exhibited the tool, then a pack of rubber suckers. "I'll use these to stick to the glass so I can pull a bit out. Then I'll reach in to undo the latch."

"We'll have to be as quiet as mice."

"I'm not so sure," he replied. "Everyone'll be asleep. Freddie and Blackie will be on leashes in their kennels, but they're on the track side of the farm. The three sheds are to the north. I think we'll be okay. There'll be cats prowling, and maybe a fox or two, but nothing I reckon that'll make enough noise to wake anyone."

"All right... if you're sure."

"You got black clothes, just in case? We might need to melt into the shadows."

Halfie felt her heartbeat race. "I suppose so. Oh, Billy... I hope this works."

"Don't worry. I know my way around with my eyes shut. We'll find the car."

"Then take back what's mine."

"Right enough."

As dusk merged with night Halfie found it difficult to sleep, but at last she drifted off, the barn joists clicking around her as they cooled after a hot day.

Her alarm beeped.

She rolled over and pressed the switch, then listened. Nothing sounded up in the mezzanine. Pitch black inside the barn.

Dressing in dark clothes, she crept outside, meeting Billy beside the tent. No hint of dawn lay in the east, but darkness would not rule for long, the Solstice little more than a month earlier. She took a few deep breaths, smelling night dew on hay.

"Ready?" he asked.

She nodded.

They struck out along the western track, navigating by starlight and the hint of a sodium glow from Ludlow, then crossed the disputed fields, gaining access to Stone Farm fields and heading west, a little north, then striking an old track down from Stone Wood. Soon they lay behind bushes, studying the buildings before them.

"That one first," Billy said, pointing.

Halfie saw little more than black shapes in the darkness. Billy put on gloves, then stood up.

Seeing her puzzled expression, he said, "In case the glass breaks."

She nodded as her anxiety rose. But he sounded confident still.

At the rear of the building he took a pencil torch and shone it through the cobwebbed window at the rear. "Nowt," he said.

Taking her hand, he led her around the building and across a path towards an adjacent shed, this one smaller, but taller.

"The old plough store," he whispered. "Balers too."

At the rear window he shone his beam inside.

"Aha!"

Halfie

Halfie looked. Inside stood the Citroën, parked with its front nearest them. Now her heartbeat raced and her hands trembled. Having checked that the shed was padlocked, Billy took out a rubber sucker, positioned it, then began scraping at the glass while Halfie held the torch for him. She glanced over her shoulder to see dawn breaking in the east.

"Hurry up," she said.

"This ain't as easy as I reckoned," he replied. "Should've practised a bit first. Oh, well, I'll get there."

After a few minutes he stopped scraping and gave an experimental push. The glass cracked, but stayed put. He pressed again. A large segment of glass broke free, but fragments fell to the floor with a crash.

They both froze.

No noise. No dogs barking.

Billy pulled the segment out, placed it on the ground then reached in to test the latch. "It's rusted shut," he said. "Should've brought some oil. Never thought of that."

"What will you do?" Halfie asked.

"Keep tugging. Ah! Felt it move. I'll have it free in a minute."

After what seemed ten minutes he muttered something then leaned back. With a squeak the whole window opened.

"Got it," he said.

He clambered in first, taking the torch then helping Halfie inside. They stood at the back of the shed, the car just feet away, Halfie swallowing to ease her dry mouth. Still her hands and arms trembled.

"You look," she said. "I daren't."

"Okay. I'm checking the back first 'cos that's where the boot is."

Halfie

Halfie followed him around the left side of the car. The remains of the canvas top lay folded at the back, so he leaned over to extract the key. In torchlight, Halfie saw two linked keys, Billy taking the second one between his thumb and forefinger.

"This one," he said.

At the back of the car he paused, took the boot clasp in his left hand, then put the key in the lock, turned it and lifted all in one motion.

Shrieking noise filled the shed.

"He alarmed it!" Billy cried, turning to stare at her.

"The boot!" she replied, leaning over. "Before it's too late."

He rummaged through the cloths, canisters and junk in the boot before grabbing a wooden box wrapped in a tea towel. Halfie snatched it away, opening it to see silver gleaming inside.

Snapping the lid shut she said, "Run!"

Now they heard dogs barking at the front of the farm. Clambering through the window first, Billy tried to take the box once he held the torch, but she refused to let him. She struggled through, falling to the ground outside the shed.

Furious barking merged with the wail of the alarm.

"Run!" she said, staggering to her feet. "There's still time!"

They sprinted away at top speed, resting beside the bushes to listen to the car alarm and barking reverberating across the land.

Then Halfie heard a door slam. "It's him," she said.

"We're goners," he replied, gripping her arm. "He'll *know*."

Halfie felt fury and fierce pride rise up. "He can guess all he likes," she said. "He can't *prove*. Run, Billy, run

311

now. We'll head for Stonewood then hop across the gap to my wood. We can get back to the farmhouse out of sight. He'll never see us."

"He might! And he's got a shotgun for rabbits."

"A gun…"

Billy turned away. "Okay, we better shut up talking and start running." He glanced over his shoulder then added, "There's a torch beam!"

Again they ran, heading for the nearest cover, a hedge partitioning the western and eastern top fields, with the east field holding Stonewood. From behind them, distant now but clear, came the sound of thuds and a voice. Still the alarm wailed.

Then it stopped.

Halfie turned to watch as the swinging torch beam approached, and she knew William must be carrying it. Alongside Billy she hid beneath briars growing out of the hedge, but it was poor cover. They both lay flat. As the torch beam approached she heard muttering, and then, most frightening of all, the odour of stale cigarettes.

He was nearby. She could hear him talking to himself.

They lay motionless.

After a few moments the beam pointed back towards Stone Farm, but it did not move. He was thinking, wondering, deciding what to do. Then he hurried away, and she could hear nothing.

Somehow, the silence terrified her even more. It brought deep foreboding. "He'll know what's happened!" she whispered. "He'll come for my dad. They'll fight. Your dad might shoot. Oh, Billy."

"Your dad don't know nothing about what we done."

Fear coursed through her now. "Billy! We'll look *guilty*." She struggled to control her emotions. "We'll have to act innocent," she added, "otherwise…"

"Yes, innocent," he repeated, getting up to peer towards Stone Farm.

"Can you do it?"

"No choice. But we could bury the necklace in Snittonwood, right? *You* bury it. In or out of the trees. Don't tell me where, then I can't lie. Reckon you're a better actor than me, and besides, my dad knows me too well. If only you know where the necklace is…"

She nodded. "All right. Deal. C'mon, we can still get home, I think. Look away – I need to find a place to bury this."

"Okay. I'll stand behind that thicket of hazels."

Halfie stuffed the necklace into a fox hole beside a huge oak, then rejoined Billy. They hurried away, saying nothing. Halfie felt afraid, yet glad she no longer carried the necklace.

Twenty minutes later, as dawn brightened the sky, they walked into the upper smallholding field, converted years ago into a vegetable plot and orchard. Halfie signalled for a halt, and silence. She listened. All she could hear was the faintest sound of an agricultural vehicle.

"I don't hear barking," she said, "nor voices."

"He'll have quieted Blackie and Freddie by now. He'll be plotting revenge though."

"We'd best keep an eye on the track down to the lane. If we see him, we'll wake Dad and warn him."

"Sounds about right," he said. "If we're all awake we can mebbe contain him a bit. But he'll be so hopping furious…"

"And he has got a gun?"

"'Course! He's a farmer. Got a rifle."

Halfie shuddered.

"It won't come to that. Doubt he'd do anything to put himself in jail."

"Billy… people do strange things when they're furious or terrified. He might come around and–"

"Shush!" He raised one hand. "What's that noise?"

She listened. "A big engine, I think."

Billy nodded. "Tractor or something."

She turned, trying to locate the direction of the sound. "It's coming from your farm."

He listened, then said, "That's a tractor. A big one, I reckon."

"Shall we go and look? Perhaps he's driving it along the lane."

"No," he replied, gazing west. "It's over there. I don't like this. Let's get to your yard, eh?"

They ran through the orchard, across the vegetable patch then over a piece of overgrown lawn, from where they rounded the house corner to the yard. But still the tractor noise was quiet, indicating distance.

Then Halfie saw her mum at the lower end of the bridleway.

She pointed. "Billy! Mum's up."

He stared. "Yes… and she's going at quite a lick for a hospital patient."

"She must be going into the wood. Perhaps it's one of her trances."

He glanced at her. "Reckon we should follow?"

But Halfie did not hear. She stared further up, at the shoulder of land adjacent to Snittonwood. "There's a massive tractor heading for our wood."

Billy looked. "Bloody *hell*. That's Dad. He's got the big tractor out with the digger on the front. That's a speedy one."

"I think Mum's seen him."

"What's he up to?"

Halfie watched for a few moments, before the tractor vanished into Snittonwood. Sudden terror impelled her. "Billy! He's going to *do* something."

She ran, but, fatigued, she could not run fast – nor could Billy. By the time she reached the end of the western track her mum was already at the top of the bridleway, the tractor long since vanished. Desperation impelled her. Ignoring Billy and his hoarse gasps for breath, she ran on, legs heavy, chest hurting, until she stood at the corner of Snittonwood.

She bent over, exhausted. Looking up she saw a pair of muddy tyre trails leading into the wood, many trees fallen where they had been wrenched out of the ground. Horror clutched her heart. Listening, she heard thuds, rumbles, and the whining, whirring noise of a tractor motor at maximum strain.

Billy staggered up, grabbing her arm. "No, Halfie! Don't go in. If he's gone crazy he might run you down."

Halfie, unable to speak for gasping, shook him off, but she could only limp on a few more steps.

"Mum!"

Billy caught her again. "He's rampaging through the wood. It's only a few trees. He'll calm down once he's had his revenge."

Halfie shook him off. "He's had time already to ruin our wood."

This time Billy would not let her go, though she tugged as hard as she could. "Leave him be, Halfie! It's got to blow itself out."

Then Halfie froze. A piercing scream sounded.

"Mum!" she yelled, pushing Billy away.

He tripped and fell to the floor. "Halfie! *No.*"

"Mum!" she cried, staggering into the wood. "Where are you?"

At the glade she paused. The tractor noise was loud now.

The shee!

She ran as best she could out of the glade, leaning forward to try and reduce the pain in her chest, coughing up phlegm, and spitting. At the shee she saw a terrible scene.

William Ordish was using the digger to demolish the mound, stones and turf flung in all directions. Already a pit lay torn out of the ground before him where the badger sett entrance lay. Her mum stood motionless ten yards away, arms raised in horror.

"Mum!"

Her mum whirled around. "Alfreda! The Elf King is being attacked!"

Halfie stared at William inside the tractor, but he looked only forwards, hair bristling like an anti-halo, grinning, shouting, urging the tractor to maximum destruction. Not once did he look away from his task.

Halfie took a few steps forward, but then something struck her from behind. Billy tackled her to the ground. "Don't do it," he gasped. "Please!"

At this, the tractor noise diminished. Halfie looked up to see William staring at her. "He's seen us!" she cried. "He'll stop now."

Billy struggled to his feet. "He's coming!"

Halfie stood up, watching William leap out of the tractor, but it was clear to her that his rage had not abated. William ran forwards, yet he too stumbled, dragging one leg, and gasping for breath, his right arm hanging loose.

"I'll kill you, Billy!" he croaked as he staggered.

Halfie stepped back, but then her mum ran forward. "The King!" she wailed. "The King is dead!"

"Mum!" Halfie shrieked. "Wait for *me*."

At her side, Billy bent over to reach for something on the ground. "Come one step nearer, Dad," he said, brandishing a stone, "and I'll drop you with this."

William stumbled on.

Halfie ran forward, passing William by the merest reach, but he ignored her.

"Billy, you bloody traitor!" he wheezed.

She halted, turned around, saw Billy aim then throw. The stone missed William, but even so he staggered, then fell. Billy stared, one hand at his mouth.

Halfie turned around. At the shee, her mum lurched this way and that, arms in the air, wailing, then screaming.

"Mum!"

Too late. Her mum tottered at the edge of the pit, cried, "It's all gone," then turned and fell, disappearing from view.

Halfie screamed and ran forwards. At the edge of the pit she looked down to see exposed rock, her mum lying motionless upon it – a crooked body at the bottom. Part of the sett chamber system had collapsed, deepening the pit, and there her mum lay. Halfie froze, unable to look away – just staring. There was blood on that rock.

Gasping at her side, Billy peered over the edge of the pit. "Oh jeez. She's fell all the way in."

"*Do* something, Billy!"

He let her go and knelt at her side, then threw himself down the edge of the pit. The near side was precipitous – he fell and rolled aside at the bottom, a landslide of earth and stones following.

"Billy! Is she all right?"

He hesitated for a few moments, uncertain.

"Is she *breathing?*"

He pulled her up by one shoulder, but then let her go. "Ugh! Oh, jeez... Halfie, what'll I do? It's blood everywhere."

"What's wrong?"

"Her head's all crooked."

"*Billy.*"

He staggered back, his face stretched into an expression of horror.

"Billy! Shall I go and call an ambulance?"

He stood up, then raised his arms and put his hands upon his head. Repulsion lined every part of his face as he stared at the body.

"I reckon it's too late."

Summer suns rose over Mortimer Forest: green-shrouded hills.

In warm scented air larks flew high, their signature song decorating every part of the Shropshire Hills. On tumbledown slopes sheep grazed, pigs grunted, cows lowed, as the tranquil, teeming matters of rural life continued. In sun-bleached barns the hay harvest was stacked: bales, sometimes stooks.

Storms trundled from horizon to horizon, hammerheads in a line, sometimes to move on, ever eastward, sometimes to deposit floods of water amidst the stink of ozone.

Halfie

Summer lay full hazy over the land. Stressed by heat and drought, silver birch leaves began to turn yellow, and drop. The River Teme sparkled from higher ground to lower, fringed with reeds, grebes and ducks. A million minnows grew up in warm shallows along the River Corve.

The summer sun gave heat and light in a breathless, continuous blaze.

Halfie

CHAPTER 17

Halfie sat on a chair in the middle of her bedroom, wearing just knickers and a slip; the morning was warm already. Wood pigeons cooed in the trees outside. A pair of blackbirds chittered and fought aerial battles, while everywhere smaller birds looked for food, hopping this way and that. Inside her room, the bed's single coverlet was thrown aside, photographs in frames lying across the floor.

On a cardboard box in front of her stood a mirror, the antique one from the main guest bedroom, which she had set upright by leaning it against a teapot. In her right hand, a pair of scissors.

She looked at her reflection. Medium length red hair, yellow at the roots; tired eyes with pale bags under them; blotchy cheeks. She had not shed a single tear since the ambulances took her mum and Billy's dad away, though the symptoms of what lay within were visible on her face. But an impenetrable, invisible barrier surrounded her, through which no hint of feeling yet passed.

Leaning forward to get the best view she began cutting, first at the sides, cutting most of the way up to the dye line,

320

then the front; then, using a hand mirror, what she could manage of the back, swinging locks around to snip the red away. After a while she saw her face framed by a haphazard mess of hair, fringed red. Now more carefully, she snipped away every last trace of red that she could see, leaving a cap of blond fuzz. The back was impossible to do in this way, so she picked up her dad's electric shaver, set it to beard trim, and removed what she could.

A cool breeze wafted over her head. She did not care.

She checked with both mirrors to see whether or not all traces of red had been removed; not quite. In the upstairs bathroom she washed her hair, cleaning away all the bits with a towel, then returning to her room.

She heard footsteps outside her door, then a tapping sound. "Maeve? Are you awake?"

It was Nancy. "Come in," she said.

Nancy opened the door, but hesitated half way through the doorway. At the far end of the corridor Halfie saw the open door of the bedroom her nana now occupied.

"You can come in," she said.

Nancy looked alarmed when she saw Halfie. "I heard noise. What have you done?"

"Cut it off."

Nancy sighed, her expression pensive. She walked over and brushed her hand against the back of Halfie's head. "You missed a few bits. Shall I tidy it up for you?"

"Yes, please."

Halfie sat mute while Nancy leaned over to trim a few places. Then she threw the scissors to the floor and sat on the bed. Halfie studied her.

"Are you all right, Nana?"

Nancy looked out of the window, and for a while only silence filled the room.

"Is Dad up yet?" she asked.

"I don't know," Nancy replied. "I'm not sure he stayed overnight."

Halfie glanced aside. "He'll be in the wood then."

"Probably."

"Yes, probably."

Nancy said, "Why did you cut it all off?"

"To get rid of the red," Halfie replied. "They made me dye my hair."

"Yes. I remember being told. Red hair for Faerie."

"So I've cut it off. It's all gone…"

Nancy winced, then looked away.

"Why don't I feel anything?" asked Halfie.

Nancy gazed at her. "I'm the same. It's shock."

"Shock."

"That's the purpose of shock, isn't it? To insulate you. The moment we start feeling things, we're connected to the world… to people. It's too early for that. So we have shock to numb us. Don't worry, dear, it's perfectly natural. When the time's right we'll all be crying our eyes out."

"Even Dad?" Halfie asked.

"Even him."

Halfie paused for thought. "Shall I go and fetch him?"

"Leave it. He's doing his own thing."

"Whatever must he be thinking? I'm–"

"No," Nancy interrupted. "Don't. Leave him be. You've got yourself to think of. Put *yourself* first. I know that's not easy for you, but it would be best."

"All right."

"He'll be in the wood anyway."

Halfie nodded. "Probably."

They both looked in opposite directions, as if appraising the room. Halfie heard her belly rumble.

"Do you think we'll hear soon when the inquest is?" she asked.

"There should be a letter today."

"I hope so." She stood up, then stretched. "I'd better fetch Billy."

"Yes. Time for a bit of breakfast."

Halfie dressed in yesterday's old clothes, pulled on a pair of trainers, then walked downstairs and out behind the house. From the yard she scanned land to the west, but saw no sign of her dad. Further away, Stone Farm was active: tractors and a couple of men.

At the tent, she tapped a metal pole and said, "Are you up, Billy?"

He poked his head out. "Hello. Wow... you cut all your hair off. Are you okay? How are you today?"

Halfie pointed beyond the barn. "There's men on your fields."

He emerged, already dressed, though his hair was tousled. "My uncle Adrian," he replied. "Came yesterday with a couple of casual agricultural labourers."

"Are they running the farm while your dad's in hospital?"

"Yes." Billy hesitated, then shrugged and added, "A history of heart trouble, you know..."

"What about your stepmum and Dave?"

He grimaced. "What about them?"

"Well..."

"Don't you think about them," he said. "Leave all that to me."

"Um... all right. It's honey on toast for breakfast in the kitchen."

He took a key from his pocket. "Got to go to the loo first," he said, indicating with his head in the direction of the barn. "Be with you in a minute."

Halfie turned and walked away, but then saw a car parking at the bottom of the track. To her surprise, Brian Speed stepped out of it.

Halfie stared. This was the least-expected visitor. Disconcerted, she ran to the kitchen, where she found Nancy.

"Brian Speed's here," she said.

"Who?"

"One of Dad's friends."

Nancy shook her head.

"From the Faerie Fayre."

Suddenly Nancy's face acquired an expression of anger. "The dealer?"

"Er... well, that's how Billy described him, yes."

Now Nancy looked furious. "How *dare* he show his face here at such a time."

Halfie shrank back, quailing. "I expect Dad asked him."

"Precisely! Maeve, I'm going to sort this criminal out once and for all. Run to the barn and get my little digital camera. On the sideboard. I'll stop Speed on the track. Join us with the camera ready. If he hands me anything, take a picture. Two, three... as many as you can. Make sure *he's* in view all the time."

"Hands you? Why–"

Nancy frogmarched her out of the kitchen. "*Do* it!" From the stand at the side of the door she grabbed a walking stick.

Halfie watched as she stepped outdoors. "But..."

"Hurry, dear! I know exactly what's going on here."

Uncomprehending, Halfie ran through the yard and down to the barn. But Brian Speed was already halfway up the track, and he waved at her. Not knowing what else to say, she called out, "My Nana's coming to meet you."

"Good-o," he replied. "Love the new hairstyle!"

Halfie grabbed the camera, then returned to the barn door to see Nancy walking down the track. Brian halted, hands in pockets.

Warily, Halfie approached them. She had no idea what was going on.

Then Nancy said, "Ah, Mr Speed. How may I help you?"

"Is Duncan around? How is he? I've come to talk to him about things. You know... man to man."

"Man to man, is it? Well, typically that *does* go a long way, man to man."

He looked at her, face blank. "Is he okay?"

"He is indisposed. What do you want?"

"To see him."

"What for?" Nancy asked.

"Like I said... to chat. He needs support."

"*I'm* doing that, thank you very much."

His expression hardened. "I'd still just like to say hello. You know... pop my head 'round the door, just for a few moments, tell him we're here for him."

"*We're?* So there's more than one of your type thinking about Duncan?"

"Well... of course. It's, like, a community. We're all shocked."

"Are you indeed?" Nancy replied. "Let me tell you, Mr Speed, you are not setting a foot any further onto this property, not while I have breath in my body. Duncan is indisposed and not receiving visitors."

He shrugged, glancing aside. Then he took an envelope from his pocket. "Look," he said, "it's pretty sentimental, I know, and not much, but we all signed a card for him. Will you give it him for me?"

Halfie held her breath. But this was only an envelope with a card inside… was it what Nancy meant?

Nancy glanced across, then reached out to accept the envelope. Halfie raised the camera, pointed and shot. Brian turned around, staring at her, while she took another picture, then a third.

"What are you doing?" he said.

Nancy flung the envelope to the ground then raised her stick. Two-handed, she dealt him a blow to the side of the head that made him stagger. "Get out of here, drug dealer!" she cried. "I've got proof now. Get away with you!"

He gasped, then dodged aside, trying to grab the envelope. Realising what might happen, Halfie pointed and shot until Nancy dealt a final blow to the retreating, wailing man.

"And you can expect a visit from the police with my evidence!" Nancy shouted.

"Nana," Halfie said, running up. "You hit him."

Nancy, face red, bent over to retrieve the envelope. "This isn't a card, Maeve! It's drugs. Look, it's squishy. There's something inside."

Halfie stared. This was all beyond her.

But now Nancy sagged, tears streaming down her cheeks. "Why did she have to get mixed up with these people? *Why?* I told her a thousand times it was dangerous. Oh, Maeve, *everything's* gone wrong that possibly could go wrong. I left it too late. I should've come here earlier. But I didn't…"

Halfie felt surprised, yet not pained. Nancy's tears almost seemed selfish, as if she was bemoaning her own lack of insight, her own troubles, her own weakness rather than everything surrounding her daughter.

"I'm going to fetch my dad," she said.

"No, Maeve! He'll only stir things up when he finds out."

"I need to see him, Nana. Everything's all *wrong.*"

She turned around and ran off, heading for the western track.

Nancy called out, "Don't tell him! Just support him."

"I won't! I will."

By the time she reached the bridleway she was already out of breath, so she walked towards Snittonwood at a slower pace, then crept into the wood. The place was quiet, cool.

"Dad?"

He would likely be near the shee. She tip-toed forward.

There he was, sitting on a tree stump a few yards away from the undamaged eastern side of the mound.

"Dad?" she said in a louder voice.

He did not turn around, notice her, nor even twitch. Sidling around him, she allowed herself to come into view, gazing down at him with a hopeful smile on her face. He sat mute, expression fixed, his mouth half-open; and his pupils were so huge his eyes seemed wholly black.

"Dad? Are you all right?"

He gazed up at her. Yet for all that he could see her, she sensed him in a trance, as if communing with spirits far beyond the strictures of the mundane world. But she herself, as she watched, and listened, and waited, knew that world was a fallacy.

She brushed her blonde fuzz. "Do you like my new hair?" she asked.

"Oh, man…" he murmured in response.

"Are you okay, Dad?"

"I'm good," he replied. "The elves… jewelled… all over the place…"

"Well… yes."

He turned away, staring into the trees.

Halfie looked in the same direction, but saw nothing of note. "Dad," she said, "I'm not sure it's… healthy for you to be up here. People might think it's not good for you. Won't you come back? We were having breakfast."

"They're not gone… not gone at all…"

She stepped back. Though she had seen him like this before – her mum too – she now felt angry. He should be *helping* her, talking to her, comforting her… hugging her. Then she would be able to do the same for him. But all he could do was watch invisible things amongst the trees.

She felt a twinge of something anguished in her heart. She stepped back. He was unreachable, she knew. Perhaps they both were now, father and daughter locked away by shock, by tragedy.

Inside the barn, Halfie sat opposite Billy.

He said, "I'm visiting Dad this afternoon at the community hospital, so I'll be away for a while."

"All right. It's pork and spuds au gratin tonight, about six-thirty."

He nodded, looking down at his lap. "I'm going to…"

She waited, but he said no more, leaning back, his gaze defocused. He looked nervous. "You're going to what?" she asked. "He had a heart attack, you said. The doctors will look after him. They know about his heart problems, don't they?"

He looked at her, pushing his chin out a little. "I've got to…"

"What?"

"Tell him what I'm going to do."

"About what?" she said. "He'll survive. It was mild, the doctors told you."

"The farm."

"What about it?"

He leaned forward again, elbows on knees, breathing fast and shallow, and now she sensed his distress.

"What are you going to tell him?" she asked in a mild voice. "About your uncle Adrian?"

"He knows about all that."

"Is your stepmum all right?"

He frowned, looking away.

"*What*, Billy? Tell me, please. We're friends, aren't we? I won't mind."

"I'm gonna tell him I'm not taking over the farm."

"Oh! Oh, I see… but why not?"

"To make a stand."

Words she had spoken to him sounded in her mind: *Tell him to speak politely to you. Make a stand. That's what I did.*

She sat up, aware now of how serious this was. "I'll come with you," she said.

"No," he replied. "Not your business."

Quick anger rose inside her. "It is, Billy."

"It ain't."

"It *is*. How can you speak to me like that? You're shutting me out. Of course I'll come, you'll need everybody there on your side. Will I get to meet your stepmum?"

He shook his head. "I decided it's only me today."

"Well, I'm definitely coming then." She paused for thought, aware that Billy's attitude to his stepmum was overly protective. "I can't believe you wouldn't have me," she said. "That's horrible, Billy, and you're not like that. No, I'm coming, I wouldn't dream of letting you do it on your own."

He studied her, face impassive, clasping his hands together.

"What are you going to do, run away from me to the bus stop?" she asked.

"Mebbe."

She jumped up from the rocking chair and knelt beside his seat, looking up at him. "Don't you remember what you told me before about being friends?"

"What?" he muttered.

"You've been such a good friend to me. I owe you a lot."

He seemed dubious. "That were what you said to me."

"Wait! I *know*. And then you said, likewise."

He looked chastened. "Well…"

"Admit it, Billy. We're not just neighbours any more, are we? We've looked out for each other like friends ought to. We couldn't have managed all this alone."

He sighed. "S'pose not."

"Well, then. Which bus are you getting?"

"Three o'clock."

"Right."

"I'll be paying both fares though," he said.

She smiled. "It's a deal."

Halfie

At three o'clock they got on the bus and sat halfway down. Although news of the tragedy had been suppressed, Halfie knew some of the town gossips had come to learn of it via hospital staff. She felt she was being watched by other passengers. Yet still her barriers contained her, supported her, aided her. She could deflect a few stares.

In Ludlow they alighted, walking the short distance uphill to the community hospital. Billy led her to the ward entrance, but there hesitated.

Halfie stood close. "You all right?"

"Nervous."

"Will he be awake? Will he understand?"

"He won't understand, but it's gotta be done before he comes back home. And he's a lot better, so that means doing it today. I just hope his heart'll stand it."

"It will. Come on, then. Together."

For a fleeting moment she wondered if she should hold his hand, but then she discarded the idea as inappropriate. So she walked near him, beside him, matching him pace for pace, breathing deep and standing up straight.

William lay in bed, alone, the bed beyond empty, the bed adjacent occupied by a sleeping patient. He looked nearly asleep himself, his chin resting on his chest, eyes gleaming behind half-closed eyelids, a tabloid newspaper in one hand. Hearing footsteps he snorted, then looked up.

"Eh, what? That you, boy?"

Billy stood silent as William reached out and patted the bedside table for something. Halfie watched, motionless. William's hair was cut and combed, his cheeks shaven.

Then Billy said, "I do have a name, Dad."

"What? Who's this?"

Billy took a step forward as his father put on a pair of spectacles. "My name's *Billy,* Dad. It's not boy."

Halfie

William stared at Halfie. "Is that you? What the bloody–
"

"Dad! *Listen* to me. And be polite, please. This is Halfie from next door. You can call her Maeve."

"What? What happened to her hair?"

Halfie took Billy by the hand and led him to a chair, pulling one from the bed adjacent for herself. "I'm Maeve now, Mr Ordish," she said. "We've come to visit you."

"Don't want no visitin'. Not from you two."

"This time, Dad," Billy said, "you ain't got no choice."

"So it seems. Bloody cheek."

Halfie glanced aside at Billy, but he looked confident. She leaned back, hoping he would take the cue and expand into her space.

At length he said, "Well, how are you, Dad?"

"Better. Nurse says I got nothin' to worry 'bout. What's Ade doin' on the farm? He still got it in order?"

"He's fine. It's all under control."

"Better had be."

Now Halfie felt impelled to speak. "What would you do if it wasn't, Mr Ordish?" she asked.

"What? Ain't nothin' to do with you."

Billy leaned forward. "You speak *proper* to her! You know what's happened to her. Have some common decency, won't you?"

He spat the words out. William stared at him, then groaned and turned half away.

Billy continued, "Dad, I got something to say to you."

"What 'bout? I already got enough on me mind, what with bein' in hospital. And idiots on the farm, spoilin' it. And thieves."

Halfie was glad to see Billy paying no attention to the remark. William might guess which household was behind

332

the missing necklace, but he could prove nothing. Now she too felt confident. He was a curbed bully.

Billy said, "Yes, the farm. I've been thinking about it lately."

"So you bloody should! You been *workin'* on it? Ade says not. Ade says you been shacked up at Chandler's all this time."

"So what if I have?"

"You got a home already."

"Really?" said Billy. "Perhaps I'd go back if it *felt* more like a home."

"What's that s'posed to mean?"

Billy sat upright. "You know well enough, Dad. But listen. I'm gonna tell you something straight. I got three years left at school, and I'll work the farm fair and square 'til then. But once I got my A Levels, I'm off. You'll have to get somebody else in to be Dave's buddy. Casual labour, like–"

"Off? Off where? Bloody idiot-i-stan?"

"Don't you talk to me like that! I won't take it no more. And you can leave the farm to Dave when you pop your clogs, because I ain't having anything to do with it."

William stared at him, then at Halfie. "Have *you* done this to him?" he asked her.

Halfie shrugged, feeling composed. Here on his back, she saw him as weak, even feeble, for all the bluster. "Not at all, Mr Ordish. You can shout as loud as you like for all I care. Billy's plan sounds sensible to me."

"You–"

"*Don't* you swear at her!" Billy interrupted. "I'm sick of your bullying, and she is too. You gone too far this time, so I've had no choice but to speak out. And I *have*. And if you don't like it, tough. I'm not going back on my word."

"I won't bloody let you!"

Billy leaned forward. "When you get back home," he said, "I'll come and join you. I'll live there, and do my best too. But I'll not forget one word of what I told you today."

William looked up, forehead sweating, mouth working: extinguished. Again Halfie sensed his insubstantial interior. He was all bellow, nothing more.

"Come on, Billy," she said, getting up.

He strode away, cheeks red, eyes staring, mouth set. He got halfway along the aisle before she caught up with him. But at the ward entrance he halted, turned, then looked back.

"Idiot," he muttered.

Halfie took him by the arm. "That's his word for you." She hesitated. "I'm sure we can do better."

"Fool, then."

"Oh, Billy..."

At the bus stop they stood in silence. At last, as the bus appeared, Billy said, "I'm gonna say this just once, then nowt. Sorry for the language. They fuck you up, your mum and dad. That's what that Larkin poem says. They may not mean to, but they do. What *I* gotta do is what you tried to, separate the man from the behaviour. But it ain't easy."

"It's not. And it might not work. I'm beginning to wonder if some people are beyond helping."

"Like your mum was?"

She shook her head. "Your dad's done everything deliberately against you, out of spite, because he can't stop himself. It's different with your dad."

He glanced at her, then took her hand and patted it. "You okay?"

"Yes. A bit shaky, but all right."

"Thanks for coming. You were totally right. I been daft not to see it. I did need you, and it went better for all that."

"It's no problem," she replied. "You got the return tickets?"

"Yep. Back home again. All done."

Halfie sat with Nancy at the kitchen table. Her dad lay asleep in the main bedroom, though it was only eight o'clock in the evening. They had eaten a supper of pork and mash, with a few overdone vegetables thrown in. Halfie sipped a mug of chamomile tea.

"Well?" Nancy said.

"Well what?"

"Penny for your thoughts."

Halfie shrugged. "Billy."

"What about him?"

"He's got a quest now."

Nancy sat up. "A what?"

"No, I didn't mean it that way. I meant... he's got a purpose to his life now, a really strong one. He'll leave home at eighteen, then be gone."

"You'll be going to university."

"I don't have to go," she said.

"You should though, if you get the grades, which you will."

"I might not want to."

"Your point?" Nancy asked.

"I need my *own* new purpose. The elves really have gone. I'll miss them."

Nancy's eyes narrowed. "Do you miss them now?"

Halfie shook her head. "Not yet."

"Hmm..."

"Are you worrying about me again?"

She hesitated. "Not yet, Maeve."

Halfie looked away. The inquest lay a few days ahead. "What about when I leave home?" she asked.

"You'll be your own woman then," Nancy replied. "Autonomous. And that will be ever so good for you."

"But I'll miss home."

"Everyone does. Part of life. You'll cope. We always do."

"We... women?"

She shook her head, then sighed. "No. People generally."

Halfie got up, unwilling to take the conversation further. "I'm going out for a walk. I want to see if I can spot Billy on Stone Farm, he went back yesterday to help get things ready for his dad's return. There's still plenty of light."

"You take care."

"All right."

Halfie strolled along the western track, enjoying the late sunshine, watching chickens scratching about in their pens, before heading out towards the spring field. At the bridleway, she shielded her eyes with one hand and scanned Stone Farm, but all lay at peace. She glanced up at Snittonwood.

Perhaps it was time to make a solitary visit.

At the edge of the wood, she paused. It looked the same, sounded the same and smelled the same; but it was not the same. It was a crucible for the past now, heavy with memories seared into her mind. Not the same place at all.

At the edge of the glade she began to feel uneasy. She hurried through, heading for the shee but stopping well away from it. The damage was considerable: Frank Griffiths would be aghast. What looked like flat stones had been exposed, and she could discern the deepest extent of the ditch. It truly was a Celtic burial mound, now half-ruined.

She wandered away, still uncomfortable with herself; but then she realised where she stood. It was the spot where, months ago, beside some dandelions, she had planted the seedling oak.

She halted.

She realised now what the source of her discomfort was.

Orienting herself, she walked forward, scanning the ground, avoiding new greenery, until she stood before the planting site. She knelt down, scrabbling amongst the leaf litter to reveal an oak sapling.

She reached out with the thumb and forefinger of her right hand to pluck it. Then stopped.

"No," she told herself. "Not quite yet."

CHAPTER 18

Halfie sat at the window in the upstairs alcove looking out over the track leading down to Woody End Lane. Her dad and Nancy had travelled to the inquest in separate transport, her dad in the car, Nancy by bus. The atmosphere between them was tense but polite. Her dad looked pale, thin, washed-out, his face lined; shock was receding. Nancy retained her ironclad defence, melancholy, yet never emotional.

As afternoon waned into evening she saw Nancy walking up the drive. She ran downstairs to meet her beside the barn.

"What happened?" she asked.

Nancy was in despondent mood. "Accidental death," she said.

"Where's Dad?"

"He said he was staying awhile to speak with court officials. He'll be back soon."

"What else did they say? Did they blame William?"

"He was named as a contributing factor," Nancy replied, "but he wasn't blamed. He couldn't be – what he did was crazed, but not manslaughter."

"What contributing factor?"

"Damaging the mound."

Halfie said, "He'll be jailed for vandalism."

"I doubt it. Come along, let's have some tea. I haven't been able to eat all day."

Halfie nodded, walking beside her. "How are you feeling?" she asked.

"Tired," Nancy replied.

"Will you carry on living in the house?"

"Of course. You're very precious to me, and I'll never trust Duncan."

This declaration made Halfie feel uncomfortable. "It wasn't his fault either. He wasn't even there when it happened."

Nancy glanced across, but made no reply.

"You don't blame him, do you?"

She looked in the other direction, as if unwilling to participate further in the conversation, but then said, "I blame all sorts of people."

Halfie decided she had heard enough of the topic. "We can have the funeral now," she said. "Have you and Dad agreed yet?"

Nancy entered the kitchen, gave an exaggerated sigh, then walked across to the Aga. "Yes we have," she said. "We'll do it his way, a humanist service in Snittonwood. A few selected guests. Provided certain persons don't turn up, I'll accept his list."

"Will he accept yours?"

She glanced back. "I won't have a list. That you, me and Billy are there is all that matters."

"I don't think Billy will want to come on his own," Halfie said. "He'll want to come with someone. He told me he's never been to a funeral."

"He can ask his stepmum or his uncle. But *nobody* else."

The name William Ordish hung in the air. Halfie considered all she had heard about Billy's recovering father, then sat down on a chair, feeling disconsolate. "No, not that old man," she murmured. "Billy'll come with his stepmum. It'll be nice to meet her at last."

"Like I said, he can come with any or all of his family," Nancy said, "so long as William isn't there."

Halfie nodded. "Even he wouldn't be so dense and callous as to come along."

"You never know with William Ordish. Twisted... didn't I tell you?"

Again, Halfie felt the need to shut down the discussion. She remained silent.

As Nancy chopped vegetables she said, "What will you do about the necklace?"

"I've decided what to do. I'll do it this evening."

"May I know?"

"Tomorrow," Halfie replied.

"Very well. I won't interfere."

The evening was gloomy under gathering cloud leaning in from the west. A cool breeze blew, and Halfie, stepping outdoors, decided to put on a light coat over her cardigan. She wore trainers and long socks, and in one hand carried the silver lantern that Billy had spoken of so long ago. On the bottom it was stamped 925.

In Snittonwood she returned to the mound, then retraced her steps to the hole where she had buried the necklace. Though it had been pushed further in by foxes, it was only a matter of moments before she retrieved it and held it in her hands again.

All that chaos and heartache just for this.

Halfie

It was beautiful though. Decorated with engraved curls, with male and female figures, and pierced through at the edges of each section, it was complete, strung upon silver links, albeit now clogged with mud. She wiped away the worst of the soil, walking to the edge of the wood to examine the thing in better light.

Surely this was worth a small fortune. She knew now from her research that the Celts of the region buried their high status deceased underneath ditched mounds, usually with grave goods. Most likely there was more jewellery to be found, making the mound a valuable addition to Britain's archaeological heritage. She smiled. She thought more highly of Frank Griffiths now, and knew it would not be long before she invited him and his team to survey the mound.

It would not be easy telling him about the destruction, of course.

She strolled down the bridleway as the light began to fail. Rents in the clouds revealed orange streamers to the west – the last of the day's illumination. Beside the spring field she turned off, walking slowly towards the bubbling water.

At the edge of the waterlogged ground, she knelt. The brook trickled away to the west, shining with orange light, and in the gloom it looked like an enchanted artery, vivid, lurid even, carrying dissolved messages of import. Yet it was a simple stream too, just water from underground; ancient rain, returning.

The spring was no wider than an oak trunk, surrounded by reeds and marsh grass, with yellow flowers dotted around it. Insects buzzed this way and that. She took the necklace in her right hand, weighed it, gave a few experimental throws, then flung it into the spring. It landed in the clear centre of the water with a splash.

She stood upright.

That necklace had come to her by accident, for all the strife and struggle of its recent history. Once, when she knew Faerie, she thought all deeds were meaningful, all purposes deliberate, all actions predestined. Now she understood that youthful attitude to be untrue. Chance ruled the world, as Billy had suggested, as Nancy had told her; and because she had acquired the necklace by accident it was best that she release it to the world for chance once again to be its master.

She could not see it now: too deep, too dark. But she felt relieved of a burden.

The funeral took place in the early evening of a sunny, blue-skied day. A breeze blew, cooling the land.

Halfie sat alone on a barrel at the smallholding end of the western track. A number of vehicles stood on the lane track verge – friends of Dad's. There had been no unpleasantness so far; no scenes.

Her dad and three other men carried the wicker coffin through the yard, behind them Nancy dressed in black. Halfie glanced down at her own costume, also black. Behind Nancy came the rest of the mourners, about twenty people in all.

She felt contained inside her head, as if coddled by invisible protection. Not one tear had leaked from her eyes; not one sniffle, nor any forlorn sigh.

The coffin-bearers passed her, then halted. As arranged, she stood beside Nancy, then waited for the procession to continue. She made sure not to catch Nancy's gaze, nor that of anybody else as they moved along the track.

At the bridleway they ascended the gentle slope up to Snittonwood. Fluffy seeds whirled through the air from Stone Farm, or beyond. At the upper hedge Halfie saw three figures, waiting, motionless, all of them dressed in dark clothes. As she neared she saw it was Billy and his brother Dave standing beside their Uncle Adrian. Surprised, she glanced aside at Nancy, but Nancy looked elsewhere, in a world of her own.

Larks sang on high, providing natural music.

The procession paused so that Adrian could lead his nephews to the rear of the group. Then it entered the wood.

They halted at the glade. Logs had been set down for people to sit on. Informality was the stipulation, and for a while people milled about, uncertain what to do or where to sit, while Halfie's dad stood alone, his back to them, beside the coffin.

Halfie slipped away to find Billy. He sat with his uncle and brother, but she took his hand and dragged him to an unoccupied log.

"Where's your stepmum?" she asked.

He looked at her sidelong, expression unreadable.

Halfie felt concerned. This was wrong; and in response she felt something leap up inside her – an emotion, a feeling, a worry. She felt light-headed now.

After a few quick breaths she said, "Won't you tell me?"

He looked away, mouth set, lips compressed.

"Is she looking after your dad? Has he had a relapse?"

Billy shook his head.

"Well... what, then?"

"I don't have a stepmum," he replied. "I had to invent her to make an explanation – not for you, no, not that. For pretty much everybody. Not Dave, obviously. And... I don't know, mebbe I made her up for myself."

Halfie stared. "No stepmum? But…"

He looked at her. "Sorry. I made her up quite a while back, after my mum left. At the time it seemed like a good idea. It really helped me. Besides, it meant I could read and talk about things boys don't, which… was an advantage."

Halfie clutched him, but as she touched him she felt something burst inside her, that rose, expanded, felt searing hot. Tears trickled down her cheeks, and when she felt them a torrent of grief followed. She clasped him, leaning into his chest, grabbing his jacket lapels and gripping them, heedless of what lay around her.

He put one arm around her shoulder. "I'm sorry," he said. "It weren't deliberate. I just had to do it, even though it were a lie, because summat deep down made me."

"But *Billy*," Halfie sobbed, "that means we've *both* lost our mums. Oh, Billy… that's the bravest, stupidest thing I've ever heard."

And she lowered her head to weep again, clutching him as tight as she could.

When later she glanced up she saw him crying too – not with sobs, nor even with many tears, but quietly, grieving old grief, teardrops running down his face.

Halfie blew her nose, then handed Billy the tissue for him to blow his. Her body felt hot, wracked, weak. She leaned into him, hardly aware of the glade, the congregation invisible to her as their shared loss continued to flow. A murmur of noise surrounded her, but she knew little of it, and cared less.

She felt freed from the cell inside her head, its invisible protection dissolved.

After a while, she felt somebody sit next to her. It was Nancy, her cheeks damp.

Halfie

"Hold my hand, dear," she said, "and hold Billy's too. I think we three should sit together now."

Halfie did as she was asked.

These were her true friends.

Evening lay deep and shadowed over Snittonwood. Ten minutes earlier Halfie had watched the sun dip below hills on the horizon, Billy to her right, nobody to her left. A few squirrels ran up and down nearby tree trunks, while in the sky a flight of geese passed by. The wood was dense with silence, full of mystery.

Before Halfie a tangled mess of briars lay, leaf litter, young trees and younger saplings. The glade was nearby, the mound a little further off. Scampering creatures rustled through the undergrowth, while on high rooks cawed.

"Has your dad written to the school, then?" Billy asked.

"To inform the headmaster. He had a reply by return. They'll allow me time off if I need it, or to miss lessons, or parts of lessons. It was a nice letter."

"The whole school will know the day we go back. Tricky."

"Yes," Halfie sighed.

"You ready for that? You know, some of my friends will sympathise."

She shook her head. "It's scary."

He nodded. "But they really will feel sorry for you. Lucy Rees, f'rinstance. A couple of her friends. One or two of my mates. My friends aren't all cavemen."

She tried to smile. "I know."

"Nobody will dare say anything horrible to you though. You'll be left alone."

"When I need to be, yes. Sometimes I'll need to talk."

He said, "You can count on me for that."

345

"I know. Thank you."

"And a few others," he added in a lighter voice. "Don't be afraid to reach out. Some of my mates act tough, but they've got broken families or whatever."

Halfie nodded.

"What now?" he asked.

"Just one more thing to do," she replied.

"Shall I come with you?"

"Yes, please."

She led the way forward, returning to the spot where the clump of dandelions grew. Reaching down, she plucked the oak sapling from the earth, a clod of soil coming up with it. Then she stood upright, cradling the lump of earth in her hand.

"What's that?" he asked.

"It was supposed to be my special tree in Snittonwood, which my spirit was tied to."

"Do you believe in that?"

"Tree, or spirit?" she asked.

"Spirit."

"I don't know now."

"Plenty of time to work it out."

"Such elven trees could never be cut down," Halfie continued. "Mum told me the King forbade it, to guarantee the permanence of the shee. I was supposed to end up inside this future oak – a home for centuries, Mum called it. Not now though."

"No."

"I'm choosing human. There never was a Faerie." She sighed. "I feel that's a terrible shame, because, somehow, Faerie meant nature to me, hills and woods, and I need those things. I love this part of Shropshire, Billy, and I think you do too."

He reached out to fold his hand over hers, so that together they supported the clod of earth and the sapling. "Listen," he said, "I feel real bad about what my dad did to this wood. You and trees, I can see that's a good thing. I s'pose I don't see woods like you do, but maybe I could learn." He hesitated. "Anyway, I got an idea."

"What?"

"Let's replant this somewhere else, for you and me. Together, eh? Now."

Halfie smiled, amazed to hear such a thing. "I'd like that so much. Yes… let's do it now."

"Where d'you reckon? In sight of that fox hole, I'd say."

"Yes! To symbolise what we did. Yes…"

Side by side they returned to the fox hole, choosing a clear spot nearby to replant the oak sapling. Billy dug the hole using a broken branch, then with both of them holding the clod of soil they raised the sapling and placed it into the hole. Halfie pressed the earth flat around it, covered it with dead leaves, then inched towards Billy.

In the fading light, she reached out for his hand, and held it.

Halfie

Printed in Great Britain
by Amazon